Part One

Part One

I

'COMRADE BRAGHIROLI WILL NOW SPEAK!'

The man stuck his chin out, trying to suggest the Duce's image to the enthusiasts around him, and took an old newspaper out of his pocket; then he cleared his throat and began reading loudly—though it was obvious he knew it by heart—Mussolini's historic speech made on October 2nd the previous year. His comrades in the local Group listened attentively and admiringly as he varied his tone, inspired by the thought of his elevated model.

'Blackshirts of the revolution! Men and women of all Italy! Italians scattered about the world, beyond the mountains and beyond the seas: listen.

'A solemn hour in the history of our country is upon us. At this very moment twenty million men are filling the piazzas of the whole of Italy. A spectacle more gigantic than this has never been seen in the history of the human race. Twenty million men with a single heart, a single will, a single decision.'

'The Duce's made us the greatest people on earth,' said a section-leader, fierce and haggard under his big black cap.

'Never as in this historic age,' Braghiroli continued, seeking to imitate the Duce's tone even better, 'have the Italian people shown the qualities of their spirit and the strength of their character. It is against these people, to whom humanity owes so many of its greatest conquests, it is against these people—poets, artists, heroes, saints, navigators, travellers—it is against these people that they now dare to speak of sanctions.

[7]

'*Fascist and proletarian Italy, Italy of Vittorio Veneto and of the revolution, arise! Let the shout of your decision fill the sky and comfort the soldiers who wait in Africa, let it be a spur to our friends and a warning to our enemies in every part of the world: a shout of justice, a shout of victory.*'

'Carry on, Mario—you're terrific! You sound exactly like him!' the section-leader burst out again.

'How can I carry on, you clown? That's the end!'

'Oh, so you've finished. Well comrades, cheers for the Duce!'

A storm of cheers and applause broke out around him.

'Fizzy drinks, sweets, ice cream. . . .' called a street-seller.

Mario Braghiroli wiped the sweat off his brow and settled himself. Entirely taken up with the solemnity of the moment and his tight woollen uniform, which, with its red stripes and decorations, made him feel important, he gazed around him, looking inspired.

His eyes met those of Giulio Govoni, a short youth with an oversized head and a face covered in freckles, lit by a pair of gentle eyes, the only handsome thing about him, who had that moment turned up in command of a GUF platoon and had lined his students up beside Braghiroli's local fascists. Braghiroli turned to him.

'Remember October 2nd?' he shouted.

'What d'you think? While the Duce was speaking I was tingling all over!'

'Fifty-two nations he defied!'

'And won—in the teeth of the defeatists!'

There was a moment's silence, then Braghiroli's eyes lit up: 'But my heart tells me he'll be even greater this evening.'

The large piazza of Padusa was quickly filling up. Waves of men and women, dressed in black, poured in from the wide streets leading into it: these were the fascist organisations, each in its special uniform, including the thirteen-year-old Balillas, thrilled with their miniature rifles. Obsessively, the hymn of the fascist revolution rang out over the loudspeakers, its warlike notes roaring into the farthest corners of the little town, spreading beyond its walls, breaking the silence of the sleeping countryside. Since morning the newspapers had been urging people to wait for the meeting of the Fascist Grand Council and for Mussolini's speech. Everywhere, indoors and

[8]

out, people had been watching the clock. What would the Duce say? It was only four days since he had announced the conquest of the Ethiopian capital, to the people's jubilation. Everyone's imagination was now fired, everyone was busy prophesying, longing to put forward his own ideas. But equally everyone agreed to wait for the historic announcement.

Giulio Govoni shared the others' excited impatience. But Braghiroli's oratory had taken him back, as he waited, to that memorable evening of October 2nd the previous year, when Mussolini miraculously carried a whole people to the heights of enthusiasm by declaring war. A few nostalgic idiots still denied the Duce's genius, and refused to recognise that this was the new democracy, with leader and followers speaking directly to each other: but they were fools.

Everything about that splendid evening, which was already so far behind them, had been enjoyable and moving—even the noisy, unrehearsed demonstration by the crazy medical students. Hoarse with cheering the Duce, they had scorched their clothes in the Renaissance-style torchlight procession led by Moro, as happy as young lions.

Then, when the demonstration was over, about fifty youngsters decided to protest against the hateful democracies who were siding with Abyssinia against Italy, and had roamed the town systematically destroying any shop-signs they found with foreign words on them: the dress shop called *New England*, the famous women's tailor Malagò, who specialised, according to his sign, in *paletots* and *tailleurs*, and the Hotel Promenade all suffered. Finally they had made an unholy row in the Arena theatre, where a great many advertisements with foreign words appeared on the safety curtain. They burst into the theatre and forced the owner, who was white with fear, to clean it up at once, thus interrupting the play for a very long time and upsetting the respectable audience.

Tongues had wagged, 'boyish pranks' and 'stupid vandalism' had been mentioned. But people who talked like that, Giulio thought, didn't understand the spirit of fascism, which meant youth, excitement, intemperance. All that student demonstration had meant was that the young wanted to be free of the feelings of inferiority that made Italians regard the French, the Germans and the English as having mastered life and civilisation. Italy had successfully defied the whole world, and was now going to come out on top!

A shrill squeak from the loudspeakers broke into Giulio's thoughts, and he looked around.

The crowd in Padusa's main piazza could no longer move, and elderly people started fuming. Some people cursed the local fascist officials, who had told them to come at half past eight, whereas now, at past ten o'clock, Mussolini had not yet appeared on the balcony of Palazzo Venezia. At last, at twenty past ten, the loudspeakers solemnly announced that the windows of the 'fateful' balcony were open. Over the piazza of Padusa rolled a powerful, distant roar—the excitement of the crowd in Rome, gathered in Piazza Venezia. Then came a sudden silence, by contrast all the greater, all the more solemn; and Mussolini spoke in his very personal, very studied way— speaking briefly and urgently—the way that had won over even the Socialist Party, which was sick with Maximilianism when he was young. And now Italians drank in his fieriness and his silences.

Numerous loudspeakers, strategically placed in the middle of Padusa, sent his words ringing round the town. In the warm evening, his voice came out into the streets through the open windows, from family radios inside. In spite of the hour, not a soul was asleep. Anyone who wanted to avoid what the Duce was saying would have had to shut himself up at home and plug his ears. But even then Mussolini's pounding words might have reached him.

Solemnly and imperiously, the Duce announced the birth of the Italian Empire in Africa. Every time he paused the vast uniformed crowd roared its frantic applause. Then, after a final, studied silence, when the people's excitement was at fever pitch, came the melodramatic ending.

'*The people of Italy have created the Empire with their own blood. They will tend it with their own labour and defend it with their arms.*

'*In this supreme certainty, O legionaries, raise your colours, your weapons and your hearts on high, and after fifteen centuries, salute the Empire that has reappeared upon the predestined hills of Rome.*

'*Will you be worthy of it?*'

[10]

The long 'Ye. . . . s' of the Roman crowd, massed in Piazza Venezia, broke violently on to the piazza in Padusa.

'*This cry is like a sacred oath, which binds you before God and before men, for life and for death!*

'*Blackshirts, legionaries, salute the king!*'

His outburst was over. Like a tenor who has touched the top note, delighting in the ovation that shakes the theatre, Mussolini was enjoying his triumph, eyes half-shut, while the enormous crowd roared exultantly, and its roar echoed from the north of Italy to the south in the same moment. A few people muttered to themselves, but most of them were convinced that they were taking part in an all-powerful movement able to defy the centuries and comparable in majesty with the ancient Roman Empire.

Throughout the speech the university students in Padusa had been roaring their approval, wild with delight. When it was over they flung up their caps, white, red, blue, and green, and a youngster with an old drum started beating time as the students, boys and girls, shouted with all the breath they could muster: 'Du—ce! Du—ce! Du—ce! Em—pire! Em—pire! Em—pire!'

The second-in-command of the girl students' group, a large, saucy second-year medical student, was shaking all over as she chatted to a friend.

'And he's so handsome, isn't he!'

'I should say so! With that forehead, with that square chest . . . they say women are always after him!'

'Well, of course! Who wouldn't be?'

'Du—ce! Du—ce! Du—ce!' the students shouted, louder and louder. What they wanted, urgently, was to show that no one valued the regime's triumphs and the birth of this gigantic reality, the Empire, more than they did. National pride was like wine—it blurred the edges of reality in their young minds. They saw Italy at the summit of its power and glory, facing the feeble democratic nations who were now quite incapable of stopping Mussolini. And when one of them said the word 'war' almost longingly—as happened that evening—no one thought of a frightful wholesale massacre, like the one in 1914-18; what everyone had in mind was a kind of triumphal march, with very few casualties and a great many speeches and fanfares:

an irresistible march against the enemies of fascism, who, inspired by no ideals, would very soon lay down their arms in order to avoid inevitable defeat. And, certain that the words interpreted their generation's great destiny, they marched happily along, singing:

> Siamo fiaccole di vita,
> siamo l'eterna gioventú
> che conquista
> l'avvenire,
> di ferro armata e di pensier.
> Per le vie del nuovo Impero,
> che si dilungano nel mar,
> marceremo,
> come il duce vuole,
> dove Roma già passò. . . .

II

At midnight the great piazza was empty. Only small groups of enthusiasts were left, among them—at the foot of the Garibaldi monument—a packed crowd of students who, conducted by Moro, were singing an indecent drinking song.

Antonio Spisani, nicknamed Moro, was probably the unruliest of the university students at Padusa. He was fat for his age and his flabby face, with a pair of bright, inquisitive eyes like holes poked in it, seemed to reflect his spirit exactly.

After a couple of disastrous failures he had managed, thanks to an indulgent friend on the board of examiners, to get through the school-leaving exams, but in six years at the university had barely got through five others.

Since he had been on his own, without his parents, he had lived alone in a furnished room, in the utmost confusion, scraping a living dealing in antiques. The other students liked him in spite of his faults because he had two good qualities: he knew everything that was going on in town and even when things were at their blackest he never asked anyone for a cent. He had a good tenor voice as well, and a kind of rough talent for the stage; in fact, he had become popular by successfully playing the bluest parts available in the shows that were often put on in Padusa. Now, he was just as proud of the Empire as the rest of them, but felt a touch of sex was hardly out of place in celebrating military triumphs, which, after all, had always expressed virility. Wasn't that what the Roman legionaries had felt?

Proud of his singing, he kept altering the pitch of his voice to break the song's monotony, while the others roared at the tops of their voices:

> Osteria numero uno,
> paraponzi ponzi po';
> una ganza per ciascuno,
> paraponzi ponzi po'.
> Osteria numero due,
> paraponzi ponzi po';
> le mie gambe con le tue. . . .

This facetious singing seemed to Giulio a profanation of the great day. He went over to Moro and said quietly 'Don't you think it's time to pack it in?'

'Why?'

'The G U F secretary went away—I don't think he approves.'

'Po-faced old idiot!' said Moro: then, as if suddenly inspired, he leapt on to a stool and cried 'It's midnight, boys—let's go to Franca's. Cut prices tonight!'

Giulio shook his head and turned away. He walked home at a steady pace and all the way kept thinking of how Italy had finally conquered *a place in the sun*.

About twenty youngsters answered Moro's rallying cry and, clearly delighted, he began marching arm in arm with a second-year law student, Piero Cavalieri d'Oro, nicknamed Uproar, a large, tough, bright-eyed boy with a powerful baritone voice, undisputed leader whenever the students went to brothels, and successful lecturer on fascist subjects in the vacations.

Triumphantly they entered Via Garibaldi, instinctively falling into step, while Cavalieri d'Oro at the top of his voice started up the young fascists' marching song.

> Duce, duce, chi non saprà morir?
> Il giuramento chi mai rinnegherà?

[13]

> Snuda la spada quando tu lo vuoi;
> gagliardetti al vento,
> tutti verremo a te. . . .

The narrow street echoed with their song and their rhythmical footsteps, and none of the wanderers they kept meeting could resist the chorus of what was one of the regime's best marches. From end to end of the street washed the wave of song:

> Una maschia gioventú,
> con romana volontà,
> combatterà!
> Verrà,
> quel dí verrà,
> che la gran madre degli eroi ci chiamerà. . . .

The song ended with cheers for the Duce and the king, then Moro started up the Irredentists' jingle:

> Quando saremo a Nizza, ci pianterem la giostra;
> diremo ai francesi che siamo a casa nostra.

'*Bombe a man, carezze col pugnal,*' the others yelled in chorus.

Cavalieri d'Oro went on:

> E noi andremo a Malta, ce pianterem la giostra;
> diremo agli inglesi che siamo a casa nostra.

And the rest thundered: '*Bombe a man, carezze col pugnal.*' Then it was the turn of Spoleto, Tunis, Djibouti, Suez, of every place these Italian students thought they would soon be entering with pennants flying, showing the gleaming blades of their knives to Frenchmen, Englishmen, Jugoslavs, and anyone else who belonged to the hated reactionary plutocratic democracies.

But, however heroic their plans, their real object just then was the hospitable brothel. So that night, instead of venting themselves on the armies of the democracies, the youngsters did so on the far friendlier tarts. Cavalieri d'Oro, having drunk rather a lot, had the fun of attacking a well-known villain from the suburbs, who had come into the brothel that fate-

[14]

ful day without his fascist badge; he was promptly kicked out
of the house.

'So end all enemies of fascism!' cried Moro, howling with
laughter.

III

'Come on, Nivola! Come on, Italy!'

But the Mantuan driver never heard it. Screaming along the
edge of the incredible curves of the Nürburgring, glued to the
wheel in his small red car, he was racing against the silver
German Mercedes and Auto-Union cars. And winning meant
everything.

This had all been a year earlier, in 1935, when Giulio—
who had won a travelling prize—had found himself in the
small group of Italians gathered to cheer on the Alfa Romeo
team, and in particular Tazio Nuvolari, king of the road.

The crowd could scarcely believe it. On the last lap, that
almost amateurish Italian car shot past the cars of the two
great German firms, those miracles of modern technology;
and little Nivola, as brave as they came, defied death and
hoisted the Italian tricolour on the tallest flagstaff.

Moved, Giulio stiffened to attention, his back like a ramrod, when the first notes of the Italian national anthem rose.
The huge German crowd pushed out, disappointed not to
see the flag with the swastika on the victors' flagstaff, and
remarks were passed, half kindly and half sarcastic, about those
everlasting Italian improvisers, who produced not just the
beggars flooding into Prussia and Bavaria to make a living,
but small, steely men like Nivola, as well.

When Giulio returned home his heart was swelling with
patriotic pride, after what was always to be his most wonderful
experience in sport. He was glad the Duce was happy too—he
had sent Nuvolari a telegram of warm congratulations—as of
course he must be, since sport was a way of fighting patriotic
battles and asserting the values of the new, fascist Italy. It
was a long way to the top of the world, but the top was there
to aim at. The triumphs of the national football team, now
world champions, with that fireball Meazza and the fantastic

Orsi, the marvellous achievements of the great cyclists—first Binda and Guerra, and now young Bartali—and the success of Tazio Nuvolari and of his great friend and rival Achille Varzi, only foreshadowed the coming prestige and triumph of fascist Italian sport.

Giulio had gone to the Nürburgring with his great friend Dionisio Cavallari, the student who was most in the public eye at the small university of Padusa, and, people said, the one most inclined to poke his nose in everywhere. The two boys had been together all the way through school, and had been friendly rivals. Each had a weak spot. Dionisio, a dedicated rationalist, was at a disadvantage with literary subjects; Giulio was not much good at mathematics.

When Giulio had decided to skip his last year at school, Dionisio, who was more than a year younger, had thought there was no point in throwing up twelve months of his youth, and had stayed on. Now he was reading law, and always stood out among the others in his faculty. But he was not exactly keen on law—in fact, his close friends said he had too many interests and was wasting his fine talents by spreading them over too many things. Among these interests, sport came first, as it did with Giulio. Since they were children and had cheered for the S P I M cycling team, of which their elder brothers had both been outstanding members, the two boys had been mad about sport.

As they had been to the Nürburgring the previous year, this year they were longing to get to the Olympic games in Berlin. Meantime, as always, they had been taking part in the *littoriali*, the annual university sporting events, and had got back to Padusa just in time to join their G U F comrades in the piazza on the evening of May 9th, to hear the speech on the Empire.

Book and gun make the perfect fascist, was the students' motto, but in order to use a gun the future ruling classes of Italy must toughen their bodies with sport—which was why the Duce had set up the *littoriali*. These, the fascists claimed with some justification, were the most comprehensive sporting events in the world, and they had become the main objective of the universities. There was a place for everyone in them: for besides the Olympic sports, there were games which were popular in the thirties, like tennis and rugby—soon to be Italianised by the regime into *pallacorda* (rope-ball) and *pallaovale* (oval-ball). And in every event the youngsters lashed themselves on to gain the coveted gold M for Mussolini.

Padusa university was small, and so was the number of its students. Yet they had to put someone in for every event at the *littoriali,* from athletics to canoeing, from boxing to fencing and skiing; and anyone with the smallest ability had to become an athlete and go into training. No one was expected to be outstanding: good will was quite enough. And so, whereas in the large universities only an athletic minority was involved in the *littoriali,* in Padusa they were a matter of general concern. But in spite of all their efforts, there were always yawning gaps. Since the rugby team had been formed, for instance, more than thirteen willing players had never been rustled up, whereas in fact they needed fifteen and a couple of reserves. So the captain had had to co-opt two stout policemen, who had immediately been promoted into students. Bombo and Cannone—as the men were nicknamed—sang in the chorus at the Arena theatre as well, but spoke a pretty rough brand of Italian. So they were told not to mix with students from other universities, and never to go out alone. 'Whenever you see students from anywhere else, make a dash for it,' the captain warned them. 'And if you can't, remember you're singers and sing at them when you answer.'

In athletics, Padusa had failed dismally, and people were always afraid that the genuine Padusa students might not manage to win a single point between them. So a thug who had been working in the anatomy room since 1933 was disguised as a medical student in order to compete in the discus and javelin throwing, and a young railwayman, who was marching champion of the province, had been turned into an engineering student. Had they won important events they would have been found out, but they were just reasonably well placed (which meant they were not too conspicuous), so everything went smoothly.

The only boxer at the university was a chemistry student nicknamed Knockout. Physically, he was not at all the type for boxing, being shortish, with high cheekbones and a narrow nose, but the other students had a healthy respect for his fists,

[17]

especially since he had knocked out the commander of the town militia outside the Duomo one day, when he had been teasing him in a friendly way. People said that if Knockout hadn't had an uncle who was high up in the party, he wouldn't have dared to go so far. But it was quite something to have routed a man like that, who was plastered with medals and had been the most arrogant of the fascist stormtroopers in Padusa. Just then, in fact, Knockout looked like a symbol of the vigorous generation that had not yet known war or revolution, but meant to go *beyond what was asked of it,* when the Duce put it to the test.

Unfortunately his rather squalid love affairs and a great dislike of training meant that he was not always fit to go into the ring. So every year he disguised a couple of boys from the Vigor gym as students and took them off to the *littoriali* with him. His judgement was sound and he always did pretty well.

The greatest difficulty in getting these bogus students to the *littoriali* was the fact that their identity cards had to be signed by the rector. But Professor Fabbri, rector of Padusa University, never refused the secretary of the G U F, especially if the fascist Federal Secretary just happened to ring up beforehand. The rector was an old liberal, who had been deputy in a couple of governments and since the beginning of the century had been known for his manoeuvres between the various political parties. At first he had regarded the fascists with a kind of remote condescension, thinking them a pack of scoundrels, but once the regime had settled in he had joined the fascist party and had been rewarded by being nominated senator. Towards important fascist officials he was deferential, both because he had an innate respect for those in authority, and because he hoped to be forgiven for having long ago been a friend of Giolitti, whose under-secretary he had been. The students thought him slightly senile but quite liked him. With his pepper-and-salt goatee, his beak nose and his melancholy ox-like eyes, he looked a real old gentleman; he had in fact a gentleman's private honesty, and the kind of formal good manners that made him seem respectable even to those who had no respect for him.

At the Arena theatre, in the last university revue, the outrageous Moro had excelled himself by appearing dressed up as Professor Fabbri. For a good ten minutes he had imitated his mannerisms marvellously well, and had ended his highly successful sketch by singing, in the rector's well known falsetto voice:

> Cominciai il cammin con Giolitti,
> rifutai i contatti con Nitti;
> ora son senator
> e magnifico rettor. . . .

There was silence, and the lights went out for half a minute; then came a roll of drums and Moro reappeared with a cudgel bigger than himself and dressed as a fascist stormtrooper in the twenties, with three or four swastikas embroidered on his chest, and yelled with all the breath in his lungs:

> e squadrista di grande valor!

The audience had doubled up with laughter. Professor Fabbri, who was there, had forced himself to smile casually and say 'These madcap students!' to people sitting near him. Then he had slumped into his seat.

IV

With some sports, like tennis and skiing, even the rector's agreement was useless, for disguise was impossible. Those who could hope to be classified at all were a select group who were on Christian-name terms from Turin to Palermo. An outsider would have been found out straight away.

So every year the Padusa G U F tried to enlist some reasonably good athletes from outside for these rather special sports; and as the man in charge of sport, a vague-looking boy, interested in literature and the cinema, seemed quite unsuited to making these arrangements, the G U F secretary, Francesco Tassinari, had to take things in hand himself. This Tassinari was not just an able young man, but a man of action, and since he became secretary of the G U F had become intensely dynamic; yet because of his appearance he found it hard to influence the students. Incredibly thin, with huge bat ears and a languid air, he was a total contrast to the fashionable sporting type, and among the sturdy students he looked just like the caricatures of weedy youths from the democratic countries turned out regularly in a well-known comic weekly. Under him, the G U F undertook to pay the fees of students taken on from outside, and allowed them to pass their exams as easily as was possible in Padusa. And, as good athletes were often not particularly bright, the Padusa G U F managed a few small deals of the kind every year.

The Padusa students enjoyed the week or ten days of the *littoriali* more than any other time of the year—it was even gayer than the freshers' rag. As the Padusa G U F could not discipline and control its students like the larger universities, they were more or less free to do as they pleased, and pretty well every evening they were out on the town—eating and drinking heartily, as boys of twenty will when they sit down together, getting free meals in certain restaurants when they produced their identity cards, and with plenty of girls for the asking.

Those were anxious days for the G U F secretary and the sports manager. Things were always going wrong: one man would go sick, another would fall in love and fail to turn up on the field in time, another would be disqualified for disobeying the rules. A man pushed into running for Padusa in the four hundred metres had once set the whole stadium bellowing with laughter by having no idea that he had to stick to his own lane: at the sound of the starting pistol he cut casually across from lane five, in which he was running, to lane one, and breasted the tape before anyone else, to the shrieks of the spectators and the scornful glares of the organisers.

This year, Giulio played in the rugby team, his enthusiasm making up for his lack of athletic talent. Dionisio was also in the team, but was more athletic, and was playing tennis as well and running in the hundred metres.

The rugby matches were extremely tough. They played with other teams from small universities, who were more or less their standard. Few players knew anything about the technique of the game, and their version depended entirely on brute force. The scrums were a matter of fisticuffs and kicks, and tackling was incredibly violent. If a man fell over it was not at all rare for his opponent to finish him off on the side. Whenever he played in a match Giulio was exhausted afterwards. After supper he went straight to bed and fell asleep, and in the morning often still felt exhausted.

This year, the games had taken place in a particularly euphoric atmosphere, owing to the triumphant ending of the campaign in Africa. Their political importance had been stressed by a visit from the national vice-secretary of the fascist party who had brought greetings from the Duce and the party secretary, Achille Starace, now in Ethiopia as a volunteer, to all the students. Starace could not honour the great meeting with his presence because he was still at the war, where he had covered himself in glory, according to the newspapers, as commander of the unit which had captured Gondar, the second most important city in Ethiopia, in April. But the students knew perfectly well that, Ethiopia or no Ethiopia, he would never have come.

Two years earlier, Achille Starace had been present at the *littoriali*. The university teams had marched past in the splendid new stadium, and then lined up on the grass. When the final halt was called the *Royal March*, followed by *Giovinezza*, rose in the enormous hollow, a thousand young voices happily singing:

> Giovinezza, giovinezza,
> primavera di bellezza!
> Nel fascismo è la salvezza
> della nostra libertà. . . .

They really believed they were living in freedom; and, perhaps for this very reason, the students from Padua were not afraid to start up their own impudent song, which so plainly referred to Starace, who was standing to attention on the grandstand, the moment the fascist song was over:

> Quell'uom dal fiero aspetto,
> non dica, non dica fregnacce.
> Vada a contarle al Kaiser;
> forse ci crederà.

In a few seconds the rest of the students joined in, the entire stadium was roaring out the stinging words, while the fascist officials on the grandstand squirmed and G U F secretaries rushed up and down the lines silencing their students, so that Starace was spared the insult of the second verse:

> Se il Kaiser non ci crede,
> vada a contarla a Starace.
> Quel fesso con l'orbace
> certo ci crederà.

But the party secretary had already had enough: too much, in fact.

Quite plainly, Starace and the majority of students were wholly incompatible. They disliked his mania for uniforms, parades and military discipline; and when, characteristically, he banned the freshers' rags, their dislike knew no bounds. The students called themselves fascists and adored the Duce: for this very reason they hated to see the regime represented by a martinet who, the current joke said, went to bed with his medals pinned on to his pyjamas.

V

'Heard the latest?'

'Go on!'

'An officer says to Prince Umberto: "How is it I'm sixty and still a colonel, whereas you're thirty and already a general?" "Ah," says the prince, "I've got on because my father's the Duce's cousin."'

Giulio and Dionisio burst out laughing, while the barber delightedly settled them in. Then he dropped his bantering tone.

'Doesn't it worry you at all to see the regime reducing the head of state to a subject for funny stories?'

Giulio wagged a finger: 'No one's trying to humiliate him; the Duce's a giant, and you're the only person who still keeps denying it.'

Before the march on Rome Aleardo Arlotti, the barber, had had his moment of glory as a provincial socialist official. Then, with the coming of fascism, the persecutions had started; only by a miracle had he managed to avoid having his shop smashed up. Once bitten, he had withdrawn from public protest, and had merely the small satisfaction of telling his most trustworthy friends that his feelings were still unchanged and anti-fascist.

In any case, wasn't that what so many who had fought in the socialist party with him were doing?—lawyers, teachers, doctors, intellectuals of all sorts among them. The most working-class socialist deputy in the province had actually made peace with the regime; the man who in 1919 and 1920 had stirred up the day-labourers of the *bassa* by promising them power through revolution and the wiping out of the bourgeoisie now quietly practised law in Rome, a paid-up party member like the good bourgeois he had become.

Did anyone still believe that the fascist regime would crumble? Well, when the Ethiopian business started a few pig-headed anti-fascists had muttered that Abyssinia would be Mussolini's grave; but the old devil had actually triumphed there instead.

The grumblers had been silenced. It would have looked absurd to complain about a man of whom a newspaper like the *New York Herald Tribune* had written: 'What Mussolini has done is still one of the wonders of the twentieth century.'

When Giulio and Dionisio came into the empty shop between twelve and one, they enjoyed talking politics with Arlotti, and even when they were arguing the tone remained friendly. Only once had Giulio lost his temper, and this was when a diploma for stormtroopers was set up.

The Duce had wanted the diploma given to fascists who had belonged to action squads who had fought against subversives at the time when fascism was coming to power. Giulio had laughed with Arlotti at the headlong rush to get these worthless decorations. In the province of Padusa stormtroopers, at the time of the punitive expeditions, could have numbered three or four hundred at the most, whereas applications ran into thousands, and although these were weeded out hundreds with 'cast-iron recommendations' had managed to get the diploma, though as far as fights with subversives went, they hadn't even read about them in the papers. The most outrageous case had been that of the provincial party secretary, who at the time of the march on Rome was barely thirteen, and had in fact been at boarding school. But his extremely powerful uncle, one of Mussolini's permanent ministers, had pulled the right strings.

The diploma was well worth having. It not only meant a cheque for a thousand lire, which corresponded to the back-dated pay of a man who had been employed by the party from the beginning, but gave anyone employed by a public or semi-public body an obvious push ahead in his career, for the magic diploma meant an important leap forward, and the sudden overtaking of colleagues who were older and better qualified.

Bachelors had exactly the opposite treatment, having no chance of promotion at all by the public authorities. It was said quite seriously, not as a funny story, that when a high fascist official told Starace how unfair this was, he replied: 'All party organs keep busy; and so should the genital organs.'

Giulio thoroughly agreed with Arlotti in disapproving of standards that had nothing to do with merit; but when Arlotti called the stormtroopers 'ruffians in the pay of the landowners, who had savagely beaten up unarmed workers under police protection,' he disagreed violently. No, he wasn't having that! In 1920, he had been seven. But he remembered the solemn funerals of the many victims of socialist violence quite well. They would leave from the church of San Carlo, opposite his father's shop, followed by ex-servicemen, old Garibaldians, representatives of all the patriotic associations, and a large, sad crowd of people. It was impossible to deny that there had been socialist violence in Padusa, for he had been a victim of it himself, as a child. He still remembered going to school after seeing the gun-carriage with the body of the Unknown Soldier passing through the station: he was wearing the bronze badge and the tricolour ribbon in his buttonhole, when a boy much taller than himself, the son of a socialist trade unionist, had ripped out the ribbon and hurled him against the wall of the school hall with two heavy blows.

So when the barber spoke of unarmed workers savagely beaten up Giulio had turned on him. The idea that socialist violence had, as Arlotti said, been a matter of odd, unimportant incidents compared with the organised terrorism of the fascist stormtroopers, paid and protected from above, never even crossed his mind. Nor did he even suspect that long ago,

[24]

when he had been so moved as he watched the fascist funerals from the church of San Carlo, far more funerals were taking place in the country, in the first light of dawn or at sunset, without priest, or flowers, or ceremonial—funerals of innocent victims who were guilty only of 'subversion'. He had hardly heard of Matteotti—the name was like the echo of something obscure and far away, and now quite without interest, some incident in which the irrational antagonism of the 'subversives' had provoked the fascists to go too far. Now the two young men were alone in the shop with Arlotti, who was longing to relieve his feelings and knew he could do so quite freely to them, as always.

'So yesterday you were celebrating your Duce's victory and the founding of the Empire,' he began.

'Of course,' said Giulio, beaming. 'Italy's really on top now!'

'Full steam ahead,' said Dionisio.

'The anti-fascists have had to climb down,' Giulio went on. 'After the sanctions, even the main supporters of the old regime said they supported the Duce: from Arturo Labriola to Vittorio Emanuele Orlando.'

'Orlando?'

'Yessir!' said Dionisio, 'Orlando, no less, the man who was head of the government when we won the war . . . There's a letter from him.'

'I know nothing about it.'

'Ah, but we do! This is what he wrote to Mussolini: *Your Excellency, at the present time, every Italian should be ready to serve.* And he offered his own services . . . whatever those grumblers and frowsty old exiles might have to say about it.'

Arlotti was rubbing the blade of an old razor backwards and forwards on the stone, pulling a gloomy face. When the young men had finished talking he spoke to them softly, jerkily, as if matching the words to the rhythm of his moving hand:

'Well yes, he's defeated the Negus, he's snapped his fingers at the sanctions, and now he's going to colonise Ethiopia. . . . All very fine, but what I say is, who's going to pay for it? Doing things on a grand scale is all very well, but you can only do what you can afford. I'd like to change this old saw of a razor myself, but I've got to economise. Far better to give a thought to those wretches in the South, who can't even write the word Empire and are dying of hunger.'

'The Empire's giving them hope as well as us!' Giulio exclaimed.

'The nonsense they get you to swallow! Why, only middle-class people support this little game, because it gives them a chance of making a packet for themselves.'

'That's defeatism, you know! You're talking as if we were a race of ignorant beggars!'

'Eight million illiterates, eight million!' said Arlotti, putting down his razor and wagging his finger to emphasise the reality of the numbers. 'That's the truth, even if Mussolini's so scared to confess it that he actually had the nerve to cut the question on illiteracy out of the censorship form.'

'Nonsense! The fact is that we're growing quickly, and we've got to foresee—'

'Too many of us, is it? Then why does your Duce keep urging a higher birthrate and giving prizes to large families? Wouldn't he do better to tell those wretches who eat only once a day to have fewer children?'

'You forget that numbers mean power.'

'They mean poverty,' retorted Arlotti.

'Now listen: Mussolini, who can see further ahead than you can, has seen what you're objecting to and given us the Empire —a place where millions of Italians will find work and plenty.'

'Giulio, lad, that's what the newspapers tell you. Now, I spent a year in Switzerland, as an emigrant: they haven't an acre of colonies and they're better off than anyone. . . . Mussolini would have done a lot better to ask the English for money and drop Ethiopia.'

'Fine hypocrites those English are, and their friends the French! They keep talking about the freedom of the people, to have a crack at us, and yet for centuries they've been tor-turing whites, yellows and blacks. They're fine ones to talk!'

'That's all ancient history. If you keep looking back there's no end to it . . .'

'But even today, are they ready to get out of those rich colonies of theirs? In India, Gandhi's being shifted from prison to prison.'

'All right, all right, I agree it's a bad thing, but let's get

[26]

back to our own case. Is this, 1935, the time to jump into an adventure of this kind? Mussolini's obviously putting the clock back.'

'What d'you mean?'

'I mean that one day, as the socialist teachers have predicted, the peoples of Asia and Africa will throw off all their bosses. We'll lay paved roads through our Empire and end up running away along them. . . . And then what? What'll we leave in Ethiopia? The fascist emblem, as a souvenir? What a farce!'

Dionisio, who had been silent for a while although he agreed with Giulio, now broke in excitedly. 'You're twenty years behind the times, Aleardo, so you can't understand! We'll never leave Ethiopia, and we'll found a single nation of Italians and Abyssinians.'

'Good idea! They're naked and black, so when they go on parade they won't need black shirts! Go ahead and solve the Ethiopian problem! Let's just hope there aren't further troubles on the way.'

'What sort?'

'The ones you were hoping for last night! From home I could hear the G U F crowd singing away outside the brothels: we'll get to Nice and Dalmatia and Corsica and Malta and Djibouti and Suez.'

'We weren't there.'

'But they're your friends and they think as you do! But if they're so keen to fight, why didn't they go to Ethiopia?'

'They're young, and they've got to finish their studies.'

'Splendid! That's exactly the bourgeois argument, and you fascists claim to despise them! But Empires were made by men who paid for them in person.'

'Fascism doesn't mean taking risks for the sake of it.'

'Then why d'you write "Live dangerously" on all the walls?'

Giulio's shave and haircut were now done. He gave the barber a friendly slap on the back and hurried out of the shop.

Dionisio was left behind, and he and Arlotti changed the subject. They started discussing Bartali and the Giro d'Italia.

VI

As he walked away, Giulio brooded over the barber's final words. He could not fail to be struck by what he had said, so sarcastically, about the war in Ethiopia. All too well he remembered what had happened less than a year before. Tassinari's predecessor as secretary of the G U F, in the late summer of 1935, when war was already in the air, had sent a circular round to the students telling them they could enrol as volunteers. After a couple of unhappy, anxious days, Giulio had not volunteered but had given a reply that came well from a lawyer: he said he would be glad to go to Africa if a unit of Padusan students were formed. After a week he had heard that the G U F in Padua had had only a single answer: his.

When the G U F secretary met him, he had slapped Giulio on the back and muttered, with a kind of grin, 'Drop it!'

Then he himself went off, without any flag-wagging, the only volunteer from the university of Padusa, certain that he was doing his duty. It had never crossed his mind that two months later, while he was fighting on an Abyssinian mountain, he would read in the *Gazzetta di Padusa* that the federal secretary had appointed Francesco Tassinari secretary of the G U F in his place.

Thinking of the ex-G U F secretary, Giulio could not overcome a feeling of shame for not having followed him. Yet the war in Africa was something he had felt profoundly, just as his whole heart had been in the Italian people's reaction against the sanctions. He remembered the 'wedding-ring' day, as if it were yesterday. His eyes had filled with tears when he saw the photograph of Queen Elena in the paper, the first to take off her wedding-ring; and, in the atmosphere of high-flown excitement, he had even given his encircled country his mother's wedding-ring, which he had kept like a relic.

His friend Cavalieri d'Oro—who for some time had been storming through his propaganda lectures—justified his failure to join up by saying there was no need for volunteers in Africa: the government had called up men born in 1910 and

1911, and they had more soldiers than they really needed. But to Giulio, this sounded phoney.

The fact was that he and his friends, with the excuse that they had to carry on studying, had found it more comfortable to sit in the café Torino and, as the Italians advanced, to move the little flags on the map of East Africa; while a great many fascists, including quite elderly ones, had sought glory and decorations on the battlefield, the students had been collecting the picture cards given away with Perugina chocolates, and had lounged about at home listening to their favourite radio programme, the homely, simple-minded *Four Musketeers*.

The fact that all the other students at Padusa had done the same did nothing to ease Giulio's conscience. At other universities, according to what was said in political circles, G U F members had fought to get into the students' battalion *Curtatone e Montanara*, and had embarked enthusiastically at Naples, singing at the tops of their voices:

> Io ti saluto e vado in Abissinia,
> cara Virginia, ma tornero.
> Ti porterò dall' Africa un bel fior. . . .

The Empire was now established, and the book of glory was for the moment closed. But Giulio realised that the fascist regime would soon get involved in further fighting, and as no one could honestly say he believed in fascist politics and at the same time carry on comfortably at home, sooner or later he would have to face danger. But the thought of falling in battle like any anonymous soldier, when he was not much more than twenty, upset him. 'So I'm a coward,' he concluded sadly. 'I'm a man of little faith, who puts his own self before the cause.'

When he got home he sat down at the table in silence, and listened reluctantly to his father and his brother, Enzo. They were talking of bad times and complaining about some of their rich customers, who had to be asked repeatedly to pay their bills. Giulio ate quickly and went straight up to his room, with the excuse that he had to work.

The previous year he had got his degree in literature, and now he was in his third year of law. He wanted to get his second degree by 1937, and in the meantime he was working hard for the competitive exam that would allow him to teach Italian and history at high-school level. A degree in literature was not enough, he considered. Ambitions, though vague and unformulated, he already had, and he felt they could be achieved only with the degree in law—the only one that opened up all possibilities.

That afternoon he could not concentrate his attention on the book of civil law. Clenching his teeth, he went through the chapter on succession and wills, but every now and then realised he was not thinking of the subject but of Mussolini's last speech, Arlotti's ideas, and the old G U F secretary who had volunteered for the war.

In the street he could hear some G I L youngsters singing loudly:

> La moglie del Negus
> ha fatto un figlio maschio.
> Appena aperti gli occhi,
> ha gridato: Viva il Fascio.
> Il General Graziani
> aspetta da più sere
> la pelle di abissini
> per far camicie nere.
> Bombe a man,
> carezze col pugnal. . . .

Giulio had been at his desk a couple of hours when the maid brought him a letter. It was from the president of the Fascist Institute of Culture, Professor Fantinuoli, asking him to lecture at the fascist headquarters in Argenziana, on May 15th, on the subject 'The conquest of the Empire.' Giulio shut his book, convinced at last that he could no longer concentrate.

He went out into the street. Late in the afternoon he was to see Linda Boari, a girl he was coaching privately for the school-leaving exam; but for the moment, with a couple of hours ahead of him, he had nothing particular to do. As a rule he was careful never to waste a moment, but for once he was going to wander about the streets. What mattered was to stop brooding over Mussolini, the barber Arlotti, or the ex-secretary of the G U F.

When he reached the public gardens, the scent of young

lime-trees was sweetening the air enticingly all around him. He dusted the fragrant yellow dust off the last bench in the garden walk, and sat down gingerly. Two shabby old men from the local authority home, bundled up in their grey cloth uniforms, which smelt of carbon paper, were enjoying the spring sun on the bench beside him. He shut his eyes and leant back, thinking of Linda Boari. She was not pretty, but her liveliness and her middle-class air made Giulio, awkwardly conscious of his own position as a tailor's son, find her attractive. The almost daily lessons had made him used to her, and he now felt he could not do without her. What was influencing him most, perhaps, was the need to break through the ring of loneliness that had so far hemmed him in, and to have someone to love who was all his own, someone he could talk to about his private worries, celebrate his successes with, confide his hopes and plans to. He kept looking up at the oil painting of his mother on the dining-room wall, but the picture was no longer much use to him. His mother had been dead for several years, and the memory of her tenderness was fading.

His father, who was now elderly, was an excellent tailor, skilful, hard-working, and well-considered by his middle-class customers. Giulio admired him, but spiritually he felt he was a stranger. As a child, he had never been fond of his father, probably because his parents' frequent quarrels upset him. Like most boys whose parents quarrel, he had taken his mother's side, and she had done her best to keep him to herself.

When she died he was seventeen, full of intellectual interests both at school and outside it. At that age he could not come close to his father with the ingenuous sorrow of a child, who instinctively took refuge in the affection of his surviving parent. In any case, he found it hard to express his feelings, and this meant he was uneasy with his father and unable to try any friendly approaches. He justified this by telling himself that his father did not seem to want any more relaxed, more familiar relationship with the son who was so much unlike him.

Giovaccino Govini, in fact, had never managed to get over the feeling of inferiority he felt towards his son. Towards his wife, an Austrian brought up in Trieste, who had never been pretty, even as a girl, but was highly intelligent, he had felt the same. So when he was left a widower he tacitly renounced his authority as a father; and if Giulio ever needed advice or a scolding he preferred Enzo, who was twelve years older than Giulio, to give it to him. With Enzo he felt easier, partly because they worked together in the shop. But even with him he was not as close as, secretly, he would have wished, since they differed too much in both temperament and education.

The seven years since his wife's death had brought the family an atmosphere of peace, but no warmth. Just occasionally the three of them would have a small row at meals; but in practice Giulio had been growing up on his own, without any guidance from his own family since he was seventeen. His father and brother seemed scared by the emptiness of their large old house, and when the meals were over they almost dashed away, each going his own way. Giulio occupied the cold rooms entirely on his own, and in the long hours studying and thinking he had only the elderly maid for company; her conversation was purely domestic.

There was too big a gap between Enzo's and Giulio's ages for them to feel as familiar as brothers who had grown up together. Enzo was extremely fond of his younger brother, but he preferred to carp at rather than encourage him. In his heart he was delighted with Giulio's success, but wanted to avoid appearing to be so. He thought it his business to scold him, especially because, as a practical man, he thought Giulio, in spite of his obvious intellectual gifts, was clearly an innocent.

Enzo had done pretty well at school himself, but his enthusiasm for sport and his lack of enthusiasm for intellectual work had meant he had not gone on to university. Officially he had started working with his father, but in practice he rarely set foot in the shop for several years, for he was an exceptional athlete, and distinguished himself as the SPIM goalkeeper, the man who could stop anything. As such, he shared the fans' admiration with Dario Cavallari, Dionisio's elder brother, a remarkable centre-forward, who could play brilliantly or feebly and whose acrobatic talents meant he could save a lost match at the last minute with one of the impossible goals that only he, out of the whole of Italy, could achieve.

After the catastrophe in 1926, when S P I M, which for years had been playing on a level with Milan, Juventus and the Internazionale—strong only in its supporters' enthusiasm —had played a disastrous final, and gone down to a lower division, Enzo retired, and when he gave up sport he flung himself into work. As partner in the family firm, he proved himself even more able than this father, and to friends who sometimes suggested he should take a degree, he invariably replied that he preferred English fashion magazines to text books. All this meant he was hardly the sort of brother to free Giulio from the weary emotional loneliness he had been suffering from for years.

VII

Outside the family Giulio had two friends from whom he occasionally sought affection and comfort—God and Dionisio Cavallari. But Dionisio did his best to uproot Giulio's faith in the Christian God. Only a few days earlier, seeing him going into church before an exam, he had attacked him bitterly.

'How can you reduce God to a kind of first-aid kit who changes the course of events to help anyone who prays to him? We each create our own destiny.'

'D'you really think you can chuck out religion with a couple of tags from your philosophers?'

'They're not tags! They're truths that are crystal clear.'

'But the churches are still full.'

'Full of women, yes.'

'Yes, because just now a lot of men are afraid of being called tepid fascists. And they're wrong—'

'That's wishful thinking, Giulio! The fact is religion's on the way out, and anyone who's young and educated just can't believe any longer.'

'The young need faith.'

'But nowadays anyone who wants to believe has got the doctrine of fascism. Then there's the idealistic philosophy, and outside Italy, there's even Marxism.'

'Well, obviously I'm not like the rest of you. . . .'

In fact, Giulio was quite unlike his friends. His mother, though not narrow-minded, had been extremely devout, and had given him a good religious education as a child. Throughout his school days he had been an active member of the Catholic youth club run by a saintly zealous old priest, Mgr Castelli, and its atmosphere had strengthened his Catholic feelings. When he went up to the university in the autumn of 1931, and, like all the others, joined the G U F, he had not joined F U C I, for the G U F disapproved of students who belonged to Catholic organisations as well, and Giulio felt unable to stand out against this disapproval, like the handful of excessively Catholic youngsters—only seven or eight—who belonged to the F U C I in Padusa. But he had remained a sincere Catholic, and though he went to communion rather less often than he had done while he was at school, he had never once missed Mass. In God's house he felt more than ever the Church's majesty and the nobility of its message of love.

So it saddened Giulio to see the fascist regime—which in 1929 had praised the Lateran treaty so highly—mistrusting the Church, and sometimes taking up attitudes that seemed to him quite unjustified. Fascism had been carried away by its determination to monopolise the young entirely. But Giulio thought its fears were pointless and kept hoping to see Catholicism and fascism in agreement—the two greatest expressions in history of the Italian genius.

In his second year at the university, when fascism and the Church had been most at loggerheads, he had once been in trouble himself. He and a friend had come rushing back from a training exercise of the student corps, and had served at the midday Mass in the church of San Gaetano, which was bang in the centre of Padusa, still wearing uniform. Both Giulio and his friend had been acting in good faith; neither had the faintest idea that he was infringing fascist regulations. But the corps commander, who came to hear of it from a fascist official who was present at the Mass, had angrily proposed severe disciplinary measures.

Religion was something quite private, he argued. The Duce had been perfectly right to curb Catholic Action, in 1931, because it was seeking to extend its own organisation outside religious matters. A student in the corps who served Mass on his own initiative, and not at any official ceremony, was humiliating his uniform and black shirt before the priest, behaving as if Italy belonged to the Pope, and not to the party.

Things hung in the balance; Giulio was saved from disciplinary action only because the G U F secretary behaved like a true friend and defended him energetically. But for some days he worried about being reprimanded, which would have lowered his standing in the eyes of the local fascist officials, without hope of redemption.

VIII

For some time Giulio had been considering proposing to Linda, but when it came to doing so he never quite dared. Appearances looked encouraging, but twice before he had thought a girl loved him, and then, when it came to proposing, he had been refused. Once he had been in love with a warm, lively, laughing girl called Rosa, who was studying Italian, like him, and seemed to adore him; and for three years at school he had been secretly and ardently in love with Dionisio's sister, Mariuccia. This was further away in time than the other, but it still stung him.

Giulio had been swept off his feet by her: with her perfect oval face, her sweeping fair hair and her large proud eyes, which sometimes had a cold, enchanting glint in them, Mariuccia was lovely. Men were attracted by her and she knew it, and her short, unanswerable refusals had saddened any number of her victims at school, and later at university.

Giulio had suffered in silence. She had treated him with a kind of motherly condescension, and every time he thought she was going to yield to the current admirer, he had been in a torment. At last he thought she had realised how he adored her in silence, and felt she was growing much warmer towards him herself; so he ventured, very timidly, to declare himself.

He was in the drawing-room at her house, and Mariuccia had looked at him with kindly astonishment. 'Why, Giulietto, whatever's bitten you?' she said softly and then straight afterwards burst out laughing in the friendliest way. 'Please, please don't be cross,' she kept saying, in her rich, fluting tone. 'But it's all so terribly funny.'

Giulio kept thinking of his own age. Maybe I'm too young, he kept telling himself, but he was really thinking: maybe I'm too ugly. A great wave of embarrassment rose hotly to his head, and seemed to make it swell, but he managed to pull himself together, said goodbye between clenched teeth, and left the house.

He was now twenty-three, he had his degree, and felt he had a dignity to uphold. Another humiliation was something he could not bear.

That day he arrived unusually early at Linda's. On the way he had thought of speaking out, but in the end decided not to. So he greeted Linda gaily and casually and sat down beside her at the table.

'Now for a little Latin translation, Signorina! You choose.'

'Oh, but I don't feel like it.'

'Why?'

'Because once in a while I'd like to talk to you about something a bit nicer. A charming teacher who doesn't wear glasses or a beard ought to—'

'Ought to flirt with his pupils?'

'Not with all his pupils. Just with one. . . .'

'You?'

Linda half shut her eyes and leant her head languidly on his shoulder. All Giulio could do was kiss her, but he did so timidly, with the embarrassment of a boy who had never yet touched a woman's lips.

That evening, as he went home, he thought that he now had a girl like everyone else at the university, and that his feelings of inferiority—because he was shy, despised tarts, and was never taken seriously by respectable girls—would now surely grow less.

His best friend, Dionisio, was not really a success with girls, either, though not at all bad-looking. He was tallish and well-built, with expressive eyes and a Charlie Chaplin moustache which he grew in order to distract attention from a long, tough chin; women liked him right away. But he liked girls for company more than for love-making, and no one else could make them laugh as he did with his jokes and tricks and the rhymes he could make up on the spot. It was not just the girls at the university who liked him but those still at school as well, because every year when they were taking their Greek and Latin exams in July and October he helped those he called *bonae puellae* with their homework, and even smuggled his help past the ushers, with generous tips from his own pocket.

At the university he flirted, not very seriously, with a couple of girls reading literature, both of whom considered themselves eggheads; but neither girl lasted and Dionisio shrugged it off. Jokingly he would say, imitating Joan Crawford in the film *Grand Hotel*, 'Love doesn't exist.'

What Dionisio really enjoyed was being leader of the student gangs in cafés, at the university, and at sports. Giulio admired his dynamic ways and the self-confidence he never managed to achieve himself.

'I'd love to be as lively and relaxed as you are,' he had said to Dionisio the previous day. It was a conversation they often had, and they knew exactly how it would go.

'All right, I hold forth, I make jokes—and what's the result? Masses of people get offended, think I think they're idiots, and everyone touchy dislikes me.'

'Who cares about touchy idiots?'

'Giulio, lad, they're the majority!'

'Well, they won't stop you getting ahead. You've really got what it takes. But I'm too timid. . . .'

'Ah, but you've got brains and you've got no enemies, whereas I've got any number. You mustn't believe Mussolini when he says "Plenty of enemies mean plenty of honour"— he's exaggerating there, you know.'

IX

On May 14th, Giulio went to see Professor Fantinuoli, president of the Fascist Cultural Institute, who was celebrating his birthday, and read him an ode on the conquest of the Empire, which he had been working at for weeks. In the excitement of the recent triumph, with forty-five million flags waving, a thousand mourning mothers had passed unnoticed; and it was their sacrifice that Giulio wished to recall.

He waited anxiously for Fantinuoli's verdict, for the professor's word was law even in matters of literary taste. Fantinuoli said that Giulio's poem was not an empty rhetorical effusion, as it might at first seem to be, but had some real lyrical originality and he himself would get it published in a good review.

Giulio was delighted. He had always had a gift for writing verse, and envied some of his contemporaries who had long ago had delicate little lyrics published in the leading reviews. Beside them, he felt like an elephant: an elephant with plenty of ideas, but able to express them only dully and woodenly.

Professor Fantinuoli took him along to the fascist headquarters, where six G U F members, chosen to give propaganda lectures in the smaller local towns, had been called to his office.

The first to arrive was Dionisio, whose impeccable logic even Fantinuoli appreciated (someone had nicknamed him Pure Reason). Cavalieri d'Oro was another: he always responded enthusiastically to any invitation of the kind, so long as he was not distracted by a girl. The young G U F members were given clear instructions about their propaganda lectures on the Empire and on the world-wide development of fascist politics. There was no doubt about it: Fantinuoli had brains, and it was hardly surprising that he had got a university chair in political economics while he was still under thirty.

'It's a great pity such a bright fellow has to click his heels every blessed time he says the word fascism, and put on his uniform when he goes dancing with his wife,' Dionisio whispered to Giulio as they left. 'No sense of humour, that's the trouble with him!'

Giulio did not reply. Probably his wish to get ahead in politics made Professor Fantinuoli lose his sense of proportion at times, he thought. But you couldn't help liking him. He was a really decent sort, and clever enough to justify being ambitious.

Some years before, when Mussolini dismissed five ministers in a few months, among them three who were extremely important in the regime (Grandi, Bottai and Balbo), and took over their ministries himself, a sharp joke went round the country: there were now very few ministers directly responsible to the Duce in the cabinet, it seemed. 'Mussolini's got the lot,' the café wags said, 'except justice, education and economy.'

Giulio had repeated this to Fantinuoli, who had laughed heartily, but had taken the opportunity of explaining that this concentration of power in the hands of a single man was part of the logic of a totalitarian state, as only the leader could keep in direct touch with the people and interpret their deepest needs. Indeed no one felt the 'revolutionary value' of the new regime as Fantinuoli did; he spent more time trying to make his pupils understand the essential reasons for totalitarianism than he did teaching them political economy.

But Giulio could not see why Fantinuoli spoke approvingly of some of the Soviet economic achievements, when the Duce so often said that communism and fascism were total opposites and even that the world would soon face a dramatic choice between Rome and Moscow. Yet Fantinuoli idolised Mussolini: Moro, the prize gossip, said he had Mussolini's photograph at his bedhead instead of the Madonna.

Next evening Giulio arrived at Argenziana half an hour ahead of time. He was greeted by the fascist secretary, an old farmer who had the stormtrooper's red stripes on the sleeve of his woollen jacket. Fifteen years before he had been the organiser every time a local red was beaten up. The important locals were all with him. If Arlotti—who in fact came from Argenziana—had been there, he could have told Giulio that all these 'comrades' were either landowners or important tenant-farmers, except for two, who were the local organisers of the fascist agricultural and industrial trade unions.

In a quarter of an hour the room filled up, Giulio was introduced by the fascist secretary and plunged into his speech. With a voice full of feeling he spoke of the injustices Italy had suffered in the past few years, compared the poor nations with those who ate five meals a day, and praised Mussolini for restoring Rome's ancient grandeur. Finally he spoke of the conquest of the Empire, with all the advantages that would come to the Italian people from it.

Every now and then his speech was interrupted by applause, and Giulio noticed that the loudest clapping came, not from the fascist officials around him, but from the audience in the front rows, by the look of them primary-school teachers, clerks, minor professional men, shopkeepers, who lapped his warm words up enthusiastically. The poor, at the back of the hall, clapped readily enough when the front rows gave them the signal to, and often smiled and nodded in agreement as well. This was striking proof, Giulio thought, that in every social class people appreciated the great conquests which the Duce had achieved with so little Italian bloodshed. Nor was he mistaken, for just then the mirage of the Empire was in fact dazzling. Ethiopia seemed like a kind of Eldorado that would soon flood fascist, proletarian Italy with inexhaustible riches. Mussolini had created a great collective illusion, and even the poor believed in it.

At the end of Giulio's speech the fascist secretary ordered the salute to the Duce. '*A noi!*' the entire hall thundered enthusiastically.

As the audience was leaving, the secretary called over a thin, bent old woman dressed in black, with a bronze medal pinned on her breast, and presented her to Giulio as the mother of the only man from Argenziana to have died gloriously in Africa. The old woman had wet eyes and muttered a few words in dialect. Quite obviously she felt uneasy playing the part of a hero's mother.

Giulio found the scene embarrassing. After a few conventional words he managed to get away and went over to the end of the hall to talk to the few people still left in the back rows. Obviously they felt shy, as if unused to talking politics with 'important' people who were socially above them. Giulio had exchanged only a few words when the secretary came over and took his arm, and dragged him away decisively, and with a touch of scorn.

'Comrade Govoni, come along to my office: the members of my committee are waiting to drink your health.'

During the same week Giulio spoke again twice, on the same subject, and each time the scene at Argenziana was repeated.

The following Monday Dionisio asked him round. He too had returned after giving three propaganda lectures on the Empire, and they swapped impressions. Giulio's direct contact with the people seemed to show up the inconsistencies in Arlotti's sarcastic criticisms, for even in the country people seemed united behind the regime.

'What's more,' Dionisio said, 'I noticed that among the very poorest of the poor, there were plenty who were dying to get out and have a stake in the Empire. One of the trade union organisers agreed with me about that, yesterday.'

'Poorest of the poor? D'you really think there's poverty among the peasants here in the province?'

'I don't know much about it, Giulio, but the day-labourers must be in a pretty bad way.'

'I suppose so. But there aren't such a lot of them, are there?'

'What? They're the majority of farm workers, you know.'

'And what d'you think they earn, on an average?'

'Search me! A married couple might get two thousand lire a year.'

'Why, that's impossible! An elderly high-school teacher gets only just under that every month.'

Both were silent, embarrassed. Giulio felt ashamed to think he had so confidently harangued the country people without any idea what an acre produced in the way of hemp or wheat, or how and when beetroot was planted, or maize. But above all he had no knowledge of the farm workers—their problems, the way they lived. The various categories into which they were divided were just so many names to him.

Dionisio knew little more, though four years of studying law at the university had made him more observant about some things. Like Giulio, he was a lower-middle-class townsman living in his own cocoon, completely out of touch with people poorer than himself and even more so with those who lived in the country. His father had a fine draper's shop in Padusa's main piazza, patronised by the rich, and this background had certainly not done anything to make Dionisio familiar with the problems of poverty.

Giulio and Dionisio were sipping iced pomegranate juice, in silence, when Dionisio's cousin, Fausto Carrettieri, came over to them, to borrow a legal textbook. Fausto was large, thickset, and fair, with a crew-cut, an enormously high forehead and a tough jaw, Mussolini-style. Undeniably he had charm and some intellectual ability, but when he started at the *liceo* he had lost interest in intellectual work, and had never recovered it; and the whole of Padusa university knew he was systematically squandering the fees his father so laboriously saved to send him there.

Like all the other students, he was a member of the G U F, but, just then, he was one of the very few (if not the only one) who occasionally spoke out against the fascists. His opposition was not obstinate and systematic, though: it was intermittent. Occasionally he would take part in some cultural event, during which he would momentarily forget the ideas he had absorbed from his father, and speak the same fascist language as the others. Francesco Tassinari, secretary of the G U F, thought Fausto sometimes posed as an anti-fascist simply because he had not done particularly well in the G U F. He must be the 'great resistance man', Tassinari suggested sarcastically, who scrawled 'Who reads Starace?' on the lavatory walls in the law faculty.

'There are too many thieves in Italy and outside it, admittedly, but it used to be worse,' Giulio said to Fausto. 'Maybe in another hundred years we'll get a world that's decent.'

'I agree about honesty; but there's something else we used to have and haven't got now.'

'What's that?' asked Dionisio, coming back with more drinks.

'You know perfectly well I mean freedom. But you don't give a damn. Your mouths are bunged up with the word *Empire*.'

Dionisio smiled as if taking no notice of what his cousin had said. But Giulio burst out: 'This freedom lark—you've been on about it for ages and now you're becoming a bore.'

'You don't care, of course. . . .'

'All I say is, it's the subversives who want freedom—to undermine the state. Real Italians want freedom from foreigners, and we've had to wait for Mussolini to get that for us.'

'What a worm's-eye view of it, Giulio! What matters in this world is freedom of speech, freedom of thought.'

'You can't eat freedom—the poor don't give a damn for it.'

'Giulio, you make me mad! A man's got to be free to say and do what he wants.'

[42]

Dionisio cut in coldly, 'Suppose you were free to do what you wanted, what would you do? Pile up more debts?'

'What's that got to do with it?'

'Of course it's got something to do with it, Fausto! Fascism's given you the freedom to take a degree, and you've profited from it by taking only three exams in four years.'

Abruptly, Fausto left them.

X

A couple of days later Giulio was sent for by the G U F secretary.

'Govoni, I need a serious chap, and that's why I've sent for you.'

'Fire away, then!'

'The Federal Secretary wants the best of the girls' G U F to lecture to women workers on the organisation of the fascist state.'

'Fine. But what's it got to do with me?'

'Don't you realise they're just not fit for it? They know damn-all about the fascist state.'

'But you can get a few elementary ideas just by reading the newspapers.'

'Newspapers, Govoni? But these girls only read film mags and the glossies.'

'So I've got to. . . .'

'I see you've guessed. I'm giving you a fortnight to teach four or five of them: the least awful.'

Tassinari had good reason to be sceptical. There was precious little revolutionary spirit in the girls of the Padusa G U F, and Mariuccia Cavallari, Dionisio's sister, who had been their leader between 1933 and 1935, had tried in vain to prod them into action. Pugnacious and pig-headed, Mariuccia had flung herself into the G U F with enthusiasm, and for those two years had bombarded the others with postcards announcing meetings. These became more and more numerous, and anyone who wanted peace with Mariuccia around had to train for the sports events and march vigorously in parades. The other girls, who might have put up with her better if she had been plainer, disliked being organised, nicknamed her 'the new broom' and stood up to her with 'elastic resistance'.

Mariuccia stopped being a new broom the day she met Efrem Mantovani, an accountant studying economics. Efrem was hard-up and hardly outstanding, but he was the best gymnast in the university team and had a body like a Greek god; and the unassailable blonde, whom the boys had nicknamed Greta Garbo, suddenly fell in love and, whatever her family said against it, was determined to marry him right away. Mariuccia gave up medicine, which she had seemed to love, and wrote to the G U F, resigning, and at last saying just what she thought of the good-for-nothing girls in it, who for two years had given her so much trouble.

After her, as leader of the girls' G U F, came Rosella, and she it was whom Giulio now approached. He wanted her to agree on a crash course that would bring the girls up to date on things, but with Rosella it was very hard to agree on anything. She was a pretty girl who, though extremely keen on her position in the G U F, had very little interest in politics. What she cared about was sport and training the others for sports events; she loved appearing at G U F dances and any other of its social affairs, too, and did well as a fascist do-gooder, a lady bountiful. But if anyone asked her about the totalitarian state or the corporations, her undisguised yawns put an end to the talk in a couple of minutes.

And the other girls were just like her. All of them felt they were fascists through and through, just because they were Italian; they wore the black G U F uniform quite happily ('it's slimming,' Rosella used to say) so long as the meetings were short; whenever enthusiasm needed to be loudly voiced they were ready to compete with the men, and they venerated the Duce as their country's god. But fascist doctrine had never entered their heads, nor had the regime's hatred for 'the cushy life' taken a hold on their hearts.

The only girl who set herself up as politically-minded in the epic year 1936 was the second-in-command of the girls' G U F (nicknamed the Mountain by everyone because of her quite remarkable size), who loathed Rosella and was cordially loathed in return, as everyone knew. The second-in-command,

[44]

in fact, was dying to kick out her superior. She regularly, though not always accurately, quoted the Duce and the party directives, and aired her views on current affairs. But no one had taken her seriously since Moro announced in the café Torino that she was larking around with the Vice-Federal Secretary, a married man twenty years older than herself, at the fascist officials' hide-out at Cardellino.

The village at Cardellino, with its blackened hovels, its hammers beating incessantly on leather (it was an old shoe-making centre), its few cars and its bicycles endlessly parading up and down the ill-kept cobbled street, was huddled along the river bank a few miles from Padusa. Where the village began stood an old brick country-house, unpretentious and just like any number of others in the Po valley, with a narrow arch over the front door, greenish shutters, and two odd portholes near the roof that looked like the dead eyes of a caryatid. Here Rosanna, the house's mature but still attractive owner, whose behaviour as a young woman had made her pretty well known in the village, had had the idea of setting up a 'house' where important people could arrange their love-affairs discreetly, and had approached a couple of fascist officials who had been her lovers in their stormtrooper days. These two had at once considered her confidential proposal, and quite soon the house, rechristened 'The house of the fatherland' by some wag, became their headquarters, erotically speaking.

Soft divans, cut-glass chandeliers that shed a diffused light, daring little statues, cushions embroidered with the languid pierrots then fashionable, warm scents, drinks, expensive cigarettes, were all provided, and Rosanna reigned in triumph as semi-official madam, arranging everything with remarkable tact. At the time arranged she would be found at the entrance, looking extremely alert and on guard as she awaited her important deliveries, till the car she was waiting for drove up, and a young woman hurried out of it. Then, after a while, another car would arrive—this time it would be the latest model—and drive up with a screeching of brakes. Solemnly the important fascist would strut out, then dive indoors, bowed in by the ceremonious Rosanna, who would then sit for the next two or three hours at the door, watching the convolutions of her cigarette smoke with apparent indifference, yet ready to give the alarm the moment anything suspicious happened. Moro, the inveterate gossip, would not rest till he had penetrated the house's erotic mysteries, and as soon as he had any news he would rush to the café Torino to tell all, gathering his friends around him and keeping their curiosity alive by winks and hints and by what he cunningly failed to tell them.

'The walls have ears,' he said, when anyone said he had too much imagination.

'Rosanna talks when she's had a few drinks,' he said one evening. 'The day before yesterday I went dancing at the Fascist Workers' Club in Cardellino and there she was, slightly on heat because of all the boys squeezing up to her and giving her the odd poke or two. When the band stopped she came to the bar with me, I bought her a couple of drinks and then we went outside for a breath of air. "Well," says I, "how's the House of the Fatherland doing?" "Fine, love," says she. "Girls, cold suppers, drinks galore, and the bigwigs crash into armchairs—or rather on to divans—and lie there snoozing till they've slept it off."'

'Not bad going for people who aren't supposed to enjoy the cushy life!'

'Cushy life, I'll say! It's for others to rough it, not them!'

Moro went on telling his friends more about his meeting with Rosanna, then lowered his voice to bring out the prize piece of gossip.

'Well,' he said, pulling his chair up to get more comfortably settled, 'the Mountain's been at it again, with the lieutenant-general of the Militia this time. Maybe she's hoping for promotion. . . . Anyway, it was November 4th and this chap, who used to command the Arditi, came along for the victory celebrations with eight medals all over his chest, and insisted on ogling the Mountain. Whereupon the Vice-Federal Secretary, who's as modern as they come and hasn't a twinge of jealousy in him, had the bright idea of suggesting a cosy little meeting, which might finally dislodge Rosella from the job she longed to get for herself.

'"This won't be forgotten," he whispered in her ear, which easily won the Mountain over. But what actually happened was, our hero couldn't make it!' and Moro roared with laughter, coarsely.

'So, when he got back to fascist H Q, d'you know what happened? The general was furious with the Vice-General Secretary and made a sign with him to come close. The Vice-Federal Secretary obeyed and his ear was pierced like a sword with the distinct metallic word *"Imbecile"*. So the Mountain'll take over from Rosella the day Starace takes over from Mussolini!'

Moro went on laughing, leaning back in his chair and banging his hands on its arms; and his friends laughed too. One of them, doubled up with it, cried: 'Imagine him getting medals on Monte Grappa, and being defeated on the lower slopes of the Mountain. . . .'

And the coarse laughter went on and on.

XI

The hot Padusan summer was earlier than usual that year and middle-class families who could afford it hurried off to take their holidays on the Adriatic or in the Dolomites.

Few of Giulio's friends spent the summer away, though. Most lower-middle-class families thought holidays a luxury for people better-off than themselves, and even when they could have sent their children to the sea or to the mountains preferred to save the expense of it. In any case, the less sophisticated students could bathe on the large sandy beach by the river called il Ghiaione. Half an hour by bicycle took them there from the middle of town. Admittedly, it was the poor man's beach, but it was the ideal relaxation for youngsters who were preparing for exams. Many of them got up early, worked till about three o'clock, then finished the day on the river beach. One of the advantages of this was the chance of uncompromising love affairs, because, apart from the plump, blooming peasant girls from the surrounding countryside, there were plenty of town girls who came there to seek summer flirtations.

Dionisio's lazy cousin Fausto Carretieri spent more time on the river beach than anyone, but he was less interested in swimming and sunbathing than in pretty girls. On the beach he would look over the ones who looked most approachable, start chatting them up and then, after a while, vanish with the one he had chosen among the willow trees that grew thickly along the banks.

Fausto, like many other students of modest means, spent his summer holidays working in the sugar industry. A couple of months' work in an office connected with it, or in the Sugar-Beet Growers' Association office, meant they could pay their year's university fees, and have a bit in hand as well. But Fausto also had to pay for his higher education taxes.

Early in June public life stopped in Padusa, and with it the fascist propaganda lectures, which involved the most prominent students, from Giulio and Dionisio onwards. First the harvest and then the threshing kept farmers, tenant-farmers and day-labourers working from morning till night. Then it was the time for sugar-beet and hemp, which involved work that was just as important and onerous. And until the heavy work was over in the country, the small town marked time.

In summer, Giulio felt happy. The heat never worried him, and he loved nothing better than the town asleep under the midday sun. What he loved best were some of its wide Renaissance streets under the sun at its highest, when the pavements were burning, the walls of the houses breathed out heat, and the shutters were all closed. Straight after lunch he would get out his ancient bicycle, and like a child enjoy himself pedalling slowly up and down the crumbling surface of the streets he loved, where only a very few people hurried past in their shirt-sleeves without looking up at him, and the odd cat might be seen chasing a lizard.

In other years he too had gone to the beach at Ghiaione for sunshine and sunburn. But he had never liked the crowded, messy, proletarian beaches, with their heaps of rubbish. Dionisio, on the other hand, stood outside the general untidiness and, with the air of a sociologist on holiday, enjoyed studying the seething humanity around him.

But this year Giulio could not go to the beach at Ghiaione; Linda would never have allowed him to be seen there, where so many students spent the day with tarts. She had failed her Italian and Latin exams, and her mother hoped that with coaching she would pass the difficult exams in October. So every day Giulio went to their house to give her lessons.

As soon as he arrived, he and Linda fell into each other's

[48]

arms on the wide, soft sofa, tormented by desire. Giulio was always the first to pull away. Perhaps his temperament made it easier for him to control himself; but what really influenced him was a sense of duty. He thought of how Linda's father, knowing nothing, was paying him to coach his daughter for the exam, and not to make her fail by wasting time like that. Sometimes her mother came downstairs (Linda's study was on the mezzanine floor) and knocked lightly at the door to warn her that it was time for lunch. She would smile kindly and affectionately at Giulio, as if apologising for having to send him away, and Giulio, blushing, would hurriedly set the next day's homework, and leave without saying any more. He was now afraid that Signora Boari had realised what he felt about Linda.

It was not only Linda that he coached. As always during the summer he was giving private lessons to a number of boys at the *liceo* who were taking school exams or university entrance, and although his main reason for doing so was to earn a little pocket money, to avoid having to ask for it at home, he really enjoyed teaching. All this did not keep him off his own work, either. He was a tremendously hard worker; and in summer, when the university was closed, the G U F activities were suspended, some of his friends were away and the city lay half-asleep, he managed to work with extraordinary intensity.

XII

At least twice a week Giulio met Dionisio at the café Torino. How pleasant it was, Dionisio always said, to enjoy the coolness of the summer evening in that well-aired spot, lying back in the comfortable, sensibly-designed metal armchairs in a row on the pavement outside the café!

When he was not at the beach at Ghiaione, Dionisio spent the hottest hours of the day at home, in vest and shorts, reading and studying. Being restless, dissatisfied and curious, he preferred books on philosophy, history and economics to his legal text-books. After supper he relaxed at last, and enjoyed listening to the café gossip, hearing the respectable towns-people mercilessly dissected, and Moro softly murmuring the latest scandals.

The café Torino, in fact, reflected the Padusan middle classes. Ever since it opened—not long before, in 1930—it had been well liked. Much of its success was owed to its position opposite the great clock tower, in the busiest street in Padusa, and because tables were spread attractively and invitingly under the welcoming porticoes; but the new American-style interior, designed by a lavish decorator, had much to do with its popularity as well—in particular the low, windowless room that customers found so relaxing and immediately christened 'the submarine'.

From the start this new type of café atmosphere had seemed to people like modernity itself, completely ignoring, as it did, the modest, old-fashioned traditions of the other Padusan cafés: the grand but run-down Folchini in Corso Gioconda, and the nineteenth-century Mozzi, with its old chintz-covered sofas, and hopelessly outdated air, both of which it quickly supplanted. Its customers were varied but friendly, and went well together. When it opened up, Signor Attilio, the amiable owner, was there to smile at everyone who crowded inside or in the porticoes outside—old and young, penniless students and rich landowners, government clerks and well-off business men. The few local intellectuals had their corner there as well; and if any writer or painter who had become known in Rome or Paris came to Padusa, he could hardly fail to drop in at the café Torino where people were having drinks before dinner.

As the whole of Padusa was represented there, its customers of course included important fascist officials. But they dropped a little of their arrogance in its atmosphere, and for an hour or so stopped feeling like uniformed overlords and became slightly more used to the everyday middle-class world, that liked dressing informally and occasionally allowed itself a grin at the gloomy fascist uniform.

It was in the late afternoon, as a rule, that the fascists hung about under the café portico, answering the slack Roman salutes of the regulars, listening absent-mindedly to whispered requests from people seeking help, but also—perhaps most importantly—eyeing the chatty middle-class girls who swarmed under the porticoes of the town's main street just at that time of day.

The café Torino was not particularly conformist. Nearly all its customers might be members of the fascist party and absolutely loyal to the regime, which was then at the height of its success, but, when there were no humourless fascist officials about, jokes went the rounds about fascism and even about 'the professor' (which was the customers' name for Mussolini). The main target, of course, was Achille Starace, who, since the conquest of the Empire, had been the subject of wilder jokes than ever.

Of course, the Empire was really something; but since its conquests Italy's role in the world had been so much exaggerated in official circles that even a great many fascists criticised an attitude that seemed quite fatuous. They roared with laughter at the imaginary conversation between Mussolini and the deputy Lanfranconi, who was famous for his flat jokes: 'Now,' the Duce told him, 'I've given you your head with funny stories so far but now we've had enough. We've conquered the Empire and the regime's looked up to all over the world, it's loved by all Italians and destined for further conquests—'

'Oh excuse me, Duce,' Lanfranconi broke in. 'This really isn't one of my jokes. . . .'

But those who loved telling their friends the latest joke, as if to prove their own broad-mindedness, often reacted very firmly if some old customer, not yet resigned to fascism, timidly tried to steer the conversation into serious non-conformity and throw doubt on whether the regime, with its faults, was really bringing Italy prestige, power and prosperity.

Politics, however, was not the main topic of conversation in the café Torino. Heads of families talked business, youngsters chatted about girls and exams, and everyone discussed sport and in particular the town's football team, the bane and delight of thousands of obdurate supporters. Anyone who wanted to talk about books and music knew where to go. In a corner of the 'submarine', even in the dog-days, Arturo Bottoni, self-taught playwright who, between dozes, wrote gay little plays in dialect, taking no notice of his job at the town hall registry, was always to be found bundled up and feeling

[51]

chilly. All he did in his office was sign his name in the register every morning, in order to draw his small salary at the end of the month. His boss had anyway given up the idea of keeping him behind his desk after Bottoni, threatened in a fatherly way, had candidly, in wide-eyed self-defence, quoted a Spanish proverb *Quien trabaja perde tiempo precioso* (the man who works wastes precious time), which made the boss burst out laughing.

Bottoni was always ready to stop writing and start interminable conversations on D'Annunzio and Pirandello, Ungaretti and Marco Praga, Mascagni and Lorenzo Perosi. At sixty, he had read everything, except (but this he confessed only to his closest friends) what the Duce had written.

As a young man he had loved women. Now he just put out a hand whenever a pretty one went by, which earned him the nickname of 'Patacake' in the café Torino. His usual companion was Moro, who loved the theatre as he did, and, also as he did, despised work as a waste of time. These two determined night-birds never left the café until the shutters were put up, and were delighted if they could then go home with someone, and stay up until three in the morning.

Bottoni's Mediterranean indolence and unsystematic culture, which puzzled Giulio, cheered Dionisio. Whenever he had time to waste, he sat down by his old friend and got him going on the eccentricities of the artistic and literary world at the beginning of the century, and listened to his unpredictable remarks on the present, with all their scepticism, their delicate irony.

Bottoni was the only customer at the café Torino who failed to take sport, and football in particular, to heart. He said he despaired to see thousands of serious people going mad over a goal and hearing respectable family men yelling curses at the referee and the referee's mother if he happened to blow a whistle.

In July Dionisio told him he was going to the Olympic games in Berlin, to spend the generous sum he had just won so brilliantly with the Mussolini prize. Bottoni turned red as a turkey-cock.

'I'm sorry I ever thought you had a brain at all,' he spluttered.

But Giulio felt envious as he said goodbye to Dionisio, wishing he could have afforded to make the journey with him. This was not just because he was thrilled by a sports event of that size, but because he longed to know the world, to meet people who spoke other languages, who belonged to other races and had other ways.

Yes, Rome and Mussolini were the light of the world; but they weren't everything.

XIII

On the first Sunday in October Giulio had to go on a training march with the university militia. Like most of the students who had not yet done their military service, he had enrolled, but the frequent meetings annoyed him.

That morning, as on every other morning, the exercise was pointless. No one wanted to run or make any effort, or march in line or do rifle drill; and the two officers training them— a fat captain and a young lieutenant—had no authority at all.

As they marched back to town that morning the students in the troop were straggling along the road like a herd of cattle, taking no notice at all of the officers' protests. Many had even taken off their jackets and tucked their caps under their arms, as if they were coming back from some gay outing, wearing ordinary clothes, and they were singing songs of all kinds, particularly enjoying the indecent ones. Had they been wearing G U F uniforms, they would have sung *Giovinezza* and other fascist songs enthusiastically; but they disliked the uniform of the university militia so much that the regime was the last thing they were thinking about.

Dionisio suddenly had the idea of striking up the old socialist song:

> Avanti popolo, alla riscossa:
> bandiera rossa trionferà. . . .

He had no intention of playing the anti-fascist, but was simply trying to be funny, trying to give the final flick of humour to this absurd exercise that made them dress up as soldiers practically every Sunday, and wear that horrible alpine cap and lug their guns along like broomsticks on their shoulders. The tail-end of the straggling column gaily joined in, and so did Giulio, who, not knowing the words, mechanically followed the tune.

Waving like madmen, the two officers at the head of the column came dashing back. They knew how these educated youngsters brought up in the fascist climate felt, and knew quite well that this was a piece of bravura, not intended to show any liking for an ideology that was now buried in shame. But they could not let them show such a marked lack of respect towards the militia. How could the troop forget, they shouted, that it was wearing the uniform of one of the armed forces, indeed the chief of the regime's armed forces? Already they had been singing untidily the whole way, making a terrible spectacle of themselves; but this was too much, this was past bearing, to be singing a provocative song like that! What would people in the road say? That the troop was idiotic, farcical!

Dionisio got the worst scolding, from the captain.

'A nice thing for a fellow who thinks he's really someone in the cultural competitions, I must say. The Federal Secretary's going to hear about this.'

'Oh, come off it, don't make such a fuss! I was only joking.'

'Joking hell! And call me *sir* when we're in uniform. D'you take this for a troop of firemen?'

Dionisio clicked his heels and stood at attention:

'Certainly not, sir!'

The officer either failed to see that this was also meant to be funny, or pretended not to see it, and muttering between his teeth turned his back on Dionisio. The incident would have been over if Giulio had not had the unfortunate idea of remarking loudly 'And what's wrong with firemen, anyway?'

He had not meant to tease, but the pointless joke made the captain furious, and he turned on Giulio, raging: 'There's nothing wrong with firemen—it's you that's the fool. Those lectures you give are just to keep the public amused.'

XIV

That evening the G U F ball, the first of the new season, took place. From the beginning of their engagement Linda had told Giulio that she would certainly go, and wanted him there.

Giulio was in a bad mood: the captain's angry answer had left a sour taste in his mouth. And he was not at all cheered by the thought of going to a dance, either. Although in his first two years at the university he had often been to dancing lessons, he had never managed to become even a passable dancer. He had no sense of rhythm, could not lead the girl, and was as stiff as a ramrod. So he felt at a disadvantage on the dance floor and envied the way so many of his friends could twirl about so elegantly, and the way the girls smiled delightedly when they accepted. Whenever he asked a girl she agreed with an air of resignation. Dionisio often urged him to get over his inferiority complex. It was all very well to talk, but Dionisio, though a cold dancer, was fairly good, and could have no idea what it was like to feel that girls were just putting up with him.

Now the situation had changed a bit, which was just as well: he had a girl! No longer would he feel alone, as he had so often done in the past, when his friends wandered off and he was left to play wallflower with the girls' mothers.

On purpose, he arrived very late. The glittering dance-hall of the Padusa hotel was full, and people were dancing to an excellent band. This first G U F dance after the holidays was considered the young people's meeting-place by the town's respectable families, and the prettiest, most noticeable girls were all there, as there was no need to be a university student in order to attend—at least as far as the girls were concerned. Every girl of 'good family'—whether at university or *liceo* or not studying at all—thought it a point of pride to be at the G U F dances. The smartest young men—those who paraded their father's wealth and had the advantages of aristocratic blood—held more exclusive and more elegant dances at the Union Club, where the fact of being at university was not enough to get one in; but they too felt bound to attend the GUF dances. The young men at the ball were not all students, though: a glittering, noisy crowd of young officers from the large garrison headquarters came as well. And youngsters from well-to-do families, though they might neglect their studies, never neglected the GUF dances. Those who avoided them were, on the contrary, poor students—sons of workmen or small shopkeepers—who disliked meeting girls who might despise their shabby clothes and rough manners, and who preferred to go to the suburban dance-halls where the 'hops' were held.

As soon as he came into the hall, Giulio began looking round for Linda. Moro he saw right away, humming softly by the band, thumbs tucked into his waistcoat pockets; he caught a glimpse of Mariuccia Cavallari with her husband; he saw the GUF Secretary, Tassinari, waltzing with his fiancée in the middle of the room, and looking round like a hen clucking over her chicks; but Linda was nowhere to be seen. Only after a couple of minutes did he find her in a side room, talking to a second lieutenant in the cavalry, whom Giulio now saw for the first time; slim, very smart, with a large nose, a pencil-thin moustache and an air that was smug and affected. He was talking into Linda's ear and both were smiling.

As soon as the dance was over Giulio joined Linda. He looked even angrier than when he had come in.

Without scolding him for being late, Linda jubilantly told him that the lieutenant had been flirting with her and had asked her to dance five times. He wasn't exactly handsome, but very polite and distinguished—and a count, from Piedmont!

Giulio was silent. The dancing began again and he led her on to the floor.

'Darling, you're awfully glum—what's the matter?'

Giulio said nothing.

'You wouldn't, by any chance, be jealous?' Linda went on. 'Who of?'

'Why, of the lieutenant! I may never meet him again. . . . So really!'

'What rubbish, Linda. I don't even know his name.'

'He's Count Parvo Passu. He's called Bob.'

[56]

'Splendid. . . . So's Moro's dog!'

'But what's got into you this evening?'

Giulio was already hurt by what the militia captain had said earlier in the day and now on top of it there was this loathsome lieutenant. But pride kept him silent.

They danced several times, and every now and then the lieutenant brushed past and smiled at Linda, elegant, sure of himself. Linda never stopped talking; Giulio listened absently and answered in monosyllables, pretending to agree.

He was thinking hard. As he brooded over what the captain had said, he was tormented by the thought that the man might have called him a fool not merely because he had lost his temper, but because he wanted to let him know that the fascists had a pretty poor opinion of him. As for tonight's smiling lieutenant, he irritated Giulio more and more. All he had was an outsize nose—but he was a count, and wearing the uniform of the smartest regiment. And here was Linda clearly pleased at his attention: Giulio had never seen her so lively.

He told Linda he had a very bad headache, and moved away, leaving her talking to another girl.

'A fool to the fascists,' he thought, 'and a yob in the ball-room, that's me. What am I doing here?'

He was going across towards the exit when Tassinari, the G U F Secretary, slapped him on the shoulder.

'Here, come along, Govoni! I want to present you to the Minister, Barboni. His Excellency's passing through Padusa and has stopped in here to see his grand-daughter's first public ball. . . .'

They went over to the Minister.

'Your Excellency, this is Comrade Dr Govoni, of our G U F: an extremely able fellow who works enthusiastically for the party and has had a splendid training.'

The Minister, though hemmed in by a group of admirers, turned at once with a wide friendly smile: 'Govoni! Any relation to Enzo?'

'He's my brother!'

The Minister slapped Giulio cordially on the back.

'He was a great athlete, and I was a fan of his. What's he doing now, though?'

'Still in the tailor's shop, with Father.'

'Give him my greetings, will you.'

'That'll be an honour, your Excellency.'

For ten minutes, while his friends looked on enviously, Giulio stayed talking to the great man, who rarely honoured his home town with his presence. When they parted, instead of leaving Giulio went back to Linda. He felt light-hearted, took her arm and led her to the buffet, reconciled and happy.

XV

The band had put up a notice saying *Interval*: the usual pause during dances. The players were swallowing a quick cup of coffee, then set to with their instruments, tuning fiddles, blowing the spittle out of the brass with a strange cacophony.

The hall was full of warm scent and the smell of sweat, and echoing with loud chatter, broken by sudden roars of laughter. Men and girls crowded round the buffet table. From above the shelf of drinks, the Duce's pop eyes looked down severely on the scene, and seemed to be staring at the small bronze eagle on top of the expresso machine. The barman was trying to serve everyone and orders were piling up.

'A peppermint soda.'

'Two rhubarb liqueurs and three coffees.'

'A cognac for me.'

'Arzente, *if* you please, comrade!' a familiar voice corrected the man who had ordered, with a light laugh. Giulio and Linda turned and saw Efrem with Mariuccia, looking extremely pleased with life.

'What a marvellous dancer you are,' Giulio told him, and moved away, with a smile at Mariuccia. As a bachelor Efrem had been an unusually good dancer, who had won diplomas, cups and medals at the Merchants' Club, the Apollo dance hall, and the Edelweiss—now rechristened the Imperial. But after marriage his enthusiasm had waned.

That evening, after a long time without dancing, he had yielded to Mariuccia's pleas and had danced uninterruptedly with her, like a real virtuoso, twirling about in perfect style and in the most elegant and complicated figures. Mariuccia, with the unmistakable femininity that dancing reveals better than anything, had followed him, and everyone was drawn by the harmonious grace of such a wonderful-looking pair. People remembered their university years—between '31 and '33—when Mariuccia would flash down the passages leaving behind her a wake of desires expressed in the tune heard everywhere in those days—on the radio, in the streets, in the theatre:

Parlami d'amore, Mariú. . . .

It was a song she might have inspired herself. When it spoke of 'Your beautiful shining eyes' everyone thought of her, and when it said 'Tell me it's not an illusion' everyone thought of the way she aroused illusions and longings in everyone by the way she flirted, and how, when her admirers became too aggressive, she stifled their hopes.

Moro was probably thinking of all this when he suddenly started whistling the tune, as if without realising he was doing so. Those around him listened, nodding to the song's rhythm in a soft silence that recalled their secret dreams. Suddenly Moro drew away from the group, and whispered something into the bandleader's ear. Then he turned quickly back to the buffet.

'The band's starting up again, boys!'

They all left their drinks and food and went back into the dance hall, delighted at the thought of dancing again after a rest. The orchestra struck up the familiar first notes of *Mariú*, and there was a soft chorus of approval. Mariuccia's face lit up. Efrem took her hand: 'Come on . . . this is always lovely. . . .'

They went on to the floor, while Moro set up a kind of fence around them and the rest

'Let her dance,' he said. 'It's her dance, after all.'

The pair were left alone on the floor while everyone watched and Mariuccia slid lightly into the first steps of the dance. Graceful and supple as a reed, sometimes standing up straight, at others flung backwards, she followed her husband in the magical circle, plunging over and over again, detaching herself slightly then clinging to the man who held her in a tender vice. For a while Moro watched them in silence; but he felt that the band alone did not give the full atmosphere, and he

[59]

started up the song, as if to wrap the dance round in it. The others immediately joined in.

It was not just a song: it was like a strange wave that lapped the heart and the senses:

> Parlami d'amore, Mariú:
> tutta la mia vita sei tu
> Gli occhi tuoi belli brillano,

The couple were now fully launched.

> Fiamme d'amore scintillano. . . .

As the old G U F members sang Mariú, meaning Mariuccia, they all felt the old fascination and were all carried away by her as they had been before. The other girls smiled, without jealousy. Mariuccia's triumph was the triumph of Woman.

XVI

October 24th 1936 was a day of celebration for the local fascists: the Duce was coming to make an important speech in the regional capital. The G U F secretary took his staff from Padusa university along, and Giulio and Dionisio could not fail to be there. The huge, crammed piazza was dominated by a gigantic poster bearing Mussolini's motto 'Live dangerously'. On the balcony the dictator appeared; there was a storm of applause, and he looked fierily at the crowd below.

'Blackshirts of the Tenth Legion! Blackshirts of my own land! Ten years have passed since our last meeting.'

'Much too long!' roared the crowd.

'In this piazza I find the same ardent faith, the same vibrant enthusiasm, the same spirit of the Tenth Legion, favourite of Julius Caesar, founder of the first Roman Empire.'

The enormous crowd in black, proud of this child of the district, who had founded a second Roman Empire, roared enthusiastically. But Mussolini knew quite well that on the outskirts of the city and in the countryside there were people expecting promises to be kept, which in fact had been forgotten, people who might not be applauding as enthusiastically. It was to them that he now spoke.

[60]

'Our love for the people, a severe love, a soldier's love, throbs with conscious, profound humanity.'

Giulio's eyes filled with tears.

Then Mussolini went back to his *leitmotiv*—the feat of which he was proudest:

'In six months, and in five battles, we have conquered an empire. We have conquered it by overthrowing, not just the enemy forces and the betrayers of European civilisation who had enrolled and armed them, but an entire coalition that had set up its general headquarters on the banks of Lake Leman.

'When we have pacified the country down south in Africa, a country six times the size of our own, there will be work and space for everyone—after the glory.'

The crowd went mad, carried away by the image of Italy powerful and feared, and promising all its people the good life. Now, Mussolini was not proposing new wars, but a policy of peace.

'From this city, which for centuries has stood as a beacon to the human mind . . . I send a message that must go beyond the mountains and beyond the seas.'

It was the olive branch of peace.

'But take care,' Mussolini declaimed deliberately, 'this olive branch comes from a great forest of eight million well-spiked bayonets, held by young and brave hearts.'

Even Dionisio thought the image sublime, though he noticed there was something odd about hearts that were . . . holding bayonets. And the youngsters gathered in piazza Maggiore went wild with delight.

Next day a lecturing competition for G U F members was held in the main hall of the fascist headquarters in Padusa. According to the Federal Secretary and Professor Fantinuoli, who had suggested it, the contest was to show the public the political maturity of the young people who had grown up under fascism and prove their ability to preach the doctrine that was destined to conquer the world.

Fewer people were competing than had been expected. The fascist faith might warm people's hearts, but fear of an audience—Dionisio said—cooled them off. Those taking part could choose their own subject of fascist propaganda from a number suggested, and every second evening the fascist head-

[61]

quarters was opened for the day's lecture. The judges, presided over by the Federal Secretary, were Professor Fantinuoli, the secretary of the women's fascist organisation, the *podestà*, and the Vice-Federal Secretary.

The Federal Secretary would pop in for a quarter of an hour, listen to the speaker for a bit and then go into his office to attend to his paperwork. Professor Fantinuoli, zealous, conscientious, concerned to see everything went well, and always in fascist uniform, turned up first every evening and left last. The provincial secretary of the women's fascist organisations, a duchess with a liberal background, as a rule sat beside him. Most people thought the old aristocrat had taken on the job to help her impoverished family, for the fascists liked having the noblest local lady at the head of their women's organisation, and treated her very handsomely. Padusa's *podestà*, an excellent Jewish doctor who looked like an Old Testament prophet, was a very good attender at the lectures. As he wore his fascist uniform only at extremely formal official ceremonies, he came to the lectures in everyday dress. A good many people wondered how such a man could support the regime. Mild, tolerant, anti-authoritarian by nature, he had never been a stormtrooper or marched on Rome, and seemed the very opposite of the ideal hero fascism was trying to mass-produce; but those in the know said that the Minister Barboni, who had been at school with the *podestà*, and was known to be one of the few fascist leaders who could get Mussolini to listen to him, insisted on keeping him in the position, if only to spite other people.

The Vice-Federal Secretary was a real Starace-type fascist official. Smart in his well-fitting uniform, self-possessed and self-important, he was an authoritarian who looked down on anyone below him in the fascist hierarchy, and let it be seen that he did so. He was a good-looking man who seemed in love with his own looks and peered furtively into shop windows to admire them. He had taken a degree in law, but gave the impression that he had not looked at a book for a very long time. All he ever read was *Il Popolo d'Italia*, the regime's official newspaper, but he was good at sensing the Federal Secretary's moods. What the party leaders said was gospel to him. Without arguing, he obeyed orders down to the last detail: 'To be-

[62]

lieve, obey and fight,' Mussolini's slogan, was apparently the main object of his life. But those who knew him well knew that he was ideologically zealous rather than hardworking. He spent as little time as possible in the office, being very busy outside it with the training of the town football club, of which he had been president for some time, and in particular with a great many complicated and time-consuming love-affairs. Exuberant virility was, he maintained, one of the signs of a true fascist, and he had even managed to persuade his poor wife that this was so.

Every evening he attended the meetings, listening rather absently, making wide gestures of support every time the Duce was mentioned, glancing at the clock and always getting out first after the lecture.

Three to four hundred others also turned up every evening: clerks, teachers, professional people, university students. Mario Braghiroli, leader of the local Felletti group, never failed to be there (listening to the speaker's tone and voice rather more than to what he had to say) as well as a great many minor fascist officials (local group-leaders and section-leaders), who might not have turned up quite so often if they had not hoped to be noticed by the senior officials in the two front rows.

The audience was mostly lower-middle-class—an audience that saw the fascist regime as a guarantee of order in the country and as a guardian of the moral values of Roman and Christian civilisation, and in particular filled with patriotic pride and therefore taken in by Mussolini's grandiose policies. If the speaker merely raised his voice slightly when he mentioned the Duce, or if his voice shook slightly at the words 'victory,' 'greatness,' or 'Italy's mission,' the audience burst into applause at once.

Giulio thought Dionisio would get the first of the three prizes, having a sound background knowledge as well as being an unusually good speaker; whereas Dionisio thought he had no chance at all. His lecture on corporativism was thought learned (no other student at Padusa could have dealt with the subject), and everyone praised his style of speaking. But the judges thought his speech too cold, and in particular they disliked the way he kept mentioning socialist theory.

[63]

'Admittedly he mentioned Marx only to criticise him,' the Federal Secretary remarked. 'But he mentioned him much too often. He gave the impression that fascism was on the defensive. What an idea!'

Dionisio was told the judges' opinion, and reacted angrily, telling his friend that such narrowness made him despair. Mussolini was colossal, a genius, but a great many fascists were so petty-minded that they stood in the way of spreading his doctrine throughout the world.

Giulio spoke warmly and eloquently of the Empire, and was often applauded. But when towards the end he spoke of the Abyssinian war, he gave the impression of failing to take seriously the Abyssinian army, against which fascism boasted of winning such an outstanding victory on the battlefield—'an ill-armed rabble of hungry blacks,' Giulio called it. It was only a small point, but it went against him, and—as Professor Fantinuoli explained to him afterwards—it was the reason why his lecture, which was in every other way excellent, got only third prize.

Cavalieri d'Oro spoke on the subject 'A book and a gun makes the perfect fascist!' This happy slogan, which the regime had thought up for fascist students, gave the imaginative Uproar the chance for an impulsive speech on the revolutionary ideas of the fascist young, whose spirit and muscles were hardened in the contest of life, unlike those of the feeble youngsters in Western democracies. He concluded his hot-headed speech by saying the Duce's slogan slowly and deliberately: 'Fascism's creed is heroism; the bourgeois creed is selfishness.' There was a storm of applause.

In spite of this success, the Federal Secretary suggested Cavalieri d'Oro should have second prize, and that the first prize should go to his secretary, a young man originally from Istria who had just got his degree and had spoken on 'The genius of the Duce.' He was steeped in fascist mysticism; his name had originally been Walter Colausig, but his father, an official at the town hall, had had to italianise the Slav surname into Colaussi, and Walter, at the time of the sanctions, had asked to be baptised Italico-Gualtiero by royal decree, and was allowed it. The Duce might always be right, but Federal Secretaries might sometimes be wrong, and on this occasion

[64]

fessor Fantinuoli be right when he said that it was silly to pity them and that the fascist policy of racial discrimination should not be dramatised?

Only once did Giulio feel uneasy; this was when he saw a teacher the same age as himself, whom he had introduced to Milazzo at the request of Linda's mother, coming out of the inner office muttering 'Money, money, money! Always the same old thing!'

Giulio pretended not to understand. 'What d'you mean?' he said.

The young Jew came over to him and murmured in his ear 'That fine lawyer of yours certainly gets all he can out of the Jews.'

'Don't say that—he's a good chap.'

'Everyone's a good chap, according to you. But I've lost my job and no one'll help me, from your Milazzo onwards. D'you know I'm actually hungry?'

And he laughed bitterly, while Giulio silently shook hands.

Next day, Giulio told Linda about it.

'Contini came to the office yesterday. It was terribly sad.'

'Don't think about it. That's the way the world is.'

'Why d'you say that? He's such a friend of your family and your mother was so worried.'

'Mother's always worried about other people.'

'But this poor chap's ruined—he hasn't even enough to eat.'

'Yes I know. But I've got too many troubles of my own to worry about the Jews.'

This reply shocked Giulio, and he went home in silence and brooded over it for a long time. What he looked for in a woman was delicacy, consideration, warm affections; but what had Linda now become?

Her good-tempered days, when she was kind and thoughtful towards Giulio, were rare; and every day her once-keen interest in his problems seemed to grow less. Sometimes, when others were there, she had generous outbursts and moments of gaiety that endeared her to everyone, but when they were alone together she became sulky and on edge.

'Those nerves of hers mean she needs a husband,' her mother sometimes grumbled.

Giulio was sometimes worried that it was he, with his shyness

[97]

and complexes, who made Linda so nervous. But he had no intention of making her his mistress. Both his religious education and his respect for her family made this impossible. So their relationship was a series of short lulls between long storms, as they waited for some event that would alter its course. Giulio now felt that this event was approaching.

XXVII

When he came home Dionisio had also decided to set up in his profession. He was in a hurry to get experience, because the higher exam for those who had taken their degrees in 1936 was coming up, and he managed to get a job in the office of Mario Scaranari, the best lawyer in Padusa. Scaranari had been a socialist deputy several times until the coming of fascism; he came from a middle-class family and was steeped in the romantic socialism of de Amicis, which had been born out of pity for the wretched poverty of the day labourers on the land in the Paduan lowlands, where he was born.

Scaranari had a fine head with a mane of nearly white hair, and strong features that always looked calm and firm, even when stormtroopers broke violently into his office and smashed it up from top to bottom. Oppressive acts against him had never made him submit to fascism in any way. He had always remained faithful to his own ideas, though he had avoided the kind of open resistance that would have made it impossible for him to carry on in his profession.

His smile was charming and his manner distinguished, and as he went along the streets or through the law courts, leaving a trail of lavender behind him, he greeted everyone with vigorous waves. Scaranari was a man of taste in behaviour and in dress, and Matteotti, who had been a great friend of his, had called him a 'silk-shirt socialist.'

No one who knocked at his office door was refused an interview and everyone was given cheering words at least. He felt that the first duty of the only true aristocracy—which was an intellectual aristocracy—was friendliness, a virtue unknown to the triumphant party officials who thought themselves the élite of the new imperial Italy. Even the fascists, except for a few fanatics, greeted him respectfully. They felt the charm of this man who was so unlike them, and who won friends with smiles and kindness.

Scaranari disliked the day-to-day work of the office, and had it done by a tall weedy man two years older than Dionisio called Vashinton Marangoni (his father, an anarchical pork-butcher who had risen in the world from nothing, had been unable to spell the name correctly). Vashinton was not at all lively, but he had a sharp brain and good legal background, and made an excellent support for Scaranari. Contact with his boss had made Vashinton lose the fascist beliefs he had held at the university, and instead of them he had absorbed Scaranari's ideas. Now he disliked the idea of being a party member so much that on public holidays he was likely to stay indoors all day to avoid wearing the obligatory black shirt.

The most frequent visitor at Scaranari's office was a large young man, slightly younger than Dionisio, called Eriberto Melloni. His father was one of the richest landowners in the province and possibly Scaranari's most important client, but he seldom came to the office himself and preferred to get in touch with Scaranari through his son. Eriberto had started at the university the year Dionisio left, and, as it suited his temperament to do, took his engineering studies pretty lightly. He was the only student in Padusa who was not a member of the G U F. Tall, strong and elegant, with fine black eyes and curving lips, Eriberto was the kind of man the girls under the porticoes of the café Torino peeped at out of the corners of their eyes. He liked an easy life and by habit and temperament was an aristocrat, who despised the regime's vulgarity in refusing to let people say what they thought, go where they wanted to, or even dress as they liked.

Scaranari's outer office was a favourite place of his, and he might spend a whole afternoon there, chatting with the typist and leafing through the magazines, waiting to tell Scaranari the latest anti-fascist joke.

Before he had done his military service, Dionisio had thought him a useless idler, like so many others. But now he began to respect and like him.

XXVIII

In the agonising spring of 1939, Eriberto had grown so bitter
about the regime that even in the café Torino he often gave
way to indiscreet outbursts and worried his friends. Giulio
understood the spiritual sufferings of a committed man, which
was why he could take Dionisio's outbursts calmly, but he
loathed the anti-fascist arguments of people who stayed in bed
till midday. So when Dionisio got him along to meet Eriberto
he made his disapproval obvious by a cold silence.

But the day the newspapers had banner headlines about
the Duce's great decision to increase wages and salaries, Giulio
wanted the satisfaction of rubbing it in.

'Have you seen the papers?' he asked.

'I don't give a damn what they say,' Eriberto replied.

'Of course! You millionaires don't like fascism because it's
trying to improve the lot of the poor.'

'You may know reams of Carducci and Leopardi but you
know damn-all about economic problems.'

'And I suppose you do—remembering how you were
shoved up by main force from form to form at school!'

'We've got a big firm and we know what's produced here
and abroad, and I can assure you the national wealth hasn't
been increasing for some time.'

'Prove it!'

'Just look around you. The cake's still the same size. So
what's the use of the Duce's generosity?'

'To increase consumption.'

'Nonsense! All it'll do is raise prices and please fools.'

Caught on the quick, Giulio was about to make an energetic retort, but just at that moment a party official came
in and, to avoid involving his friend in trouble, he swallowed
his reply. But a few days later, Eriberto involved himself.

It was March 16th and the newspapers, in enormous headlines, gave the news that what was left of poor Czechoslovakia
had been occupied by German troops. Eriberto was thumbing
nervously through the *Corriere della Sera*, deathly pale, whis-
pering something to Dionisio. Behind him, Mario Braghiroli,

distinguished reciter of the Duce's speeches, was holding court, and had begun explaining loudly to a group of friends that the occupation of Czechoslovakia was a decisive stage in the setting up of the new order in Europe. When he raised his glass to toast 'the success of our German comrades,' Eriberto whirled round and shouted in his face:

'In this atmosphere of *obligatory enthusiasm* we needn't actually cheer the aggression of bandits!'

The glass fell from Braghiroli's hand.

'Bandits? Have you gone mad?'

'I'm not the one who's mad, it's that whey-faced Hitler, who doesn't even respect Mussolini.'

'How dare you? No one's more respected than the Duce.'

'Have you forgotten the guarantee he gave at Munich?'

'That's old hat! We're on the march now, to make Europe fascist—'

'Hand-in-glove with those crooks!'

'That's enough!' shouted Braghiroli, grabbing Eriberto's jacket. 'Idle bastards who spit poison are best locked up.'

One of Eriberto's tough fists shot out, hit Braghiroli on the jaw and knocked him down.

That afternoon Eriberto quickly packed his bags and left for Milan, and his father rushed round to his cousin—who was fascist secretary in their local town—with a generous offer to the party funds, and so managed to hush up the incident.

The party might ignore Eriberto—who was thought to be just an idler—but it took it out on the café Torino. The Braghiroli incident had shown that too much 'anti-national' talk went on there, and this was not to be borne. So all known grumblers were given a good talking to, and Dionisio got special treatment. He clenched his fists to keep from answering, because if he had opened his mouth he too would have had to voice his disgust at the vicious happenings in Prague.

A few days later Giulio was at Dionisio's, and during the meal Mariuccia attacked her brother. She was not asking him to give up his own ideas, she said, but simply to be prudent and less childish.

Giulio supported her.

'Why have you of all people lost your head? Haven't you always preached realism and rationalism?'

[101]

'Of course! But it drives me crazy to see the Middle Ages coming back into the twentieth century, and being treated as real and rational. . . .'

'The Middle Ages, my eye! The world's getting better, it's progressing.'

'How can you say that? Why, only yesterday Mussolini said perpetual peace was a catastrophe for human civilisation.'

'That's just talk. A totalitarian regime wants life for its people, not death. And that's why it speaks directly to them.'

'But it takes away freedom of speech and freedom of thought. It's worse than it was under the Inquisition.'

'Oh, don't make such a tragedy out of it! Most of the world's still run by the democracies, who say they love your precious freedom.'

'But totalitarianism's advancing, and I'm watching it with terror. The last stage was the fall of Barcelona, where Franco's cannons were blessed by the priests. The world's upside down and that's why I'm exploding.'

As Giulio went home Dionisio's words kept whirling about in his head. His friend's opinions and analysis of events seemed to him pessimistic, but not totally untrue. Giulio tried to take his mind off things. He went into the imposing Via Grande and started walking slowly along it, looking at the marble reminders of noble families—though he knew them all by heart already—at the great sixteenth-century buildings, with their wonderful ornaments, at the old medieval brick houses, with their fascinating jumble of windows large and small, Romanesque and Gothic. And at last he managed to think of other things.

Then he reached the middle of town, and in the large piazza, with its noble Lombard Gothic church, a beam of light was turned on one of Mussolini's sayings, written in enormous letters on the front of the Palace of Justice: 'Only God can bow the fascist will: men and events never can!'

Giulio remembered seeing these words on the front of the primary school by the church, outside Porta San Giorgio, until a few days before; but one night some unknown hand had scrawled across them in pitch 'Let's hope in God!'

XXIX

A few days later Giulio had a telephone call at the office from Mariuccia, Dionisio's sister. Since her marriage he had not seen much of her—for one thing, she had seemed to be avoiding her old friends. Besides, he had never really understood her sudden marriage. She was beautiful and rich and not at all domesticated, and she could have quietly finished her studies and then have made a brilliant marriage. It seemed absurd that Efrem Mantovani, of all people, could have made such a gifted girl lose her head—handsome though he was.

Mariuccia now asked Giulio to call in the middle of the afternoon, when she would be alone, so that she could talk to him about Dionisio. He turned up punctually with a bunch of flowers and Mariuccia asked him to sit down beside her on a big sofa.

'Dionisio's hopelessly ruined,' she said.

'Oh now, don't exaggerate!'

'Don't you see that when he talks about fascism he just doesn't control himself any longer? Even Scaranari disapproves of his outbursts and his lack of prudence.'

'It's the sudden disillusion that's embittered him. He'll quieten down soon.'

'But suppose he keeps talking nonsense in the meantime and gets himself chucked out of the party?'

'Don't worry. No one dislikes him all that much.'

'But he's ruining himself.'

'I told you he'll soon quieten down.'

'That's not enough, Giulio. He'll never become a fascist again, and anyone who's not a fascist never gets on.'

'Scaranari's done well. Don't you think he may do the same?'

'But Dionisio's got a first-class brain, he ought to go even further.'

'Well, who's to say he won't be way up there in ten years? The world's changing, you know.'

'Giulio, don't tease. I've failed as a woman but I don't want my brother to fail as well. All my hopes are centred on him.'

[103]

They were silent a while; then Mariuccia moved away for a few minutes. When she came back her eyes were shining, and she began talking to Giulio again.

Just as Dionisio was now going irrevocably wrong, so she had been wrong in her time. She had rushed into marriage stupidly cutting short her studies, in the belief that marriage was in itself the crown of life. If she had had children she might have found a different balance in life. But so far she hadn't, and she might never have any. She could not limit her own interests to domestic affairs, and thought of taking up medicine again. What right had Efrem to oppose this so obstinately, when he did nothing that could possibly interest her? She could be interested in painting, too (in fact, as a means of escape, she had been painting surrealistically for some time), but at home they talked shop from morning till night, and it meant nothing to her. It almost looked as if her marriage had been a business deal of her father's: he had found a son-in-law as much in love with fabrics and designs as he was, but his daughter wasn't happy.

'But your father didn't force you to marry Efrem! And Efrem didn't go running after you. It was you yourself who wanted it.'

'What could a girl brought up without a mother know about these things?'

Mariuccia got up suddenly, went over and closed the shutters, which let a tiresome gleam of sunshine in, and continued talking excitedly.

She had now forgotten her brother, and was thinking only of explaining her own dramatic situation—that of a woman who had made a mistake and now felt stifled by her narrow household circle. She and Giulio were sitting together on the sofa. As she grew more excited she became less composed, and inside the low-cut dress he could see her breasts swelling with her growing excitement. Giulio was now only pretending to listen, and secretly thinking how attractive she was, how full of life and spirit, and comparing her with his own Linda, who had no beauty, no excitement, no poetry about her. Had he been less timid he would have seized her hands and told her that this outburst of hers had revived the passionate adoration of his early years, as if by magic; and he would have reproached her for having discouraged him when he was her only admirer who had really understood her. But he kept silent, and tried to leave as soon as possible.

At the front door Mariuccia stared into his eyes: 'I know what you were thinking.'

Giulio blushed and looked down.

'But you were wrong,' she said.

'Why?'

'I told you before. You're like Dionisio to me, like a brother. You could never have been anything else.'

That night Giulio slept very little. At four in the morning he was wide awake and had made up his mind.

For some time he had been seeking something to put an end to his weary relationship with Linda. This bewildering plunge into the past, this contact with a woman who was in so many ways his ideal, had made him see that his love for Linda was quite dead and that it was hypocritical not to admit it.

He warmed up half a pot of coffee and sat down at the table to write a long farewell letter. After a couple of hours he got up, put the letter in his pocket and set off slowly for school.

XXX

Linda never got the letter. The more Giulio thought of it, the more he was persuaded that it was neither dignified nor decent to say goodbye to her like that. He could not avoid having it out with her, particularly because of her family.

Early in the afternoon he plucked up courage and rang the bell at the Boari's house. He asked the maid not for Linda (who was always resting at that time) but for her mother.

The old lady was sitting in her favourite room, doing embroidery on a frame, her slender hand going up and down as she passed the thread through, stitching a coloured flower pattern. The room seemed to suit this harmless, old-fashioned pastime, for it summed up all sorts of old family memories: the style was *art nouveau*, with plenty of rounded consoles, portraits of grandparents and great-aunts and landscapes in oils. On a calendar was a girl with long fair hair, and in a

[105]

corner the baby grand piano still seemed to vibrate with the last notes of Toselli's *Serenade,* as if time had stopped in 1910.

'You want to speak to me?' Linda's mother asked gently.

'Yes, signora, I must.'

Giulio did not need to say much. Linda's mother herself brought up the subject.

'Things haven't been going well between you and Linda for some time, have they?'

'That's quite true.'

'Linda's grown very nervous.'

'Linda's not happy, signora. We don't understand each other.'

'So it's better to think it over, while there's still time, don't you think?'

'Signora, you embarrass me. You see things better than we do.'

'Well of course, old age gives you something! And that's why I'm telling you you mustn't be afraid of failing in respect towards me or my husband.'

'If only you were involved, I'd never leave her.'

'But it needn't be a definite goodbye. People change, you know.'

'D'you believe in coming back, signora?'

'In your case I'd always be glad of it, because I think so well of you, Giulio. I've got used to thinking of you as one of the family.'

'Thank you, signora. So have I.'

'From now on we shan't meet very often. But don't forget us.'

At the end Giulio was moved, overwhelmed by her gentleness.

When he met Linda, things were not at all dramatic. For some time she had felt that he would one day say goodbye. When he told her about his talk with her mother, and calmly and firmly confirmed his own decision, Linda's eyes filled slightly with tears. She held his hand as she told him, with a calmness that was rare in her, that she realised how wrong she had been. But she had been born nervous, and it would always make her unhappy. Could a man help her to change? Experience had taught her he couldn't.

XXXI

On the evening of April 1st Giulio turned up at the café Torino, after several days away from it. He was sure he would not find Dionisio, who was very busy preparing for his next exam.

But Dionisio was in fact there, and came straight over to him.

'Is this the way to behave? We thought you were dead.'

Giulio looked down.

'What's happened to you?'

'I've broken off with Linda and I'm a bit upset. I'm sorry!'

'You might have rung me up. . . . But if you come to supper tomorrow we can talk quietly.'

In his mind Giulio saw Mariuccia again, and the memory of her was disturbing.

'Thanks. But please don't insist.'

'Damn it, breaking off with Linda isn't such a cosmic drama!'

'No, but let's wait a few days.'

Just then Moro turned up, and asked for silence and attention so that he could tell his friends about the brilliant April Fool joke played on Tassinari, the G U F Secretary.

Everyone respected Tassinari's brain and his long training and many remembered how the president of the law faculty had told him: 'If you go in for law you'll soon be the town's chief lawyer.' But what the Padusa students disliked was his ill-concealed wish to follow those who had climbed high in the party through the G U F. So on March 31st, a few wags had had some mysterious telegrams of congratulation sent to him from Rome. Then on the morning of April 1st, at eight o'clock sharp, they woke him with a fake trunk call from Palazzo Vidoni: the office of the National Fascist party officially announced that Tassinari had been appointed Federal Secretary of Matera. On the other end of the line the students could hear him stammering with emotion.

At nine he was at the Federal Secretary's house to bring him the good news. But the Federal Secretary had been warned in advance by an anonymous telephone call, and when

Tassinari, looking pale, announced that the Duce had deigned to consider him, he did not even let him finish, but pointed to the calendar and burst out laughing in his face.

Poor Tassinari! He could not even avenge himself on those responsible, because the Federal Secretary, who knew his colleague's weakness, had forgiven them in advance. In fact at midday he had already told half the people in the office about what seemed to him the year's most successful April Fool joke.

But a joke of quite another kind had been played that morning on Guido Coen, a shy Jewish medical student whom everyone liked. Fausto Carrettieri, who had arrived while Moro was speaking, told them about it.

At dawn three ex-law-students, dressed up as policemen and armed with pistols loaded with blanks, had turned up at his house to carry him off. One of the three, putting on a typical policeman's southern accent, told him they were arresting him for seditious action against the state. His old parents fainted, and Guido was stupefied. They pushed and punched him downstairs half-dressed, and when they reached the front door dumped him on the ground like a sack of potatoes and went off sniggering.

'I've teased him myself in the past,' said Fausto, 'but now that the Jews can't defend themselves that sort of filthy trick just isn't on.'

Everyone was silent. Only Dionisio hissed: 'Imbeciles!'

About eleven someone suggested walking to the rampart of San Rocco, at the end of the long straight Renaissance street in which the café Torino stood. Six or seven of them set off. Moro began talking about the Bologna football team, which was now almost sure to win the championship, and Giulio emphasised the recent triumphs of the national team, which had grown almost invincible ('thanks to some imported South Americans,' Dionisio muttered).

They were at the end of the road, about ten yards from the rampart. That part of the street, which ran between some fine gardens, was poorly lit and very dark, but Giulio recognised a small man walking jerkily ahead of them with his hands behind his back. He nudged Fausto Carrettieri and murmured in his ear 'It's him!'

Fausto did not hesitate. He quickly caught up with Coen and in a friendly way dragged him over to the group.

Guido Coen stood in silence, hanging his head. Clearly he wanted to be alone and was annoyed by this unexpected meeting. When the first minute's embarrassment was over the others told him not to make too much of the stupid joke that morning, and to stick to his friends, which was what they wanted to be, and keep politics out of it altogether.

'Do believe me, we're more friendly towards you than ever,' said Dionisio.

'You're very kind, but your friendliness can't change the wretched reality. D'you know I'm being chucked out of the university because I'm a Jew? D'you know my father's been dismissed by the Council with a pension he can't live on?'

'Haven't you any savings to stand up to all this?' said Giulio.

'No, I swear we haven't. And what can I do to help my parents and myself? I can't be a labourer, I couldn't stand up to it.'

'No, of course not. What you need is a good private job.'

'Yes, but who'll give me one in this atmosphere?'

'Not everyone is a coward,' said Dionisio.

'All the same, if I came to the café Torino three-quarters of the customers would avoid me.'

'Oh, don't be too depressed,' said Giulio. 'Wherever we are, you can always come too, and no one'll turn their backs on you.'

'Obviously you don't know Mario Braghiroli pushed me out of the tennis club. And no one said a thing.'

Moro coughed, and the others looked at the ground.

XXXII

Next day, as soon as Giulio got to the office, Milazzo spoke to him.

'Have you seen the town's plastered in posters announcing Cavalieri d'Oro's lecture on the Protocols of the Elders of Zion? What a fuss! It's not even as if he were a nationally famous speaker.'

'Quite!'

'You may call him Uproar but he's getting ahead, Govoni. You're worth much more than he is, but you keep slaving between my poor office and the school. . . . Take a leaf out of his book!'

What could he answer? The man with so many Jewish clients seemed actually to be praising an anti-semitic action. Was he serious, or was he trying to be funny about Cavalieri d'Oro's ambitions? It was not easy to interpret his everlasting half-smile.

'Men aren't judged by their success as speakers,' said Giulio. 'You've got ahead in life, sir, but you've never made a speech in public.'

Milazzo laughed slyly. 'All the same, don't miss his lecture. If you do I'll think you're envious of his success.'

Giulio nearly retorted 'I thought you'd be staying away so as not to upset your Jewish clients,' which Milazzo deserved, but he only smiled evasively.

On the evening of April 4th Giulio was in the lecture room at the headquarters of the Merlanti group, a few minutes before the lecture was due to begin. He greeted Milazzo, who was talking to some party officials, but avoided going in with him; then he noticed that the first row of seats was already taken by the Federal Secretary Professor Fantinuoli and the Secretary of the G U F, Tassinari.

Many officials, high and low, were wearing their black uniforms with flashes and decorations, like the Federal Secretary. Local society was also represented in the crowded room, and several smart local ladies, elegantly dressed, were prominent in the audience. Crouching against a wall near the entrance was the barber Arlotti. Giulio, who was amazed to see him, went over and murmured in his ear 'You here?'

'Yes, I am! I'm not interested in the subject but I'm curious to see how people react.'

'So you're representing the opposition.'

'I'm certainly the only proletarian. D'you see there's not a single workman or artisan here? It's the great gala of the middle classes.'

At that moment Dionisio came in, with his cousin Fausto Carrettieri. Giulio saw them out of the corner of his eye and tried to avoid them. This was hardly the place to be seen with two 'heretics.'

Loud applause broke out when Cavalieri appeared, and stiffened in the Roman salute. When he began speaking he sounded a little uncertain, possibly intimidated by the unusual size of his audience, but after a couple of minutes he was perfectly at ease. He spoke well and fluently, and with studied pauses and gestures, as if he were on the stage. But enthusiasm was the best thing about his delivery, and it was this that really carried his audience with him.

His speech was a harsh, terrible indictment of the Jews. It would seem, from what he said, that, despising other races for theological reasons of their own, the Jews thought of nothing but the domination of the world. Pitiless and unscrupulous towards anyone who did not belong to the chosen people, the leaders of Judaism had—according to Cavalieri d'Oro—been undermining Aryan society for nearly two thousand years, in the hope of finally dominating it; and the Jews had crept in everywhere, like an enormous freemasonry, trying to take over all the key positions, one after the other. It was not cleverness that got them ahead, but push and unscrupulousness. The now declining western democracies were not strong enough to stand up against them, so Judaism was conquering the United States, England and France. Wall Street, the great temple of world capitalism, was a Jewish domain. But healthy nations, upheld by vigorous regimes, must necessarily react against them. This had led to the 'sacrosanct' racial laws of fascist Italy, not to mention those in Germany.

Gradually, as his speech proceeded, Cavalieri captured his audience. Every three or four minutes there was warm applause for something he said. Giulio watched the audience's reactions: delighted faces, nodding heads, smiles of agreement. Cavalieri's political arguments, and his power as a speaker, had won people over. At the end of the speech there was long, loud applause and a number of fascist officials ran up to embrace him. A little girl, dressed in the uniform of the Young Italians, interpreted the general enthusiasm by presenting him with a splendid bunch of roses and kissing him on both cheeks.

The crowd dispersed slowly because people hung about in

the hall to discuss the lecture—which was certainly going to be remembered.

As he was going down the stairs alone, Giulio felt someone tapping him on the shoulder. He turned and saw Dionisio and Fausto. It was impossible to avoid going out with them; but he could see they were soon going to burst out. Together the three went out in silence, and walked along a side street, and as soon as they were in the dark alleyway Dionisio spoke. 'Cavalieri d'Oro's so irresponsible! When he stirs up hatred against the Jews like that he gives an outlet to people's lowest instincts, and there's a risk we'll have a situation like the one in Germany, where the Jews are quite literally hunted down.'

'Mussolini isn't Hitler—don't worry, for goodness sake,' said Giulio.

Fausto interposed sarcastically 'Mussolini's a thief in kid gloves, and Hitler's a highwayman. But they do the same job.'

'You must be blind to talk such nonsense,' Giulio said, caught on the quick and raising his voice. 'Mussolini may make mistakes at times, but he's a balanced man.'

'Oh, he is, is he? And d'you know the latest idiocy of this balanced man of yours?'

'What is it?'

'A few days ago he ordered dance bands to stop playing *Little black face*, because of the racial law forbidding Italian soldiers to go after coloured girls.'

And he laughed harshly, leaning on Dionisio's shoulder.

They had reached a corner of the street, and Giulio, making some excuse, left them there. In the darkness he heard Fausto calling after him: 'Maybe you keep venerating that racialist Mussolini because those priests of yours keep their eyes shut to what's going on. I wish I knew how the church can be a friend of the friends of that German Anti-Christ!'

XXXIII

That night Giulio hardly slept at all: Fausto's last barb had really disturbed him. His friend had accused the Church of lacking the Christian spirit, no less; and Giulio was now thinking for the first time that racialism, with its discriminations, was the antithesis of the spirit of brotherhood and charity that was the essence of the Gospel message.

He knew that the Vatican and Germany had been quarrelling quietly over the paganising Nazi theories and the persecution of the Jews, even of those who had been baptised; but why didn't the Church openly denounce racialism in Italy, so as to make Mussolini, who was a reasonable man, draw back? Politics and morality were two very different things, of course, and the Church could not avoid politics altogether. But if Giulio still felt he was a Catholic, it was above all because he saw the Church's divinity reflected in its moral leadership; any doubt thrown on this was a blow to the faith of his childhood.

At twenty-seven Giulio was still a good Catholic, but he often felt uneasy about religious problems. It was as if his conscience, and his old habits of belief, were being slowly torn apart.

'There are distinguished men who believe without ever doubting,' he thought, and tried to gain strength from this idea and overcome his worst moments of uncertainty. His religious spirit had weakened as he left childhood behind him, and he identified it more and more with those early years.

Without realising it, he began re-living that time: the mornings when his mother took him to Mass in the church of St Catherine opposite the house. He could still feel her hand holding his, warmly and jealously, as they crossed the small, still empty piazza; and then he was again in the big church gazing round-eyed at the flying buttresses and the high arches where angels in wind-blown veils floated in a soft blue sky. The smell of incense rose and the organ shuddered and the mystery of the priest's nasal voice struck his scared, bird-like heart.

A single thought from those wonderful years persisted: Christ among men, with his love. It was a domestic, consoling image. 'Christ had my mother's goodness,' he often told himself, and it did not seem blasphemous to him, as a priest he had once confessed this thought to had told him it was.

Perhaps it was this vision of a familiar Christ that took him

[113]

to church when he was most depressed, even if his reason found it harder to accept dogma. Since his broken engagement had flung him into a kind of dismayed loneliness, he had been to church more often. Usually he went to the first Mass in the cathedral, at six in the morning, when there were few people there and an elderly canon said Mass at a small altar in the transept. There, in the front benches, were the usual attenders, those known to be pious, whereas in the back benches he occasionally saw people who were obviously suffering.

That morning Giulio got up very early and arrived in good time at the six o'clock Mass. It was not just the previous night's thoughts on the Church's moral teaching that were tormenting him, he was still shaken by the tragic fate of an uncle on his father's side—a building contractor—who a few days before had been attacked and killed on a building site by a total stranger just out of a lunatic asylum. This irresponsible crime, which had thrown a large family into desperate poverty, had made him deny divine providence; and he was sorry for it. He now wanted to go to communion, in the hope that the effort of faith necessary would make him calmer and settle his doubts.

During Mass he went to confession and prepared to go to communion, together with a few old women. He covered his eyes with his hands, and concentrated on his prayers. Slowly he said the Our Father, over and over again, meditating on the concepts of this loveliest of Christian prayers. But every time he came to the end and repeated the words 'lead us not into temptation,' temptation crept into his soul in the form of total doubt.

When the priest approached him with the consecrated host, he suddenly drew back.

Part Two

Part Two

XXXIV

MAY 1940: THE GERMAN OFFENSIVE against France was proceeding relentlessly. Every day the wireless gave news of lightning victories, and the banner headlines of the fascist papers gave prominence to the Germans' galloping advance. The morale of the few anti-fascists in Padusa was very low. Every day before supper Scaranari shut himself up in his office with a few close friends to discuss the situation. There was always someone anxious to show—more for his own sake than for that of the others—that the French troops would be able to launch a decisive counter-attack on this or that front. But no one believed it. Every day the hypothetical front was pushed back further and further, and to Hitler's armies, now launched on the conquest of the world, nothing seemed impossible.

Nothing annoyed Dionisio more than the attitude of a number of old professional men, who, in the days of his enthusiasm for the GUF, had seemed to him unpatriotic defeatists. Now he saw these mummified anti-fascists apparently thunderstruck by the sweeping success of the totalitarian machine, listening guiltily in the central cafés to broadcasts of pro-German tirades and summaries of Hitler's victories. Whether the change was due to opportunism, the power of suggestion, stupidity, or all of them combined, he did not know. To Vashinton Marangoni, his colleague in the office, he burst out: 'We've swapped round parts, the way they do in plays at times: the opposition now comes from young people brought up in the regime!'

But he realised himself that he was exaggerating. Scaranari was there to show that not all anti-fascists had weakened, even if totalitarianism seemed to triumph.

Overwhelmed by Hitler's spectacular victories, most people really seemed carried away by the German success. In Padusa, the café Torino's customers seemed to take it calmly. Hitler was fast liquidating France with his *Blitzkrieg*, and soon it would be the turn of 'proud Albion,' which had no real defences. The war was nearly over. . . .

Cavalieri d'Oro, whose anti-semitic lectures and articles had brought him fame and prestige, was not afraid to add in a sententious tone—with most people's agreement—that Italy's now inevitable entry into the war should not worry anyone with a family. It was just a case of walking up to an enemy already on his knees.

Giulio shared the optimism of the café Torino but could not become enthusiastic, as he had done in the days of the campaigns in Africa and Spain. Perhaps this was the effect of Dionisio's furious anti-fascism.

One day he went to the barber Arlotti's at about one o'clock. The old man was about to shut up shop but seemed glad to put his apron on again. As soon as Giulio was seated he burst out 'D'you know what those . . . comrades have done tonight?'

'No, I don't know a thing. What've they done?'

'They went and scrawled on people's houses in pitch—including mine. They wrote "Life is out there, where people are fighting and dying!" Begging your Duce's pardon, this remark of his is a bloody great blasphemy!'

'Well, you know what propaganda's like.'

'Yes, propaganda for this war which few people want. Tell me though—are you glad to be going into this cauldron?'

'Glad? No—I can't say I am. But I think it'll soon be over.'

'Well!' exclaimed the barber, with a deep sigh.

'The people trust Mussolini, and they'll agree to war,' said Giulio.

'The people! Who d'you think all those special tribunals are trying?'

XXXV

On June 10th everyone in Padusa heard that Mussolini would speak from the balcony of Palazzo Venezia late in the afternoon. Clearly it had come to war.

The huge crowd that gathered in the main piazza was not, perhaps, as enthusiastic as it had been at other times, but it was certainly calm. The Duce was a wise man, and if he went into war he was not doing it to send young men to be butchered, but to get a secure place at the conference table when peace was made. Dionisio listened to the speech in Scaranari's office. The windows overlooked the town's main piazza, and through the half-closed shutters he could look out on the sea of men and women in black uniforms. Scaranari, pale and silent, was sitting at the table with Vashinton opposite him. Every time the radio transmitted the frantic applause in Rome, which echoed noisily round the piazza in Padusa, Scaranari put his brow on to the palm of his hand and shook his head. The old anti-fascist fighter was thinking desolately not so much of the terrifying risks of a world war as of the defeat of the democracies and the triumph of the new barbarians, which no force now seemed able to contain. At the end of Mussolini's speech he had to sit down. He was sweating and his face was drawn.

Dionisio had been walking nervously up and down the big office during Mussolini's speech, and as soon as the loudspeakers were silent he shook hands silently with Scaranari and went out, slamming the door. He needed light and air, and went down to the piazza as the people were still moving noisily away. There he pushed through the crowd and met his cousin Carrettieri.

'See, Fausto?' he murmured. 'Mussolini was scared of getting in too late. These bloody Nazis are really going ahead. Sometimes I'm afraid it's all over. Scaranari's terribly depressed as well.'

'Cheer up, we're only at the beginning. Hitler'll lose, I tell you.'

'I didn't know you were a strategist.'

'I'm always wrong, according to you. Can't I have an idea of my own occasionally?'

'Of course you can.'

Dionisio prepared to leave him.

'Wait a minute, I've got a joke to tell you.'

'D'you think it's quite the time for it?'

'It's my way of letting off steam, you know. . . .'

'Well if you really want to, go ahead. . . .'

'Well, there was this man who went up to a newsvendor every day, bought a paper, looked at the first page, and then handed it back. One morning the newsvendor was so curious that he asked him what he read in the paper. "I'm looking at the deaths," the man replied. "But the obituaries are on the last page." "No, no," said the man, "the ones I'm looking for are on page one."'

'That's fine, but don't kid yourself. Not many people think like that about Mussolini.'

'Oh, there'll be more of them as time goes on.'

'But meantime he'll kill the lot of us and the idea of risking *my* life for him makes me ill.'

'You think too much of your own wretched skin. I got my call-up papers this morning and I'm leaving quite calmly.'

'With your ideas? I can't understand you!'

'The peasants can't get out of it. D'you think we should leave them to fight on their own?'

Giulio had not wanted to hear the speech broadcast in public. Milazzo had wanted to take him along to the piazza but he said he preferred to stay in the office. He closed the shutters and switched the radio on very low, and stayed alone in the dark, thinking. He could not keep calm.

Next morning he found the town centre filled with young men. Although the schools were already closed, his ex-pupil Rodolfo Accorsi, as full of enthusiasm and initiative as ever, had gathered a fair number of students in the grass-covered piazza. About twenty university students were grouped round him, and on the sides of the piazza, ready to answer the call, were groups of younger boys; most of them were just passing by, but some had stopped as soon as they saw the large tricolour flag waved by Rodolfo Accorsi. Giulio was just going to turn off towards his office when Accorsi loudly struck up the hymn of the Empire. The youngsters joined in and the piazza echoed with:

> Salve, o re
> imperator!
> Nuova legge
> il duce die
> al mondo, a Roma,
> al nuovo Imper. . . .

Rodolfo Accorsi quickly took command, looking as pleased as a victorious commander, and led the noisy procession to the main piazza where the victory monument stood. He was wearing a black silk shirt, with a skull embroidered on the left and under it the fateful words: *Me ne frego.*

Giulio followed the procession from a distance and could see what Accorsi was up to. When he reached the monument, he started shouting at the top of his voice till he had stopped the traffic and had a good half of the piazza to himself.

'On your knees!' he ordered sharply.

At once hypnotised and amused, the youngsters knelt down before the monument, while Accorsi solemnly climbed the monument steps and shouted his literary speech—a kind of baroque oath which involved the young in giving up their studies, taking up arms, and offering the Duce their own youth as a sacrifice.

Out of all the shouting not many of them managed to grasp what he was saying, but when Accorsi loudly asked them to swear the huge piazza echoed with the answer of the electrified crowd of students: 'I swear, I swear, I swear. . . .'

Accorsi was beside himself. He felt that in a few hours he had really become someone. Everything would have gone well if a few youngsters had not wanted to do something out of the ordinary to demonstrate their pure fascist faith.

Not far from the monument stood a few shops belonging to old Jewish firms. The owners were mostly of mixed blood and had recently been baptised, but the students knew nothing of the subtleties of the fascist racial law that had turned them into Aryans. Pisa, Pesaro, Fano and Ancona were Jewish names, and Accorsi's most excited followers, who had just sworn to take up arms against the 'plutocratic democracies' and even to sacrifice their lives, could not let slip the chance of raging against an enemy so much more conveniently close. Shop signs were thrown about and windows smashed. When the police intervened, it was nearly all over, and the students quickly dispersed. A Jewish shopkeeper called Pisa, who had won the silver medal in the First World War, was taken to the hospital's casualty department. He had protested when the students smashed his windows, and one of them had given him 'a good lesson.'

About midday Giulio met Dionisio at the law courts and could not help telling him about the incident. He supported the regime but hated bullying.

'Poor Pisa!' said Dionisio. 'His father called him Italico, he tried to do honour to his name, and now he's beaten up as anti-Italian.'

XXXVI

Next day Giulio saw Dionisio again at the Palace of Justice, helping Scaranari in an important trial at the Assizes. They were defending a day-labourer called Schincaglia, who had killed his mistress and her daughter. The man was only a little over forty but he looked sixty, toothless, rheumy-eyed, bent and with a shambling walk: so much had poverty, drink and want worn him down. As a young man he had been a socialist, but for years he had not had enough sense to reason about politics or anything else.

Dionisio had prepared the defence and Scaranari was sure he could have made a magnificent speech. But unfortunately he was unable to do so at the Assizes. Dionisio was hoping for a pardon on the grounds of complete mental infirmity. The wretched man accused had grabbed a knife that was lying on the kitchen table during a family quarrel and had stabbed the two women, who were both pushing him out of the door of his own house.

'A man who kills is always mad,' Dionisio said to Giulio. 'But Schincaglia's a lot madder than the Marchesa de Dominicis, who got off last month by pleading mental infirmity.'

'They say she was obsessed.'

'Yes, but she went out into society quite normally, like a woman of the world, and killed her lover with unusual coolness.'

But in spite of Scaranari's passionate defence Schincaglia was not even admitted to be partially insane, and was condemned to thirty years' imprisonment.

'Anyway, in prison he'll have enough to eat,' Milazzo, who was prosecuting, remarked.

On the evening of the sentence Dionisio asked Giulio to his home: he was extremely upset.

'A tough chap like you mustn't give way like this over a small professional failure,' Giulio told him.

'But if you're disillusioned over criminal law, what's left in the profession?'

Although he had to take on civil cases (a purely criminal lawyer did not exist in a small town like Padusa), Dionisio hated that side of the law. His temperament was unsuited to nursing private interests and defending selfishness, and his innate sense of justice was outraged by legal quibbles. He would not admit that a man who thought his client in the wrong should use shameful legal tricks to make him win.

'You see, Giulio, it isn't right that prevails in Italy, but legal quibbles. We think legal subtlety's a good thing, whereas in fact it's our curse.'

In his heart he believed that Scaranari thought as he did, although after the collapse of his political ideals he had found his only refuge in the law.

'You'll all say I'm restless. I gave up Rome and came back to Padusa to practise law and now I'm thinking of giving that up as well. But don't judge me too harshly, I know what I want.'

And the words came pouring out, as if he were addressing a meeting. He read books on history, politics and social science with so much interest because he was really passionately excited by the problems of collectivism. If he could have solved them he would have worked for nothing, whereas not all the money in the world was enough to pay for the time he wasted on private quarrels. He might have worked willingly at the law if he could have had the distraction of political activity, as so many lawyers had in pre-fascist days.

'I may be a special case,' he went on, 'but I'd never advise a friend of mine to take up law. To get ahead in the profession you've got to take on all the clients you can get and adapt yourself to whatever each case demands, you've got to be involved and advise on tax fiddles, you've got to charge steep fees to poor wretches who've got to sweat blood to pay you. . . . And I can't see you doing that sort of thing either, Giulio.'

That night it was a couple of hours before Giulio could get to sleep. Dionisio had dug deep into him, and had made him examine his conscience—a thing he had avoided doing for some time. Yes, Dionisio was right. He was not born for the law either, and had been wrong not to listen to his brother. Gino had often urged him to concentrate on teaching and make a university post his final goal. But it was too late: he could not turn back now.

XXXVII

On June 13th Giulio was having supper at the Cavallari's to celebrate Dionisio's birthday. When he arrived Dionisio had not yet got home and he sat down in the dining-room to talk to Mariuccia.

'Well, what d'you think of Balbo's death?'

'Italians shooting down their commander-in-chief's plane! It's disgusting.'

'People say they did it on purpose, but I think that's a bit much.'

'So do I. . . . Anyway, I'll hear the truth from Efrem.'

'How is he? How's he getting on in the African heat?'

'He's written to me only four times in the two months he's been in Libya. That shows he's all right.'

'And what about you, Mariuccia?'

'I'm vegetating.'

'D'you still paint?'

'I've just finished a gigantic painting called Defeat.'

'Meaning the war?'

'No, meaning me.'

Just then Dionisio came in, carrying a military letter form.

'Hey, listen to what Mussolini's been up to!'

And he began reading:

'Dear Dionisio,

A few days ago we were together and now here I am
writing to you from the Western front, after being in
action and scraping through alive by some miracle. I got
to the front from the depot in two days, and they assigned
me to a company composed mostly of Calabrian peasants.

The day after I arrived we had orders to advance. The
French were nowhere to be seen: they were high up,
with their guns hidden behind the rocks. In front of us
was a bare, open road. The minute the first soldiers got
out on it they were mown down from up there. My boys
stopped: they weren't having any. So it was my turn to
decide. But I couldn't retreat without danger of being
tried for cowardice.

So, under cover of the rocks, I gathered my fifty men
round me and spoke plainly to them. "Boys," I said, "we've
got to advance: orders are orders. I'll go first and you
follow me. Two hundred yards ahead of us there's a rock
we can shelter behind. We'll have to run, and God help
us." "Sir," said a little chap, "I've got a wife and two kids
at home. Why don't we wait, seeing the radio says France
is already beaten?" Dear Dionisio, what could I reply? He
was right! But I'm an officer of His Majesty and I had
to pretend I was cross and say "War takes a bit of courage,
you know."

The men made the sign of the cross (and out of solidarity
with them I made one too, though I believe even less
than you do) and we dashed down the road which the
artillery was covering. The French started firing hard.
It was quite pointless for them to kill a hundred or a
thousand Italians now, but like my Colonel they had those
famous higher orders. So seven men lay on the ground before we got to the rock we were aiming for.

I know seven isn't much in the economy of the war.
But is it human to send them to be killed in a war that's
practically over, just to show the Germans we've conquered a few square miles?

Send me your news and tell me how our friends from

the café Torino are doing. I need to feel I'm close to you. All the same I can see that we shan't be here long.

All the best,

Fausto.

P.S. It seems the Colonel's going to recommend me for the silver medal for valour. Who'd ever have thought this would happen to the rottenest G U F member in Padusa?'

'That idiot cousin of yours is a brave chap,' said Giulio. 'If the censors had read that letter he'd have had it: no silver medals then!'

'There's one detail you've overlooked: only his parents and I can read his terrible writing.'

XXXVIII

Among the few hundred who fell on the French front was Padusa's Federal Secretary.

He had gone out as a volunteer, as if going on a sporting holiday, and had arranged appointments for the following month. But a solitary grenade had landed on his inoffensive tent at night and blown it to pieces. Even Scaranari regretted his death. He was a good fellow, really, believing in the Duce and in fascism yet treating even the lowliest comrade kindly and leaving to the police the difficult task of bullying the anti-fascists.

It was only at the begining of June that his successor's name was announced. The Duce, it was said, had a special regard for the cradle of the fascist stormtroopers and had avoided nominating a Federal Secretary from outside, chosen from among the new fascist bureaucracy. The new Federal Secretary, Antonio Puglioli, was in fact an old stormtrooper from Padusa, a man who enjoyed great prestige and had won all kinds of medals for valour.

But Dionisio was astounded when he heard from his friend and colleague Vashinton Marangoni that he was leaving Scaranari's office to work for the new Federal Secretary.

'How can you be secretary to that man when you're disgusted by totalitarianism?' he shouted at Marangoni.

'He knows I'm a heretic, but we're family friends, and Puglioli needs someone he can trust.'

'But you won't have to do with anything but politics.'

'I know, but my ideas won't change, even if I have to mind what I say.'

'You'll have to do more than mind it. . . .'

'You don't know the Federal Secretary. He's a moderate, and I'll make him more moderate still.'

'Just wait till you hear what your friends say. . . .'

Dionisio brooded sadly over this. Could you call Italy a serious-minded country, when the fascist party entrusted a province to a man who chose his closest collaborator from among the opponents of the regime? And where a young anti-fascist without money troubles could quite openly sacrifice all his principles for the prestige of a minor fascist job? Fascism and anti-fascism thus came to seem equally evil.

The Federal Secretary had been installed for a few days when Professor Fantinuoli, in his position as president of the Fascist Institute of Culture, turned up to propose a series of propaganda lectures that would stress recent triumphs and strengthen people's faith in imminent victory. Britain, unable to expect help either from America, which was too far away, or from Bolshevik Russia, which was now friendly with the fascist states, was at the mercy of the Axis.

The discussion turned to the Soviet Union.

'What I can't stand is that now we can't say just what we think about Russia,' the Federal Secretary said.

'You're quite mistaken in your attitude, you know,' said Fantinuoli. 'Have you seen what Hitler and Goebbels said after the German-Soviet pact? They praised Stalin and the regime—'

'I don't give a damn what that cripple Goebbels said. And as for Hitler, he may be all very fine, and leader of a great people, but he's not fit to wipe Mussolini's boots.'

'But I assure you the Duce himself has said that even Soviet totalitarianism is evolving towards fascism.'

'Has he, now? Well, let me tell you, we stormtroopers fought for the revolution against the subversives and the communists—'

'Yes, but the Italian communists aren't Russia. The regime in Russia's got this much in common with ours—it's anti-bourgeois and anti-democratic.'

'If you intellectuals are trying to let communism in by the back door, you'd better remember that we old stormtroopers just won't have it!' the Federal Secretary exploded, banging his fist angrily on the table, and upsetting an inkwell over the astounded professor's white jacket.

Pale with anger, Fantinuoli left the office without a word. That evening he sent in his resignation—irrevocably—as President of the Fascist Institute of Culture, and a few days later moved to the nearby town of Sàvena, where the chair of Economics was vacant and he had asked to be transferred. He told Giulio that, as long as the party was represented in Padusa by that boorish lout, he'd never set foot there again.

The news of the clash between the Federal Secretary and Fantinuoli went the round of all the local groups, and Mario Braghiroli suddenly found himself considering the conflicts at that odd moment of history: on the one hand was the Federal Secretary, who refused to hear any good of Russia, and on the other the party's official newspaper *Il Popolo d'Italia*, which was now urging people to forget their old ill-will towards the Soviet regime.

'How's it going to end?' he wondered, marching up and down his office. For the past ten months, since it took effect, he had been trying to understand the German-Soviet alliance, but any approach towards the country of Bolshevism still seemed to him quite nonsensical.

'What's happened?' he wondered anxiously. 'We've been beating up the communists, smashing up their headquarters, putting them in prison, exiling them, bashing them, giving them the castor-oil treatment—and now, because Hitler's become friendly with them, we've got to back them up and look on them as allies! It's just crazy!'

XXXIX

In July 1940, when the euphoria of the phoney war still lingered and ruling circles in Italy were still determined to think England would very soon submit, young men born in 1922 (the year Mussolini came to power) formed the 'voluntary battalions of the G I L.' Each province sent its own battalion to what were called exercise and training camps in the Po valley.

'Youth on the march' was the name the regime's propagandists had thought up for what was to be a proud, martial demonstration. Instead, to an unprejudiced observer, it was a pathetic business. Sure of their own heroism, the regime's eighteen-year-old sprigs marched and sweated in the heat and the dust, in dirty, smelly uniforms, with no exact object and no serious discipline, humping old guns and singing military songs at the tops of their voices.

Anyone with a sense of humour, seeing these weary boys having a rest, would have compared them with an untidy mob of extras in a war film. But the regime had no sense of humour, and the press poured out its tritest official rhetoric on the subject. Still less did the regime realise that this clumsy, theatrical training gave the young exactly the opposite idea from that intended: the war was already being fought, but they felt they were being fobbed off with the most amateur sort of preparation.

The boys of the Padusa G I L had left enthusiastically, led by Rodolfo Accorsi. Since he had made the students kneel down in the piazza the day war was declared, Accorsi had become quite a local character. More than anything he wanted to get ahead. His father had been highly decorated in the First World War, and, while waiting to emulate him in the field, he kept drawing attention to himself as best he could: it was hardly wise to leave things entirely to the future, because with the Germans so anxious to finish off the war, it might be over any day, leaving aspiring heroes high and dry.

When they returned, the 'volunteer battalions' were not welcomed as warmly as they had been seen off, possibly because the regime's many admirers had meanwhile realised how totally unserious the whole enterprise was. But no one expected to see 'Youth on the march' sent up in a sketch in the sparkling students' revue put on by the Padusa G U F at the beginning of September.

Moro was star of the show as usual, and took several parts. His liveliest was at the end, when he played a young activist showing off for all he was worth as he dragged the boys born in 1922 along the dusty provincial roads of the Paduan low-lands. From the very first jokes Giulio, who was at the show with his brother, realised what a blunder had been made, and looked around him, waiting for the storm to break.

Accorsi, who had recognised himself at once, charged furiously on to the stage before the sketch was even over. Goggling with rage, he roared his protest at the insult, not so much to himself, he said, as to the regime. Indescribable confusion then broke out: catcalls, whistles, protests it was hard to understand. The show was interrupted for a good half hour.

Unfortunately, the local G U F leaders, who had taken over from Tassinari when he was called up, had handed over the arrangements of the show to Dionisio. They were not really up in politics and had trusted him entirely, knowing his talent for such things; he had evidently lost his head.

An enquiry was held, and the three G U F leaders were sacked. That the man secretly responsible was not involved was all due to Vashinton, who persuaded his boss, the Federal Secretary, that according to fascist ethics only leaders were responsible, and must answer for anyone who might have advised and influenced them.

One evening, when he got home, Dionisio found Rodolfo Accorsi outside his front door. The young lion posed as he always did on solemn occasions: long chin stuck forward, hands on hips, legs wide; being a frail, weedy youth, he looked grotesque. Raising his index finger accusingly and trying to find the right deep-throated tone, he shouted 'That sketch in the revue was disgusting!'

'Was it really?' Dionisio retorted ironically.

'Pseudo-literary anti-fascist filth!'

'Well, well!'

'Don't try and be funny. You ought to be ashamed of your-self!'

'Well, well, well. . . . And what authority have you got to lecture me?'

'I'm a fascist who really believes in it.'

'Prove it!'

'I've proved it a thousand times.'

'On parade, yes. But not in war!'

'I'll volunteer, you can be sure of that. Let's see if you do.'

'If I'm not a fascist, as you say, why should I play the hero?'

'You're playing on words to justify your cowardice,' spluttered Accorsi.

Dionisio lost his temper, and though he was longing to smash the boy's face in he merely shoved him hard into the middle of the road.

'Keep off,' he told him softly, standing at the door, 'or I might wring your neck. And remember, you ape, scenes like this don't solve problems that are a lot bigger than you.'

Next morning Dionisio had a telephone call from Vashinton, at the fascist federal office: 'That creep came along this morning at nine. He wanted the boss to see him. I packed him off with a flea in his ear—told him he hadn't a leg to stand on. But you've got to be more careful, you know. Else you'll come to a bad end.'

XL

About midday on Saturday October 26th, the café Torino was crammed, and voices and accents mingled in the big room as sport, business and women were discussed. Cavalieri d'Oro's sudden entry was like a gust of wind; roughly he slammed the heavy glass door with its brass ornaments and in his usual loud 'public' voice called for attention by slowly reading the banner headlines on the first page of the *Popolo d'Italia*: 'The Roman eagles fly across the Channel.'

'Now we'll be bombing the English,' said the young racialist, while fascist supporters applauded noisily.

Giulio was puzzled. The previous June, he remembered, those who had bombed Turin had been called criminals by the fascist press. So couldn't the Italian air force now be called equally criminal, since the Duce had requested the 'honour' of taking part in the bombing of English cities?

Every day came further sensational news. Giulio had not digested the news that Italy was taking part in the raids on Britain when there was another bombshell—much larger this time. It was October 28th, a holiday on which the anniversary of the March on Rome was being celebrated with special solemnity. Towards evening Giulio was on his way home when he met a friend, who worked on the editorial side of the paper, outside the door of the *Gazzetta di Padusa*, and heard the latest news. During the day Mussolini and Hitler had met unexpectedly in Florence, and at the same time Italian troops from Albania had invaded Greece.

His friend was wild with excitement.

'Isn't the Duce marvellous! This year we're celebrating the anniversary of the fascist revolution and settling accounts with another *provocateur* . . . Soon we'll see our flag flying on the Acropolis!'

Giulio listened in silence, and then hurried home. He could not understand why a weak, poor nation that was no threat to anyone and wanted only to be left alone, had unexpectedly been attacked.

Even the café Torino heard the news with surprise. But no one was worried, because most people thought the campaign in Greece would be over in a few weeks. Italy was the warlike nation of eight million bayonets, that had so bravely defeated its enemies in East Africa and Spain, after all. Even the regime's opponents, who guessed that from a military point of view Mussolini was a phoney, never thought the Italian forces could stumble over a pebble like Greece.

Then the incredible happened. For a few days the news bulletins spoke of rapid Italian advances; then they dried up. But Radio London broadcast the truth, and its increasingly large audience in Italy thus came to hear of the humiliating Italian failure. These defeats sounded the alarm; and in the café Torino, as in the whole of Italy, many respectable souls who had been dozing quietly for years, blindly trusting Mussolini to see to everything, suddenly opened their eyes, and realised that the war was not going to be a matter of walking easily ahead, as people had said it was in the early months of the fighting.

The reverses on the Greek front depressed Giulio. He could not believe Italian soldiers were too cowardly and hopeless to stand up to the wretched Greek peasants who had suddenly been flung into the fighting in the mountains of Epirus. He realised that the regime could get out of some of its responsibility by blaming the generals, but he still believed that Italian officers were no worse than those of other nations, except for Germany. As for arms and equipment, they had enough to defeat Greece ten times over, however little was at the front, so the conclusion was inescapable: defeat was the result of inexcusable amateurishness, and a total lack of foresight in undertaking the invasion before being prepared for it.

The disaster in Albania had affected Italy's military prestige irrevocably, Giulio thought. On either side, in Germany as in England, people would say once more that the Italians, as ever, made poor soldiers. Those now fighting were the sons and grandsons of those who had been defeated at Lissa, at Custoza, at Adua, at Caporetto. The triumph of Vittorio Veneto was wiped out, and Mussolini was now responsible for the most burning humiliation in the history of Italy since its unification. The pedestal on which he had set Mussolini and idolised him was crumbling; only a great feeling of emptiness was left in Giulio's heart.

How could he have been so stupid as not to realise it before? He had quarrelled a thousand times with Dionisio in his defence of Mussolini, and lately had even quarrelled with his brother, who listened to Radio London, because hearing those broadcasts, which spat poison at Mussolini, had seemed to Giulio an act of disloyalty to his country at war. It was sad, now, to have to be ashamed of his own zealousness.

Only on November 22nd was defeat officially confessed in war bulletin 168, which admitted the loss of the Albanian city of Coriza. Giulio was in the café Torino when the news was broadcast. When the bulletin announced the defeat, people leapt to their feet, and many actually stood to attention. Just as well to look keen, whatever happened! Even the two barmen stopped making coffee and pouring drinks and moved over to the radio.

An embarrassed silence followed, when the broadcast ended, with people trying to avoid one another's eyes. After a good minute Bottoni the playwright broke the silence.

'Where *is* this Coriza, anyway?' he asked loudly.

Nobody answered.

XLI

The very day that operations against Greece began Fausto Carrettieri was posted to Albania. Although he was coming to despise fascism more and more, he did nothing to get out of it. With his men he felt comfortable and being at the front had made him forget his elusive degree, his never-ending debts, and all the other troubles of his unruly life.

From Albania he started writing to his cousin, giving his impressions of the war. All the feelings he could not show to his men, who needed encouragement and moral support, went into these letters. On the feast of Santa Lucia it was Dionisio's father's birthday, and Giulio was invited to supper by the Cavallaris that evening.

'Well, what's the news, Giulio?' Dionisio asked him at the door of his study.

'I heard that general's speech yesterday—threatening the defeatists with blue murder for spreading black news about the front.'

'Then read this, if you want a laugh,' said Dionisio, holding out a letter.

'Read it to me, I can't understand his scrawl.'

In his peculiar hieroglyphics Fausto wrote:

Z.O. 4th December 1940.

'Dear Dionisio,

Let me tell you at once I'm going to call a spade a spade. You may think there's danger from the censors. But no one can say a word against me now I've got all these medals. Anyone risking his own skin in the front line has a right to speak out, after all.

You'll have heard we've withdrawn. To put it bluntly, we've taken some terrible knocks. This isn't surprising considering the Greeks are pretty well armed and especially considering they've got heavy mortars that get in everywhere. And they put all they've got into the fighting, as well.

Whereas we came here with practically nothing, as if we were just out for a stroll. I don't think we even had enough divisions to cover the front. Our chaps may not be Germans, but they can fight. It's true that one division, caught by surprise immediately after disembarking, shot off at such a pace outside Coriza that it got itself nick-named The Bolters; but that's more or less by the way and we mustn't make too much of it. On the whole it's not the men who are failing to do the job. It's everything else! We're badly armed, badly equipped, badly supplied, and every day we're forced to muddle along as best we can, the way Italians traditionally do.

It's winter already, in practice. These loathsome moun-tains, without a street, a house or a plant on them, are the next best thing to hell. The rain's teeming down now and we're wallowing in mud. Flu or pneumonia's nothing. Yesterday a chap slumped down beside me, just overcome by all the hardships.

But what shocks me most isn't the fact that we're defeated by all these troubles. The really horrible thing about war is the bestiality of hand-to-hand fighting.

A few days ago a small Greek gun set up in a dominant position was banging away at a path our soldiers had to retreat along. They were being butchered, so we just had to get rid of it. It was our battalion's job and the major asked who'd take charge of a picked bunch to try and do it.

I did. I thought I'd be lucky because a bad penny always turns up again. Anyway, I managed the job and should have been proud of it, but the way the Greek N C O manning the gun died left me feeling sick to my stomach. Poor chap! My corporal, who'd gone a few steps ahead, jumped on him suddenly from behind and bayonetted him. He was the most wonderful-looking boy, with a profile like an ancient coin, and he died the most ghastly death, calling for a girl, Elena, and looking at me with his dying eyes, asking me to help, while his right hand kept clutching spasmodically at my overcoat. He didn't want to die, but after ten minutes blood came pouring out of his mouth, and he did.

I've been proposed for the silver medal for valour. It's the second, after the one I got on the French front, and it'll come right away, the major says, because it was won "on the field."

Don't think I'm pulling your leg when I add that they're just going to propose me for a third medal. So I'm a bit of a marvel as a fighter—but don't worry, I shan't get stuck up about it. All I need do to keep a sense of proportion is remember that one of the most decorated men in Italy is that creep Ettore Muti, whom grandfather had the dubious honour of seeing born in his house.

Which reminds me, I'm really all for the Boss since I heard he sacked that bully in a pretty nasty way. The only good thing our Ettore did in a year as party secretary was give us the year's best joke. Remember his telegram when he got the job? *"Duce, I will make Italians as you wish them, Muti."*

But to get on to more serious subjects, I've at last read your Benedetto Croce. It's a pity he fell a bit from grace in '35, if what I hear's true: it seems he handed in his senator's medal when the Boss made everyone dizzy with his speech about gold for the fatherland.

But he's really something, all the same! No one else can make you see that truth's not a monopoly of any single man and is built up day by day through all men. It's the most eloquent indictment of those who presume they have the whole truth themselves, and so persecute, condemn and kill their enemies.

> Love,
> Fausto.'

Giulio stared at Dionisio. 'I didn't need this letter to be convinced that Mussolini's incapable of leading a nation or an army. My eyes have been opened . . . but I can't agree with you when you keep cheering on our enemies.'

'I've told you a thousand times, this is a crusade of freedom against tyranny.'

'No, Dionisio. Those who are beaten are always wrong. And when our country's at war we should stick to it. Even Fausto thinks so.'

'But don't you see that we can have freedom again only if the other side wins?'

'Freedom! Like the Negroes in the States, like the Indians in the British Empire, like the subjects of the Red Czar of all the Russias!'

And Giulio laughed bitterly.

XLII

In June 1940 Scaranari had taken on a new secretary, a girl of about twenty-five who was already an experienced book-keeper. Like her predecessor she had to keep the office books, see that Scaranari's fees were paid to him, and keep an eye on the administration of over two hundred fertile acres he owned. Besides this, she had to deal personally with the correspondence from clients, which the lawyer refused to read.

She was a quiet girl who never spoke ill of anyone, understood people's weaknesses, and could cover up their mistakes. It was her nature to see the best in things, to take life in a positive sort of way, and her clear, tidy mind—not very lively or imaginative, perhaps—seemed made to simplify problems. She worked so unremittingly and quietly in the office chaos that some people nicknamed her 'the ant.'

Pina Ferrioli was not pretty, but she had a good figure. She had a round face, a broad nose, and sparkling eyes behind thick spectacles. But anyone who got to know her found that her moral and intellectual qualities made up for her lack of beauty. Scaranari was soon delighted with her, and often said, in a jolly, fatherly way, 'You're a splendid girl, and if I was a youngster I'd marry you tomorrow: what an investment that'd be!'

Dionisio was entirely taken up with his reading of English and American political books, which he discovered in private libraries, and by his new work as assistant in financial law at the university. So he had no time to think of Pina, although he liked her more and more and their relations were growing friendlier all the time. Although she was not a typist, Pina often stayed on in the office with Dionisio until nine in the evening, typing out his comments on the political books he was reading, or articles for a new economics review he was writing for. She was calm and patient, and quite ready to sit quietly for ten or fifteen minutes while he found the right idea or the right phrase; and when he went on dictating she would smile happily. Whenever Dionisio needed any legal research done (one of the things that bored him most) Pina would offer to give him a hand. She understood not only his temperament but his secret ambitions, and when he complained that he found his legal work extremely dry, she told him fervently that he wasn't the man to waste his life in the fiddling details of private practice. When fascism fell, he would have the important political post in the province which Scaranari had filled before the March on Rome.

In a few months Pina's infatuation had become common gossip in Scaranari's office. Lawyers and typists winked slyly every time she found an excuse to go into Dionisio's room.

One day, when they were working together, Scaranari suddenly looked up from his papers.

'You deserve a hiding!' he told Dionisio. 'You're not interested in girls, yet you make one fall in love with you in my office.'

And he roared with laughter, boyishly.

That evening, when Pina brought in some papers, Dionisio stared at her for a long time; and as he did so he thought she might make a model wife. Neither pretty nor ugly, intelligent, gentle, restful, she would give anyone who married her a life without conflict. And gradually, as he continued to think this, while Pina stood in front of him, he felt an unexpected, agreeable tenderness.

'Am I falling in love with her?' he wondered. In the days that followed he asked himself the same question several times and tried to think about it coolly. If love meant thinking constantly of a woman, and desiring her passionately, then he certainly did not love Pina now, and had not loved other girls in the past. But to a man of his temperament, might not the feeling of mingled tenderness and respect that a man may feel for a woman when he appreciates her inner qualities, and

[138]

shares her tastes, be love? If so, then he loved Pina, with all her gentleness.

But approaching a girl like Pina meant committing himself for life, and the idea of marriage, at that particular time, did not attract him. But there are imponderable factors that even the most rational temperament cannot control; and so it was that Pina's love suddenly and unexpectedly won him over.

One evening he was dictating fast when she suddenly stopped.

'Is it true you're nearly engaged to a beautiful girl from Porto?' she asked abruptly.

'Why, who told you that?'

'A friend of yours.'

'A friend of mine? He must have been joking. I'm surprised you swallowed such nonsense!'

'Why, there'd be nothing odd about it.'

'That's true, but I'm in no hurry. Anyway, you gave us all the impression you were engaged yourself, when you first came to the office.'

Pina was silent for a few seconds, her head bent over the typewriter. Then she turned suddenly to Dionisio, who was sitting behind her, and stared into his eyes.

'That's not true!'

'What about that cousin of yours at Sàvena, then?'

'Oh, he doesn't care in the least! A couple of years ago, when I was staying with my uncle, he did chase me a bit—because he hadn't anything better to do, I expect.'

'And then what happened?'

'Nothing. But I don't mind. It's not easy to get on together.'

Pina stared intensely into Dionisio's eyes, and they sat for a few minutes in silence. Then, as if they had been talking for a long time and explaining a great many things, Dionisio moved his chair beside Pina's, and she laid her head on his shoulder.

'You'll hear my thoughts better like this,' she murmured. For a long time they were silent; how long, neither of them could have said. The clock striking on the town hall tower roused them.

'Twelve or eleven o'clock?' Pina said at last.

'Twelve o'clock; it's midnight,' replied Dionisio.

They left the office and went down the long staircase. Pina timidly took Dionisio's arm. Then, when they reached the dark hall, she flung herself on his neck and nervously kissed him.

'Why don't you say anything?' he asked her.

'Doesn't this silence speak for us? Maybe this is what we needed to tell each other everything.'

'Maybe.'

'Words measure time,' Pina went on. 'And I don't want this moment to end.'

'Why should it end?'

'Just because . . . because very beautiful things are soon spoilt. In any case, I've been happy, and that matters to a girl like me.'

'It matters to me as well,' said Dionisio, and turned up the collar of his overcoat to go out into the street. But Pina kept him in the doorway. She felt as if a hand were pressing her heart; suddenly she laughed and cried, and, in her nervous tremulousness, hid the deep joy she had felt and her fear of losing him.

They were married at the beginning of February. The spring of 1941 looked as if it would be a busy one for the Italian army in North Africa and Greece, and Dionisio had already heard locally that he would soon be called up; and he would rather leave a wife behind than a fiancée. In any case Pina would stay with her parents because, while waiting to be called up, Dionisio had agreed to live in their house.

They were married in the presence of a few friends in a small empty church near Pina's home. Pina was not particularly religious and would have been quite willing to forgo the religious ceremony, but Dionisio wanted to respect her mother's feelings, and her mother was very devout.

XLIII

On February 20th, when Dionisio had just returned from his short honeymoon, his brother-in-law arrived home, sent back from North Africa on a long convalescent leave.

Efrem was one of the few officers in the front-line units of Graziani's army who had managed to escape captivity. His family had heard that he had been sent to hospital in Africa suffering from nervous exhaustion, but had put it down to the incredible hardships of the retreat and had taken it quite calmly, certain that all he needed was rest. Only Mariuccia had forebodings, which she kept to herself. And these forebodings were painfully confirmed when Efrem appeared. Bent, shattered, he was a shadow of his old self: his eyes were glassy, his voice strangely metallic.

As soon as he arrived he went to bed for twenty-four hours on end, seeing no one but his wife. Late in the afternoon of the second day he got up, but only because Dionisio and Pina were coming to supper that evening, and the family was celebrating his return.

Dionisio had not even had time to ask him for his impressions of the North African campaign when Efrem started talking in a wildly excited way, using confused images and occasionally bursting into meaningless laughter.

It was pitiful to hear him.

'Graziani's an outsize idiot,' he began. 'He thought he'd got a handful of English ahead of him and could scatter them with a few shots.'

'Impossible!' Dionisio interrupted. 'Only a corporal like Mussolini could think that sort of thing.'

'I tell you Graziani believed it too,' said Efrem, laughing. 'The clot was supposed to take us to Alexandria. But we stopped at Sidi Barani . . . stuck there sweating in those heavy uniforms . . . we were to make a triumphal march along the Nile, the Egyptians were to come out and meet us . . . with the Pharaohs marching out in front!'

He laughed again, freezing Dionisio and Mariuccia, who were suffering as they listened.

'Everything went well,' Efrem went on seriously, 'until the beginning of December, when the great English tanks appeared. We had the odd couple or so ourselves, but they were just tin-pot tanks.'

'I know them,' said Dionisio. 'Their steel plate's much too light.'

'Steel? What are you talking about? I tell you they're made of tin, real tin, just like tin cans—'

'Oh, don't be funny,' said Dionisio, but Mariuccia, who was

sitting beside him, gave him a nudge, and Dionisio realised he must stop contradicting.

'I'm telling you seriously, they were made of tin. And even the prize clot realised we couldn't use them in a fight. So when the English tanks turned up we had to give in. What else could we do? Fire at their tanks with our rifles? Might as well try and knock down a bull with a paint-brush. Yes, we had artillery too, but they were light cannon that hardly scratched their tanks' armour.

'Anyway, being taken prisoner by the English meant saving one's skin and ending the war for good, and that's quite something to a man who's risking his life every day. But think how humiliating to see a few thousand carting tens of thousands off to prison! It was like belonging to an inferior race.

'Those of us who were in Graziani's army will be called cowards forever. No one's said so publicly, but everyone thinks it. A woman in the Red Cross, a war widow, yelled it at me once. She was hysterical, and shouted that if we'd had any sort of courage we'd have formed a square with our rifles and cannon and fired and fired till they killed the lot of us. That's the sort of thing that's said and even written, but it's not done. Even the Germans, who are the finest soldiers in the world, wouldn't commit collective suicide like that.

'No one felt like copying the G U F secretary from Sàvena; when his company was surrounded by tanks, he hurled himself at them all alone. He had a bag of hand grenades and that famous clenched fist of his and didn't give a damn when those steel monsters fired at him. Even when he was mortally wounded he managed to chuck a bomb into one of the tanks' turrets. They crushed him to pulp under their caterpillar tracks, while his soldiers stood there unarmed. Poor Viani! He taught fascist mysticism and championed the war for all he was worth and wasn't going to end up a prisoner, smeared as a rotten soldier.

'Whereas I'm what's left of Rodolfo Graziani's rotten army: an army that'll be a black stain forever, though not through my fault or the fault of my wretched companions.

'We were prisoners only of the desert and the distances; there weren't enough English to guard us all. So one night, with a couple of others, I decided to steal a vehicle and get away. When we thought we were out of range we met a British motorised patrol. There were two white men and a Negro about seven feet high.'

'But the English don't have Negroes in their army,' Dionisio broke in. 'And no one's seven feet high.'

'Why don't you believe me when I tell you what happened?' Efrem said violently. 'D'you think I'm mad?'

Dionisio looked at his brother-in-law, whose eyes were starting out of his head. He bit his lip and was silent.

'Well,' Efrem went on, 'they came up to nab us and they were pretty well armed. We let them come up till they were a couple of yards away and thought we were giving in, then we flung ourselves on them like tigers. I didn't know what was happening. Pistols, bayonets, kicks, punches—we used the lot. I broke an Englishman's skull with my gun, but the gigantic Negro got me immobilised: he had his knee on my chest and was strangling me when suddenly, I don't know how, he tumbled over. If it's true that God cares about these things, I'd say the Lord saved me miraculously, when I was three-quarters into the next world.

'There'd been three of us and now there were two. The third, a quiet chap from Friuli, wasn't breathing. The English were all lying on the ground. The other chap with me, a lieutenant from Naples, said "Now, when they get to Heaven, they'll be able to say the Italians aren't cowards."

'We could now go on safely enough. But I couldn't follow what was happening. I could smell the sweetish blood of the Englishman I'd killed on my hands. That smell haunted me, and took away all my strength. I put myself in the other man's hands, like an automaton. I remember those clear nights in the desert like a nightmare, with the stars that seemed to be falling on us, and the hot hours of the day when the burning sun made my head boil. I no sooner fell asleep than the gigantic Negro would appear before me, his great hands on my throat, and the dead Italian, too, with his red guts bulging out of his belly.

'War's so foul. You stick your bayonet in a man's guts and break his skull open in a flash without knowing him, for no reason at all. My whole life won't be long enough to free me of those men's deaths. Every night they come and visit me.'

[143]

Mariuccia saw Pina and Dionisio out. Dionisio stopped in the doorway.

'I think Efrem's very sick,' he said. 'You must have him properly attended to.'

'Professor Boschi's coming tomorrow. He's eccentric, but he's very clever. We'll see what he says.'

As Dionisio was setting off, Mariuccia took Pina's hand, and smiled wryly.

'This was all we needed! You see what marriage is!' she said.

Next day Dionisio went round to his father's shop.

The old man was very depressed, and even Guido Coen's kind words had not cheered him. Guido had been his closest collaborator since Dionisio had persuaded him to take the boy on, at the time of the racial legislation.

'You know, Signor Cavallari,' Coen was saying, 'I studied medicine for several years and I do know something about it. Your son-in-law's had a severe shock, admittedly, but nowadays there are excellent ways of curing people.'

'That's all talk, Guido. When a man goes out of his mind he stays there,' said old Cavallari, sticking firmly to what he believed. 'And the one who'll pay for it will be poor Mariuccia.'

XLIV

On March 27th, about a month after his marriage, Dionisio was called up, and sent to an artillery regiment near Sàvena. Before he left he told Giulio how pleased he was: a more convenient place he could hardly wish for—only about fifty kilometres from home, and hardly like being away at all.

Pina took it calmly and continued to work at Scaranari's office. She said she would leave only if she had a baby. Perhaps she felt closer to Dionisio in that office, so full of his things, than in the dull rooms at home.

Scaranari understood, and when she was near him never failed to whisper in her ear 'You really are a lovesick pussycat, aren't you?'

Military service at Sàvena might seem to Dionisio much like

ordinary life in a pre-war barracks, but elsewhere young men were suffering and dying. Dionisio had been in the army only a few days when he had a visit at the barracks from his uncle Emilio, Fausto Carrettieri's father, who was worried about the boy. Fausto was still in the front line of the terrible battle in Albania, and they had had no news of him for three weeks. The old man had come to ask Dionisio if he at least had had a letter; but Dionisio had had no news either.

'I can manage to take it quietly—it's my old girl who just can't. She's got a fluttery heart, you know,' he told Dionisio.

'Try and explain to her how disorganised they are over there—three weeks just doesn't mean a thing.'

'It's not easy to persuade her. You should try.'

'But uncle, what could I say to persuade her? The fact is that last time Fausto wrote he told me that the column he's with is in retreat, and that it was in a narrow mountain road with another one—a supply column; and although they were terribly hungry they had to get the trucks bringing up supplies off the road and burn them. Now, if they're having to lose valuable stuff like that, you can imagine how easily letters may be going astray.'

Dionisio meant to be comforting, but realised he had had the opposite effect. Next day, though, he had a letter from Albania, and sent a telegram straight off to reassure his uncle. Fausto, with his usual brutal frankness, told him what had happened when Mussolini visited them, in a letter dated March 15th:

'Dear Dionisio,
    They haven't said a word on the radio about it—maybe because it wasn't such a wild success—but I'll tell you the great news: the Boss's been here. He visited lots of positions and got well ahead, looking proud and martial and frowning. When he came to my battalion, as luck would have it, he stopped in front of poor me. First he stared at me for a while, with his lips pushed forward, then asked abruptly "How's this division getting along, lieutenant?" I said we were still short of all sorts of things, but compared with the way things had been before everything was rosy. Then he saw my decorations. "Decorated

[145]

for valour, eh? That's splendid!" Then he turned to the general with him and whispered something in his ear and as he was leaving he yelled at me, as a sort of good-bye, sounding terribly sure of himself: "Be of good heart, lieutenant! Everything's ready for the great leap forward."

In front of us there's a horrible great mountain with an unpronounceable name. The day after this historic visit, after a terrifying lot of attacks and counter-attacks, we managed to occupy the top and the Greeks fell back at last for a few kilometres. I thought it was over and breathed again. But towards evening those devils leaped on us suddenly and took the mountain back again. They died like flies but still they came on, not giving a damn for their losses. And so they took it.

Our men banged away for all they were worth along the whole front, knowing they were losing, and I even thought we'd get through, because now we've got all we need to beat this little Greece of theirs. But it was no go!

"All will be well in spring," the Boss said, "and we'll break the back of Greece." But spring's here and Greece's back is still unbroken!

Love,

Fausto.'

XLV

There are gloomy times in life when the few things that happen are all unpleasant. For Giulio, the winter of 1940–41 was like that.

Milazzo politely began to ease him out of his office.

'You see, Govoni, my work's grown. I could use the room you're in.'

'You mean I'm to leave it free?'

'I'm not saying that. But if you could just adapt your-self. . . .'

'How, exactly?'

'Well, in the morning you're nearly always busy at school. What I need is someone who'll get around for me.'

'You're quite right, I'm no use to you here.'

'On the contrary, you're very useful, but on a higher level. You're a first-class jurist.'

Giulio realised that Milazzo was right, from his own point of view, and that he must pack up as fast as he could and get out with dignity.

By paying a small rent he managed to find a room in the office of a lawyer called Ravalli. But it was an old office, and gloomy, and everything depended on an old clerk-typist of over seventy, whose clothes had been bought around 1910 and who tottered about with arteriosclerosis. The walls were lined with dusty books that had not been touched for years, and dust lay everywhere else as well: on the furniture, on the pictures, on the shelves, on the faded curtains, even on the telephone.

The lawyer, a rich man, worked only when he had nothing better to do, and never spent more than two or three hours a day in the office. He was so tight-fisted that he actually seemed to enjoy the squalid conditions he worked in. The clerk came in at about ten o'clock and never left the office all day except to go to the café four or five times. When he went out he locked the door and hung a rectangular piece of cardboard on the handle with 'Back soon' written on it.

But by now Giulio had fallen out of love with the legal profession, and it was only inertia that kept him going. His interest was all in the school, and there lay his few satisfactions.

A few days before Christmas he was called home in the middle of a lesson: his father was apparently dying.

A fews years earlier Signor Govoni had already had a slight heart attack, but the family doctor had applied leeches and in a week he had recovered. For a very short time he had dieted, then he went back to eating and smoking as before, and took no notice of what the doctor ordered.

But this time it was serious. In the first days after his attack he could hardly speak and could not move the right side of his body. A medical consultation was held at his bedside and energetic measures were taken, and after a month, surprisingly, he was able to go back to the shop. But he walked with difficulty and his reflexes were slow.

This went on until the beginning of March, when he had a third attack. After that he was no longer his old self. The right side of his body was seriously damaged, and his mind grew dull. What he needed was a nurse night and day, as happened in such cases in well-off families. But to save expense he was entrusted to the dubious care of a distant relation, who was out of work and was paid a small wage.

Giulio felt profoundly bitter.

XLVI

Some days after Dionisio was called up, Giulio went into the shop to see old Cavallari. He took care to enquire first of all about Efrem's health, which was deteriorating, and then they discussed Dionisio, the army, and the war.

It was late, and the shop was empty; the assistants had left. Suddenly Guido Coen came out from the back, and Giulio greeted him warmly.

'What ages since we met! You seem more relaxed,' he said.

Coen's morale did in fact seem very much better than it had been when Giulio had last seen him. Now, after the terrible shock of being thrown out of the university and the life of Padusa, he seemed resigned to his state. Fortunately he was not worried about money, because old Cavallari, who was as generous as his son, gave him a decent salary.

Lately, Coen told Giulio, he had really managed to resign himself to the lot of Italian Jews. Admittedly they were no longer citizens—they were a subject race. But on the other hand, those of his own age from Aryan families were now nearly all of them in the army and far from home; several of those they had known at the university were already on the list of dead or missing. The world was crumbling, and plenty of people were very much worse off than he was.

But Coen had something else to tell Giulio. He coughed, as if to overcome his embarrassment, then asked abruptly: 'Heard my news?'

'What news?'

'I've been baptised!'

Giulio could not help looking startled.

'Don't think badly of me. My being converted doesn't help me at all, because both my parents are Jews.'

'Of course. I wasn't thinking. . . . It's only the children of mixed marriages that can be Aryanised like that.'

'But mine's a real baptism,' said Guido.

'A real conversion, you mean?'

'Judge for yourself. Till yesterday I was a Jew in name, but in fact I've never practised. Now I believe in Christ and in his church.'

When war broke out, Guido explained, he had begun reading the *Osservatore romano*. It seemed to him the only newspaper in the world that condemned the war, with all its violence and its evil, and stood right outside the contest. In its pages he had found the equality of all men and all races solemnly affirmed, and all discrimination condemned, and this had brought him towards the Catholic religion and had made him start studying its doctrine and liturgy. What had finally bound him to it was the sublimity of the Christian message, a universal call to men to love their neighbour as themselves.

Taking on the Christian religion had made him feel at last that he had emerged from the terrible spiritual isolation in which he had been living since the beginning of the anti-Jewish laws. He had become a conscious member of a human community based on love, which in the future, as in the past, would be able to stand up to the violence of tyrants.

Giulio listened to Guido in silent amazement, and old Cavallari smoked his pipe impassively, firm in his religious scepticism. Then Guido was suddenly silent, as if to let Giulio speak.

'But becoming a Catholic doesn't just mean accepting the message of the Gospel,' Giulio burst out, unable to restrain himself. 'You've got to accept the Church's dogmas, even the hardest.'

'I know. But if you believe in the message, it means that Christ is God. And if Christ is God, then the Church is divine. Its dogmas are only a result of that.'

Giulio was disconcerted, touched. He thought of himself, and of the increasingly hard battle against doubt which he had been fighting for years, to avoid losing his childhood faith; and then of Guido, who had come to Catholicism from outside so enthusiastically, so calmly. Guido's example made him determined to hold out, not to give up his faith in Christ and in his Church.

XLVII

Before the end of the spring, Giulio was called up. He was given his military checkup, declared fit for service, and sent away from Padusa on a crash course for wartime officer cadets.

When he left home he was spiritually prostrated, knowing he would now never go back to the law, and feeling that his life was a failure. His only success, in fact, had been getting the job teaching Italian and history. His personal life was a failure as well. No girl had come into his life since Linda, and on the evening he left he looked down to avoid the humiliation of watching the others embracing mothers, wives, girl friends, and sisters on the station platform.

He was now hurrying into uniform, but with very little enthusiasm. At one time he had dreamt of glories and triumphs in the army that was awaiting him, but he now saw it routed in North Africa, unable to redeem its humiliating defeats at the beginning of the campaign in Greece, and openly despised by its German allies. It meant total ruin.

It was months since he had lost faith entirely in Mussolini and in fascism, but he had not managed to adopt the democratic beliefs of the anti-fascists. He felt he had no ideals and no plans, that he was staggering about in a world he could not understand, in which he could not get his bearings.

It was when he left so disconsolately that Giulio for the first time saw his brother in a gentler mood than usual.

'I'm going to be terribly lonely in that empty house,' Enzo said.

'Now don't lay it on, Enzo . . .'

'I'm not laying it on. For years I've been thinking of getting married and not doing it; for years I've been meaning to modernise the firm and I can never get down to doing it. And so the years go by and I'm over forty. . . . Maybe I've got no initiative, no courage. . . .'

'In life you've got to make a choice and then fling yourself into it.'

But Giulio realised that his life and Enzo's, which on the surface looked so different, were linked by an invisible bond. Indecision and uncertainty must be family failings: that was why none of them ever succeeded.

Saying goodbye to his father was particularly painful. Giulio stood by the bed and thought how life disintegrated inexorably, and in the old man's moist eyes he felt he could read his old secret suffering at being kept at a distance by everyone in the family.

Filled with remorse, Giulio leant over his father's face, trying to give him a physical feeling of his own love, and to do away with so many years' coldness. Suffering silently and perhaps for the last time, old Govoni seemed comforted by the gentleness and closeness of his son, and, with a burst of energy, muttered some clumsy words. When Giulio murmured that he was forced to leave, though very reluctant to do so, he pressed his hand with the little strength he had left.

'Come back . . . soon. . . .'

'Yes Dad, very soon. . . .'

The old man did not answer. His lips moved into a faint, disbelieving smile, then his head fell weakly back on the pillow.

Before leaving, Giulio went to the cemetery to visit his mother's grave. Marta Govoni was buried in a modest grave under a high arcade that for most of the day was sunlit, and smelt strongly of box-wood and dead flowers. From childhood, this had seemed the smell of death to Giulio.

He stood before the grave holding a small bunch of anemones (those awkward flowers his mother once grew in the small garden at home) and read the simple inscription he had so often read before: 'Marta Meier Govoni, never forgotten by her family.' The tombs around had elaborate inscriptions, praising the dead person, and whenever he was there Giulio could not avoid comparisons. Yet he always ended up thinking it was better for his mother to be recalled so simply. In the first years after her death he had managed to divorce himself entirely from reality when he stood by that stone. He would question his mother as if she were still alive, confide his most secret thoughts to her and seek comfort from her. Then, as time went by, it grew harder to do this, and he felt guilty, thinking that unworthy affections and interests had distracted him; and he would try to recall the most vivid memories of his childhood, times in which he had been helped by his mother's love, in which she had cheered his early sorrows. And even if he could not re-establish direct contact with her, as he had done in the early days, he could still feel the one person he had really loved was alive within him, and this made him feel at peace with himself.

Now, for the first time, he was leaving home without knowing that he would soon be back. So he stayed longer than usual under the arcade, and when he left he squeezed the bronze candlesticks on the grave so hard that his hand was blackened.

XLVIII

The summer of 1941 in Padusa differed from that of 1940. The previous year everyone had been caught up in the euphoria of the Germans' lightning advance, and most young men were still at home in civilian clothes. Few of them thought that they would one day really be fighting.

Now the war had taken a new turn. The German armies, having lost hope of landing in Britain, had invaded Russia, and Italian troops were fighting in North Africa and occupying Greece and Yugoslavia after their capitulation.

Those between twenty and twenty-three had been called up, and the café Torino missed their carefree gaiety. It now had a settled, melancholy air occasionally enlivened by witticisms from the playwright Bottoni, who, between dozes, still scribbled dialect comedies and teased the 'nobs' with his mock-ingenuous air.

Among Giulio's few friends left in Padusa the one most in evidence was Vashinton. Exempted from military service because of a weak chest, he carried on working as private secretary to the Federal Secretary, and every day, in fascist uniform (which was obligatory), he turned up punctually at the café Torino, when it was time for apéritifs. His new job had made him more reserved, but he still kept his natural friendliness. Almost as regular a customer was Eriberto Melloni, who had been graded fit for sedentary work only and wore the uniform of the town's recruiting office; his time was spent in the quartermaster's office, doing as little as possible. On Sundays Dionisio usually turned up, having wangled a few hours leave from Sàvena.

But these old friends would hardly have bothered to meet at the café Torino if Moro's unmistakable figure had not been seen by the door for at least four or five hours a day. There he was, delightedly recalling their adventures a few years earlier, giving detailed news of all old friends, in North Africa, Yugoslavia, or Greece, and regaling those on leave with the latest local gossip. His warmth, humanity and good humour disarmed the shyest and no one failed to hang about and hear his jumbled chat for half an hour or so— chat that was spiced with scandals, nonsense and ironical digs.

The German advance in Russia revived the propagandist action of the fascist federation in Padusa, which flooded the province with lecturers. Puglioli, the Federal Secretary, was at last feeling comfortable: now he could proclaim the genuinely fascist aims of the anti-Soviet war, in which Italian troops, under General Messe, were going to take part. Propaganda found a more fertile soil in Padusa than elsewhere, because the province was a rich farming district in which food rationing was easily arranged, and so far there had been no shortages.

'War doesn't look so bad on a full belly,' Moro used to say.

After his trip abroad the previous autumn, Moro had reappeared at the Torino the very day the Italian press was excitedly announcing the entry of German troops into Zagreb and Salonika: April 11th 1941. He had spent a short time in Spain and had then travelled all over the United States, where he had lived like a millionaire by selling, for astronomical sums, a few mediocre paintings he had brought from Italy. On this long journey he had performed three miracles: first, though he knew nothing about it, he had passed himself off as an expert on art; second, he had failed to learn a word of English; and third, in spite of his Italian citizenship he had crossed the Atlantic in wartime as easily as could be.

He had left a fascist and returned a democrat—or so it seemed, and now he agreed with Dionisio in everything.

Among the things that made Dionisio angriest just then were the requests from well-known anti-fascists to join the fascist party. On January 22nd 1941 the fascist leaders decided to allow veterans of the First World War to apply for membership, after about ten years: and so the phoney democrats—as Dionisio called them—took out an insurance policy against what was then the likelihood of a German victory, which would have consolidated Mussolini's regime for years.

'You get too upset over it,' Moro told him one day. 'We've got such bendable backs that Churchill was right when he said Italians deserved Mussolini. And remember, if the whole might of America were thrown against us tomorrow, these people would be the first to stick the stars and stripes in their buttonhole, instead of the swastika.'

And he spat scornfully on the ground.

'D'you really think the Americans will come in, Moro?'

'I certainly do! And if they do, with all their power, the Germans will have had it.'

'D'you think that prize fool of ours ever thought of that?'

'Who? That farsighted leader of ours? Why, he's so provincial he actually underestimates the U.S. Maybe he thinks they're too rich to get seriously involved in a war.'

Dionisio smiled.

'I agree. He's got absolutely no sense of proportion.'

'Just now, in fact, he's drooling over the conquest of Yugoslavia and Greece, which aren't worth a fig, and anyway the whole credit for them goes to the Germans.'

'Quite. The only real success this spring is in North Africa, where that old devil Rommel's really pushed the Axis ahead.'

Moro grinned.

'On a return ticket, though . . . and meantime the British have swept us out of East Africa.'

'I ask you! After all the fanfares and the millions they poured into it, who'd have thought we'd have lost Ethiopia in a mere five years?'

[154]

But Moro's critical attitude was short-lived. The German advance in Russia, which began at the beginning of June with fantastic successes, was enough to make him change his mind. He forgot about America and began to make it clear that he believed in an Axis victory, and once again gave the Roman salute in the café Torino. Dionisio, who knew him well, merely smiled.

But the swift German advance in Russia failed to arouse the enthusiasm among the café Torino's respectable customers that the tremendous campaign in France had done the previous year. Most believed that Germany's marvellous war machine would crush Russia—though occasionally someone would remember the precedent of Napoleon—but the war itself now looked quite different. It was like a patch of oil on water, spreading everywhere, covering new nations and continents. Of course they were going to win it; but when?

In public, everyone still declared his faith in the Duce's genius, and his trust in victory. But in fact Mussolini's prestige had obviously fallen, and the jokes murmured about him became more biting. For years the regime's propaganda had spoken of Italy as a great, strong nation, on a par with any other country in both military and civil terms. The alliance between Germany and Italy had at first appeared to be a pact of friendship between two equally strong nations, destined to advance on an absolutely equal level. But the burning humiliations suffered in Greece and in North Africa, where the Germans had had to come in and lend a hand, had altered the image of Italy, and therefore of its leader. Where were the fine times of the Abyssinian war and the sanctions, when the Duce had been Europe's leading figure?

Now, in the café Torino, though they kept affirming their 'unbreakable faith' in final victory, the truth about Italy's role could actually be stated—as Eriberto Melloni stated it one Sunday morning.

Rodolfo Accorsi, the leader of the patriotic scenes in the summer of 1940, had unexpectedly turned up in the café. He had carried out his promise to volunteer, and when the Germans and Italians had advanced in North Africa in the spring he had been noticeably courageous. As a reward he had been given a short leave and there he was, dressed in civilian clothes, to tell what had happened. In the left lapel of his jacket he wore an expensive, fussy pin bearing Mussolini's words: *We shall conquer.*

As soon as Eriberto saw him he went across to him, smiling and holding out a glass of vermouth.

'Why, what an original idea, that pin of yours, Accorsi! We shall win, of course, but we shall have to give grateful thanks to St Hitler, St Rommel, and the entire German Valhalla.'

'On our own!'

'If we were on our own, I don't know what'd happen. We may have eight million shining bayonets, but war's not fought with metal polish.'

The others round them laughed, and even Accorsi didn't answer.

'So, you'd hand over your land to the Germans to save,' he grunted.

A pair of minor fascist officials were there, and must have heard what Eriberto said. A year before they would have leaped on him like dogs whose tails had been trodden on. Now they pretended not to hear.

XLIX

One Sunday afternoon at the end of August, Dionisio was at home trying, with a map, to explain to Pina what was happening on the Russian front (fear that Hitler might destroy the Soviet army was worrying him more than ever), when he was called to the telephone by the landlord. Annoyed, he went upstairs; but when he heard his father's voice, he was much more than annoyed.

Stammering with emotion, his father told him to come straight home: Mariuccia was hurt, Efrem raging mad.

Dionisio had been expecting some ugly accident for some time. In spite of medical care, Efrem had shown no improvement. Weeks of calm, during which he went to the shop almost regularly, alternated with black weeks in which he shut himself up, feeling persecuted by everyone and refusing to speak to anyone. When he was depressed Mariuccia not only failed to soothe him: everything she did irritated him.

Dionisio felt he could not blame her for losing patience with him occasionally and yelling louder than he did.

Though it was not really unexpected, the news horrified Dionisio. He leaped on to his bicycle and was at his father's house in a few minutes. There he heard that, after a large meal, Efrem had gone to lie down with Mariuccia, but after half an hour had woken up and begun hitting her. Finally he had grabbed her by the throat and tried to strangle her. On hearing her screams her father and the maid had rushed in; a scuffle followed, which ended with Efrem lying exhausted on the floor, in a state of stupor.

While Mariuccia was attending to her injuries Dionisio went into the bedroom. Efrem had got up again, and he went across and tried to pacify him. But Efrem refused to listen, and spoke in jerky, broken sentences, accusing Mariuccia of betraying him and Marshal Graziani of persecuting him in some absurdly melodramatic way. Suddenly and violently, he leapt for a revolver hidden under a tile in the floor, but Dionisio quickly disarmed him.

The same day Efrem was taken to the psychiatric hospital, where the director said his case was very serious. This terrible blow was made even more painful for the Cavallaris by the ungenerous attitude of Efrem's sisters, who thought it was all Mariuccia's fault for treating her sick husband so intolerantly. It was about this that Dionisio had his first disagreement with Pina.

'Those two old maids are mean and unfair, but Mariuccia hasn't got the best temperament for helping the sick— especially someone sick in that way,' Pina said.

'You'd do a lot better to stick to things you know about,' Dionisio told her, 'and stop poking your nose into something as delicate as this.'

'I wasn't trying to judge her.'

'I am, though. And I can assure you that Mariuccia's a responsible woman who's done everything that could possibly be done for Efrem. She's no saint, but then neither are we!'

When her husband had gone, Mariuccia had a bad time, grew thinner, and shut herself up in herself. Nothing but painting seemed to interest her, and she flung herself into it with a kind of voluptuousness, taking up the surrealistic experiments she had started some time before and then dropped. She said she felt terribly alone: childless, without any serious hope of getting her husband back, without any activity that could really distract her, that might give her life a real purpose. But after so many years she disliked the thought of studying again, and still more that of working in an office, shut up there till she died of gloom.

So she thought of taking up country life. Out of doors, away from the depressing atmosphere of the city, she might breathe at last, and by painting, and being in close touch with nature, might find some peace of mind again. So she asked her father to use some of the money that would eventually come to her to buy her a farm. That she hadn't the smallest experience of farming was no matter: she was a good administrator and had always known how to manage money. In any case, as time went by, she would gain experience; what she wanted to do was grow fruit in an up-to-date way. Her father and Dionisio went into the whole thing carefully, and finally agreed.

'The longer this war goes on, the more money loses its value,' Dionisio said. 'Our savings are going down all the time. Land means real wealth, and buying Mariuccia a farm will guarantee her against the uncertainties of the war.'

So, at the end of the summer Vito Cavallari bought an eighty-acre farm about twenty kilometres from Padusa, near the village of Guarda; and Mariuccia took to the new life, which, it was hoped, might restore her peace of mind.

L

Giulio's army course was slackly run, without any of the patriotic enthusiasm which the official propaganda was still trying to encourage. The instructors jogged along feebly, and the few headaches were caused only by the odd N C O who, by shouting and bullying, tried to make up for his own lack of intelligence.

Giulio seldom went out with the other cadets, who were nearly all students. They were gay, healthy boys who liked the cinema, pretty girls and trips to country inns. But when Giulio was free he liked to lie on his bed in the large empty barracks, and read. Suddenly the great gaps in his exclusively literary and legal knowledge had become clear to him, and he was now busy trying to catch up a little in social questions and economics. He even tried reading the first book of Karl Marx's *Capital*, which was freely available, but did not get very far with it.

The chance of testing his new interests came suddenly, when he was posted to Sicily. Until then, he had known nothing at all about the South of Italy; two short trips to Naples and Bari, when he had seen merely their chief buildings, were his whole experience of it. Suddenly flung down in Catania, Giulio found an Italy he had never suspected. The squalor, the horrifying filth of its outlying districts, where people seemed to live entirely out in the streets; the neglect of the buildings themselves, right in the centre of Catania; the poverty-stricken look of shops and shop windows—except for a very few smart ones—all made him wonder. And when curiosity urged him to look more closely at the outlying houses, he felt he had tumbled into hell: dark, narrow rooms crowded with great iron bedsteads, without any bedclothes; a few rickety cane chairs and, in a corner, a stove made out of an old tin can; the latrine in the bedroom, or else missing altogether. 'We just nip outside,' a dark boy sitting outside one of these hovels told Giulio one day. The contrast between the real Italy and the Italy put across by the propagandists was now all too clear.

Giulio was even more profoundly shaken when he began going further outside Catania. At Valguarnera, Caropepe, Raddussa, Mirabella Imbaccari, at Gramminchele and at San Cono he found the same unimaginable people—exhausted, bony, just like those in the pictures in late nineteenth-century books in the library at Padusa, dealing with plague and floods; men and women dulled by privations, surrounded by troops of filthy children whose bellies stuck out like drums.

Only a few of them grumbled openly.

'Believe me, sir, the chap who dies gets the best of things here!' a peasant in the village piazza told him one day. 'Well water, no electric light, no drains—we live like animals, worse than animals!'

The other echoed his protest in a faint murmur but their

[159]

faces remained expressionless, hardened by resignation.

'A few years ago we started hoping, but with this Africa business and the war. . . .'

'You mustn't get too depressed,' Giulio tried to console them. 'Things will be a lot better after the war.'

The men were silent, and shook their heads.

'To earn a crust of bread we have to tear at the ground with our bare hands,' one of them said.

'But isn't there any light industry about here which might help you?' asked Giulio.

'Even the mechanic's shop's been shut down! We're all on the land, as thick as flies, even now when the youngsters are all in the army. . . . Believe me, sir, I wish I was tubercular like my cousin, then at least I'd have two meals a day on my war pension.'

The others round him nodded.

So this was Italy: not the swiftly rising nation the propagandists spoke of, but a country where millions lived little better than the African Negroes, and where the day-labourers in the province of Padusa, who lived on bread and vegetables in houses with broken floors and no drinking water, were well off compared with those in the depths of poverty. For years Giulio had thought that the industrial cities of the Paduan lowlands reflected the nation, and had firmly believed that within ten years the passionate eagerness and hard work of the entire nation would enable Italy not merely to cancel the difference between itself and the richer European nations, but to surpass them. Now, seeing the squalid reality that spoke for itself, he was ashamed of his own presumptuous ignorance.

One day, when he went into one of the wretched hovels to wash his hands, he could not even find a piece of soap.

'Who'd use it?' said the woman, embarrassed, exhausted by child-bearing and hard work.

'But don't you ever wash these children with soap?'

'We can't! When they go off to be soldiers they'll wash better. They'll be fine there, if the war's over.'

'Really? Don't you mind them living in barracks, then?'

'Why, barracks is the sort of place rich people live in. My husband's always telling me how well he did when he was called up and sent to Turin. They had meat every day and got cigarettes free. They even taught him to read and write.'

'Don't your children go to school?'

'What for?'

So it was not only the old who were illiterate, as Giulio had always believed. Even a few months earlier he would have laughed had he been told that in many parts of Italy even fascist children never went to school. And in his mind he saw the fascist motto so often written on walls: 'A book and a gun makes the perfect fascist.'

Giulio smiled bitterly when he thought how, to these desolate people, a book was something quite unknown, and when he remembered the 1891 gun that now looked so ridiculous when compared with the new German and Anglo-Saxon weapons.

He kept remembering what Arlotti had said at the time of the Ethiopian war. The old socialist barber had unsuccessfully tried to make him see that a serious-minded government, which was aware of the people's needs, would have raised the standard of millions of the poor, instead of gleefully pouring out money on colonial wars. What was the use of all he had learnt? Giulio wondered. It was only now that he realised how a cultivated man very often understands social matters rather less than the intelligent uneducated man.

Mussolini urged all classes to collaborate. Indeed, harmonious co-operation between the classes, organised into contrasting unions of employers and workers, was the fundamental principle of the corporative system. Giulio had always believed in this arrangement, and in fact had thought that the workers' unions in the province of Padusa were fairly active and effective. They protected wage agreements, looked carefully into individual disputes, and could be quite aggressive in the case of defaulting employers. But what on earth did such things mean here?

'Don't you get the union rates?' he asked.

'Whatever's that? Here, we take what the boss likes to throw us, and lump it.'

'Hasn't anyone ever told you about corporativism?'

The man thought for a moment and then shook his head.

'I've heard the word once or twice when people were talking in the piazza, but it's only a word to us.'

If this was the result of corporativism and collaboration between the classes, what on earth would ever alter this atmosphere of poverty and resignation? Arlotti would have had an instant remedy: Karl Marx.

Marx? But he had described the class struggle of English workers exploited by leaders of industry. Here, in this desolate land, Giulio wondered what kind of class struggle could ever possibly develop. In many villages the big landlords never showed their faces; still less were there leaders of industry or rich tradesmen. In others there were, admittedly, a few large landowners, greedy, selfish men who paraded their wealth and looked down on the poor. But, when you got down to it, how could a few hundred acres of mediocre land appease the appetites of thousands who had nothing at all?

Situations of this kind might arouse rancour towards the useless landowning classes in the minds of peasants less resigned than most, but a Marxist class struggle could draw no nourishment from that. The struggle against the few rich seemed completely hopeless when poverty and despair were everywhere. So what was needed? A revolution? And if so, what sort?

Giulio found the problems too big to face—much bigger than himself.

It was only then that he could say he had really known Italy—but not, alas, the inheritor of Rome's imperial greatness, as he had been told so emphatically it was on the radio and in the press since he was a boy. Nearly two thousand years had passed since Rome was at its height, and every nation had gone its own way since then: others had gone ahead much faster than the Italians.

Giulio realised fully the disastrous nature of the wars in Ethiopia and in Spain, which had given Italians their naïve delusions of grandeur. Very few people had realised that victory against the barefoot Abyssinian armies, against the Spanish republicans, who were left entirely on their own, meant nothing; and those who had been at the university between 1936 and 1938 were now in touch with harsh reality, and paying bitterly for the euphoria of that bogus imperial atmosphere. The humiliating disaster on the front in Albania and Greece had turned Giulio entirely against the regime; but now his rejection of fascism turned to indignant disgust when he saw this new aspect of its lies and deceit.

Meanwhile the war was spreading further. In the summer the Germans had advanced swiftly in Russia; but in the autumn they came to a standstill on this front, which was a sure sign that the Soviet army was gathering its strength. At the beginning of December, the British, using the most modern weapons, had begun to advance in North Africa and took Cyrenaica for the second time. The Italian war bulletins, which at one time had spoken of the enemy smugly and scornfully, now admitted that the Axis forces were 'fighting hard against an enemy far superior in numbers and equipment.' Admittedly the Japanese had taken the Americans and the British in the Pacific by surprise, attacking them stealthily and inflicting frightful losses; but their aggression had dragged the world's richest nation into the conflict.

To avoid collapse under the strain, a man needed faith. The fascists who still believed in the myth of Mussolini had a faith; Dionisio and others like him who saw the enemy as champions of freedom and longed for his victory had a faith. But what had Giulio?

He could not support Dionisio, because he still believed that invasion and defeat would bring greater hardships to Italy; and he believed this all the more because he still failed to believe that the enemy was freedom-loving and altruistic. He kept saying that the dictator Stalin, the President elected by those who persecuted the Negroes, and the nation that imprisoned Ghandi and held India in slavery, had no right to talk of freedom. But longing for Italy's victory meant longing for the triumph of the two dictators he hated; and this tormented him. Sometimes he would tell himself that there must be a third way, and that maybe the Lord would show one. But if he looked back he had to admit that divine providence had never intervened to change the course of history in its most dramatic moments.

[163]

LI

When he was first in Catania Giulio lived in an hotel. But it was neither comfortable nor cheap, so that when a brother officer from Catania suggested he should rent a small apartment from a family he knew, Giulio was easily persuaded.

Late one winter afternoon he appeared at the front door of the large house where he was to live, owned by the family of Baron Caminiti. He did not even have the trouble of ringing, because Rosa, the maid, was already in the hall, ready to receive him. She leaped forward to pick up his army bag, smiling broadly, anxious to please.

'Welcome, sir . . . come in, sir . . . the Baronessa is expecting you,' she kept saying as they crossed the hall, where carriages had once driven up, and which still showed the marks of their wheels on its floor.

The Caminiti family consisted of Baronessa Maria, who, though old, still ran the household, her son Rosario, who had a degree in law, and her daughter Agata.

Rosario spent the night gambling and usually came home at dawn. But he never staked a great deal, realising that if he did so he might be ruined, after which nothing would be left but suicide or—a scarcely more pleasant prospect—a suitable job. For years his mother had pleaded with him to take up law or at least sit for one of the competitive state exams. But she was now sure that Rosario was suffering from a constitutional illness.

Her daughter's situation was also painful. Fifteen years before, when she was only twenty, Agata had married an enterprising and ambitious young lawyer. But after three years of marriage he had suddenly left her without a word, and had emigrated to the States. Since then, Agata had seen no one. Friends she had known in happier times were now humiliating to meet, and she spent her time either at home or in church. Every morning she was up early for Mass, which she heard devoutly, and she never missed the afternoon Benediction either. She was the most zealous do-gooder in the parish, and let it be known that if she were free to do so she would become a nun. At home, times of total idleness alternated with periods of intense activity, when she would help Rosa with the housework. As a girl she had been to the university, but gradually she had lost any intellectual interests, and now it was rare for her even to read the newspaper; the few books she read were lives of saints.

The Caminitis had at one time owned a good deal of property, but the late Baron had sold off parts of it, and all that was now left of it was some orange groves on the slopes of Mount Etna, which, since the outbreak of war, had not been paying too well. Government bonds were no more encouraging, for while the income they provided stayed where it was, the cost of living soared daily.

Baronessa Maria, though worried about the future, was not prepared to sell an acre of land or a single bond. So, overcoming her aristocratic pride, she had decided to rent Giulio a small furnished apartment with an entrance of its own. His two rooms communicated with the Caminitis' on the inside, so the maid could get in to clean in the mornings. It seemed a respectable arrangement.

Followed by the chatty, ceremonious maid, Giulio climbed the main staircase of the old palace. There were two flights made of old marble, with heavy baroque banisters, on which stood elaborate wrought-iron lampstands at each landing, with a skilfully made clump of plants and snakes curling peculiarly round the main pillar. The faded walls were covered in decrepit old paintings of bearded ancestors with parchment-like faces, ruffs and velvet doublets; others with pointed beards; ladies tightly laced into heavy dresses that fell in folds like dusty curtains, and men with swords and wigs; and so on until the most recent, a nineteenth-century ancestor with whiskers sunk deep in his hard high collar.

All were imposing, very serious, almost grim—a painted history of the Spanish spirit of the Sicilian upper classes. Giulio could not help smiling at the contrast between the rhetorically displayed, immovable world shown in these paintings, and the present world of war, in which everything was crumbling and changing. He turned to Rosa as if to confirm his impression, and she was flattered by his smile, which she put down to quite another reason.

'If you need me at all . . . don't fail to ask, sir,' she said mischievously.

They were now at the top of the stairs, outside the main apartment. Giulio was taken into the drawing room, where Rosa asked him to wait while she took the luggage into his room. When she had gone he gazed round at the room which was so unlike anything he had so far been used to. The walls were covered with faded brown material, with the emblem of Sicily embossed all over it in green. In a dark, Renaissance bookcase were a great many books in old bindings. Impressive Spanish looking-glasses, curved eighteenth-century consoles, armchairs upholstered in crimson velvet, severe leather chairs with the Caminiti crest gilded on them, Empire-style columns on gilt pedestals surmounted by onyx jars—all these furnished the rich room which seemed to symbolise the Sicilian aristocrats' determined attachment to the past.

Baronessa Maria, whose manner showed her aristocratic background, came in, holding her hand out to Giulio in a friendly way. Agata followed her, and when her mother had spoken to him she was introduced. Obviously she had once been beautiful. She had striking black eyes, wavy hair, a Greek nose, and rather thick lips; the lines of her body were harmonious, but she was rather fat and carelessly dressed.

The Baronessa took to Giulio from the first. She liked his intelligence, his interest in every problem, his modesty. In him she saw a man who was alive, someone entirely different from her own two children, who lived in a merely vegetative sort of way.

'Do come in and have a little chat with us after supper, lieutenant, if you don't mind our horrible wartime coffee,' she took to saying quite often. Some evenings she insisted on his staying for dinner as well.

'It's no trouble to us,' she would say. 'You can eat here, or at the officers' mess.'

Giulio talked to the old lady about literature and politics, but more often about agriculture. The island's desolate poverty had made such a strong impression on him that he was trying to discover the reasons for it. Donna Maria did not mince her words. She knew what she was talking about and was well aware, too, of the limitations and faults of the land-owning class she belonged to.

'My dear lieutenant,' she actually told him one day, 'we're eating up the ground under our feet. Defending the present order, which is in Mussolini's hands, won't save us. Look at my children, if you want an example. When I'm dead, where will they be?'

Agata listened, nearly always in silence. Sometimes, when Giulio led the conversation on to nineteenth-century poetry, which she had loved when she was younger, she became more animated; but then she would quickly fall back into her habitual apathy. Occasionally, if her mother urged her to, she would make a cake for Giulio, but would offer it to him with a submissive air and all kinds of apologies, as if certain he could not possibly like it. The only thing she seemed to enjoy was playing cards, and her mother loved it too. When Giulio came in for coffee he nearly always found them busy playing at the table, which was still laid, while Rosa stood behind the Baronessa, giving her support and following every move. But as soon as Giulio sat down they stopped playing, knowing he disliked cards.

On the last day of January the Baronessa was seventy-five, and she celebrated her birthday in the evening by inviting her nieces, Carmela and Gaetana, Carmela's husband, a lawyer called Libra, and Giulio. The Libras were both about thirty and apparently very much in love; they were a likable pair, and Giulio had already had a chance of enjoying their intelligence and culture. Rosario had to stay to supper with his family, and to put a good face on it. It would make him late for his gambling, and this was no small sacrifice.

The conversation at dinner was very lively. They talked about the war, which Libra, unlike Rosario, was not too optimistic about; about food shortages—not serious, but noticeable—that were beginning to make themselves felt in large towns; about the poverty of the Sicilian land workers who, Libra said, had not noticeably advanced at all since the First World War. It was only just before war broke out, he said, that Mussolini did anything to alter the large, under-cultivated Sicilian estates; but there was now not enough capital for investment in anything of the kind.

[167]

There were not many courses but the food was plentiful and delicious, and the meal ended with two excellent desserts Agata had made. Rosa was on her toes and kept filling up the glasses with some very good wine from Etna.

Giulio immediately noticed that everyone drank fairly freely: he himself was the most abstemious. By the end of the evening they were all very gay. Even Rosario was oddly euphoric, and kept joking with his cousin Gaetana, who seemed to like his jokes a good deal; and the Libra cousins were gazing ardently at each other.

The only person whose mood seemed unchanged was Agata, though she had eaten and drunk no less than the others.

At midnight Libra left, with his wife and sister-in-law, and Rosario, who was off to meet his usual crowd, went downstairs with them.

After a few minutes Giulio left too and went into his own apartment. The large meal and strong wine had made him drowsy. Absently he watched Rosa preparing his bed, leaning across the bedclothes, her breasts visible where her dress hung forward, and then going round to the other side of the bed to smooth out the clothes, and mischievously displaying her thighs. But love affairs with servants had no attraction for Giulio, who made this plain by his sleepy silence.

After five minutes Rosa left the room, murmuring disappointedly 'Well then, goodnight sir.'

The house was plunged in silence. Only Agata had stayed on in the drawing room, unusually excited. She took a book from the bookcase and opened it haphazardly, stretched out in a large velvet armchair by the marble fireplace. The fire was still crackling in the grate, and warmed her blood as she sat there, close to it.

She stretched her hand out along the back of the chair, flung back her head, and dropped the book. She was not asleep, but day-dreaming. Through half-shut eyes she could see the small figures on the old rococo clock on the chimney-piece gleaming in the firelight. They were of Cupid and Psyche; but now they seemed to have come out of their frozen, centuries-old stillness to kiss and embrace and clutch at each other.

Distractedly, Agata thought of her past. For a long time she had been trying to forget it: the church and good works had hidden it from her. But now, after that evening, she was disturbed by her cousins' warmth and desire; and the fact that, in her loneliness, a young man was now nearby made her blood run languidly, as it had done in the past; and she was terrified.

Giulio had not been asleep for long when he woke up suddenly to find a body pressed close to his. Instinctively he tried to get free, but at once felt warm lips on his face. He dropped his head back on the pillow inertly, and murmured 'Why Rosa, what are you doing?'

'My God!' the woman murmured, pulling slightly away.

Giulio froze. There was no doubt about it: it was Agata. What man would have hesitated? He could only take her in his arms. But Giulio was clumsy. Only when he felt her yielding did he relax. Agata stayed with him till nearly dawn, and left him overwhelmed by his first experience.

He was late at the barracks and his colleague on duty saw in his eyes how uneasy he was. After a strange day, during which he wondered more than once if he had been dreaming, he went home at eleven, his heart thudding. Would she be back? Because it had something morbid in it, he feared her coming; but because it was exciting too, he longed for it. At midnight he was waiting, suffering, when Agata came rustling in, barefoot in the darkness; and it was all as it had been the previous night.

For two weeks she came every night, and stayed for several hours; and in all this time Giulio could never get her to speak. Every time he tried to talk to her she put a hand over his mouth and with the light out began her ardent caresses again.

During these two weeks Giulio politely refused Baronessa Maria's invitations and avoided having coffee with the family after dinner. When her mother was there he could not even greet Agata. Her obstinate silence while they were together at night made her seem strange and different; and he was terrified, as if it were all the result of some spell she had cast over him.

At last, one night, Agata turned on the light.

'I want to talk to you,' she said decisively.

'Please do,' said Giulio.

'Looking at a person is sometimes harder than anything. . . .'

'I understand, you know.'

'D'you understand everything? D'you understand my coming the first night?'

'Of course. You couldn't go on doing violence to your own nature.'

'That's true. For years I've kept to myself, so as to hold out. But since you came to us, everything's changed. You were under my own roof—d'you see?—and you filled everything. You were a man's smell I had to breathe, and everywhere. . . . Why is it that here, men call you a bitch if this happens to you, whereas *they* boast about it?'

'Don't ask me, Agata. I refuse to accept this double standard of morality.'

'You aren't like the others,' she said, and wept softly.

Her visits continued. She no longer feared the light, she no longer feared conversation. Punctually, at the same time every night, she would arrive, and often she sat on Giulio's bed and talked. She no longer neglected her appearance, as she had done before. Now her hair was done charmingly, and she used scent. Much of her lost beauty had returned.

Giulio now needed her. He had once thought her soulless; now he knew that she was not only ardent in love but had a strong temperament: and she had won his love. If she had suggested that they should set up a family together, and have illegitimate children, he would not have hesitated. But Agata had a sense of reality. She herself brought up the subject one night.

'Giulio, are you tired of me?'

'On the contrary, I wanted you to know that—'

He had no time to finish the sentence. Agata put her hand over his lips.

'Don't say anything. Our relationship has no future.'

He pressed her to him, gently.

Some nights later he asked her a question he had never dared ask before.

'How is it you still go to church every day, even now, when this is happening between us?'

'You're right, Giulio,' she said slowly, hesitantly. 'But this is the atmosphere we live in.'

[170]

'What atmosphere?'

'You come from the mainland. But our roots are in this country, which refuses to forgive certain things that happen. You've got to pretend and seem to be as others want you to be.'

'As far as society's concerned, I can see that. But what about religion?' he said.

One day, of course, orders came for Giulio's transfer. Two and a half months had passed since their first night together.

That evening he was invited to coffee, and when he came in he told the two women the news, trying to hide his own feelings. Agata could control herself, and, looking carefully calm, expressed her regret; but half an hour later, with the excuse that she had a headache, she left Giulio alone with her mother.

The Baronessa went up to him and looked into his eyes. 'I know everything,' she said suddenly.

Giulio was silent.

'I've known from the beginning,' she said, saving him embarrassment. 'But I had no right to be harsher to my daughter than her fate was.'

Giulio remembered Linda's mother: maybe all mothers were as understanding as this. What could he say? He managed a banal sentence.

'I beg you to believe I'm a gentleman, signora.'

'I have no doubt of it.'

'And I'd be ready. . . .'

'Oh no, please. The problem's quite different.'

'What are you thinking of, signora?'

'What Agata will do when you've left.'

That night Agata stayed away: it was the first time she had failed to visit him.

Next morning she telephoned him at the barracks. When he tried to tell her that her mother knew everything, Agata abruptly stopped the conversation and said angrily that she didn't care. All she wanted to say was that she had not come the previous evening because she would rather end it this way. After supper, when Giulio went into the drawing room for coffee, as usual, Agata was quite openly familiar to him in front of her mother. The two women's roles seemed to have

[171]

been reversed: now it was Agata who was strong, and was giving her mother courage. And the old lady began to hope that Agata would find a new life in some work.

When he was leaving Agata went downstairs with him to the hall. For a long time they stood in silence, gazing at each other, their hands clasped together; then Giulio kissed Agata's forehead and left, unwillingly walking over to the waiting carriage. High above them, Rosa stood at the window, red-eyed.

Alone with his own thoughts, in an old first-class carriage, lulled by the rhythm of the train, Giulio thought it all over. Gradually he was persuaded that it was best for it to end like this, although he felt Agata's loss acutely. But the thought that in Catania he had left a woman who was not desperate, but would rise above it, consoled him.

LII

At the end of April Giulio went home again.

With a few colleagues he was sent to the big depot at Sàvena, where he was joyfully welcomed by Dionisio, who was still there with his old artillery unit. And he was already thinking of a short trip to Padusa when he had a telegram from Enzo, telling him their father was desperately ill. He rushed to the train and arrived just in time to see him die.

Death, for a man in his condition, was obviously a release; but Giulio's heart was wrenched to see him laid in his modest coffin, wrapped in a white shroud. He looked as if he was relieving them of a burden.

Giulio could not get over a feeling of guilt that he had not always been fair to his father. When he was dead, his face reflected a life of hardship and sacrifices. The funeral was a wretched affair. Apart from the wreath from his sons, the only other was from Uncle Fritz, their mother's rich brother, who was always considerate and kind. Few signatures appeared in the big exercise book left on the black hall table; few telegrams of condolence arrived; few friends and acquaintances followed the hearse, and those who did looked bored. The small procession went quickly by, in the drizzling rain.

If no one tried to hide the fact that his presence there was purely conventional, it was because no one thought his death was much of a loss. But Giulio was hurt by this air of indifference, as he was hurt by the absence of so many people they had known. As they left the cemetery he took his brother's arm, and they walked in silence along the damp, empty road. Each knew the other's thoughts. Only when they were back in town, outside the shop, did Enzo break the silence.

'We'll discuss the property at home,' he said.

'I don't see why,' said Giulio.

'Why not?'

'Because everything's yours, Enzo. I've had too much already: my two degrees are worth much more than you have.'

'But there's the shop, which. . . .'

'It's yours, and yours only—you've kept it going. I don't come into it.'

Enzo did not reply; Giulio added no more. He could see they would never talk about it again.

LIII

At Sàvena a large unit with modern weapons was being formed, which Giulio joined at once. He never understood, either then or later, why a junior officer without any special qualifications had suddenly been brought up there from a place like Sicily, to start his training all over again. But Dionisio found it all quite natural.

'Giulio, our armed forces are commanded by the Duce—an ex-corporal. Sometimes someone amuses himself shunting us around, and then we get our orders to move.'

There were all kinds of training units and army groups in the handsome, comfortable town. The cafés, inns and cinemas were crowded with soldiers off-duty. A young colleague told Giulio he was amazed at the large number of officers there: there were enough men at Sàvena to make up several regiments.

'Before I went to Sicily I was surprised at this sort of thing,' Giulio said. 'But now I see how it is. A modern war's a war of equipment. If we haven't got tanks, guns, vehicles and everything else we need, there's absolutely no use forming regiments.'

'Then why don't they send all these chaps home?'

Giulio did not answer. But he had already heard that at some airports, where they had no planes, this had in fact been done.

Meeting officers from every sort of unit made Giulio realise that many of them welcomed the idea of rotting out the war there, a long way from any battlefield. In fact, when officers for the front were called for, a great many pleaded illness or family matters as an excuse for not going. Very few set off in a disciplined way.

In everyday life there were plenty of keen garrison officers, who fully did their duty; but there were plenty of slackers as well. These were not just conscientious objectors like Dionisio, who were secretly opposed to the Axis war, but, for the most part, temperamental slackers, always ready with excuses to get out of doing what they should. Among these, of course, there were a good many spoilt rich boys, pushed ahead by important patrons, either military or civilian, or sometimes favoured for the duller reason that their fathers had given some solid material benefit to someone in the depot itself.

But there were youngsters who came on from the cadet schools with some enthusiasm, and were later weakened by garrison life—young bachelor lieutenants with probably more money than they had ever had to spend at home, who found that the glamour of their uniform brought them amazing success with women. Had they felt that the whole country was working hard to defend its future, they too would have worked at their training; but in an atmosphere steeped in hypocrisy and indifference their early enthusiasm soon slackened, they lived for the moment and avoided asking themselves questions that might be too worrying.

Most of the officers were still loyal to the regime and hoped for victory, but very few gave the impression that they felt the war was something that really concerned them. Hitler had managed to plant the idea of Germany's imperial destiny in the soul of most Germans, and the soldiers of the Wehrmacht were convinced that they were fighting for a splendid plan of conquest and domination. On the other side of the barricades, the Russian soldiers were fighting for their national survival, and hoping that victory would in the end allow communism to spread as a force of freedom. And the British and American soldiers, brought up in the school of democracy, knew that they were fighting not only for their flag but for the values of human freedom, now threatened by the most appalling dictatorship in history. But what sort of ideal could the Italians in uniform fight for? They had fought well in the Ethiopian war, but all dreams of the empire were now over, buried in the humiliating defeats they had suffered; and there was not the patriotic myth of Trento and Trieste to warm their hearts, as there had been in the First World War. Italy was now only a feeble tool to forward Hitler's dreams, and very few Italians felt like dying for these.

More and more clearly Giulio guessed that this was how people felt; and it gave him further cause for sorrow.

LIV

Giulio now realised that everything was over with Agata. Since he left Sicily he had written to her about twenty times, and had had only a single short letter in reply. In heartfelt words she begged him to stop writing, so as to help her to regain her peace of mind. But he still longed for her, and every night, before he went to sleep, could not help thinking about her. What made him suffer most was not sensual desire but the need to have a woman with him, to save him from the terrible sense of emptiness in his heart, from which he had suffered already, when he broke with Linda.

To escape this loneliness, and the dreariness of army life, which now held out no hope, he often went on short trips to Padusa, sometimes with Dionisio, and sometimes even without having leave. Dionisio's time there was spent mostly with his wife, but Giulio had plenty of time to spend at the café Torino. But it was now unrecognisable: Bottoni and Moro, still protected by his certificate of discharge from the forces, though they still went there as much as ever, were unable to blot out the dreary impression it made on anyone who had known it as the living heart of Padusa.

Giulio saw his brother at meal times in the empty house, where their old servant skimped the housework more and more. They would sit together for about an hour, chatting about nothing in particular, and then each would go off on his own. They were fond of each other, but their interests differed.

Giulio heard from Enzo that Mariuccia was now the mistress of a man called Russo, who had an important post at the Prefecture, a rich talented Neapolitan who had been living a gay life in Padusa for several years. He had been legally separated from his wife for some time; in fact, many people thought he was a bachelor.

One day Dionisio himself brought up the subject. 'If I were left a widower I could give up women for the rest of my life,' he said, sounding understandably embarrassed. 'But we're not all made the same way, Giulio, we've got our own nature. It's easy to be censorious about others.'

For a year Dionisio had been adjutant of the artillery unit, and the commander's right-hand man. Colonel Mammi was a sceptical, intelligent old officer who disliked the barracks, despised fanatics, loved reading, quail shooting and pretty women, and liked his assistant's wit and culture. The bustle of administrative detail bored him to distraction—he would flick absently through the post, glance wearily through his monocle at the endless circulars sent round by the district command, and hand the papers over to Dionisio with a sigh of relief.

'You see to it, Cavallari, you were born for this dreary old desk-work.'

He was quite sure that, in practical terms, it would alter nothing to hand over everything to Dionisio; so he himself dealt only with technical training problems. The senior officers grumbled, for it was an affront to the principles of army seniority, but he was amused and merely shrugged. So for the past year Dionisio had been slaving for a lost cause, but with the priceless satisfaction of showing himself and the others his attitude to the command and his talent for organisation.

Dionisio saw no contradiction between the job he was doing and his anti-fascist feelings. He was, in effect, looking after two thousand Italians in uniform, and it was his duty to do the job as well as he could. The outcome of the war was quite another thing, and Hitler's victory (Hitler still seemed to him the greatest threat to human civilisation) could hardly be said to depend on his bureaucratic work in the artillery depot.

But soon after Giulio's arrival this peaceful state of affairs came to an end: fifteen university students and schoolboys in Padusa were suddenly arrested for anti-fascist activities and sent before the Special Tribunal. They had only broken a few windows in the centre of Padusa and poked through some hand-written anti-fascist leaflets, but now that the Axis tide had turned, even childish tricks of this kind seemed dangerously subversive. From one of the boys arrested the police learnt that his own spiritual crisis and that of the others had arisen from talks with Dionisio a couple of years before and from books he had lent them.

It was a hard blow for Dionisio when the colonel told him confidentially that the military authorities had ordered a top secret inquiry into his career. He went to Giulio for comfort, and told him just how worried he was.

Fortunately Colonel Mammi, who was generous both by nature and because of his background, did everything he could to defend Dionisio, whatever it might cost him personally. Another equally useful ally was Vashinton, who was still working for the Federal Secretary in Padusa, and could make him do just what he wanted. Vashinton persuaded his boss to sign a report that was substantially favourable to Dionisio, in which the present was played down and the not very distant past was emphasised—the time in which Dionisio had worked fervently for the G U F and done so well in the fascist cultural competitions. The Federal Secretary failed to realise—or pretended he did so—that during the past few years many young intellectuals had changed their ideas a good deal.

Dionisio said nothing to his father or his sister, and certainly nothing to his wife. Since he was a boy he had been telling Giulio that it was selfish to confide bad news to those you loved, simply to share your suffering.

LV

In the uneasy spring of 1942, people watched what they said, but bad news got about all the same, on a sort of nervous grapevine. And so one day Mariuccia heard that her brother was in trouble.

It was no good asking Dionisio; she knew he would tell her nothing. She could only try Giulio, who was too close a friend not to know all about it. She telephoned the shop and heard that Giulio would very likely be coming to Padusa on a short leave next day.

'What time does he get here?'

'On the usual train, at seven o'clock.'

Giulio arrived a few minutes late and was hurrying out of the station when he heard someone calling his name, and saw Mariuccia in the crowd, beckoning to him. Surprised and embarrassed, he joined her.

'Giulio, I've got to talk to you.'

Without another word Mariuccia took his arm and led him out of the station, unable to hide her anxiety, in spite of her charming ways. The old Fiat Balilla was parked in the piazza and they went over to it. Mariuccia sat down at the wheel, started up the engine, and drove out on to the circular road, which was nearly empty at that time of day.

'Surprised, Giulio?'

'Well, frankly, I am a bit.'

'What's happening has made me get over my reluctance, you see.'

'Tell me, then.'

Mariuccia did not reply. She drove on for a few hundred yards, then stopped the car by the road in the space between two large plane trees. Giulio became more and more surprised. She realised this, looked at him, and said decisively: 'D'you know about Dionisio's troubles?'

Her abrupt question dried him up completely. He felt he could not tell her what he knew, yet disliked lying to her.

'Do you know or don't you?' Mariuccia said peremptorily.

'I don't know anything exactly. I've heard something, but

I don't think it's anything important or anything to worry about.'

'I don't know how to help Dionisio. We ought to have some-one powerful . . . but who can you turn to, at a time like this? You can't tell who's a friend or who's an enemy.'

For a few minutes, she was silent and then murmured, as if scared, 'Maybe I could get help at the Prefecture. . . .'

And she looked at him sidelong, as if to judge her effect.

'Certainly, they could help a great deal, if they really want to,' was all Giulio said; but he used a significant tone that Mariuccia understood. Suddenly encouraged, she looked straight up at him and said 'You know, don't you?'

'Yes, I know.'

'What d'you think of it?'

'I can't blame you. What matters is choosing someone who's worthy of you.'

Without answering, Mariuccia hung her head and smiled bitterly. She lit a cigarette, blew some smoke rings, and said lightly, 'I don't know: it just happened. It's just the way things are, especially nowadays. It's a shelter, but I must admit I'm often uneasy about it, because I've got a husband, even though he's locked up.'

'That's your cross, Mariuccia. I've talked about it to Dionisio.'

'Then . . . d'you think I'm right?'

'I understand you.'

'If we were in another country—somewhere unprejudiced —I could get a divorce and avoid this unjust slavery.'

'Well, it would be fine if you could marry Dr Russo and have a family.'

'All the same, I don't know. . . .'

'What?'

'I'm afraid Russo wouldn't be my ideal companion for life.'

'But you love him.'

'Oh, that's something quite different! An exciting man who takes you out of your loneliness is one thing. A man who gives you an object in life is quite another.'

'And what sort of man would that be?'

'A man who's got something to achieve. Then you get caught up in it, with your love.'

[179]

'So you're still dissatisfied?'

'I shouldn't feel this dissatisfaction if I'd managed to fill my life with an ideal.'

'I see. You haven't found one or the other.'

'Maybe I did meet the man and didn't realise it. . . . But let's not talk about these things.'

Giulio looked down. Mariuccia hurriedly switched on the engine and jerked the car away, staring at the road ahead of her, her lips trembling, her fingers moving nervously on the wheel.

But she soon came back to reality.

'Tell me, Giulio, what can we do for Dionisio?' she said.

LVI

On May 2nd Giulio, while he was having lunch at the officers' mess, was called urgently to the telephone. It was Moro, asking him to supper with Dionisio that evening, at a well-known restaurant in Sàvena. Moro had been in funds for some time, selling sixteenth- or seventeenth-century 'daubs' from country churches and aristrocratic houses to war profiteers. It was rumoured that he was making a great deal, among other reasons because there was an old countess who, flattered by his gallantry, handed over her pictures at rock-bottom prices. But this might all have been malicious gossip and the countess might have been making profits as large as his.

'Sensational news from Padusa!' Moro said loudly, when he met his two friends in a small room at the restaurant.

'We've been waiting for you nearly an hour. You might at least apologise before anything else,' said Giulio, looking at Moro's splendid suit with an ironical smile.

'Like it? It's pre-war English cloth.'

'At a price, I bet!'

'I work hard and can allow myself these luxuries.'

'D'you think anyone notices what you're wearing,' said Dionisio, 'when you eat garlic and puff it out over them?'

'Garlic's healthy,' retorted Moro, sententiously smug.

'Well, tell us this sensational news,' said Giulio impatiently.

Moro's smile faded, and he looked sad.

[180]

'Guido Coen's father jumped off the bell tower of San Callisto!'

'No! But why?'

'It was his protest against racialism.'

The two friends were speechless. Moro looked at them with an oddly sinister grin, half-sad, half-pleased; it was hard to say whether sorrow at what had happened predominated, or pleasure at being the first to tell of it. He rang to order drinks and started talking hard, his chest against the table. Dionisio already knew the Coen family's troubles, but let him carry on.

A few months earlier, Moro told them, the authorities in Padusa had arrested some Jews, those who were most hostile to the regime. The ministry's orders were fairly elastic and in other places things had been let slide, but the Jewish community in Padusa was too important for that. Isaac Coen was one of those arrested, though no one knew him as an anti-fascist. Until the coming of the regime he had been a militant socialist, but he had soon resigned himself to the new state of affairs and when the tenth anniversary of fascism was celebrated he had been among those who had asked for party membership. No one would reasonably have attacked such a harmless old fellow, but Isaac had no useful friends or protectors, as others had, who were much more prominent than he was.

So he had been sent away alone, leaving his wife to her grief. The sick woman's fear, when they parted, was frozen into the look she gave him, which stayed in poor Isaac's thoughts, and in his heart.

He was exiled to a small bare village in the mountains of Calabria—a huddle of dark huts belonging to peasants and shepherds, who were nearer to the animals they lived close to than to the few landowners shut up in large shabby houses which attempted, at least on the outside, to look grand. Isaac found it impossible to talk to these people, who were naturally fascists, and equally impossible to make contact with the wretched peasants, who were totally indifferent to everything and even to other people in any way unlike themselves.

So the poor old man could only take refuge in himself, tasting his own sorrow, like wormwood. In his room at the inn he spent the long lonely days lying on the bed, staring at

[181]

the oppressive beams overhead, occasionally hearing mice scuttering above the light ceiling. It was the only sound he heard, and it increased his tragic loneliness.

When he heard the news of his wife's death, his health deteriorated: having lost the centre of his thoughts and feelings, he felt more alone than ever. His son belonged to another generation.

'I am alone in a soundless world,' he kept saying, when solitude weighed so heavily on him that, to feel his own presence, he had to talk to himself. His only comfort came from his landlady, a strong woman who looked after him and urged him to eat in the friendly way that comes naturally to humble people faced with human suffering.

Guido, meantime, had pleaded with the minister for his release, and the Prefect of Padusa, urged on by Vashinton Marangoni on behalf of the Federal Secretary, at last gave a favourable reply, convinced that it was pointless and cruel to keep such a wreck of a man in exile. When the order for his release was expected any day, the old man suddenly escaped. The police at Padusa were told on May 1st, but Isaac had reached home and embraced his son again a few hours earlier.

A police sergeant knocked at the old door in Via Pallone, but the house was empty. Guido had to open Cavallari's shop up early, and his father had gone out with him, saying he wanted some country air. Out in the open he would be safe from the police as well.

He said goodbye to his son and moved quickly away, keeping close to the walls; but instead of going out to the country he went to the Jewish cemetery, which lay in the sun and the silence, and at the end of which ran the stout city walls, with their great horse-chestnut trees. There, Isaac flung himself down wearily in the high grass by his wife's tomb, and he had fallen into a tired doze when the air was shaken by bells at midday. Decisively, he rose, and went to the nearby church of San Callisto, where he painfully climbed the stone steps and then the wooden corkscrew staircase to the bell tower— round and round—till he reached the top. Through the narrow door he went out and over to the low rail; below him lay Padusa, with its brown, felt-like roofs, its wide streets, beauti-

ful and beloved and serene, and immediately beneath him
the geometrical piazza opening out, as welcoming as a drawing
room. On Sundays, when high Mass was over, the best families
in town stood about there, exchanging greetings and chat;
but now it was deserted, terribly empty. The old man bent
over the rail, and then leant still further. Suddenly he saw
the piazza coming up towards him, huge and fast, broken
up in his staring eyes like a grey, colourless kaleidoscope.

He lay on the paved road: a wretched little bundle that
looked like a jacket dropped from a bicycle. A quarter of an
hour later the police chief was on the spot, removing the
corpse in a hurry: the suicide must be kept hidden as far
as possible. But it was impossible to do so, and that evening
it was being whispered in all the cafés. That same afternoon
two copies of Isaac Coen's will were delivered, one to the
Prefect and the other to Scaranari. Moro had, surprisingly,
seen the first, and he now told Giulio and Dionisio about it.

Sir, it said, *I have come back to my own town to die.
The restrictions and privations of my present sad life,
though severe, are not what induce me to take this step.
What does so is the humiliation of no longer being a
citizen of my own country, where, through no fault of
my own, I am exposed to ridicule. The Coens have lived
in Padusa for four centuries, and very few families share
this privilege with me. Yet I have lost the right to live
in my own city, and I am not even allowed to visit the
graves of my family.*

*In the days of absolute rule my ancestors lived in the
ghetto, but, like other citizens, they enjoyed the protection of the law, went where they pleased, exercised
any profession. But progress and civilisation seem to have
been a curse to us, for we have now been thrown back a
thousand years.*

*I respect the laws of the state, whatever they are, and
I respect the authorities. This I learnt from Socrates,
when I sat at my desk at school. I have never thought of
rebelling against the rightful government of the country
nor did it ever cross my mind to sabotage its efforts in
difficult times like these. The authorities can make me*

do anything in the name of the king's laws, but they can-
not, fortunately, make me, against my will, live a life that
is not worthy to be lived. That is entirely my affair.

I recommend my son, who will carry on the family, to
respect the law as he has done until now.

You, sir, who will receive this letter, I ask to apply the
legislation concerning my forsaken co-religionists with
humanity, and may Heaven hasten the day when you
will be relieved of this painful duty. Laws like these vio-
late the principles of charity and human brother-
liness, which are the eternal leaven of your Christian
religion.

Isaac Coen, son of Abraham.

'Poor Guido,' murmured Giulio, after a few moments
silence.

Next day Giulio managed to get to Padusa. The usual crowd
was outside the café Torino discussing the news, and Moro,
delighted to be the centre of attention, was giving the tragic
details for the thousandth time.

Among his listeners, home on sick leave, was Cavalieri d'Oro,
the pre-war propagandist of the anti-semitic campaign. Giulio
was surprised to hear him express regret, like the others, but
said nothing. Eriberto Melloni, however, was longing to get
his fangs into him and the moment Moro stopped talking he
went into the attack.

'I'd really be interested to hear what you feel about it,' he
said to Cavalieri d'Oro. 'After all, you're an expert.'

Giulio held his breath, certain that they would come to
blows. But time and experience had obviously altered even
the racialist orator.

'My friends, we all talked and wrote nonsense when we
were in the GUF,' he said, with studied calm. 'Let anyone
who's quite guiltless come forward.'

Nobody breathed.

'When I gave those lectures,' he went on, 'I wasn't trying
to play the Nazi, I was just trying to cut down these ever-
spreading, ever-ravenous people a bit.'

'But . . .' said Eriberto, trying to break in.

'You're the only one who can say *but*, because with your

[184]

millions you could refuse to join the G U F and could back up the plutocrats instead.'

Everyone smiled at his retort.

'The rest of us,' Cavalieri d'Oro went on smugly, 'carried the party card in our pockets, and still do. As fascists we're aiming for a victory that's just and Italian. When we've won, once and for all, the restrictions will be over and the Jews can breathe again as well.'

'If they're not all dead,' hissed Eriberto.

The argument had become dangerous again and no one dared take it up. It was Moro who broke the deadlock.

'Boys, I'm flush. Drinks all round on me. So let's drink to victory, which'll let Uproar go on lecturing and Eriberto multiply his millions.'

LVII

It was evening. With a chorus of 'so long,' the friends had scattered to their homes for supper. At the café Torino only Giulio and Eriberto were left at a small table. Eriberto stubbed a freshly lit cigarette out in the ash-tray so hard he broke it to pieces. Giulio watched him, realising how much on edge he was, and then, to break the tension, burst out laughing.

'Wasting that cigarette, in the present shortage. . . .'

'Listen Giulio, I don't give a damn if that fool Uproar tries to be funny at my expense by saying I sympathise with the plutocratic countries because I'm rich.'

'Then why are you so annoyed?'

'I'm annoyed because right-thinking people pick on my dislike of fascism and say I'm being disloyal to my own class.'

'They don't understand you, that's all.'

'I know. Because my father's one of the richest landowners in the province, because his money gives me a comfortable life as well, I ought to swallow every dirty, rubbishy thing they go in for . . . I ought to be on the side of this new order, as they call it—whereas. . . .'

'Oh, carry on, Eriberto! You know perfectly well I lost all my illusions about fascism long ago.'

That evening Giulio missed both the late evening trains. Eriberto asked him to dinner at the Giovanni, where they sat in a secluded corner, quietly discussing their reasons for being disillusioned.

'As you know, my father's no fool,' said Eriberto.

'He certainly isn't. Everyone knows he's one of the most go-ahead landowners in the province, way ahead of the rest in his farming methods.'

'You agree, then, my father's no fool. And he's no fool even when he opposes the Duce. But—people object—he supported and financed the stormtroopers.'

'That was quite another thing. It was a reaction against the revolutionary riots in 1919.'

'Right! But when the movement became a "party," when it became a tyranny and a gag in 1926, when it denied all individual freedom, then my father said: "This is disgusting."'

The waiter arrived with two 'disguised' steaks and carefully covered them with lettuce and radishes. Giulio signalled to Eriberto to stop talking.

When they were alone again, Eriberto continued.

'D'you see? We're forced to shut up because even the waiter might talk and get us into trouble. That's what those scoundrels have reduced Italy to.'

'You're right, Eriberto. There are some things I've only recently understood, and I envy you.'

'It's my father who's so farsighted; he can already foresee how things will go when this roundabout of imperial miracles is overthrown. D'you know who'll get the worst of it then? The landowners!'

'I can well believe it. Fascism's kept you landowners in clover, after all.'

'If any trade unionist ever dared ask for the agricultural agreements to be revised, he's been tripped up by the political blokes.'

'Slavery, some people call it.'

'That's right, slavery: a system that keeps wages down, guarantees prices, and lets any fool play the farmer, even if he hands his land over to an agent and spends his time in town playing poker and messing around with tarts. My father's put his heart and soul into his land and pays his men more than the minimum.'

'That's why the other landowners don't agree with him.'

'They loathe him! But he doesn't give a damn and he's longing for this ignominy to finish—even if it means communism.'

'Communism! Why, that's impossible!'

'Maybe. But the red law'll be back, and that'll start retaliations and strikes off again.'

'But not anarchy, like we had in 1919.'

'It'll be worse, I tell you, after twenty years' repression. Father keeps saying he'll have to retire to the Riviera and grow carnations, but he's quite resigned to it so long as we get rid of that scoundrel in Palazzo Venezia.'

They got up, paid the bill and left. In the fine, calm, lime-scented night they walked along to the station. After a long pause Eriberto burst out: 'Fascism's not the only answer for the rich! In America they're doing fine.'

'I agree. Fascism's a concept of society, of the state.'

'That's right, Giulio. And that's why we Mellonis don't go for it. Yet, you know, I feel I'm a bourgeois! Bourgeois in my bones! But I'd sooner be a beggar with the right to speak out than a slave dressed in silk.'

They had now reached the half-empty piazza outside the station. Curled up on the box of his old *fiacre*, a coachman was dozing. On the steps up to the station a well-known eccentric, the local drunk, was muttering a hoarse, barely audible song. As they passed close by him, Eriberto roared with laughter.

'Hear him, Giulio? He's humming *Giovinezza*!'

'Why, so he is!'

'Isn't it absurd? It's like a symbol of today's fascism . . . he drinks, sings, and can't foresee the paralysis that'll soon choke him. . . .'

LVIII

On the third Sunday in June, Giulio was sunning himself beside a pillar near the café Torino when people were having their drinks before lunch. The smartest Mass in town was just over, and, spreading fan-wise across the wide pavement, possibly considering the ideas in Mgr Formigatti's patriotic sermon, were the wives and daughters of fascist officials, conscious of their importance, and the female members of the few noble families in Padusa, the most important local landowners, and professional men. It was a point of honour for them all to attend the midday Mass.

In spite of the war, the ladies' dresses were still impeccable. Womanisers and those who appreciated clothes smiled as they watched them go by. No one, faced with such elegance, would have thought Italy had been at war for two years. Had it not been for the youngsters in uniform outside the café Torino, it would all have looked like the peaceful, pre-war Italy. Upper-class ladies were still, in this third wartime summer, hastening to the gay Adriatic beaches. In fact, this was probably the last really elegant Mass of the summer. Next Sunday several families would be away at Rimini, Riccione and Cortina d'Ampezzo.

The procession ended rather grotesquely when Contessina Tonarelli went by, sixty years old, plastered in theatrical make up, and wearing clothes that had been fashionable thirty years before; Giulio reflected that this worldly, superficial sort of scene could scarcely survive a war that was overthrowing the whole world. He stood very still, deep in thought, his eyes half-shut, and the sun beating down on his face.

Suddenly, someone tapped his cheek. Giulio shook himself: it was Moro, predictably with the playwright Bottoni.

'Know the week's scandal? It's one in a million.'

'Go ahead, I'm all ears.'

Moro delightedly recounted the latest story, but instead of the loud laugh Moro was expecting, Giulio gave him a conventional smile.

'Anything wrong, Giulio?'

'No. But my battalion's been ordered south.'

'North Africa?'

'Very likely.'

'Then what are you worried about?' cried Moro. 'The North African front's the best place for us, because Rommel's a wizard. This morning the radio woke us announcing that Tobruk had been recaptured.'

[188]

'D'you think that matters so much?'

'Why, it's a terrific blow, everyone's wild with excitement . . . that fellow may get to Alexandria before you're in North Africa at all.'

'You're suddenly optimistic, aren't you? Have you forgotten what you were saying just recently?'

'Oh, don't lecture me, Giulio!'

'All right then, you go ahead.'

'Well, this morning in the café Torino people were saying that if the German offensive brings Russia to her knees, and we get to Suez, we shan't lose the war. At least we'll be quits and everyone'll keep what he's got.'

'But if Russia keeps on her feet and Rommel's stopped, what are we going to do about the Americans, who are coming along so fast?'

'Look, Giulio, the Axis is like an old boxer who's got to finish it off fast and has doped himself up to the gills to keep his title. It's all or nothing . . . if we don't win now, the Axis is *kaputt*.'

'Either way, we'll be the losers,' said Giulio.

LIX

When Giulio left Sàvena with his motorised battalion in September, there was still a euphoric atmosphere. Officers and men were afraid that when they reached North Africa it would be all over. Every day they expected Rommel's army, which was now within range of Alexandria, to take the decisive leap to the Nile delta and final triumph. Some of the youngsters talked of nothing but the beauty of the Egyptian women, who were said to be as seductive and voluptuous as Cleopatra, and were scared others would get in first and leave them only the rejects.

But, within a couple of months, from the time the first grapes were picked until the time the first leaves fell, the Italians passed from the excitement of renewed success to the realisation that they had irrevocably lost the war.

It was in the port of Naples, where he had been waiting to embark for weeks, that Giulio heard the dramatic war bulletin of November 5th 1942. The Italian High Command had been forced to admit the decisive defeat of El Alamein. German and Italian troops, defeated after a long hard battle in which they had fought with great courage against a better-armed enemy, were withdrawing quickly towards Libya.

'We shan't sail,' said the soldiers, easily resigned to losing Cleopatra; and washed their hands of it.

But the major thought otherwise.

'It's the usual swing in Africa,' he kept saying. 'We'll go over to North Africa and the Axis will get on top again, just as it happened in '40 and '41.'

But Giulio felt this third British offensive was unanswerable. The atmosphere had changed.

After less than three days even the major was silenced by the announcement that a new Anglo-American army, under the command of General Eisenhower, was disembarking on the coasts of Morocco and Algeria. So Giulio never saw Libya. On a night of storm and terror his battalion was hurled at the coast of Tunis in a small convoy. Italian and German troops were going to defend the declining fortunes of the Axis, with Marshal Pétain's agreement, on the ancient soil of Carthage.

At that same time, at the artillery training post at Sàvena, Dionisio, who had been predicting the catastrophic events in North Africa for some time, saw his prestige visibly growing.

'We always knew he had a good head on his shoulders,' the colonel confided to his friends. 'But I'd never have thought he'd get as near the mark as this.'

When the mess radio broadcast the news at mealtimes, the officers looked sadly and silently at one another, and things became worse in the second half of November, when Radio London announced that the Soviet army had launched a tremendous offensive on the Don. For the first time the Russian front was moving westwards.

Overnight the most conformist captain at the depot, who had always been carefully cold to Dionisio, began being friendly and started taking work off his hands and offering him drinks.

But Dionisio could not really carry on at Sàvena. The colonel had behaved in a really fatherly way over the inquiry, and had got him through it unscathed; but now it was up to

Dionisio to remove his embarrassing self. The regime was now tottering, all kinds of things looked ominous, and the 'anti-fascist lieutenant' was very much in the public eye. He could not go on lying low in that comfortable depot, so he got himself transferred to France, which the Vichy government was allowing the Italian Fourth Army to enter.

Pina, realising she had been only too lucky so far, made no fuss about his leaving her. Dionisio was, after all, not going to the front, where so many young men had lost their lives. The South of France was out of the war and might continue to be so.

LX

At dawn on November 16th 1942 Giulio disembarked with his battalion on the coast of the Gulf of Tunis. Axis planes from the aerodromes of Sicily and Sardinia were able to protect the landing by hammering at the French positions.

At midday the regiment had taken over the coast, and, undisturbed, had formed a solid bridgehead. Clearly, the officers thought, the French did not mean to resist. This was an enormous piece of luck for the weary Italian troops. Fifty tanks were sent ahead, as far as the slopes of the hills, to make a wide reconnaissance. Everything was going well. Easy success at last, people said.

The other Italian and German units had also landed without much difficulty. So, having overcome some hardly more than symbolic resistance, they took Tunis and Bizerta, where, on the 25th, reinforcements they needed for the advance came up. As they marched through the outskirts of Tunis, through a silent crowd, the men were in a good mood again and sang:

> Vincere, vincere, vincere!
> e vinceremo in terra, in cielo e in mare.
> È la parola d'ordine
> d'una suprema volontà. . . .

It was the gay song of victory they had sung when the war looked easy, in the days when the amazing German feats had given so many Italians the idea that success was just around the corner. For months now, no one had sung it; as if by some tacit understanding, they had all forgotten it. Now, here it was again. . . .

'Poor boys,' thought Giulio. 'They're so excited they don't realise we're going to meet an even worse disaster than the rest. Here we've got the Americans ahead of us!'

The battalion was ordered south. A few skirmishes, a few casualties. Throughout November the enemy did very little and aerial reconnaissance kept sending back 'nothing to report.' This worried the officers, because in wartime silence is more disturbing than action.

Lieutenant Pisarri, a bright lad from Rome whom Giulio had quickly become friendly with, was among those who wondered why the advance was going so slowly when there were no solid enemy troops ahead of the Italians. He was ingenuous enough to believe in Mussolini still, and he failed to realise that things were already very much in favour of the enemy coalition.

The Tunisians idly watched the troops and vehicles going by; they grinned at the *Bersaglieri*'s plumes and turned to stare at the tanks, obviously struck by their bulk; but, apparently speechless with oriental resignation, they never said a word. Officers and men kept their eyes open and their ears cocked for any signs of hatred or friendliness, but in vain: these people, dressed in rags and depressed by poverty and ignorance, took the war with complete fatalism.

'Italians come, French go . . . Italians go, English and French come . . . French and English go, Italians come back . . . Italians go, Americans come . . . Men pass, but Allah remains,' a pedlar of sheepskins said one day.

Giulio wondered why the people were so completely indifferent to what was happening. Clearly, to the Tunisians, French, British, Germans, Italians and Americans were all one: Europeans fighting among themselves, but all treating them as inferiors. So why take sides? Why care who won?

But would these poor ragged creatures have cared if their own fate had been in the balance? If, for instance, they had really been promised independence, freedom, a decent life? He tried to feel that they would have, but could not really convince himself, for he felt it impossible that a real will to improve could arise, with a new sense of human dignity, from such depths of ignorance, squalor and poverty.

The easy days—during which Giulio spent several hours a day trying to discover something about the local population—did not last long. At the beginning of December the battalion's losses first showed the power of General Eisenhower's equipment. For four days they fought furiously to take an important crossroads, then lost it when the enemy brought up their powerful armour. Sometimes it looked like a fight between men and machines; and the losses they suffered were heavy.

Anyone who, after the initial advances, had deluded himself that the Italian troops would do great things in Tunisia now had to face the facts. The enemy had enormously superior equipment; and the fact that it had not yet been seriously used was no reason to imagine a rosy future.

In the last ten days of December the battalion dug itself in on the mountains, not far from the crossroads where it had been so harshly repulsed. Instead of moving ahead, they now held on to their positions. From the low, inaccessible hills where they were entrenched, the battalion went in for short, sharp attacks on the enemy troops moving about ahead of it.

In rickety shacks or even in caves which reminded old officers of the dug-outs on the Carso during the First World War, the Italians slept worse than ever. A further discomfort was the great difference in temperature between day and night, which most of them found very hard to bear. Their uniforms were ragged and their shoes worn out, and only one man in three had a change of clothing. All these discomforts might have been bearable if the food had been decent. But the food was the worst thing of all.

So from morning till night there were complaints. Some complained that the men were dying of thirst while the officers (according to them) had crates of mineral water; some furiously declared that the medical officer had ordered bitter coffee to be served to the men because it cooled the mouth and cleaned out the intestines; some cursed the uneatable tinned food which had to be thrown to the animals, and described their friends' stomach disorders; others complained that Mussolini's personal orders that equal rations should be

[193]

given to officers and men on all fronts had been sabotaged.

Not all these complaints were justified. Very often—as Giulio realised—the men thought that what was in fact physically impossible was due to the officers' ill-will or lack of interest. The main reason for all their troubles was the difficulty of getting supplies by sea. Although the coast of Sicily was not far away, the obvious superiority of the enemy's air-power made transporting them more and more hazardous, and often, when the necessities of life were lacking, it was not because the officers had been negligent or the colonel had washed his hands of it all, as the men tended to believe, but because the fresh supplies had ended up at the bottom of the sea.

Giulio, who was at the battalion command post, was one of the few officers who was friendly with his men. Pisarri, a good, sincerely religious man, disapproved of this.

'If you treat the men familiarly you end up losing their respect,' he said. 'We should keep our distance even when we feel like being friendly with them.'

It was best not to argue—any discussion would have gone too far, so Giulio just shook his head. In the system Pisarri believed in he saw the fundamental obstacle to good under-standing between officers and men that might have helped an army with such low morale and so little equipment. But the idea that dignity and in a way even rights progressively diminished as one went down the scale of importance was a corollary of the fascist concept of society; and the way the army was divided into two castes, officers and men, with the N C Os as a colourless link between them, was accepted, even at the front, as a firm, indisputable fact.

The men liked Giulio's way of treating them politely, as equals. Sometimes this gave him the advantage of being listened to and believed when other officers, no less honest and sincere, would have been heard with suspicion. So he was able to persuade the men and ease the tension when, maddened and demoralised by their privations, they began accusing those who were neither guilty nor responsible.

It was not only the men but the Italian officers who felt they were being treated with a kind of remote condescension by the Germans. Relations between them soon became cold and

[194]

distant, and collaboration weak. Every Italian plan seemed to be opposed and delayed. This was very probably not true; but once an atmosphere of suspicion had been established between armies of different nationalities fighting side by side, any piece of nonsense was believed and the most unlikely insinuations seemed plausible to people prepared to accept them.

Junior officers often let slip expressions of hatred for the Germans, and so did the men. There was nothing surprising in this; the youngsters were sons of those who had fought against Germany from 1915 to 1918 and had grown up in the atmosphere engendered by their fathers' memories of the war. But these outbursts annoyed Giulio no less than the gushing praise showered on Germany by some of the fascists. He felt that the great majority of German soldiers were the unthinking tools of a machine infinitely bigger than themselves, victims of a diabolical propaganda that taught them to despise and humiliate others. Among them, there must be any number of Austrians like his mother. Hating the Germans was like hating her.

For a couple of weeks a German unit bivouacked a few hundred yards from the huts where Giulio and his men were encamped. Every evening as soon as darkness fell NCOs and men, with typically German punctuality, would start singing together; and they always sang their favourite:

> Vor der Kaserne
> bei dem grossen Tor,
> stand eine Laterne,
> und steht sie noch davor. . . .

Who could fail to understand their profoundly melancholy tone? These terrible German soldiers were only poor boys flung down thousands of miles from home, singing *Lili Marlene* because, behind Lale Andersen's blonde bony face and horsey teeth, they saw some distant woman who was waiting for them; mother, wife, or sweetheart. Of course they longed to fling down their arms and go home! Otherwise they would hardly have put so much passion into the song broadcast every evening from Radio Belgrade and sung by the now familiar, favourite voice. All over Europe, now going up in flames,

[195]

its soft, melting, melancholy tune seemed like an indictment of Hitler's barbaric inhumanity.

For a while Giulio's men would listen to the Germans; then they too would start singing:

Tutte le sere
sotto quel fanal. . . .

The words of the Italian translation were nothing much; but the tune was still the same, spontaneous, fascinating. And the Italians sang melodiously.

'They may be better at fighting than we are,' said a small Neapolitan, 'but we're better at singing.'

Before going to bed Giulio never missed listening to the radio. There was a good one at the Italian headquarters, which a young sergeant who was an excellent electrician had managed to get going even under those difficult conditions. Occasionally an Italian military broadcast for soldiers far from home would come through from somewhere or other; and then Moro's familiar, unmistakable voice would boom through Giulio's head. Obviously Moro's brashness had got him the job of sending out these unpretentious broadcasts. Then for a few minutes Giulio would feel he was home again in Padusa, at the theatre watching the G U F reviews with a cruelly satirical Moro on stage, or at the Freshers' Rag, when they carried a corpse round the town with lighted candles, and Dionisio led the procession while Moro intoned his grotesque litanies for the imaginary dead. Whereas now the dead were real men around him, consumed by the indifferent sands of the desert.

Giulio would then feel crushed with gloom and sadness, and would have to switch off.

Towards the end of January the enemy began to give signs of offensive action. This was only to be expected. The fall of Tripoli had meant the loss of the last city of the Italian colonial empire, and if the Americans and British could only conquer Tunisia, they would have complete control of an enormous bridgehead from the continent of Africa.

After a few attacks on land and in the air, which caused no serious damage, the battalion, together with some other units, was ordered to counter-attack. From their mountain positions, where they had been waiting for over a month, they had to go down and face the enemy below. But the fight to maintain their positions had weakened the fighting units' strength, and in order to counter-attack they needed to be in really good shape.

Meanwhile, the regimental command had asked for the necessary replacements of equipment, weapons and supplies, and it was confirmed that these would be arriving from Sfax. Fresh troops would also be coming from there: a unit of blackshirts and a battalion of Alpini, who would climb the single mountain slope, and join those waiting to counter-attack.

At Sfax, a town of only a few tens of thousands, a centre had been set up behind the lines for troops, vehicles and men coming from Tripoli, after the evacuation of Libya, to join those coming from the North after the landing in Tunis. Infantry units that had suffered heavy losses in Egypt and Cyrenaica, isolated artillery batteries, Italian and German officers without men, and the remnants of tank units were all waiting to be reorganised and used, and the improvised hospitals were crammed with sick and wounded.

The battalion commander said that inevitably the men and materials crowded together at Sfax would attract the enemy; especially as they had no anti-aircraft protection at all. And, as he had foretold, the day before the troop movements were planned, enemy aircraft launched a massive, terrifying, completely unanswerable attack. This gave the Italian and German army its first mortal blow, delivered on the new troops and supplies: it was the start of a haemorrhage that was to bleed the troops till they were totally paralysed.

The enemy now felt sure of himself, and during the first half of February struck ceaselessly and fast. On February 17th, just when the troops were hearing with horror about the appalling raids on Naples and Palermo, the attack on land and in the air was launched with indescribable ferocity. Italian troops tried to counter-attack, and, at the price of enormous losses, managed to capture Gafsa and Sbeitla for a time.

A series of murderous attacks and counter-attacks, during which Giulio risked his life several times, meant that there were fearful gaps in the battalion, never to be filled again. A few more days would have crushed the unit and others nearby, but the enemy did not press his advantage although he had complete control of the sky, from which Axis aircraft were now vanishing. The Italian and German troops used the lull, which continued until about the middle of March, to consolidate their positions, take advantage of a few local successes in the west and form a strong line of defence against the offensive that a great many formidable signs suggested was not far ahead.

The atmosphere was one of nervous expectancy. Everyone tried to do his duty, but both officers and men had lost every scrap of good humour. What worried them most of all was the enemy's increasing air strength: when the great offensive began they would hurl fire and slaughter out of the undefended sky. Giulio realised that the end of the Tunisian adventure was at hand and that, unless some miracle happened, the entire Italian army would be captured. Not that this seemed a good reason for stopping the fight: it was a matter of honour and of duty.

The war was now on a downward slope, and it was quite certain that the Axis would be defeated in the end, but after so many Italian reversals, Giulio thought that the army in Tunis must hold out as long as possible. Too quick a submission would be another heavy blow to Italian prestige, which was already so low, and he was ready to lead his own men to the end. Many of them, of course, would fall in this final defence of African territory. But in the fire that had already swallowed up millions, what was the sacrifice of a handful of youngsters?

That was all very well: but he might be one of them!

It was at sunset, when he was alone, that the thought of death mostly came to him. He envied the few men who could face danger boldly, who on the eve of an attack could eat gaily, as if they were at a party. Giulio himself was afraid. It was not so much physical fear as regret at the thought of dying before his time, before doing what he dreamed of, before becoming the man he wished to be. The thought of what came after death could not cheer him, either; for something within him kept telling him that the day he fell on the dry soil of Africa, everything would be over for him forever.

The stars glittered as they never did at home. He would gaze at them, as if to escape his own thoughts. But after a while the faint echo of a song would recall him to reality. It was sung by the Tuscan soldiers of the first company, who every evening gave vent to their longings:

> Sull' Arno d'argento
> si specchia il firmamento,
> mentre un sospiro, un canto
> si perde lontan. . . .

LXI

Suddenly the battalion was sent south-east, where the main part of the first Italian-German army, commanded by General Messe, was operating. Messe's troops were racing to hold the British Eighth Army offensive on the Mareth line—an offensive obviously meant to break through the front along the coast, and push north decisively.

On the evening of March 17th the artillery fire that preceded all the British offensives in Africa, and left no doubt of the enemy's intentions, started drumming along the Mareth front. Next day the Eighth Army, commanded by Montgomery, launched an attack all along the line, and fire rained down from sky and land along the whole front, causing enormous losses. The enemy offensive was too powerful to be repelled. It could only be contained for a few days, and after that it was a case of trying to fall back in good order, without too much haste.

In the entire Italian and German army, at that crucial moment of the battle, only about forty armoured vehicles were in working order; these were drawn up in a semi-circle across the main highway to try and halt at least two hundred British tanks advancing fast across the yellow plain to cut off the entire Axis army.

Sick at heart, Giulio thought of the friend he had shared a tent with, and others involved in that final effort to cover the retreat; and he thought how this fine March morning was no time to die.

Meantime, obeying orders, he was going north beside a shattered vehicle, in appalling confusion, with bombarded villages and ruined olive groves as a sad backcloth to the retreat. Occasionally he saw exhausted soldiers dropping out from the lines and the chaos, to wait for the Americans and the British. For them the war was over. But he was determined to do his duty to the end, although terrified by the enemy planes in the undefended sky that might swoop down on the road at any minute. So he carried on, suffering.

Very few tanks and armoured cars returned to the new lines set up after the retreat, at the end of the battle. The losses had been frightful. On one of the two surviving tanks, Rodolfo Accorsi suddenly appeared, thin, wasted, and with his arm roughly bandaged. It was so extraordinary to see him that Giulio went over to make sure, and it was, in fact, the young fanatic from Padusa. Two years at least had passed since Giulio had seen him, and now he saw him again thousands of miles from home at the end of a day of great sadness, which had shown quite definitely that the army was incapable of resistance.

Accorsi saw him. Above the noise of men and trucks, he shouted 'Hallo sir! I'm still on form, as you see!'

'How on earth did you get here?'

'I've been fighting all the way from the gates of Alexandria! Two thousand five hundred kilometres of desert! Tell that to those creeps in the café Torino!'

'Well done and good luck!' shouted Giulio. 'We'll meet again in Padusa some day, if these damnable planes spare us. . . .'

At that moment a shell whistled down, Giulio flung himself on the ground, and where Accorsi's tank had been standing he saw a huge pile of dust rise.

'Poor wretch!' he thought, and shut his eyes.

The dust settled and Giulio went over to the tank. But once again Accorsi had escaped: he was bawling at one of the men and seemed livelier and more elated than ever. The shell had burst half a yard from the tank, hurting no one.

Accorsi looked out for Giulio again and shouted triumphantly 'See that, sir? Fascists are tough-skinned!'

And he carried on along the road.

On April 6th the British Eighth Army attacked again to break the Sciott line, where General Messe had set up other defences. An avalanche of shells and bombs was dropped again on the Italian and German troops.

On the night of April 7th the Axis troops were forced to retreat again, and began to fall back on the line of Enfidaville, over two hundred and fifty kilometres to the north.

It took a week to reach the new lines, a week that seemed as long as a year, during which the exhausted Italian troops, with very few vehicles and practically no supplies, suffered unspeakably. The remains of the army fell back fighting, pursued all the way by enemy aircraft and tanks. Many died in skirmishes with the enemy vanguard, but still more were the victims of air attacks.

Giulio, never very robust, dragged himself along like an automaton. When he could finally rest, on the 13th, he was at the end of his resistance. Around him were dull faces, eyes either empty or desperate.

One blackshirt kept repeating the fascist motto 'We shall conquer,' like a worn record. Grunts, bitter laughter, ironical jokes, were his answer. But he continued. A lieutenant, with a bandaged, bleeding thigh shouted 'Shut up, you fool.'

A big Alpino suddenly gave him a powerful kick in the pants, and only this silenced the blackshirt.

On the line at Enfidaville they had to hold out. Orders were given for a desperate last defence. The battalion commander confided sadly to Giulio:

'We're to answer the enemy fire for another few days, for prestige reasons.'

But how could they make the men understand these reasons? Prestige was an elastic concept, one that could be lost and found again. But life could be lost only once. . . .

Yet the first battle to break through the line, which had started on April 29th, was not as successful as the British Eighth Army had hoped it would be. The wasted Italian troops, without reinforcements and forced to count every scrap of ammunition, fought with the courage of despair during the last days of the month.

A corporal told Giulio that, apart from the men who had lost the will to fight, there were others who could hold out. They were doing so, not because they thought they could avoid submission in the end, but because they did not want to be branded as cowards and were trying to show their sarcastic German 'comrades' that they were as good as they were.

These were the Romagnoli of the second division, who sat round in a circle in the evenings; and perhaps because they felt deeply how similar was their present condition and the whole dramatic story, now ending, of the Libyan oases, they sang the song of Giarabub with anger and with melancholy:

> Colonello, non voglio pane;
> dammi fuoco pel mio moschetto.
> Ho la terra nel sacchetto,
> che per oggi mi basterà.
> Colonello, non voglio l'acqua;
> dammi il fuoco distruggitore.
>
> Con la febbre di questo cuore
> la mia sete si spegnerà.
> Colonello, non voglio il cambio:
> qui nessuno ritorna indietro.
> Non si cede neppure un metro,
> se la morte non passerà. . . .

At last, on May 1st, they had a respite: the enemy concentrated his efforts elsewhere, on the front of the American Fifth Army. Then, on May 5th, came unexpected news: Mussolini was to speak on the radio.

'*Seven years ago,*' he said, from the balcony of Palazzo Venezia, '*we came together to celebrate the triumphal conclusion of the Ethiopian campaign.*'

So they had! On May 5th, 1936, during the sports contests, Giulio too had listened to Mussolini at the height of his glory and success. What would the leader who, in seven years, had taken the nation from that to the shameful, humiliating present have to say?

For a moment he thought that Mussolini might abruptly announce the defeat in Tunisia and unite the regime's friends and enemies with a pathetic appeal to defend their own native soil. For once, perhaps, he might be human and sincere. But no: with a complicated play on words, he made it clear that the campaign in Tunis was now at an end, but he was careful not to face up to reality, as Churchill had done in 1940. It was just the sort of bluff that might be expected of him.

At the end of his feeble speech the unshakable orator cried: 'We shall be back in Africa!'

'You may be,' yelled one of the soldiers, gesturing rudely.

'How could he think of appearing on the balcony of Palazzo Venezia, while the remains of an Italian army's dying out here, completely abandoned!' cried a captain who was supposed to be a fascist; he spat noisily on the ground.

'If the King doesn't get rid of that demi-god quite soon, there won't be a stone left in Italy,' said an aristocratic lieutenant.

On May 8th resistance in Tunis and Bizerta, attacked on the west, was overcome, and Messe's soldiers lost any chance, however theoretical, of escaping capture. But, surrounded and pushed together into an ever-diminishing space, the remnant of the army continued to hold out, while the Allies, who were not prepared to sacrifice men and equipment against troops who were bound to surrender, slowed down their attacks.

Officers and men now had a single topic of conversation.

'What's General Messe waiting for before surrendering?'

'He must be waiting for orders from Mussolini.'

'Then why can't the idiot make up his mind? Does he still believe in a counter-attack?'

'Well, he's in no hurry, that's clear. In Rome they're not as hot as we are here.'

On May 12th, in the chaos of defeat (waiting for the orders to cease resistance, which were to come the following day), while the troops were huddled untidily together, out of touch with their officers and without orders, a group of seventeen officers and men of the battalion managed to get hold of an abandoned lorry with its tanks full, and to dash away from that terrifying pit where the smoke of fires and explosions hid and protected them as they fled.

Giulio, drained with fatigue, was one of the group. He hardly realised what the others were trying to do, but was too tired to ask, and certainly too tired to argue. Had he known what he was doing he would probably have thought the flight pointless. But the others were not reasoning, they simply wanted to make a final effort to escape the prison camp and get home. How, they had no idea.

The group was led by a major who looked after the maps and led them to the coast. It was the only district not in the whirl-pool of battle. Occasionally a patrol would fire at the crazy lorry, the driver zigzagging to avoid the shots, tearing along the road with his foot hard on the accelerator. With the lorry's radiator boiling, its engine losing power, the group of rebels against the war's destiny, their nerves stretched to the limit, came in sight of an anchorage under the lower slopes of the Tunisian mountain chain that at that point went down almost to the sea. They were about 400 kilometres from Hammamet.

On the left, far away, they saw the outline of Cape Bon. The major got his bearings at once. Two lieutenants and an NCO crept forward, exploring cautiously. Giulio did not move, but stayed in the lorry exhausted.

Suddenly someone shouted 'Sir . . . quick . . . come and see . . . a wreck!'

Everyone rushed frantically over, taking no notice of the dangers in the difficult ground ahead. Giulio arrived last, a few minutes after the others. A half-beached motorboat was lying there. They all looked at one another, smiling, as if the wreck were a gift from heaven. Two tank drivers flung them-selves into the craft, examined the engine and the keel, and worked out what it might do.

'We can try. . . .'

Everyone felt encouraged. While the mechanics started work on the engine, all the others ran to the lorry, took out the fuel drums, and, forming a hasty chain, carried the precious liquid to the motorboat's tanks.

After an anxious, expectant hour, the chief mechanic said 'Let's have a try.'

At the first effort, the motor failed to fire.

'It wants priming again.'

They poured a little petrol into the carburettor, and gave the starter another violent tug, while everyone watched out for British patrols. This time the engine fired—feebly and intermittently at first, then more and more regularly.

'That's it!' yelled the chief mechanic, radiantly.

A shout of joy broke from the others. They stood in the water and pushed the motorboat vigorously out. It was not really watertight, but could hold out for several hours.

Excitedly they climbed in, packed tight in the small space, Giulio the last of them, privately thinking the whole adventure was crazy. But he said nothing to dissuade the others, who were all keyed up at the idea of getting home. He followed them, and trusted to fate.

The engine was revved up and, in a wide, foaming crescent, the boat set out towards the open sea. The sea air went to their heads: made them breathe deeply and take heart.

They made for Sardinia, as the sea routes to Sicily were controlled by the enemy. Through sheer good luck they sighted the Italian side and they landed at Cagliari, not as prisoners, but still as soldiers.

A few days later Giulio was in Naples.

LXII

The day after his arrival Giulio was walking in the centre of Naples when he suddenly met an old friend he had thought was dead—Mario Salatini. At the time of the Ethiopian war Salatini had been about the most impressive and admired of the Padusa students, but now he seemed to have deteriorated surprisingly. When he greeted him Giulio noticed that his left hand was stiff, encased in a black glove, but Salatini saw his glance and at once put him at ease by saying 'I'll tell you about my hand later.'

They went into a café and ordered hot drinks.

'D'you remember the way we used to get so drunk and excited singing student songs and fascist songs?' Salatini said with a melancholy smile.

'Even when we were drunk, as we were at your famous degree supper!'

'No, that was a horrible evening, the way it ended, with that business about the queer. But d'you remember what a one I was at the parades?'

'Moro could sing as well, though.'

'Ah, but he sang lyrics in the reviews. My strong point was Fascist hymns. How I worked everyone up with the Hymn of Rome! *Sole che sorgi libero e giocondo. . . .*'

'Yes . . . I remember the day you made even Starace sing it, in the Anatomy theatre!'

'With words—d'you remember?—about conquering Nice, Corsica, Malta, Tunisia, Djibouti, Suez and Dalmatia.'

'Dalmatia was your strong point, I remember.'

'Well, I didn't invent Dalmatian irredentism. The GUF wore its blue kerchief in honour of Italian Dalmatia, didn't it?'

'But you were Dalmatian by birth. I remember your special kerchief with the golden lions printed on a blue background.'

'My grandfather came from Zara, you see, and the Dalmatian question was like a piece of my family history. And then I thought there'd be Italians there. . . .'

'Whereas. . . .'

'Whereas when I was sent there in the war I got to know the Dalmatians. And they're Croatians . . . Croatians born and bred. That's where I left my hand.'

'It's sad: but they were fighting their war as well.'

'I know, Giulio. Don't think I hate them for it. Yugoslavia hasn't done us any harm, and we attacked it.'

'Worse still! The Axis meant to destroy their national unity.'

'Perhaps that's why everyone's for the partisans there. And I couldn't agree with repressive action, though our men were being killed in ambushes. That's how I lost my hand.'

'In an ambush?'

'Yes. We were stationed in a large town, and one day, on the way to the station, as I was greeting a colleague I was suddenly fired at. . . . But it might have been worse.'

For a while both were silent, each absorbed in his own thoughts. Then suddenly Salatini exclaimed, with a bitter smile, 'But losing my hand may bring me luck, after all, as it did that fool Vidussoni.'

'Don't say that! You're a clever chap and won't need to be pushed forward to get ahead. Whereas Vidussoni's a masterpiece—one of Mussolini's real grotesques!'

'To think he actually appointed him party secretary—it seems incredible. D'you know this twenty-seventh party secretary, by any chance?'

'Never seen him. But everyone says the same—that he's a

good soul but hopelessly mediocre. Puglioli said that when someone mentioned Balbo's *Le speranze d'Italia,* poor Vidussoni thought the author was our late marshal. He heard him himself.'

'No need to tell me! We fought in Spain together, and one day someone was being sarcastic about the way Roosevelt defended the Jews all over the place but put up with the blackest racialism in the Southern states, and up he bounced and asked how the Government in Washington could impose its authority on South America.'

'And to think we used to joke about Starace, when we were in the G U F!'

LXIII

In Naples Giulio heard that Dionisio had been sent to the military war tribunal and was under arrest. The news worried him profoundly. He was living in a depressing atmosphere that induced worry, and where anyone who was not out of his mind could smell decay.

That morning he had had a refusal in reply to his urgent request for a hundred pairs of shoes, for his men's shoes were in pieces.

'But this is crazy! The imperial army marching barefoot, and they have the nerve to end their letter with *We shall conquer!*'

His colleague the Marchese Ameglio, who had also got back from the front, looked deliberately grave and gestured to them to look up above their heads.

'What is it?'

'Look at that!'

Giulio looked up and once again saw the unfortunate poster which was stuck up everywhere—from police stations to public lavatories: the ugly head of a British soldier, and the words *'Be quiet, the enemy is listening!'*

Giulio burst out laughing.

This sentence, under the Tommy's incredible monkeyish face, had become a stock joke. It was applied to everything— an invitation to a good dinner, pre-war style, a packet of smuggled cigarettes, a black-market ham; and people laughed. They also laughed at the man who, on the poster saying 'We do not discuss high strategy here—we work!' had crossed out 'we work' and written 'we swallow whatever we're told'— clearly alluding to what the fascist radio was every day asking Italians to swallow. All the ordinary man could do was make jokes out of the slogans hammered into the ears of over forty million Italians for twenty years.

'What can you do about it, Govoni? Everything's going to the dogs. . . . Better stop worrying!'

Enzo's unexpected arrival in Naples, bringing his forty-year-old fiancée to introduce to Giulio, confirmed the uncomfortable things they said. As far as Enzo was concerned, Mussolini and the regime were now buried deep in ridicule.

'Here's a joke from Rome,' he told Giulio and Ameglio. 'On Via dell'Impero there's a finger pointing to the statue of Julius Caesar, and on this finger someone's stuck a slice of black bread, and written underneath it: "O Caesar, who ruled the whole world, here's what's left of our slice of empire."'

'Even if it's not true it's good,' said Ameglio. 'As good as the medal for valour in food rationing.'

Giulio looked at him inquiringly: 'Which is?'

'It's Mussolini's new decoration for people who don't buy any food except the official rations. But the first medals have all been awarded posthumously.' He laughed, but with a tinge of melancholy.

Enzo then told Giulio that a number of soldiers, led by Eriberto Melloni, had been arrested in Padusa.

'What had they got up to?' asked Giulio, worried.

'Melloni was a bit too casual: a sergeant caught him in the quartermaster's office dictating the text of an anti-fascist manifesto to a typist—it was to be handed round the barracks.'

'Poor Eriberto! What on earth'll happen to him!'

'You needn't worry too much about these arrests. The barracks'll soon crumble, anyway.'

'Not as soon as all that.'

'I think it will.'

Enzo then told them in detail about some powerful strikes that had broken out in Turin and Milan during March, while Giulio was fighting in Tunisia. Ameglio was amazed.

'We did hear something about it, but I thought it was all exaggeration. The newspapers didn't even mention it.'

'Ah, but d'you think they would, just when fascism's been beaten? Because if people strike in the middle of the war, after it's been forbidden for years, it means the regime's collapsed. Don't you agree?'

'I do. But I suppose they were striking over pay. . . .'

'On the face of it they were. And the workers got decent pay out of it. But underneath it all the motive was political. Obviously it was all organised.'

'And who organised it so well?' Giulio asked.

'As you can imagine: the communists. They were even giving orders in an underground edition of *Unità*. Believe me, at this very moment the balance is beginning to tilt to the other side. Fascism's on the way down, Communism on the way up.'

In fact, official Italy was rapidly collapsing; and Giulio realised it, even from his inquiries in military circles. The few officers who wanted to be sent to the front and spoke fervently of the war were thought crazy, and, as far as victory was concerned, only a very few kept their hopes up, after the Germans' disastrous defeat in Russia and the total withdrawal in North Africa.

'What really gets me is that the King still supports this old has-been enchanter, with the nonsense he talks non-stop,' said Ameglio after a pause.

'Quite,' said Enzo, and then laughed. 'He's even changed the name of victory. He now calls it the hypotenuse.'

'What d'you mean?'

'I can see you haven't been reading the papers while you were at the front. Don't you know the Duce's invented a *geometrical* victory?' Enzo then told them that Mussolini had sent for the editors of the daily papers on April 18th, for a special statement. 'They'd run out of nonsense and needed something new. Well, the best bit of nonsense came from the old soothsayer himself. It's such an outsize idiocy that I learnt it by heart, so listen if you want a good laugh: *The war will be long and we shall conquer, that is mathematical; just like Pythagoras's theorem that the angles of a triangle are equal to two right angles; or the other theorem that the square*

[209]

on the hypotenuse of a right-angled triangle is equal to the sum of the squares on the other two sides. It is just as certain that we shall win, in fact it is already clear that we are advancing towards victory.'

Giulio was silent, as if stunned by this unexpected rhetoric.

'But that's crazy!' exclaimed Ameglio. 'The fellow's not just murdering common sense, he's murdering mathematics!'

The brothers left the barracks together and went into a bar. The radio was babbling the usual propaganda about spring having come and with it good times. But what hadn't come, Giulio thought, were a hundred pairs of shoes for his barefoot men. People went in and out, bored, incredulous, on edge. A few muttered: 'Stinking stuff,' but it was not the disgusting ersatz coffee they were grumbling about.

Among the officers flooding the town, very few dared profess anti-fascism openly. But the regime's intense propaganda was now met with shrugs, and at the stupidest broadcasts people would hum a tune which was then popular: *Illusione, dolce chimera sei tu. . . .* Then they would go to their rooms, shut the windows tight and tune in to Radio London.

But the troops' morale was much worse; and one day his corporal made this quite clear to Giulio. 'Excuse me sir, but we're the ones who are suffering in this war.'

'Well, so are the officers, after all . . .'

'The officers grumble, but their life's not really too bad. They've got their pay and decent food that isn't expensive, and they know their families aren't suffering because pretty well all of them come from middle-class homes. But we're poor and wretched, we have filthy food and not a penny in our pockets, and they write to us from home and say: if you don't get back soon we'll die of hunger. All we can do is take our guns and chuck them in the canal.'

'Don't worry so much, the war will come to an end.'

'Let's hope so. Else we'll have to end it ourselves.'

'Come on, have an *Africa*. It's a miracle to find any.'

'That's it: from the whole of Africa there's just a few fags left.'

Giulio wondered where Italy, now floating about quite rudderless, could find an anchorage. From Churchill and Roosevelt, who kept demanding unconditional surrender, there was little hope. How could Hitler's and Mussolini's enemies at home dare risk a *coup d'état* with such a prospect before them? So it was to be war to the end, a war that would come on to the soil of Italy itself, leaving terrible desolation behind it. The militant anti-fascists were delighted at the thought of seeing the fall of the regime they hated, and seemed to consider the rest was pretty unimportant. Perhaps they were more long-sighted.

But Giulio could not reason as they did. He suffered, and could see only darkness ahead.

LXIV

On July 5th Giulio heard confidentially from a colleague that their men were on the point of being sent to Sicily, where an enemy landing was expected at any moment. Since the island of Pantelleria had been occupied—the first piece of Italian territory lost—the idea of invasion had become an obsession.

Giulio was still shocked by the unwelcome news (he had no wish to repeat his Tunisian experience), when he was surprised, one morning, to see in the paper the banner headlines used only for Mussolini's speeches. Astonished, he read that the speech had been made some ten days before in Palazzo Venezia, to the regime's top officials, and thought that possibly it had been dug out in a final effort to restore the Italians' lost confidence. Mussolini's speech from the balcony of Palazzo Venezia had been made two months before. In it he had said firmly that although Italy was preparing to submit in Tunis, she would return to Africa; and, although carefully coached, the audience had not been exactly delirious in its applause. Now, after the string of swift disasters, he could no longer face the public himself.

Giulio read the long text carefully.

Mussolini finally admitted that a great many people were doubtful; and it was to these people in particular that he tried to show how defeat would be something apocalyptic, which would condemn generations of Italians to wretchedness and slavery. With this spectre he hoped to shake a people who now distrusted him profoundly into some sort of patriotic fervour.

When he spoke of the dreaded enemy landings, he tried to play on people's feelings: '*The Italian people now know that it is a question of life and death*,' he said. '*As soon as our enemies try to land, they must be stopped on the sands, where the water ends and the land begins. If they happen to penetrate further, our reserve forces must fling themselves on them and destroy them to the last man. So that people may say they have occupied a piece of our country, but occupied it horizontally, not vertically.*'

Giulio's arms fell to his side. Was this Mussolini's eloquence, which had seduced Italians for twenty years? Imprecise, vulgar and childish, his weary outburst betrayed the state of mind of a man who saw the ephemeral structure of the system he had created crumbling beneath him.

Giulio was still with his men in Naples, when, amid general excitement, the expected Allied landing in Sicily was announced. It was June 10th 1943. After a couple of days the invaders' success was already quite clear. The gaps in the Italian news bulletins could not hide the truth: everyone listened for the broadcast from London.

These Allied divisions, Giulio thought to himself, were those he had faced in Tunis; and there they had had a hard fight to overcome General Messe's army. If they were now advancing so easily, it was clear that the Italians were no longer fighting.

Everyone in the regiment realised this, except for a couple of madmen who hoped for a counter-offensive. A young second lieutenant from Milan, the son of one of the regime's official journalists, refused to accept defeat. He was angry with the Sicilian population, which were said to be greeting the invaders with delight; angry with the local soldiers opposing them; angry with the defeatists, who had undermined the morale of the armed forces. One evening a Sicilian captain lost his temper at dinner. 'The strength to resist comes from within,' he said. 'It came to our fathers after Caporetto, and to the English after Dunkirk. But in order to get it one's own country must be in danger, not just one's own party.'

'In Italy they're the same thing.'

[212]

'Where did they teach you that?'

'The Duce taught me, and twenty years of history have proved it. Fascism has made Italy into a great nation.'

'Go and tell that to the Sicilians—wretched, ragged creatures living in almost African hovels and now seeing an enemy land who gives them food, fags and freedom.'

'But the Duce gave them—'

'He made a lot of speeches but he left them hungry, and then he took their sons to die in North Africa or in Russia—'

'You're a lousy defeatist,' shouted the youngster. 'You're one of those the Duce attacked in his last speech!'

The Captain got up, furiously, and the pair would have come to blows, but the commander stepped in and stopped the quarrel.

LXV

On the warm, damp night of July 25th a number of officers had stayed in the mess. Most of them were out in the pleasant garden, sitting in cane armchairs, and trying to enjoy the faint night breeze that occasionally filtered through the stagnant air. Inside, a handful were playing poker and bridge. Everyone looked patiently resigned to the heat, the boredom and the increasingly bad news. Yet secretly everyone was waiting for something.

'D'you think we can go on like this?'

'Lord knows!'

'My own feeling is that Mussolini's had it.'

'Right, but what next?'

'Better not think about it.'

In order to avoid thinking about it, each man shut himself up in his own silence.

'Gentlemen, the radio's repaired,' the head waiter called.

Lazily those in the garden got up, straightened their crumpled uniforms and went indoors.

'Might as well hear the usual rubbish,' muttered a lieutenant.

'No, it's music at this time.'

But the radio announced a special communiqué: it was twenty-five minutes past ten.

'Etna must have erupted on the Anglo-Americans,' murmured a captain ironically.

But it was much more than that: a voice that seemed unreal stated that the King had 'accepted the dismissal of Cavalier Benito Mussolini' and had assumed supreme command of the armed forces, appointing Badoglio head of the government.

A shiver ran down everyone's spine. The small crowd of officers clustered in a tense silence round the radio, anxious not to miss a word. But Badoglio's proclamation—read after the King's—concluded with 'The war continues,' which increased the general bewilderment.

The colonel cried 'Long live the King!' and all the officers echoed it. Then, in an atmosphere of feverish surprise, and hope, and fear, comment and discussion burst out. Giulio joined in for a while, then went into the garden to hide in the darkness. His temples were thudding.

Anyone who had heard the Duce's universal genius exalted, as Giulio had, since he was at his primary school, was bound to feel his inglorious end, however anxiously awaited, as something remarkable and dramatic, as if the earth had suddenly caved in under his feet. Giulio could hardly persuade himself the news was true.

He listened. From a distance, in the street that ran below the garden wall, a band was playing a tuneful serenade.

A street singer was singing *Summer night,* a seductive old Neapolitan love song, using all kinds of trills and flourishes.

Curious, Giulio went through the garden gate and towards the music. Suddenly a door opened on to a balcony, and a man wearing pyjamas and a woollen skull-cap, like those worn by fishermen in Amalfi, stepped out. He waved nervously and pointlessly, turning about in every direction as if to call people, and then shouted rhythmically: 'The swine's brought down . . . they've brought the swine down!'

'What swine?' called a voice in the street.

'Mussolini—Mussolini himself. I'm going to bed with democracy tonight!'

Everyone roared with laughter.

'That your wife's name?' asked a merry young voice.

'My wife's Maria,' said the man.

The street became alive with chatter and gossip. The

musicians, wonderingly, moved off together to the streets of lower Naples. One of them started singing *Avanti, popolo, alla riscossa!* softly, accompanying it by plucking at the mandolin, then the whole band joined in and the lead singer's voice rose above the rest, still trilling elaborately.

In the distance the noise was growing—people were calling from door to door and from street to street. As if a single hand were switching on lights everywhere, windows lit up. The city was awakening to the great news and sleep was impossible in all the talk and laughter, the shouting and tears.

'The war's over!' people cried, swarming through the bomb-damaged streets.

Men were dashing about, not knowing exactly where they were going. They looked as if they were chasing someone, yet in fact they were not following anything except joy, which in Naples is something solid, material, tangible. Many tore off their gloomy clothes; blind people ran decisively along, as if by a miracle, borne by the human tide, and paralytics shared the excitement, carried along by relations and friends. Even quite casual acquaintances sobbed and embraced when they met.

Giulio, used to people who controlled their feelings and passions, was amazed by the whole outburst, by the way people poured out of their houses and dashed about seeking others, calling them, shouting nonsense. He wanted to see more, and followed the crowd of maniacs, realising that the fall of fascism meant the end of the war to them, the end of a nightmare. He tried to stop one of the men and explain that Badoglio's proclamation had said 'the war continues.'

'But he's mad!' the man replied.

No one believed the war would continue: the war meant fascism, and if fascism had fallen, the war could not go on. The flood of people rose higher, more uncontrolled and more excited.

In Via Chiaia, in a smart district, Giulio stopped, wonderingly. Outside a grand house with a wide marble doorway stood an impressive-looking man wearing a homburg hat and carrying a cane, surrounded by eleven urchins and every ten seconds chanting: 'Colonel!'

'Bang-bang-bang!' roared the urchins.

[215]

'Colonel!'

'Bang-bang-bang!' cried the boys, again.

It was all done in a staid, dignified sort of way; and the urchins behaved as if taking part in some public function. The oldest was adding up accounts with a piece of charcoal on the pavement.

'125 . . . 126 . . . 127 . . .'

'That's enough,' said the man.

'Such-and-such and such-and-such makes such-and-such,' said the boy. 'Then there's overtime for night-work and danger money (seeing it's wartime, sir), which makes 100 lire.'

He pocketed the money quickly, and moved off. Giulio stood there, speechless.

The man came over to him with the usual Neopolitan friendliness.

'You're not from these parts, I take it?' he said.

'No, I'm from the north,' said Giulio.

'Maybe you don't understand.'

'I certainly don't!'

'It's not easy to follow, but . . . think of an execution. Yes, I wanted to execute that swine the colonel exactly according to the rules.'

'I see,' said Giulio, 'so the kids are your guns.'

'Guns indeed!' the man snorted. 'I'm only sorry I disturbed the . . . colonel's wife, asleep.'

Then he said goodbye and went down a side street, in the direction of the port.

Giulio was astounded. He kept wondering what sort of people these were; the atmosphere around him seemed completely surrealist. All the harsh evidence of the war—the damaged streets, the scarred houses, the tangled ruins—seemed an absurd theatrical background for people who were all too gay, whose riotous feeling for life and death prevented any real trouble touching them.

His mind was in a turmoil as he thought all this over. As he climbed up the Vomero, he looked over the tops of the houses. In the distance, the sea was edged with its dawn pallor. Giulio felt the morning coolness, but his ideas were no clearer.

What were these people really after?

Suddenly he became alarmed. Tomorrow, he thought, they'll go out into the streets and greet the American planes, and the planes will shoot them down like flies.

LXVI

Giulio went to bed for a couple of hours without sleeping, and was up early next morning, with orders to take over public duties. Everyone seemed to have been roped into this—officers and men—and it was clear that the new government was afraid of serious difficulties.

The day was a long series of demonstrations. Students and workers marched about, followed by troops of children, waving tricolour flags, singing songs to the King, to Badoglio, to freedom and to peace. News reached the barracks by telephone, from other places, near or far; and everywhere there were the same scenes, the same exultation.

From the Alps to the outlying islands, portraits of Mussolini, flung delightedly out of the windows, meant a great many things to the unhappy Italians: the end of the war, the end of hardships, the end of injustice. Suddenly, millions of men who for years had accepted and endured, identified the regime with everything that had gone wrong in the present Italy; and among those who railed against the defeated regime there were any number who, till the day before, had actually said that all Italy's wrongs were a result of sabotaging the Duce's orders. But in their excitement those who burnt a black-shirted guy in piazzas all over Italy thought they saw the nation's troubles, symbolised in the regime, blown away in a puff of wind.

Towards evening, Giulio had to intervene to rescue a man from the claws of an excited group hurling insults at him. He was a small dark man of about sixty, who looked the typical harmless little clerk.

Giulio took him into a chemist's, but luckily the man needed no first aid. He had just been shoved about a bit.

'Why were those youngsters after you?' Giulio asked him with a friendly smile.

'Let's not talk about it, sir.'

'Are you afraid to tell me you're a fascist?'

'Me a fascist? For heaven's sake! The trouble is, there are just too many cowards and turncoats around.'

'Well, are you a fascist or aren't you?'

'I did take their wretched party card in 1941, when it was offered to veterans of the First World War. Before that I had nothing to do with it—I was loyal to the socialism of my youth.'

'Then I don't see—'

'I'll explain. I work in the registrar's office, up on the third floor, and this morning when I went to work I was still wearing my fascist badge in my buttonhole. During the night a hundred thousand Neapolitans had chucked theirs out—but I'd forgotten. So a chap in the office met me with a flood of curses and told me to take the badge off at once. I refused.'

'But why did you refuse? Are you becoming a fascist at this very moment?'

'Fascist my eye! That's got nothing to do with it. This young chap who told me to take my badge off is the very same swine who kicked me when I wasn't a party member. Even last summer, when we were advancing in Egypt, that wretch got up a subscription in the office to have a bumper supper to celebrate the conquest of the Suez canal! It's disgusting! Any excuse was good enough to come to the office in his black uniform, with the wretched fascist eagle on his cap. And now he has the cheek. . . .'

'Well, there's nothing so odd about that—he's just changed his mind . . .'

'Yes, he changed his mind a few weeks ago because the wind changed. He makes me sick! And he's not going to get me to take my fascist badge off, just with his threats.'

'Oh, so you're wearing it just out of pig-headedness?'

'Certainly. And because the others in the office started beating me and asking me if I'd stuck to Mussolini because we were both originally socialists. So I lost my temper and shouted straight at those who'd all supported Mussolini till the day before that I was staying a fascist, just to save their honour.'

'You're paradoxical, aren't you!'

'I'm serious, that's what I am. Even fascist officials woke up this morning quite convinced they were victims of the regime, so I'm the only fascist left around here.'

'And was that why those boys were so angry with you?'

'They found a scapegoat for their own folly.'

'You're looking for trouble, you know, with a character like yours. Don't forget that fascism made a great many people suffer.'

'I've got my own character, lieutenant, and above all I've got my own dignity. And if they keep making me so angry, I may become a fascist and really mean it.'

LXVII

Giulio had no time to feel happy over Mussolini's downfall before he began suffering over the new situation: the war that was going on, with apparently no object, and the nation that was simply drifting.

He longed to know what was happening around the King and Badoglio and the leaders of the new parties. But being a mere junior officer on the very edge of things, without political contacts, he had to get his information from the press, which was still censored, or, when he was lucky, from some colleague who had come from Rome and could tell him roughly what was being said in its political cafés.

With his old major, he gave vent to his feelings.

'D'you think it's possible that Badoglio hasn't any plans for getting us out of this terrible impasse?'

'Let's hope he has! But haven't you seen the number of Germans turning up?'

'But they've got enough on their plate in the rest of Europe. They can't send many big divisions here.'

'They can send enough to wipe us out.'

'We've got the remains of the army, which can do its best in the circumstances, while we're waiting for Eisenhower.'

'And where's our equipment?'

'In a case like this you've got to take account of people's spirit!'

'Of course! Spiritual against . . . material. That's one of Mussolini's expressions.'

'It mightn't do so badly for us, if we were decisive and properly led.'

Giulio had never lived through days so intense, so baffling. The atmosphere seemed totally unreal. What struck him most was the free political debates in the newspapers, which were now no longer the tools of a totalitarian regime. But he was saddened by the blanks the censor left on the front page of the dailies, which made it seem that the Government had all kinds of mysteries to hide from ordinary people. One day *Il Popolo di Roma* opened with a political article by the editor, Corrado Alvaro, censored entirely except for a few short sentences, and Giulio wondered all day what new ideas this pugnacious paper might be proposing, and was amazed at the fact that he now demanded to know the truth. Unknown ideas and concepts, which came out of this democratic discussion, he seized on with admiration and astonishment, and he followed the intense, febrile activity of the local party leaders, shot suddenly out of hiding into the limelight. The names of the anti-fascist political leaders—De Nicola, De Gasperi, Sforza, Nenni, Saragat, Ruini, De Vittorio, Togliatti—had meant nothing to him until July 25th. To him, pre-fascist politics meant four old men, Orlando, Nitti, Bonomi and Don Sturzo, whom history books called feeble and inept.

One day the old major, shaking his head, said: 'They say Togliatti's got a very good brain. If only his ideas were different, that's the sort of man we could do with, instead of Badoglio,' and Giulio, deeply embarrassed, had to ask 'Who's this Togliatti, then?'

'Are you interested in politics or are you living in the clouds?' the major asked with an air of fatherly pity. 'Don't you know Togliatti is Ercole Ercoli, alias Mario Correnti, the leader of the Italian Communists?'

Halfway through August Giulio's men were transferred to Rome. A rumour went round that Badoglio meant to mass troops round the capital, to defend it from the Germans if there was an armistice. But no one knew the truth.

Giulio found the journey appalling. He went by lorry; his forehead was burning hot, and he felt exhausted. He tried to sleep but when he dozed he was disturbed by the soldiers singing, venting all their anxiety on the sun-steeped countryside:

Col governo Mussolini
paraponzi ponzi po,'
ci mancavano i quattrini,
paraponzi ponzi po',
col governo di Badoglio
manca pure il pane e l'olio . . .

Questo è proprio un mondo cane,
paraponzi ponzi po',
niente donne e niente pane,
paraponzi ponzi po';
ma in compenso abbiam la guerra,
che ci manda sotto terra.
Daghela ben biondina,
daghela ben biondaaa.

When they reached Rome Giulio found he had a temperature of 101°. The doctor diagnosed bronchitis, and he was sent
to a military hospital. It was only a primary school, built in
King Umberto's reign, and very roughly adapted. The class-
rooms on the second floor had been turned into wards and were
crammed with officers from all the services.

Hospital life, to anyone not really ill (and there were few
who really were) could not be called uncomfortable. The
war seemed very far away, and the hospital a kind of secluded
harbour in the present storm. The patients exchanged chat
from their beds.

'Got your parcel from home?'

'This very minute.'

'What did your mother send you?'

'Fags is the only good thing.'

'I've had some cake. . . .'

Not only was there less discipline: even the patient's conditions were only formally checked and no one was sent back
on duty. Towards evening, when they whispered about the
escapades they were plotting, the relaxed atmosphere became
quite amusing.

'Lend me your suit and I'll bring you back some fags.'

'There's a brunette in Trastevere expecting me and. . . .
Get up!'

'Lucky dog!'

Those who slipped out at night were mainly rosy, well-fed young Romans; their pockets were full, and they had grown used to living without any sort of control.

'Whew—just look at Isa Miranda!' said a spoilt youth, turning over the pages of *Cinema illustrato* as he lay in bed.

'When I was in Croatia, a girl like that. . . .'

'I've never been at the front.'

'Rotten slacker, eh?'

'I've spent three years in hospital, on convalescent leave, and short spells on duty.'

'And you've got a medal, I bet.'

'Well, you never can tell.'

Everyone laughed.

'Well, who'd I have risked my skin for? La Petacci's fat lover?'

'Mussolini's done with, praise be. Now things are different.'

'D'you want to fight for Badoglio?'

'Are you joking? After two years in Libya and Egypt all I want is sleep. In any case, he's only carrying on the war while he prepares to end it.'

'One of these days, peace'll break out.'

'Let's hope it breaks out soon.'

'Suppose the Germans break us up first?' Giulio suggested.

There was an icy silence. No one wanted to think of anything so terrible. And to soften their fears of it, the boys ate up the cakes their mothers had sent them.

LXVIII

On September 7th, Giulio was sent on convalescent leave, and he rushed to the station to get the first train he could catch. It was the worst journey of his life. The stations were cluttered, the carriages jammed, the stops frequent and interminable. Everywhere he saw the oppressive green of the Wehrmacht uniform.

He got home on the evening of the 8th, just in time to hear the dramatic news of the Armistice. Next morning he went round to the piazza, and found Scaranari at his office window, trying to calm down a crowd of workmen who had been fighting a military patrol. But by evening there were no longer any patrols about, in spite of orders from the local commander.

By dawn on the 10th, even the command had ceased to exist: outside the imposing colonnade of the great old house, between the two marble lions, a German soldier, legs wide apart, stood on guard. Late in the evening and during the night German troops—without firing a shot—had occupied all the barracks in town, while officers and men, left to themselves, had tried to slip away in civilian clothes. The greenest of them, who had stayed in the barracks awaiting orders, had been taken prisoner.

At midday, when he reached the café Torino, Giulio had to avoid German tanks insolently moving down Corso Gioconda. And the soldiers wearing civilian clothes and making their way home by whatever transport they could find confirmed that everything was going exactly the same in other towns nearby.

Giulio was reluctant to believe his own eyes, but the truth forced itself crudely home. In a few hours the Italian army in the Paduan lowlands had vanished!

He cursed the King, Badoglio's ineptness, and the British and American armies who had done nothing to help the new government. The final action of the king and this government, who had fled to Brindisi at night with their lights out like smugglers, depressed him. The whole humiliation of Italy flooded his soul.

That evening at supper he kept staring at his plate.

'What are you thinking about?' Enzo asked him.

'I'm thinking that for at least sixty years, if anyone in Europe wants to be funny about the Italians, they'll talk about our military valour. . . .'

LXIX

The third day after the armistice Moro panted into the café Torino with the news that Dionisio, wearing civilian clothes, had arrived at the station at dawn. It was nearly one o'clock but Giulio rushed straight round to Dionisio's, without a thought for the lunch awaiting him at home, and stayed with him till supper time. Pina, who had had a baby a fortnight before, was in her room with the child, who was roaring its head off, and the two friends, delighted to meet again after a year's separation, exchanged all the latest news.

Dionisio's interesting time in France had started in Nice. In the first months of 1943, he told Giulio, Nice had none of its usual cosmopolitan airs—no millionaires on holiday or anything of the kind. But it was still a tonic to be there—it was still a restful oasis in the midst of chaos. The charming city had not lost its style or its taste, and was keeping its elegance and luxury for the days when peace returned. Its natural beauty meant that it could survive food rationing, military occupation and poverty; even in its privations it managed to be impressive, and never lost its charm, which was partly the charm of its women. The magnificent hotels, which had lost nothing but their customers, were the undamaged frames of a self-contained world that seemed to have escaped the cataclysm of the rest of Europe.

The watchword was '*Je m'en fiche*'; and the Italian junior officers heard it from any number of gorgeous girls, whose sole idea of spiritual comfort was Caron scent, Elizabeth Arden make-up and Coty powder. In that pool of tranquillity they forgot the war, and re-lived the days when, in peacetime, in Milan or Naples or Genoa or Palermo, they had pursued the girl they loved or desired.

'*Ninon, ou allons-nous ce soir?*'

'*Ou tu veux, mon Italien. . . .*'

and Ninon would take her escort—already thrilled at the thought of the adventure he was involved in—into fashionable shops, where cigarettes could be bartered for something particularly smart, into the impressive Galleries Lafayette, with glittering, still amazing windows; into the attractive bookshops, which sold books on politics and sex that were strictly forbidden in Italy; or into seductive cabarets, where, in some back room, they might even see the blue films that were only whispered about at home.

In spite of the war, love affairs between Italians and French-women flourished in the sunshine, like the most natural thing in the world. Wives and girl-friends seemed thousands of miles away.

Dionisio had been assigned to a military command which had its headquarters in one of the most luxurious hotels at Nice. The rooms used as offices looked out over a magnificent garden, with great hundred-year-old palm-trees in the centre and Mediterranean plants of every kind bursting out into flower all round them. Desks were almost crowded out by sofas, arm-chairs, carpets and mirrors, and it was hard to withstand the temptation to dump military documents on a gilded console table or delicate Louis Quinze chair, and imagine the holiday-makers who had once filled those luminous rooms.

The officers took their meals in a splendid dining-room, served by immaculate orderlies. Between four and eight of them sat at each table, the most senior with the C.O. at the end, next to the great window, majors and captains in the middle of the room, and lieutenants near the door. The tone of the mess was grandly old-fashioned—many of the regular officers had aristocratic backgrounds.

In spite of the war the food was often excellent, but in particular there were plenty of good French and Italian wines. When courtesies were exchanged hardly a day went by with-out one of the officers offering the others at his table a fine wine at dessert. They drank the health of their friends and toasted their return home, and sometimes—in low tones— they drank to victory.

Next to the dining-room were splendid drawing rooms, once used by American millionaires. Now their chief occupants were those few officers who stayed in in the evenings, playing poker. But the imposing lamps and majestic furniture, the satin and damask armchairs, and above all the superb car-pets which they hardly dared desecrate with their heavy boots, all weighed on them, and it took a couple of drinks to put them at their ease.

When the weather was fine, the officers met after lunch outside the Hotel Negresco, at the beginning of the almost de-serted Promenade des Anglais. On wooden armchairs they sat in the sun, some staring at the blue sea, absorbed, isolated in their own thoughts, some eyeing the girls mincing along a few yards away, some telling a friend about a magni-ficent villa or a marvellous view admired the previous day. They looked relaxed and rested, as if it were peacetime and they were on the sea-front at Rimini or Viareggio.

News of the tragic storm overwhelming the rest of the world seemed muted by the time it reached them in that land of forgetfulness.

'*Ça ne va pas*: in Russia they're turning back, in Africa we've been pushed out . . . farewell forever, Tripoli, *bel suol d'amore*. . . .'

'Oh, stop worrying: what's to come will come, in any case.'

'Good God, are we Italian soldiers or Swiss holiday-makers?'

'What a bore you are! You're ruining the peace, and this perfect sky. . . . Shut up about the war: look what we've got here.'

'But how will it end?'

'One fine day they'll both get tired of fighting, and they'll realise that the war was idiotic on both sides.'

'Let's hope they do, and that they don't trample on us instead.'

This was the kind of talk that prevailed: a few fanatics sometimes tried to adopt a heroic tone, but the mood was soon demolished by the others' lack of interest.

The command handled the local people very gently, and, except for the odd lout, officers and men behaved with perfect politeness and respect, tiptoeing round the town as if apologising for occupying it at all. Perhaps subconsciously they knew that they must behave themselves in other people's houses, now that the enemy was almost in their own.

The French civilians were equally respectful, and sometimes friendly.

'*Bonjour, monsieur le capitaine!*'

'*Bonjour, monsieur Dupont!*'

The officer would salute, and M. Dupont courteously raise his pre-war hat.

The worse the war went for Italy, the closer people drew to these kindly, ill-armed youngsters, who were there playing the part of provisional victors. The citizens of Nice seemed to feel sincerely for them, and sometimes expressed their solidarity in terms that were brutally sincere. 'Don't be depressed,' they would say. 'France collapsed in 1940, and now it's Italy's turn. Wars end, the world starts turning again, and there'll always be room for our civilisation!'

All public places and shop windows showed portraits of the chief of state, Marshal Pétain. During his first weeks there Dionisio had thought that this symbol of defeat and betrayal was being displayed under strict orders from the police. But he was wrong. Many people in Nice saw Pétain as a fine old man who had sacrificed himself for his defeated country, and was trying to save it from further trouble.

In his anti-fascist fervour, Dionisio had come to France convinced that all the French were openly supporting the Anglo-Saxons. But the situation was hideously complex. In middle-class families hatred of the Germans was mitigated by fear of Communism, and everywhere there was barely concealed suspicion of the Anglo-Saxons.

Dionisio had become friendly with the few officers who openly shared his hatred of fascism. Day after day they discussed the military situation, made prophecies for the future, discussed freedom, democracy and social justice. But while his friends avoided giving themselves away in public, Dionisio became increasingly indiscreet.

It was not only politics that made things difficult for him. Pride came into it, too. Coming from the depot at Sàvena, where he had been a sort of little king, Dionisio could not stand being treated as the small fry he was. When treated familiarly by his seniors he turned scarlet with rage, and having to behave deferentially to some fool of a captain, who might actually be younger than himself, was bitter. Occasionally he lost patience and exploded.

After barely three months at the command, Dionisio had made himself unpopular, and the authorities transferred him to a divisional artillery regiment stationed in the district. Its officers were billeted in a group of elegant villas just over a kilometre from the sea, on a green hill. Their fine Italian-style gardens had run wild through neglect during the last few years, but Dionisio thought their strange untidiness enchanting, a kind of botanical return to nature. Each officer had a splendid room to himself, the sort none of them would have dreamt of having at home. The men were less luxuriously housed, but they too were comfortable and there were few complaints.

But they all longed for their homes and families, and in

the evening sat round in a semi-circle in a kind of natural amphitheatre looking down over the sea, and sang nostalgic songs. Then finally, to throw off their gloom, they would strike up the current popular march, the one they used to set the pace when they were out on manoeuvres:

È lui! È lui! Sì, sì, è proprio lui!
Il tamburo principal della banda d'Affori,
che comanda cinquecentocinquanta pifferi. . . .
Che emozion, che passion,
quando fa bon-bon. . . .
Guarda qua,
mentre van,
le oche fan qua qua. . . .
Le ragazze nel vederlo diventan timide,
lui confonde il Trovator con la Semiramide.
Bella figlia dell'amor,
schiavo son,
schiavo son,
dei vezzi tuoi. . . .

Here too, as at Nice, they lived for the moment. Idleness, in the liquid Mediterranean spring sunshine, made the young officers feel languid and resigned. Even the news on the radio —which grew daily worse—could not shake them out of it, and they seemed to be living outside the harsh realities around them. The catastrophic wind blowing over Italy seemed to avoid them and their leisurely life.

Dionisio thought military collapse could not be far off, and felt it was cowardly to hang about, waiting on events. But, without contacts in anti-fascist organisations, he had no means of action. So, to let off steam, he wrote to relations, friends and colleagues. And he talked: to his men, to civilians, even to the French gendarmes; in fact, he talked too much. He was warned, but he went on doing it, and so the day came when his pompous C.O. denounced him to the military war tribunal for defeatism, and had him imprisoned.

But it was only for a few weeks. When Mussolini fell Dionisio shut the prison door behind him and, in the small piazza outside it, held the first free meeting of his life.

Part Three

LXX

ASHEN DAYS FOLLOWED the armistice. The terrible enigma facing the country seemed to have paralysed everyone's will-power. Even at the café Torino, few of the old customers turned up. The only old supporter of fascism there was Mario Brag-hiroli, ex-leader of the local 'Felletti' group. But after a slight heart attack in June, he no longer seemed the man he once had been.

In the 'submarine' they discussed the Allied advances, but flights of fantasy were more frequent than well-reasoned ideas. Someone always had the 'latest' news, mysteriously obtained.

'They're just going to land at Livorno.'

'No, they've attacked La Spezia.'

'Who told you?'

'My cousin, who. . . .'

It was a kind of optimistic grapevine that, for a few hours, deluded those who were waiting impatiently; but soon they were disappointed by hearing nothing about the rumour from Radio London.

'I can't see it's all going smoothly,' someone would say.

And Dionisio, aggressively hopeful, would retort, 'Oh come, the war's virtually over.'

'But don't you see those Nazi pigs getting more and more insolent every day?'

'Well, what d'you expect? Hitler found Mussolini a dead weight militarily speaking, but for the strategic policy of the war he was indispensable. Today, without him, he's done for.'

'But he won't give way.'

'He will! It's a matter of another two or three weeks in Italy.'

High hopes alternated with discouragement and suspicion, and the *'Achtung!'* of the German Command began to be heard around the town.

Every day Giulio went to the Torino before meals to hear the latest news, but he had not set himself up there, like Dionisio. He preferred spending hours in his study, especially since the old house had become so much more attractive since Enzo's marriage and the arrival of Bianca, who was such an excellent, warm-hearted housekeeper. There Giulio would read and make notes on what he read, frightened by his lack of preparation for democratic life, without a thought of starting up his professional work again. He did not even know whether to take up teaching in October. With the country a prey to anarchy, and the war coming up the peninsula, who would want to do a job?

He never forgot to tune in to Radio London on the short wave, waiting for the good news that never came. But on September 16th he had an ugly surprise.

It was Enzo who heard the broadcast.

'This was all we needed!' he cried. 'Mussolini's back.'

'Did you really hear it right?'

'Yes I did—damn it! He's taking on the leadership of fascism again and he's appointed Pavalini party secretary.'

'The lousy. . . .'

'I told you it wouldn't be over so fast. We'll be spending Christmas with the Germans.'

When the freed tyrant broadcast on September 18th through Radio Munich, his voice sounded weary and distant, like a portent of disaster to the many who no longed believed in him.

And now, with fascism restored, what was to be done? No one at the café Torino had yet thought of fighting fascism and its Nazi masters who kept it in power. The way the king's army had melted away so fast had left Italians mistrustful of their own capacity to fight back.

One man who seemed not at all discouraged was Fausto Carrettieri, who had got back to Padusa after the armistice

in an adventurous fashion, and was keeping up his reputation
as a man of action. Far from sitting about in the café Torino,
he spent his time collecting weapons. Mario Salatini, full of
keenness and initiative, in spite of his lost hand, went with
him.

Dionisio teased them about it: 'What use d'you think this
old junk is, when you think what the Allies have got?'

'Oh, they might come in useful.'

'How on earth?'

'If the Americans don't come soon, we can't fight fascism
with café chat.'

LXXI

A month after the armistice Giulio and Dionisio had to admit
that they had been wrong. It was now quite clear that in spite
of their overwhelming military superiority the Allies were in
no hurry to advance up the peninsula. There was no point in
racking one's brain to seek a reason for this exasperating
strategy: it was better to face up to the new situation.

The fascists, meanwhile, had drawn breath. On September
22nd Rodolfo Graziani had spoken on the radio as commander-
in-chief of the new armed forces, appealing to officers and
men to join up again. In spite of the North African defeat in
1940 he still had some prestige and there was no denying that
his unexpected intervention beside Mussolini had had some
effect.

Mussolini had done all he could to get a council of 'Republican' ministers on its feet, and, having quarrelled with
the King, had assumed the office of Head of State. At the
beginning of October the fascist party had been more or less
re-established; in fact on the 5th Pavalini, the party secretary,
clearly anxious to put teeth into the newly restored party
and give its leaders a chance of revenge, threatened that the
new Republic would make a harsh example of all traitors to
fascism and to the country at war.

This counter-attack was felt in the café Torino. People who
half-way through September had hung about there listening
to Dionisio's anti-fascist talk now listened to the propagandist

speeches on Mussolini's radio; and those same respectable people, who immediately after the armistice had declared themselves faithful to the house of Savoy and had cursed Mussolini as the author of all the country's ills, now pitied him for being victimised and called those who had arranged the armistice traitors. In fact, within a few weeks thousands of Padusan citizens had turned from fascism to anti-fascism, and then back again.

While his friends despised this wavering, Dionisio managed to find a certain amount of amusement in it. The *coup* on July 25th had restored his old sense of humour, lost in the long years of opposition.

The fascist party in Padusa was quickly re-established; but the old Federal Secretary took no part in it. Puglioli could smell danger; with Germany on its knees, the whole thing looked to him like a perilous enterprise. So, to avoid getting involved, he bolted to a remote mountain hamlet.

The town's main supporters of fascism had withdrawn or actually disappeared before July 25th. They were wealthy middle-class people, who could also smell danger. So the job of Federal Secretary was taken on by one Umberto Tagliavini, an engineer who had never carried any weight in the fascist organisation of the province. He was not a politician but a war hero, highly decorated during the First World War. With his pointed beard and piercing eyes, his sporty clothes and jerky, athletic walk, he looked exactly like one of Dumas' musketeers. As a young man he had been a fascist. Between 1919 and 1922 fascism had appealed to the patriotism of officers home from the front, and, like so many university students from middle-class families, who took their exams in uniform and were worried at the rise of the 'red tide,' he had identified fascism with Italy.

Later he had remained faithful to the regime, ready to leave home and wife (he was childless) at any moment in answer to the Duce's call; and so he had fought in all the fascist wars, without asking the reason why. In fact he was born to fight, not to build houses or roads. Fighting displayed his qualities of sincerity, decisiveness and outstanding courage, whereas in everyday life his rough countrified manners, his laboured speech, and his feelings of inferiority when faced with his superiors in the party made him perpetually clumsy. Totally loyal, indifferent to recognition and money, and indeed proud of his poverty, Tagliavini was respected by everyone for his moral qualities.

Now, when he saw those who until recently had been important in the party prudently withdrawing, he felt obliged to accept the heavy responsibility of his new post, and once again showed he was born to live dangerously. What the prospects of the war were, and what chance the fascist party had of rising again, were things he neither knew nor wondered about. Political considerations and values were not for him, and, as always, he trusted in his instinct rather than in his reason. Temperamentally he disliked bullying and violence, as many who are noticeably courageous in war often do, and no one had anything against him. For this reason his appointment was greeted with relief in Padusa.

But a dubious, dangerous group immediately began to grow up around him. In it were doubtful characters who had never got ahead in the fascist party and hoped to do so now; unscrupulous youngsters who saw a chance of living it up in a world of total upheaval; individual fanatics, certain of final victory, who seemed determined to continue with methods like Hitler's.

Among Tagliavini's new staff were a very few disinterested men. These were honest in their way, but drunk with nationalism—so much so that they failed to realise the horrors perpetrated by Hitler. To them their country came first, and its honour could be saved only by keeping faith with the alliance with Hitler, and fighting on to the end. Their plan was to build up everything that had been destroyed by the betrayal on September 8th, to win over waverers and approach anti-fascists in the hope that all men of good faith would answer their country's call.

'These people,' Giulio said, 'make me angrier than the others. I'd sooner have adventurers than fools.'

LXXII

In the face of the harsh reality of the fascist restoration, no one could just do nothing. But what was to be done? Scaranari, whose moral authority was higher than anyone's, was opposed to the use of force. They could, of course, have a few whacks at the Germans; but what result would it have, except to provoke reprisals?

Scaranari put forward this view, which Dionisio shared completely, at a meeting held in his office to set up the Socialist party again. Among the many old party members there were only three youngsters—Giulio, Dionisio and Guido Coen. Moro had got as far as the office door, but had suddenly turned and left.

The most authoritative of the old socialists was Gabriele Palumbo, an ex-exile who had been born near Naples but was married and living in Padusa. He was the only one who seemed not to be in awe of Scaranari.

'So there isn't a party,' Scaranari said, after they had examined the situation. 'We've got to start it up again from scratch.'

'You guide us and we'll make it work,' exclaimed Giulio.

'Ah, but I'm too old.'

'What d'you mean?'

'That I'd slow you down. . . . So think of me just as a father ready to advise you if you need advice. Gabriele's the man to be provincial organiser—it's exactly the job for him. He's the right age—not too old like me, nor too young like Dionisio.'

The meeting was over at eight in the evening, and Giulio was on the way home when he met Arlotti. Without attempting to hide his own pleasure he went up to him, took his arm and whispered in his ear: 'We had an important meeting at Scaranari's today, you know. We're starting to organise the socialist party, and Scaranari spoke to me about you and obviously thought highly of you.'

'I believe you. He's always condescended to think well of me.'

'So we'll be working together. . . .'

[236]

The old barber shook his head in a melancholy way, and stared at the ground. Perhaps he was moved to hear the sort of fighting talk he used to hear when he was young, Giulio thought at once. But there was something dejected about his refusal.

'What? Are you going to refuse—you of all people?' Giulio asked.

'But I'm old . . . practically seventy. And since my only son was killed in the war I've been feeling a hundred. I'm on your side, of course . . . how could I fail to be? And you can tell that to Scaranari and the others. But worn-out old socialists like me aren't any use. You're the ones who count. Boys like you. . . .'

Immediately after the armistice Giulio had enthusiastically joined the socialist party. His experience in Sicily in 1942 had convinced him that it was not enough to recover freedom in Italy: social justice must be fought for energetically as well. But he found himself disagreeing with Dionisio on the party's objective and methods.

Dionisio asked Giulio to visit him at home the morning after the meeting. Giulio let him speak for a good half-hour, but hardly seemed persuaded by his arguments.

'You're talking like your boss, Scaranari. You're all for un-limited freedom, even if it allows social injustices. Why, you seem more of a Crocian than Benedetto Croce. But what about Marx?'

'Whatever happens, we can't give up freedom. If the principle of freedom's in jeopardy, everything's justified—even Nazi tyranny.'

'So you refute the dictatorship of the proletariat?'

'It's a fraud! Even the communists will refute it soon.'

Mariuccia appeared at the open door.

'Can't you talk more quietly? Even in my room I can hear you.'

'Sorry. But we were having an important talk.'

'A fat lot of use that is.'

'Why?'

'Because you hang around talking like a bunch of paralytics, whereas this is the time for action. If you stop at home spinning your theories, sooner or later they'll sling you in prison.'

'In the whole of Italy there's not a single group taking action against the Germans,' said Dionisio, 'and *you* talk about action.'

'Things are moving in the mountains. . . . In any case, if I were a man, I'd know what to do.'

And she went out, slamming the door.

LXXIII

In the growing dusk of the afternoon, Giulio was sitting quietly at a table in the municipal library, consulting some old newspapers, when someone slapped him on the back. It was Moro.

After the armistice Moro had stopped selling pictures and had gone in for the more lucrative business of dealing in gold coins. Giulio was in fact meeting him in the library at five: he was to bring him a couple of Victorian sovereigns.

But the clock said four, and Giulio wondered why Moro was so early. Moro, however, signed to him to come along, so Giulio quickly put the files away and went out.

Moro took him to an inn opposite then briefly gave him the news. Between midday and three o'clock the police had been rounding people up and to help themselves in doing so had cut off all local telephones. Scaranari had been arrested first, and with him about thirty anti-fascists, old and new, were now in prison. A few they had been seeking were lucky enough to be out when the search was made, and so had escaped arrest.

'How about Dionisio?' Giulio asked anxiously.

'They weren't after him or you, as far as I can make out. But they nabbed Arturo Bottoni instead—imagine! What the hell can those idiots want with a harmless old bloke like that?'

'The new officials obviously remember his jokes in the café Torino after July 25th. His *faux-naïf* air couldn't save him.'

'That means I too. . . .'

Giulio smiled half-maliciously. 'After all the funny stories you've been telling these last few weeks about the regime's thieving ways and the blue funk the fascists were in. . . .'

'D'you think so? That's just what my sister says, too.'

And he dashed away.

A few minutes later Giulio was at Dionisio's.

'They're filling up the prisons,' he told him. 'Mariuccia was right.'

'If we're not to be caught like rats in a trap, we ought to get out into the country.'

'No, I'm staying at home for the moment. If those swine come and get me I can slip out through the courtyard.'

That same evening Dionisio left home, and went to stay with a friend of the family who had a small farm. Pina would have liked to suggest his going south, through the lines, to get away from the nightmare of the Nazis and fascists. But she dared not, scared that Dionisio would be upset and think she was suggesting desertion.

Pina loved the way Dionisio was fired by civil and social ideals, and did not want him to feel that his family put a brake on his political activities. She was already upset about her baby, who had been born crippled, with some deformity of the lower limbs; and now she saw further suffering ahead of her, in the dangers Dionisio seemed likely to face. But she managed to keep a hold on herself, with the serenity and dignity that ennobled her whole character.

Dionisio seemed pleased with the present solution of his problems. From his hiding place, which was barely five kilometres from the old walls of the town, he could keep in touch with his friends and go into Padusa unnoticed, to see Pina. He was still present, but outside the trap.

When Giulio told Enzo he meant to stay put, his brother was angrier than he had ever been before. Republican fascism he despised, but he saw no point in risking life just to put a very small spanner in the German works. One Allied airraid, he often said, would do more than all the anti-fascists could achieve from Rome to the Alps in six months. Nazi Germany and Mussolini's new regime would be swept away by the Allied armies when the time came—and it would be the Allies who chose the right moment.

As an example to Giulio, Enzo mentioned Cavalieri d'Oro. Until war broke out, he was a roaring propagandist for the G U F; then he served as an officer in the Balkans. Now, he had been careful to support neither Mussolini's new republic nor the anti-fascists, and to keep out of trouble he had gone to Abruzzo to await the Allies. Now there was a prudent chap, who knew just how to manage his own affairs!

And what about Eriberto Melloni? When he was let out of gaol after July 25th, he had pulled in his horns and vanished and no one had heard of him since.

Another wise man, according to Enzo, was Moro. It was only on the surface that he was casual, and the very day after his meeting with Giulio he had left Padusa. Enzo had met him outside Porta Nuova, cycling along in a thick woollen over-coat, and he had confided to him that he was going to shelter in a monastery in Tuscany.

'You don't expect me to put on a monk's habit, I hope!' cried Giulio.

'Keep you hair on! They say the monasteries in Rome are crammed with anti-fascist bigwigs.'

'In Rome they may be. But there it's just the sort of play-acting that suits Moro. I can just see him with a flowing beard, deafening the monks with the Gregorian chant he's always been so hot on.'

'Then why don't you go to Milan, and teach in a private school? Or else to Rome, where they'll soon be seeing the Allies? There, if you really want to, you can start getting into political circles as well.'

His sister-in-law nodded in agreement with everything Enzo said. Had she been able to give her real opinion, Bianca would have gone even further, and said that politics were a dirty, dangerous business that Giulio would do well to avoid. But she lacked the confidence to speak out.

But Giulio had already decided. Mariuccia's violent tirade had made him think things over during the past few days, and he had decided to go straight out to the country, to prove himself worthy of the freedom he yearned for.

Mariuccia was right: his place was there, in the thick of the fight.

[240]

LXXIV

A few days after the anti-fascists had been rounded up, Giulio had an unexpected telephone call. It was Linda's mother, asking him to come and see her that afternoon.

It was four years since they had met. Between the breaking of his engagement and his departure from Padusa he had occasionally met Linda in the street or at the houses of friends they had in common. But they had just chatted conventionally.

It was only recently, after the armistice, that something new had happened. At the local tax office they had met by chance and she had insisted on his sitting down on a bench in a long, ill-lit passage and telling her the tale of his army adventures. After nearly a couple of hours she had said a very friendly goodbye and, holding his hand, had murmured 'I hope it won't be another two years before we meet again.'

Poor Linda: he had felt rather sorry for her in her school-marm clothes (she now taught natural science), and with her half-resigned old maid's air.

As he now approached her home he wondered why he had suddenly been invited there. Unless Linda had engineered it and wanted to renew their relationship, what possible reason could Signora Boari—so level-headed and dignified—have for asking him to the house? He thought of every possible reason, but none of them seemed plausible. When he rang the bell lightly an elderly maid he knew well appeared at once and without speaking took him to the drawing room, where Linda and her mother were expecting him.

Signora Boari avoided embarrassment by going across to him with a friendly smile and holding out both hands.

'Giulio, you'll realise that I've only asked you round because of something pretty important,' she said. 'From your point of view, that is.'

'Thank you for thinking of me, signora.'

'A close friend of mine I've known since we were children is married to a party official, and yesterday she told me you're on the October 13th black list.'

'The list of arrests?'

'Exactly. They had some pretty hard things to say about you, because until the war you'd been a propagandist for fascism, so they now call you a traitor.'

'Fools! As if nothing had happened in the meantime. . . .'

'Oh, they just work it all out logically. But the night the list of arrests was drawn up, luckily for you, a well-known stormtrooper spoke up in your favour—a leader of one of the local groups.'

'Ah, that would be Braghiroli.'

'But you must see that if they start rounding people up again you won't get away next time.'

'That's just what my brother keeps saying.'

'Of course! So you must leave town at once—straight away.'

For a moment her decisive words froze him: then he thought it all over.

'I'll take your advice,' he said.

'Splendid! You're absolutely right.'

To hide his embarrassment Giulio lit a cigarette.

'Signora, would you mind telling me why it was your friend spoke to you about me?'

'Through a lucky mistake. She saw you at the tax office with Linda and thought you must be engaged again.'

Giulio gazed into the two women's loving eyes and said nothing.

'But I don't want to leave the province,' he said after a minute. 'I'll shelter in the country nearby.'

'Well, find somewhere really safe.'

'I hope so. I can't think of anywhere just like that, but when I've had time to think it over. . . .'

Linda broke in impetuously: 'If you've got nowhere to hide, why not go to our place at Fuocovivo? It's not far from Padusa but it's well off the main roads.'

'And stay with your factor? I wouldn't dream of it!'

'There's a couple of spare rooms—my parents would love you to have them.'

'But you might need them yourselves, the ways things are going.'

'Well, take them for a few days, till you find somewhere better.'

Giulio turned to her mother, who smiled at him and agreed.

[242]

'Anyone who shelters an enemy of the fascists these days is compromised, you know,' he said.

'At a time like this we may as well speak plainly, Giulio,' she said. 'My boys are in prison, but you might end up very much worse—so do think it over!'

Agreeing, he realised, meant renewed contact with the Boaris, and, he saw in Linda's eyes, rather more than that. But in spite of it he accepted.

LXXV

The arrests made by the fascist police had shaken the old socialists in Padusa. Although many of them had been tough, brave fighters before the advent of fascism, it was now hard to make them into activists: during the twenty years of dictatorship, when the party had ceased fighting inside Italy, their anti-fascism had in many cases become just a conventional attitude.

But by good luck the dark bespectacled Neapolitan, Gabriele Palumbo, a quick, decisive man although he was over fifty, was full of ideas and never still for a moment: on foot, by bicycle, or by bus he got all over the province, keeping in touch. As a rule all this activity came to nothing, but this did not discourage him at all; in fact, as time passed and things grew harder he became more and more enthusiastic—coughing continuously and convulsively but still calmly smoking and, if advised to take care of himself, merely shrugging.

Giulio and Dionisio were constantly worried at the thought of being recognised, but Gabriele had nothing to fear and could get about quite easily. For no one would recognise a man who had fled from Padusa fifteen years earlier and had come back to his family only after July 25th.

In France he had known Turati well, and the nobility of his thought and his warmth and humanity had made him seem both a teacher and a father to Gabriele. He loved telling Giulio about him, and through his talk, and the veneration he felt for Turati's memory, Giulio came to understand something of a world he had so far known nothing about.

'What a man Turati was!' Gabriele would exclaim. 'No one knew Italian society as he did.'

'What about Treves?' Giulio asked him one day, remembering the name.

'A marvellous brain, but less of an aura of passion about him.'

'And who is there now?' Giulio asked.

'Now, there are the men they taught, men exiled by fascism when they were still young. Just names for the moment—Nenni, Saragat. . . .'

'So you think the socialist tradition will continue?' Giulio asked.

'Of course, it's already continuing. History's stronger than fascism. You'll see, when we've got rid of fascism, Nenni and Saragat'll start socialism up again. They'll be the link across this empty time, and that'll be the real meaning of their exile abroad. Maybe Turati and Treves had some personal qualities we shan't find in them—but times change. They'll bring back the rigorous ideals their masters taught them, anyway.'

Giulio felt encouraged. Gabriele's confident talk filled the emptiness fascism seemed to have made when it exiled all the socialist leaders. His still unformed ideas now had a guide, and this made him feel safer.

'Gabriele'd be the ideal comrade if he weren't so obsessed by sex,' Dionisio said. 'But if you gave him a ticking bomb to hold and a pretty girl went by he'd let it blow up in his hands.'

'Oh come, you don't understand a thing!' Gabriele replied. 'Take women away and what's left in the world?'

'I know that's what Italians tend to think. But foreigners . . .'

'More fools they! Anyway, if you give their women a taste of it, they won't let you alone.'

'But really, you make too much of it. The fact is that making love so often just becomes monotonous. The same old thing. . . .'

'Oh, what a dunce!' Gabriele cried, and his thick lips parted with amused, scornful laughter. 'The same old thing, is it? Why, even Paganini made his . . . variations on the theme he liked best.'

'Variations or no variations, in time relations between the

[244]

sexes will become much less important in people's lives.'

'I hope I'm dead by then!'

'You'll certainly be exhausted, the way you carry on.'

'Make hay while the sun shines, I say!'

'But there are other things in life: sport, travel, good books, communing with nature.'

'Communing? I'd go a bit further than that,' said Gabriele, and roared with laughter again. Dionisio said it all to annoy him, he knew, but he refused to listen to what he called 'heresies.'

'Yes—heresies!' he said, between bouts of coughing, his face congested with indignation and chronic bronchitis.

Dionisio, Giulio and Gabriele, the ruling trio of the party, met almost every day in a tenant farmer's house not far from Padusa, on the road to the set; a stout peasant woman of about thirty-five, who was neither particularly attractive nor particularly polished, lived there. She had an enormous mouth, huge muscular arms, and a tough, masculine-looking frame; she could not speak a word of correct Italian, and shouted in dialect in the most terrible accent Giulio had ever heard.

'Comrade' Rina had two children of about ten. Her husband had been reported missing, believed killed, in North Africa at the time of Graziani's defeat, and she had quickly resigned herself to it, being strong enough to take over his work quite easily. Love presented no difficulties either, and she had already changed lovers more than once: it was now Gabriele's turn.

But even to Giulio Gabriele pretended that his relations with Rina were a matter of pure political friendship. He addressed her with the familiar *tu* because she was a comrade, daughter of the late socialist leader Mario Pontecchiani, nicknamed Lenin, one of the best-known extremist agitators after the First World War, who in Alberone in 1920 had expelled from the union all day-labourers who let their wives go to church. He had named his daughter Scioperina (without having her baptised, of course) but after the coming of fascism and her father's death, Scioperina had turned into Rina.

Gabriele said she was completely trustworthy, the sort of woman the Socialist movement could rely on.

[245]

'If they stuck her in front of a firing squad she'd never betray her friends,' he used to say.

Dionisio knew that until a few weeks before Rina's lover had been a lusty young local landowner, and was curious to know why she had given him up for Gabriele, who was no longer young and for all his talk hardly gave the impression of being a great lover.

One day, when they were alone in the kitchen, he started teasing her: 'That chap Aimone was really something, wasn't he?'

'He was, indeed,' said Rina.

'He was nicknamed *non-stop*, wasn't he?'

'Well, he's limping along now.'

'Why, what d'you mean, Rina?'

'The fool put on a black shirt, and I don't have anything to do with creeps like that.'

'So you took up with the asthmatic Gabriele instead.'

Rina stopped in the doorway.

'Gabriele's got the fire of his ideals!'

And she hurried out into the courtyard, gurgling with laughter.

LXXVI

Backed by German troops, the fascists now tried to consolidate the new regime's authority and organise the administration of the young republic. On October 28th, the twenty-first anniversary of the March on Rome, the newspapers had big headlines about the meeting of the new Council of Ministers, which had decided to set up the Republican armed forces and established special tribunals in every province. These would judge which fascists had betrayed the regime and who had run it down after July 25th or acted violently against individual fascists. Next day the papers reported the speech made by the party secretary, Alessandro Pavalini, who announced that before the end of the year the new state's constituent assembly would be summoned, and finally, on November 3rd, the law on the Republic's armed forces was announced, which clearly meant that Mussolini wanted to make a military contribution to Hitler's war effort.

This was the atmosphere in which the action of the Padusa fascists took place; and with the new regime obstinately determined to restore itself, the federal secretary Tagliavini, with his woolly idealism, was just a figurehead. Determined to live up to the splendours of 1920-21, when the Padusa fascist party had been the strongest in Italy, they wanted to show the Duce that the people were behind him. Old party members were curtly invited to rejoin the resurgent party, and employees of the state and of public corporations were given no choice at all. The feeblest submitted right away—anything for a quiet life. But their weakness incited others to copy them, and many who in private still cursed Mussolini hurriedly applied for membership, for fear of reprisals. All those who, after July 25th, had quietly withdrawn the 'diplomas' they had held as stormtroopers or marchers on Rome now hurried to present them again, just to be on the safe side.

In any case, the Allies now seemed to have stopped just north of Naples, and the Germans were thicker than ever in Padusa, with tanks and guns to protect the fascists. Anyone who wanted a quiet life—and most people did, especially the lower middle classes—wanted no trouble with their current masters, who seemed capable of anything. Later, they could always adapt themselves to something else.

All public places in Padusa—cafés, cinemas and the rest—were now nearly empty, as people kept themselves more and more to themselves. Shopkeepers shut up shop the moment they could, and as soon as their work was over clerks and workmen sheltered inside their own four walls. The new masters were suspicious of any sort of meeting, so crowds were no longer seen in the streets—only busy people dashing past on bicycles. Even people with cars were now reduced to a modest two-wheeler—after years in eclipse, the bicycle had come into its own again.

Industrial goods were growing scarce, and food ever scarcer. Anyone wanting to feed a family had to get out into the country for food, and, without fussing over how he got it, bring home flour, pork, pork-fat, apples and onions.

The nightmare of air-raids weighed over everyone and

when the siren sounded the damp underground shelters were filled in a flash. But a great many people disliked them, and those in the suburbs would leap on to their bicycles when the alarm first sounded and dash out into the open country-side. Fatalists stayed put, hoping the Allied planes would spare Padusa once again.

Many families who could afford it went out into the country. But most people simply kept indoors. Leaving home often meant leaving work, and losing every chance of earning, and those without savings could not possibly take such a step. They waited for the first bombs to fall before making a decision.

On November 2nd, Giulio went to the cemetery to visit his mother's grave. He thought he might be seen by some fascist, but was sure they would not choose such a time and place to make arrests. In fact he did meet a couple of minor officials, but they seemed not to notice him.

A tremendous crowd thronged round the cemetery entrance and exit. There was now an atmosphere the country had never known before: Italy had been profoundly shaken by recent events—the dizzying way in which sudden freedom had been followed by new restrictions; and to this was added the terror of worse things to come, the fearful threat of air-raids, and the shortage of fuel and food.

Everyone was carrying flowers, mostly faded chrysanthe-mums which few would have taken to the graves at any other time. The cemetery paths, which heavy rain during the last few days had turned into swamps, were full of plainly dressed women, young and middle-aged, all wearing thick woollen stockings and the hideous cork platforms called 'orthopaedic' shoes. The men were even shabbier, in worn shoes and suits, made more pitiable than usual by the mud that now stuck to them. Weary and worried in those clothes that abolished all social and financial distinctions, they looked like a crowd of loitering beggars. Giulio watched them all busy among the arches and cloisters of the cemetery, decorating the graves with renovated candles and tin cans lovingly filled with flowers. Children who understood little of it gazed curiously at the small majolica portraits stuck on the grave stones, picked up dropped flowers, nosed around wherever they could and rushed about splashing happily in the dark puddles while their parents kept calling them. Their gaiety failed to stir their elders' sad thoughts, and seemed not the least irreverent—for after all, the dead knew nothing of the sufferings of men.

Giulio found his mother's grave neglected. The flowers Enzo had brought were scattered about the ground, the vase had disappeared and the bronze candlestick had nearly been pulled out of place. For a moment, he was angry: then he thought that his mother would have understood and forgiven it. It was all the fault of the horrible war, in which people all became wolves and jackals.

LXXVII

The most authoritative members of the Communist party seemed to be a café owner called Mario Massarenti and a greengrocer called Lucio Zanellati.

Massarenti carried on his business in the middle of Padusa and was well known there. Giulio was astonished to find that he was one of the communist leaders. He had always thought of him as an unprejudiced merchant, who minded his own business—the sort of person who hardly bothered to read the papers.

Massarenti and Zanellati were both quite modestly educated men, but sensible and well balanced. In the last half of October they began meeting the socialists. Being under orders from the party they could take no steps on their own initiative, and for the moment their behaviour seemed discreet enough. Massarenti was always saying that they must be in full agreement with the others over any action taken, and that they ought to trust and collaborate with all other political parties, without exception.

'You talk about collaborating with everyone,' Gabriele burst out one day, 'but let's be quite clear we're not talking about landowners and industrialists.'

'You're an extremist, you know! We believe in the principle of uniting against the common enemy on as wide a front as possible. The rest can come later when we've got time to quarrel.'

'Why, that's just tactics!'

'No, it's realism!'

Giulio was struck by Massarenti's rational attitude.

November 8th was Gabriele's birthday. He spent the afternoon with Rina and in the evening invited Giulio and Dionisio to Rina's to meet the two communist leaders.

Dionisio seemed uneasy, and as soon as he was sitting at the table with a big coffee-cake and bottles of clear Albana on it, he took a two-day-old *Corriere della Sera* from his pocket and pointed out a piece of news in it.

Persons unknown, the papers reported, had killed two fascist party members in Brescia, after which the party secretary had issued strict orders. A special tribunal had announced that from now on all those who killed fascists must be handed over within twenty-four hours. The *Corriere* called this the party's answer to 'repeated acts of aggression against the Republican fascists, from anti-national elements in the enemy's pay.'

'Hey, Massarenti, what d'you think about this?' Dionisio asked, staring straight at him.

'It's the beginning of the resistance, I think.'

'Of course. But I can't approve of killing off anonymous people just out for a walk. I can understand a bloke firing at the S S, or the fascist police in action. . . .'

'You're right, Dionisio. We don't approve of anarchical terrorism, either.'

'So you won't spring any surprises like that on us here in Padusa?'

'You can take my word for it.'

Giulio, who had followed the conversation uneasily, now turned to Massarenti.

'I'm glad we're guided by the same principles. We'll get along together after the war as well.'

Gabriele gave him a kick under the table.

LXXVIII

A few days later Gabriele held a big meeting of socialist supporters at his wife's house. He saw the communists were on the move and was afraid his own people would be left behind. In leaflets which he handed round and asked everyone at the meeting to distribute as widely as possible, he set out what was to be done in case of emergency and ended with a long harangue on political proselytising and the need to fight the fascist tyranny to the end. For all his faults he undoubtedly had qualities of leadership.

That evening both Giulio and Dionisio decided to sleep in Padusa. The meeting was over by eight, and at that hour it was hardly wise to go out into the country. Giulio told Bianca what to do in case of danger.

'If the bell rings go and open it, and if there are fascists or Germans there call out "Enzo, do come."'

'And what'll you do?'

'Don't worry, I can get across the roofs perfectly well.'

Bianca had invited an old friend of hers to supper that evening—a schoolmistress who was intelligent but uncommonly ugly. This poor woman was distracted. For months she had had no news of her adored only son, Nino, who was in one of the regiments overwhelmed by the Soviet offensive the previous winter, and she was obsessed with the idea that he had died in the frozen hell of Russia. She said—and it was quite credible—that if she lost hope of seeing him again, she would go mad.

It was a sad supper. Enzo was sunk in his own thoughts, in silence. Bianca tried to cheer her friend up, but the main weight of the conversation fell on Giulio, whom the wretched mother kept questioning. She asked him what the Russian peasants were like, and about the anti-fascist fanaticism of the Russians, and the physical effects of the cold Russian winters. Giulio knew few of the answers, but tried to tell her what she hoped to hear.

At nine supper was over, and everyone was beginning to peep at the clock, as they drank their ersatz coffee. A long, hard peal on the doorbell suddenly stopped the talk. Respectable people could hardly be expected at that hour.

Bianca got up and went to the front door.

After a few minutes they heard her calling from the hall: 'Enzo, do come!'

Giulio leaped up and rushed to the back stairs. A fascist

in uniform, two policemen and two German soldiers came into the dining-room. The policeman spoke to Enzo.

'We're looking for Giulio Govoni. Who are you?'

'I'm his brother, Enzo Govoni. Here's my identity card.'

The policeman glanced at it.

'Your brother's here, isn't he?'

'Search away, if you think so. Since the armistice he hasn't been living here, because I got married.'

'Where does he live, then?'

'In Via Palestro.'

'What number?'

'I'm not quite sure. A while ago he got a small flat there, and I still haven't been to see him. In any case he comes here to lunch pretty well every day.'

'Govoni, don't play the fool. You're looking for trouble.'

'Me? Why certainly not! I've got nothing to do with politics.

'You're certainly not telling the truth. D'you mean to say you don't know your own brother's address? D'you think we're idiots?'

'Well, I know it's at the end of the road, going down towards the cemetery.'

The man in the fascist uniform, who had been listening, now lost patience.

'Oh, stop this pointless questioning!' he cried. 'We won't get a thing out of this creep. Let's see if the other one's here.'

The two men searched the flat, pistols in hand, roughly overturned the furniture, kicked open a door that was stiff and went up to the attic, but they found nothing. Giulio had got out through a trap-door and escaped across the roofs.

'You haven't heard the last of this. We'll be seeing you again,' the fascist shouted threateningly to Enzo as he was leaving.

Enzo shrugged. But the schoolmistress, who until then had sat there pointedly ignoring the four intruders, suddenly burst out: 'Get out of here, you slobs! Instead of spending the night looking for boys the war's spared, give me back my son, who's lost in Russia.'

The fascist whirled round, clutching his pistol, but one of the German soldiers pushed him roughly ahead of him, shouting 'Get on, get on! No fights with women.'

Next morning Giulio was dozing in his hiding place at Fuocovivo when he was woken up by two hard knocks at the door. Dionisio was there, to tell him about the previous night's tragedy.

Tagliavini, the Federal Secretary, had been assassinated. At eight in the evening he had been found dead on a country road, at the wheel of his car. The local fascists and the police had immediately pulled a noose round the city, to arrest all elements hostile to the regime: pre-July 25th fascists, who had rejected the Republican fascist party, and anti-fascists of every political shade. During the night the national party secretary had ordered a large number of tanks into Padusa, filled with soldiers who were drunk with sleepiness and wine. Local leaders were in permanent session at the fascist headquarters, organising operations and reprisals.

Before dawn eleven men had been killed. Some were taken from prison, others had been arrested that same night. Their corpses, Dionisio said, were still lying on the pavement in pools of blood, in front of the clock tower, and people walked as far from them as possible, appalled.

'Who was killed?' Giulio asked.

Dionisio told him the names of the dead, and each one came as a shock to Giulio.

'Murderers, criminals!' he yelled, striking out furiously at the furniture with a switch of elder. When their nervous tension had slackened, he and Dionisio sat silently in the protective shadow of the country stove. Outside, autumn rain fell persistently; the swollen, stained plaster on the walls held the dampness, and they felt wet to their bones.

Giulio, his head hung down, munched gloomily at a large apple from the orchard nearby. Dionisio poked at the embers of the dying fire, and with his other hand nervously fiddled with his moustache. Suddenly he got up, stretched untidily and put on his coat. Then, staring into Giulio's eyes, he said hotly 'But they shouldn't have killed Tagliavini, even though he was Federal Secretary!'

LXXIX

The national party secretary replaced Tagliavini that same murderous night, with an outsider, one Mario Golfarini.

Golfarini was one of the desperate men determined to carry on until victory. And he was pitiless. His arrival in Padusa meant the outbreak of civil war. Compromise was now impossible. Life became dangerous not just for the anti-fascists, who were now to be hunted down mercilessly, but for the fascists themselves. In the first weeks many had deluded themselves that they could go back to the easy life they had once led, risking nothing; but now they began to see how things would really go.

Golfarini was known for his sudden rash acts. One of the first surprises he sprang was his decision to make Vashinton Marangoni Vice-Federal Secretary. It was pointed out to him that Vashinton, though admittedly Puglioli's secretary, had been known as a fairly tepid fascist, but Golfarini only shrugged. He knew what he was doing, and the others would understand later.

Exactly a week after Tagliavini's death, Vashinton was summoned to Golfarini's office. He had been called up at the beginning of 1943 and had come home after September 8th, and had since been in touch with his old boss Scaranari and with Dionisio. But he had not joined the underground; in fact he had kept out of politics, in which his interest had waned. In any case, he had never been noticeably courageous and in such harsh times no one could go in for politics without running terrible risks. Vashinton declared he was neither a friend of the regime, nor a traitor to it, and when the Federal Secretary summoned him it seemed to him the oddest thing possible. He went reluctantly; as he had foreseen, he found himself facing a man very different from the fat, smiling Puglioli. Tall, bony, wild-eyed, Golfarini stood behind his desk, arms crossed, motionless.

Vashinton raised his arm in the Roman salute and stopped halfway across the room. Golfarini stared at him for a moment and then, without preamble, went into the attack.

'Why didn't you ask for membership of the P F R?'

'Well—'

'Because you want to keep out of trouble. But with me, no one can be neutral.'

'What do you mean by that, sir?'

'I mean you worked with Puglioli, and if you're not a traitor you must now come and work with us.'

'I was just a technical assistant. I wrote letters and received people. I've got nothing to do with politics.'

'You want to keep out of trouble.'

'No, sir! Tell me to respect the laws of the Republic, but don't ask me to become a party activist.'

'Now, now, don't try and be clever! I know all about you.'

'What d'you know, sir?'

'I know that you worked in Scaranari's office for years and opposed the regime, and I know that your closest chums from those days are now the filthiest anti-fascist swine.'

'But what have I got to do with them?'

'You're to persuade them not to bother the Republic.'

'They'll be killed sooner than give way. In any case, d'you suppose they'd listen to a nonentity like me?'

'You're not a nonentity to me. What I want's an honest, intelligent youngster who wasn't known as an orthodox fascist in the past. You'll be Vice-Federal Secretary of Padusa.'

'Vice-Federal Secretary?'

'Certainly!'

'Me? Are you joking, sir?'

'Golfarini never jokes. And if you refuse, I'll get you, you know.'

'But there are so many better men than me.'

'Stop drivelling, man. All I want is yes or no.'

'But I don't think this is the way—'

'I'll be the judge of that, young man. If you don't like my proposal,' he ended, shouting, 'there's the door.'

Vashinton gazed at Golfarini, whose eyes were flashing. A telephone call from the Duce's secretary was announced, and Vashinton was dismissed.

'I shall expect you tomorrow at midday to settle things,' Golfarini called after him.

Next day Vashinton returned, firmly determined to refuse.

He had even prepared a short speech. But as soon as he was inside the door, Golfarini attacked him again.

'What d'you think of double-crossers?' he asked.

'They're dishonest.'

'Right. Then I trust your loyalty.'

'But—'

'No buts. There's work to be done here. We're going back to fascism as it was at the beginning. For twenty years the industrialists and the landowners have been betraying Mussolini. Now we've had enough: we're on the side of the poor.'

LXXX

A few days later Golfarini summoned the four directors of the province of Padusa to his office in the fascist headquarters, to tell them about the eighteen points of the manifesto approved in Verona by the Party Congress on November 15th.

Vashinton Marangoni sat beside him, feeling that all eyes were upon him. To avoid them he looked up, above the heads of the audience; this made him look inspired, but in fact he was terrified.

The previous day he had heard that, as in fact he had suspected from the start, Tagliavini had not been killed by anti-fascists. The suspect was a wild young man who had been working for him, and whom he had angrily criticised for serious offences, such as claiming falsely that he had been an officer. But now, after such fierce reprisals—it was the first time so many prominent people had been killed—it would have seriously discredited the new regime to admit that the murder had not been the work of anti-fascists. So Golfarini had the man responsible sent secretly away, hoping that the incident would be done with, once and for all.

Vashinton now reflected that the murder committed by this young adventurer had very probably opened a new chapter in Italian history, and had started off a chain of reprisals and revenge that would arouse hatred to the pitch of madness and put everyone's life in danger. Terror seized him.

Golfarini began by talking about the part of the manifesto that called Jews foreigners in the Italian nation. Italy and her allies, he explained, were fighting to the last drop of their blood in a battle that would decide their destiny for centuries. So there was no place for indulgence towards a race that was promoting hatred of the Axis throughout the world. Anyone who allowed personal feelings of friendship to come into it was undermining the orders of the Verona meeting, and he was not going to stand for that.

Having disposed of the Jews with no great enthusiasm from his audience, he went on to talk as eloquently as he could about the social basis of the new Republican state. The Verona meeting, he said, had decided to make for a European community of proletarian nations. Only thus could it stand up to communism with an ideal capable of attracting and holding the workers. From now on, only labour would justify property. The workers would become shareholders in the firms they worked in, and owners of their own houses through mortgages.

Freed of all opportunists, and purified by the hard ordeals it had been through, the regime would march ahead, without further hindrance, to build a more just and more prosperous Italy, based on the strength of labour. Victory could be attained only by supporting the German war effort as strongly as possible, by establishing order and the rule of law within the country again, by setting up the armed forces and by sending them to the front to fight with honour for the common cause.

'So long as our German allies feel that our Republic isn't trusted by the people, and that the Italians have not been fully involved in the war,' Golfarini concluded, 'we shan't re-establish Italy's prestige, and when victory comes it will be the Führer's victory, not ours. This is why I demand that you interpret the orders of the Verona meeting faithfully. Put new trust and new enthusiasm into the people; teach the young, and make them realise the honour of serving this new Italy, whose spirit and whose institutions have all been renewed; approach those who used to oppose fascism, with whom we have broken off all contact, and try to persuade them of the revolutionary truth of these eighteen points; and above all, remember to be pitiless with traitors.'

A storm of applause greeted his last words. Before it had died down a group of very young boys lined up behind Golfarini had struck up *Giovinezza*. In a moment the whole hall joined in. *Giovinezza* was followed by the hymn of the Arditi. The old fascists roared, as they had done in the old days *'Pugnal tra i denti e bombe a mano.'* Everyone thrilled with morbid enthusiasm.

Vashinton looked round, and felt alarmingly alone.

LXXXI

In the climate of terror created by Golfarini, many anti-fascists went into hiding. Others, worried about their own safety, drew in their horns and tried to stop seeing anyone who was still putting up a fight.

To avoid being seen, Giulio and Dionisio had to take further precautions. Their code-names in the resistance, Todeschini and Tiberio, could certainly not hide them from the fascists.

Two days after the big meeting at the fascist headquarters, representatives of the anti-fascist parties met at Rina's. Dionisio and Giulio went with Gabriele, and the communists, as always, were represented by Massarenti and Zanellati, and with them a big, strong, gloomy-looking man with a country accent. He introduced himself as Spartaco, which was his resistance name —no one knew his real one. He had been an underground fighter for years and the regional headquarters thought highly of him. Representatives of the Action Party and the Catholic movement were there as well, among them Giorgio Luminasi, who had been at the university with Giulio.

Spartaco named himself chairman of the meeting—to Gabriele's discomfiture—and began by saying that they must immediately set up two serviceable military groups. Golfarini, he said, was dynamic and pitiless and with such an enemy they must be prepared for any eventuality if they were to avoid extinction.

Everyone accepted his proposal without objections. After the massacre of November 12th and Golfarini's appointment, even Dionisio had been persuaded that a small military group must be set up. Spartaco offered to command the first group, and asked the others to appoint a second leader. Giulio thought the right man would have been Gianni Carrettieri, but he had been arrested by the police on that tragic night in November.

It was embarrassing to find that no one really had any practical experience of underground fighting. It was Gabriele who proposed Giulio, who was startled, feeling he was not up to it. But he did not want to appear afraid, and when he saw everyone was in favour of it, he nodded silently.

Dionisio and Luminasi, the Catholic, were together put in charge of helping the Jews. They were to help them escape to large cities, where they could easily be hidden, in particular Milan, from where they could move on to Switzerland.

LXXXII

One misty dawn at the end of November, Dionisio and Luminasi were in the office of Don Renzo Tedeschi, the young curate of the outlying parish of San Giovanni, who for a couple of days had been hiding five elderly Jews in his house—two men and three women. They had to be taken to Sàvena, and from there other friends would take them to safety in Switzerland. Officially the new government was no harsher towards the Jews, but the way the new regime was speaking, and the presence of the Germans as masters, made it seem likely that the cruellest measures would soon be taken.

Dionisio had never spoken to Don Renzo, although they were the same age, and knew him only by sight. But he was immediately struck by his firm spirit. The presence of the Jews in the presbytery did not seem to worry him at all, for he was sure it was part of his mission to help them and to do so he was ready to face any risk.

The study was cold, for Don Renzo had no fuel. He was wearing a shabby, non-clerical overcoat and was blowing on his hands to warm them. His eyes were red and tired—for two nights he had been sleeping in his clothes in an uncomfortable armchair, so as to let one of the guests have his own bed. He was a close friend of Luminasi's, and the pair of them started talking softly. The priest kept besieging Luminasi with questions, to be sure the Jews were being handed over to an organisation that really worked.

Bored with the discussion, Dionisio looked at the walls of the study. A crucifix hung over the old desk, but there were no pictures of the Madonna or of the saints about. On the yellowing, damp-swollen wallpaper he could see the marks made by pictures that had been taken down. There was no furniture except a low worm-eaten bookcase with about a hundred books in it. The room—severe and unadorned as it was—seemed worthy of respect.

At about eight a large old Fiat came into the courtyard of the presbytery. The driver handed the car over to Luminasi and hurried off on foot towards the middle of Padusa. Don Renzo brought the five Jews quickly downstairs. The oldest of the women seized his hand and tried to kiss it, and one of the men embraced him with tears in his eyes. Then in silence the Jews packed themselves into the back of the big car, and Dionisio sat beside Luminasi, who was driving.

During the journey neither of them managed to speak to the Jews, not even to old Professor Contini, whom they had both respected since their university days. Pity and embarrassment made them tongue-tied.

To avoid the main roads they went a very long way round, using quieter by-roads. It had been raining for some time and mud kept shooting up from holes in the road as they splashed through. Whenever they met people, Luminasi whistled, in order to appear relaxed.

They were on the outskirts of Sàvena and thought they had got through safely when the car was stopped near the old town gate. Two German soldiers asked politely for documents. Behind them, an Italian policeman came up. Nothing was said about the car papers, and the young men's false identity cards passed muster as well. But the five Jews' documents made the Germans suspicious, and they kept consulting the policeman and seeming to argue.

Finally one of the soldiers turned to Dionisio and said, in good Italian, 'These five people must come with us. Things have been crossed out on their identity cards, and the names seem to be Jewish.'

'Oh come, take a look at them,' said Dionisio. 'They're old and exhausted by the journey, and they've got to get back home. If you stop them they'll have to stay for at least a couple of days. . . . And I assure you they're Catholics, sergeant.'

'I'm a corporal, not a sergeant.'

'I'm sorry.'

'Did you think you'd get what you wanted by flattering me?'

'No, it was just a mistake, that's all.'

'Of course, of course,' the soldier said ironically. 'Well, I've got my orders and I've got to carry them out. Then we'll see if they're really Catholics.'

'But can't you see the state they're in, poor souls?'

'Well, stay with them if you like and go along and tell the commandant about it. But my advice to you is, get out!'

Dionisio was astounded, and stared into the corporal's face for a few seconds, trying to understand. It was Luminasi who got him out of it.

'We've got urgent business in Sàvena, unfortunately, corporal, so we'll hand our friends over to you and we're sure you'll do all you can to help them.'

Dionisio was about to speak when Professor Contini, who had got out of the car meantime, nodded at what Luminasi was saying and suddenly squeezed Dionisio's wrist hard, actually digging his nails into the flesh.

'If you want a word together,' the corporal said, 'we shan't disturb you.'

He walked a few steps away with the other soldiers, and Dionisio heard him mutter, in his guttural German, 'Poor old buggers—but they're Jews all right, and orders are orders.'

The four others, who had stayed in the car during the talk, now climbed out slowly, stiff with cold, bringing their small suitcases with them. The oldest lady, who had tried to kiss Don Renzo's hand, kept trembling all the time; her eyes looked stupefied.

As Professor Contini embraced Dionisio, he whispered in his ear 'It would have been madness to stay with us. Get away at once and greet my colleague Scaranari. I'll never see him again.'

As soon as the corporal gave the car the signal to go Luminasi nervously started up the engine and shot away. He was biting on a Tuscan cigar, without noticing it had gone out, and staring ahead, ignoring Dionisio beside him.

'They'll bundle the poor old things off to a concentration camp, you'll see,' he said after ten minutes.

Dionisio looked up.

'But what could we do? End up in prison ourselves?'

'I feel terrible about it, all the same.'

'D'you think I don't?'

Luminasi went on smoking until the end of the journey. Dionisio half shut his eyes and finally dropped off.

In his uneasy sleep he could not get away from the image of the old Jewish woman with her stupefied eyes, trembling with fear and cold. Sometimes she seemed to be imploring him, sometimes cursing him, sometimes pulling his hair to drag him away with her. Then he saw her behind a barbed-wire fence, guarded by fierce Alsatian dogs. Suddenly the barrel of a machine-gun appeared before him. Terrified, he tried to take shelter, to make himself tiny; but it was no use. Pitilessly, the weapon kept following him like a snake, then it fired at him. With a yell he banged his head against the hood of the car, then opened his eyes to find himself in the courtyard of the presbytery.

Don Renzo had already come down and Luminasi rushed up to him, agitatedly.

'Don Renzo, I feel so terrible: I've got to go to confession.'

The three of them went upstairs and drank a glass of wine. Then Dionisio sat down on Don Renzo's bed while Luminasi shut himself up with the priest in his study. After half an hour the door opened again.

'This is a serious matter of conscience, there's no doubt about that,' Don Renzo told Dionisio. 'But I think you were right. For me it would have been quite different: I'm a priest and I've got special duties.'

'That's like saying fear and selfishness are sins for you, and not for the rest of us.'

'Don't pretend you don't understand and don't torment yourself more than you have to. We've got a duty to live: there are other tasks and other risks in store for you.'

LXXXIII

Next evening, December 1st, Dionisio met Giulio and Gabriele at Rina's and, without hiding his own bitterness, told them what had happened to the Jews.

'You had no choice,' said Gabriele. 'These are times of action—remorse is a luxury.'

Dionisio shook his head.

'Have you read this morning's papers?' Giulio asked him.

'Not yet.'

'Look here, then.'

And he held out the *Corriere della Sera*.

Across three columns was the headline: 'All Jews arrested. Their property taken over to help bomb victims.'

Dionisio glowered and read the article intently, frowning. Almost without noticing, he began to read aloud:

'No better use could have been found for the obviously enormous sums that will be taken over. The main burden of responsibility for this war falls upon the tribes of Israel. Having seized power through their command of the world's economy, they plan aggression in order to keep down the proletarian peoples. Through them, a world war broke out, whose purpose is to bleed Europe to death and open the door to absolute power for the chosen race. It is not so much fair retaliation as plain human justice that the riches accumulated through usury and the systematic exploitation of our people by this evil race should go to heal the wounds inflicted by the terrorists of the air.'

Dionisio sat down, dismayed.

'I've never read anything more disgusting,' he said.

'I agree,' said Giulio. 'It's a wretched demagogic appeal to the proletariat, an attempt to turn Italians into receivers of stolen goods. It means cashing in on poverty and suffering in order to increase racial hatred.'

'It's premeditated murder, that's what it is.'

There was a long silence. Then Gabriele spoke slowly: 'From now on it's going to be a manhunt, so we must change our methods of saving these poor people. What we need is someone really high up who'll play a double game.'

[263]

It seemed an excellent idea.

'We could try with that hairbrained Vashinton,' said Dionisio.

'D'you know him well?' asked Gabriele.

'Of course! He used to work with me at Scaranari's. The times we cursed the regime together! Whereas now. . . .'

'Could you approach this turncoat?'

'I couldn't very well myself. We're too friendly, and he'd feel embarrassed with me. It'd be better for Giulio to do it.'

'I could, if you think so,' said Giulio. 'But how?'

'You could tell Moro,' said Dionisio. 'They often meet.'

'Moro?' said Gabriele. 'Is that degenerate bastard a friend of yours—the fellow who dressed up as a monk for fear of the fascists?'

'Yes, but after five days he got fed up and reappeared in Padusa under the protection of a German major.'

By that evening Giulio was talking to Vashinton at Cardallino, on the banks of the river, at Moro's father's house. Moro had co-operated enthusiastically, in fact had gone out of his way to help and had given his guests a meal of the sort that was almost impossible to find in those days. Giulio could not help remarking ironically that the delicious food showed Moro's connections with the black market, whatever the present laws and restrictions had to say about it. Moro burst out laughing, apparently highly complimented; he explained that his friend the major had put him in touch with several German officers, to whom he was selling silver and all kinds of *objets d'art* in exchange for pretty well anything. Nor did he feel this trading was dishonourable. On the contrary, it meant he was helping a great many poor families who could only survive in such a way.

In any case, he never talked to the Germans about politics. They knew he was not a fascist and thought him a harmless businessman. And they too, he insisted, were mostly poor wretches who were sick of the war, longed for a bit of peace and quiet, and above all wanted to avoid trouble and get safely home.

'I can't bear the hate propaganda against the Germans. No people are good or bad, and anyone who says so is a racialist like Hitler, though the other way round.'

'You're quite right,' Giulio said.

[264]

Moro grinned: 'Well, you've got to agree, otherwise you'd be half hated yourself.'

'Because of my mother, you mean?'

'D'you mind?'

'No, I never mind what you say.'

There were a few moments of embarrassed silence, and then Giulio spoke slowly: 'Maybe I understand them better. The German's no more vulgar of soul than anyone else. But his ideas about order, duty and precedence are perfectly absurd. So when he puts on a uniform he'll obey any order . . . even if it's entirely against his conscience.'

A small girl came in carrying a plate piled high with delicious-smelling salami.

Moro sniffed for a moment, settled down in his chair again, and slapped Giulio on the back.

'I've told that idiot Vashinton that he's got to be some use to our cause. I say "our" because my only contact with the Germans is commercial. My heart's with Italy, in fact it's with the cause of universal freedom.'

'Stop making speeches,' Giulio broke in. 'And leave me to talk to Vashinton.'

'I'm sorry to be embarrassing you,' he told Vashinton, 'but finding you in such a position. . . .'

'You know how I wish I could get out of it, in fact get out of everything. But seeing I'm stuck with it I'll try and help soften the blows.'

'Fine. Then see you help us with a humanitarian job— saving the Jews.'

'By persuading the Federal Secretary?'

'No, behind his back.'

'I'm sorry, but I can't double-cross Golfarini.'

'Scared of him?'

'Scared or not, I'm not going to do it.'

'So there's nothing more to be said?'

'No. But I've got a bit of advice for you.'

'Let's hear it, then.'

'Giulio, you know the elder Lazzari in the Militia, that fat asthmatic old boy up to his neck in debts?'

'Who doesn't?'

'Well, a bit of cash right away and a guarantee he'll be in

the clear when it's all over will soon soften him up for you.'

'Who could fix it up with him?'

'Moro better than anyone. But I know nothing about it—
I beseech you.'

Moro smiled, feeling important. Silently they sipped their
genuine coffee: then Vashinton looked up at Giulio.

'Couldn't we have a truce here in the province? If the anti-
fascists lie low, Golfarini'll ignore them.'

'Oh, splendid! So the anti-fascists'd stand by while Golfarini
sent boys into the army, materials and foodstuffs to Germany,
and Jews into Nazi camps.'

'Of course. . . . I see what you mean. Oh, the mess I'm in!'

'You're still in time to come back to us. You used to preach
anti-fascism to us, remember.'

Vashinton rose, a bitter smile creasing his pale face. He
gulped down a final glass of Aquavite, held a limp hand out to
his friend, and left.

His advice turned out to be very valuable: Moro quickly got
in touch with the commander of the Militia, a fellow halfway
between a caryatid and a cartoonist's fat man. With his huge
bulk he waddled rather than walked round the streets of
Padusa, and his plump round figure and comically immobile,
inexpressive face, under the cap with its golden eagle, got
him nicknamed the Easter Egg. Money was something he
adored, and the thought of being out of trouble when accounts
were finally settled was just as attractive to him. He had a certain amount of peasant cunning and found the right man to
arrange safe-conducts—an S S officer who had been wounded in
the war and highly decorated for valour, and was considered
the most terrible man in the German command. But this man
insisted on getting two-thirds of the money for himself.

In this way, Giulio, Luminasi and Don Renzo Tedeschi
managed to save a good many Jews, including Guido Coen, who
had wanted to stay on with his friends in Padusa and contribute
to the resistance, but was dissuaded from doing so. Dionisio
foresaw Guido's difficulties if he stayed, and with his father's
agreement made him accept some gold and ready cash. This
was not something that need humiliate him, he told Guido,
because it was merely a loan he would some day repay.

LXXXIV

Shortly after Christmas came the anniversary of the 'glorious exploits' of Padusa's stormtroopers, and Golfarini, who for a few days had combined the roles of Federal Secretary and provincial leader, was in touch with those under him in the province. He was now sole master of Padusa, and wanted to galvanise it into action.

To show that Germany's power was still unbroken, he spoke of the recent German conquest of the Aegean islands and the firm resistance of Hitler's troops north of Naples; of the ten thousand Italian volunteers who had returned from Germany on December 10th to fight with their German allies; of the naval volunteers organised by Prince Valerio Borghese in the Tenth Fleet; of those who had joined the *Bersaglieri* in the Benito Mussolini battalion; of the call-up a few days before of those born in 1924 and '25; and finally of the birth of the fourth army, the National Republican Guard that was to take over the functions of the police and the fascist Militia.

He warned fascists to remain faithful, vigilant and inexorable, ready to give their all to help consolidate the success of the new state, which from November 25th had borne the great name of the Italian Social Republic.

Towards evening young soldiers, scarcely more than adolescents, came into Padusa. Nobody knew whether they were the newly called-up recruits Golfarini had mentioned or even younger volunteers. They wore a kind of red fez with a black tassel and a uniform no one had ever seen, and their eyes were full of youthful awareness. Gaily and excitedly they marched up and down the streets in the middle of Padusa, arm-in-arm, singing the song of the 'desperadoes' of the Social Republic at the tops of their voices;

> Battaglioni della vita,
> battaglioni della morte,
> vince sempre chi è piú forte,
> chi piú a lungo sa patir. . . .
> Contro guida, contro l'oro
> sarà la sangue a far la storia:

[267]

ti daremo la vittoria,
Duce, o l'ultimo respir!
Emme rossa, uguale sorte!
fiocco nero alla squadrista!
Noi la morte, l'abbiam vista,
con due bombe e in bocca un fior. . . .

Passers-by tried to avoid them by slipping away round the nearest corner: there was something disturbing in those faces, and in that song that had no light in it.

That same evening Spartaco had decided to attack a wing of the local prison in which important political prisoners, including Scaranari, were held, for he was determined to get them out.

Gabriele had tried in vain to dissuade him, telling the pig-headed peasant that it was mad to hope for success. Spartaco refused to listen to reason. He said he knew for certain that there were no Germans in the prison, which was in the charge of men who would run like rabbits at the first sign of danger. Giulio, being commander of the second fighting group, was involved in the whole business, and had been unable to support Gabriele. Zanellati and Massarenti had backed up their party comrade, but not very warmly, and Giulio was sure they had done so only out of loyalty.

So the expedition was agreed upon.

The two small groups converged from separate directions at ten in the evening on the edge of a large grassy space behind the prison. Spartaco had four peasants with him, and Giulio two students and two workmen from the sugar refinery at Zerbini. Spartaco was giving out orders when some German soldiers shouted 'Halt!' from a watch-tower, and a powerful searchlight began to swing round, trying to catch the group.

Giulio approached Spartaco and murmured in his ear: 'They've got us. Let's get out, while there's time.'

Spartaco took no notice and ordered the others to squat down separately, not in a bunch; but the searchlight had caught two of the peasants in his group. In a few seconds they were mown down by machine-gun fire.

Only then did Spartaco order a retreat, creeping along a small ditch that crossed the ground no more than three yards away. The Germans fired a few more shots into the two wretches lying on the ground, and kept on sweeping their beam round: but they must have thought there was no one else, because they stopped.

The group managed to get away without trouble. Obviously the alarm had not been sounded outside the prison.

But on the way back, Spartaco had trouble in getting along, as Giulio realised at once. He suggested the others should get away quickly, while he and Lampo, a young medical student, took the wounded man slowly to Gabriele's wife's house.

Signora Palumbo greeted her unexpected visitors warmly. Spartaco was laid on a bed, and they took off his shirt. A bullet had entered his body on the left, above the heart.

The house had no telephone, and Lampo hurried out to get a doctor. After a few moments of uncertainty Signora Palumbo decided to defy the curfew and go out as well, for she was afraid Lampo would not manage to arrange anything.

Giulio stayed alone with the wounded man. As he was unable to do anything useful he walked up and down the room, head bent, occasionally going over to the bed. After a while Spartaco tugged at his jacket and motioned him to sit down in an armchair beside him. The poor man had tears in his eyes and was panting. Giulio saw in his eyes that he wanted to talk.

'You don't know me,' he said at last, speaking with difficulty. 'You don't even know my name. It's Benito Menegatti. I was born at Massa in 1913, when Mussolini used to come and preach hay-rick firing and revolution. My father was a socialist day-labourer. Now I'm dying, I can feel it. And I'm dying badly, with a bad conscience.'

'Oh come, don't say that.'

'Yes, I killed those two youngsters. Gabriele was right in saying this couldn't be done.'

'No, really—'

'Yes he was! I thought there weren't any Germans there. I've been a fool and it's right I should pay for it.'

Giulio urged him not to worry and not to talk, because he was very weak. The doctor would be there in a few minutes and everything would be all right. Spartaco shut his eyes and stayed still and silent for a few minutes. Giulio wiped his sweating face with a handkerchief.

[269]

The pendulum clock struck eleven, and Spartaco opened his eyes again.

'Listen,' he murmured in a weak voice. 'My wife lives at Ospitale. She's called Geffa, poor soul. Promise you'll go and see her.'

'Of course I will. But you must be quiet now.'

'No, let me go on . . . Geffa works on the land—she's a day-labourer herself and she's got three children to support. When I was in prison she had to look after them entirely, because I quarrelled with the party—they said I was an anarchist . . . now I've made my peace with the party so they'll look after my children. Tell her I died for the working classes, like my father, and for Italy. But don't tell her I killed myself making a lousy mistake!'

Spartaco was silent again, and seemed to be dozing. But after a couple of moments he turned to Giulio again.

'Please give me some water,' he said. 'And if any swine ever whispers that I killed Tagliavini, I tell you Benito never fired treacherously at anyone.'

Giulio's eyes filled with tears, and he remained there staring at Spartaco as, quietly, he died.

LXXXV

Next morning the *Gazzetta de Padusa* splashed the news that two outlaws had been killed during the night trying to approach the prison, and this was a warning to anyone who might dare to defy the Social Republic's institutions. The tone of the article made it clear that the fascists and the German authorities considered the incident closed.

At ten o'clock a meeting was held at Rina's, and attended by the communist leaders. It began very late, since everyone felt weighed down with sadness, and sought relief in talking about Spartaco.

At about midday Massarenti cleared his throat ostentatiously, and after a couple of false starts, managed to get things going by dealing with the subject of the meeting—the situation in the factories. The communist party was calling on young new members to support its old activists, and secretly carrying on propaganda in industrial firms, but the Federal Secretary was taking strong action against it and refused to admit defeat even there.

Golfarini had repeatedly sent for trade union leaders to get them to see that the bureaucratic idea of trade unionism was dead and buried. From now on, he insisted, they must go along with the workers, interpret their wishes and consider themselves at the disposal of the workers. He had even said that they must try and make use of the most intelligent factory workers, even if their past was not exactly fascist.

Massarenti said that the Social Republic's conveniently popular image was puzzling some of the world. In a nation like Italy, where strikes, internal committees and the right to choose trade union representatives had all been forbidden for the past twenty years, Golfarini's demagogic way of interpreting the Verona programme socially might, at first, make some impression on people—even though, outside the factories, he might be quite ready to pack any of the Social Republic's opponents into the army. Not everyone realised that all parts of this ridiculous and reckless policy must necessarily be connected.

Giulio and Gabriele knew little about the atmosphere in the factories. The Socialist party had not yet managed to recruit dynamic young men and was represented in industry by a few elderly workers, who might have moral prestige but had quite lost the attitude of active resistance. This meant that they had little to contribute, and, having said that both they and their party would collaborate unconditionally, they rose. But Massarenti stopped them.

'Mind you,' he said, 'resistance against the Germans and fascists can only succeed in any concrete sort of way if it has the complete support of the working class.'

'But we agree with you!' Gabriele retorted impatiently.

'That's not enough: all the popular parties must carry on propaganda in the factories. You socialists must get moving.'

'Mind your own business,' Gabriele burst out. 'That's really too much to expect me to stomach.'

LXXXVI

Saint Stephen's day fell on a Sunday, which made it a feast-day twice over, and around one o'clock Giulio was idly sunning himself by a well in the courtyard at Fuocovivo. He had nothing planned for the day.

The factor brought him a cup of ersatz coffee laced with brandy from the house, but before he had time to drink it he looked up to see a large formation of Allied planes.

'It'll be Padusa's turn one of these days,' he grumbled. 'We're no more valuable than the rest.'

'I'm afraid it may be our turn this time, sir. I don't know much about it, but those planes are flying low.'

'So what?'

'It might mean they're going to drop their bombs.'

The planes were passing overhead in the direction of Padusa and they looked at them, silent and apprehensive. The last plane was still above them when the first started dropping their bombs on the southern side of the city. They distinctly saw the bombs emerging from the planes' fat bellies.

'There you are!' yelled the factor, and flung himself into a ditch.

Left alone, Giulio nervously lit a cigarette and kept looking at the planes, thinking anxiously that at that hour his brother would be having a meal. But then he remembered that his house was at the far north end of town, outside the target area, and gave a sigh of relief.

Next morning, about eight o'clock, he was awakened by Gabriele knocking energetically at his door; he got up quickly and let him in.

'What's the hurry, Gabriele?'

'Heard about the bombing?'

'Yes and no. The factor went into town after the raid and told me a bit about it. I know my brother was all right.'

'Have you heard about the prison?'

'I know they bombed it. But what happened?'

Gabriele told him that a large number, including many political prisoners, had escaped during the raid. Among the

[272]

first to get away was Fausto Carrettieri, who was now safe. He had begged Scaranari, who had shared a cell with him, to escape as well, but Scaranari refused, saying he was too old and physically feeble. Now they must get going, because some of those who had fled might need to be found safe hiding places.

Gabriele opened the *Gazzetta di Padusa*. It contained a list of buildings damaged and a preliminary list of the dead, which was apparently incomplete. Giulio knew a number of them, although none was a friend.

After a description of mothers in anguish at the sight of their dead children and husbands, and families in despair at the sight of their ruined homes, the paper went on to say that the patriotic war against the barbarous killers of civilians was now more justified than ever, and it was a sacred duty to hate the enemy. All right-thinking Italians must gather around the flag of the Social Republic, and fight beside their German allies until victory.

'This filthy rag is worse than the bombs: and its bombs hit their target, you know. Especially among simple-minded people.'

'Mussolini's the man to thank for any bombing we get.'

'Yes, but that's not everyone's view, Gabriele. D'you know what the factor was saying, and he's no fascist? He was cursing the Allies for killing civilians.'

'As if we hadn't bombed England! Mussolini himself asked for the honour of taking part in the raids with our aircraft.'

'Go and persuade the factor that bombing London justified bombing Padusa. And convince the others, if you can.'

'You're right. Today's raid may help the fascists. If only a bomb would land on the Federal Secretary and wipe out all his filthy propaganda. . . .'

LXXXVII

It was eight in the evening and after a full day Giulio was tired, and having a smoke by candlelight after a supper of bread and apples. He had on his knees an old book on agricultural problems in the province of Padusa, but could not concentrate. As always, the cigarette smoke was making him feel sleepy.

Suddenly he heard a violent knocking at the door, and his heart jumped, because neither the factor nor his wife would have knocked so hard. Who on earth could it be at this time of day? Fascists? Or Gabriele back again?

After a moment's hesitation he opened the door, holding his revolver, and saw a plump woman, all bundled up, with a suitcase on the handlebars of her bicycle. For a moment he failed to recognise her, but as soon as she came into the room he recognised Linda's features in the half-light. He took the bicycle from her, propped it against the wall, and stood staring at her, astounded.

Linda took the scarf off her head, unbuttoned her heavy woollen cardigan, and cried gaily 'Hello, Giulio! You haven't even greeted me.'

'I was too surprised. Sit down!'

They sat down at the table, their faces lit faintly by the candlelight.

'Tell me why you're here,' Giulio said anxiously. 'Is it anything serious? You don't seem worried, though.'

'No, we're all safe and sound. But our house was hit in yesterday's raid, and it's uninhabitable.'

'I'm terribly sorry.'

'Just after midday today my parents left for Milan. They're old and creaky and can't take refuge in the country, but I refused to go with them.'

'Why not?'

'Because . . . because . . . that's the way it was.'

Those 'becauses' sounded nervous, and her tone showed clearly that she was uneasy.

'I can go to my uncle's villa at Montesanto, where it would be just like being at home: and this is my house as well, isn't it?'

'Of course!'

'And I'm my own mistress, and can do as I please.'

Both were silent for a while.

'So what did you want to tell me, Linda?'

'I can imagine what you're doing. I'd love to work with you.'

[274]

'Would you? But are you going to Montesanto, or staying here at Fuocovivo?'

'What d'you think?'

'Me? I can easily let you have the rooms, at least. . . .'

Both were silent with embarrassment again.

'Linda, in times like these, when everything's upside down,' Giulio said, 'we might live together. Would you like to?'

Linda looked down.

'Would you despise me?'

'Why should I?'

Linda rose, picked up her suitcase and went into the next room. After ten minutes she suddenly reappeared in the door.

'But you mustn't think I did it on purpose. I'll stay with you, but you've no obligation to marry me. You'll be perfectly free. . . .'

Her voice trembled, and she shut the door again.

Giulio thought about his own weakness, and the way he had let desire, born out of loneliness, prevail over reason. Linda might say she would never consider marriage; but if he kept her here now, he was tying himself to her for life. Was this an unforgivable mistake, after their old engagement had foundered?

Giulio argued to himself that it was pointless worrying about the future when everyone's life was in danger and the whole world had been overturned; but he knew this was false reasoning. He picked up a book and tried to read, but none of it stayed in his head. The words seemed to hover in a kind of mist, through which glimmered the image of Linda.

For ten minutes he made an effort to continue; then he shut the book, and knocked at the door of the next room.

A few days later he took Linda secretly to the parish church at Fuocovivo; and they were married.

LXXXVIII

It was a misty morning, halfway through January, and Rina's house, where the anti-fascists were meeting, seemed submerged in the mist.

The previous day the radio had played the Fascist hymn

before announcing the execution of Galeazzo Ciano and other members of the Grand Council; the newspapers had banner headlines about the death sentence pronounced on those who had voted against Mussolini on the dramatic night of July 25th.

The shock had been tremendous, both in Padusa itself and throughout the province; even the majority of those who had joined the new fascist party were bewildered, and quite unable to understand the swaggering delight of the Federal Secretary's few fanatical supporters.

A professor of literature, who had been a sincere fascist until July 25th, confided to Giulio: 'The Duce who kills is the Duce who dies.'

'What d'you mean?'

'I mean that if he's allowed his own son-in-law to be murdered, it means he no longer counts for anything.'

'You think too well of him—d'you really suppose he didn't want this appalling revenge?'

'Then he must be really mad, tearing his own family apart with a crime as horrible as anything in Greek tragedy. However will Ciano's children call him grandfather?'

'Ah, now you're reasoning like a normal man. But he's a superman, and that makes him delude himself that he'll go down in history as a just man.'

'If that's so, it's even more depressing.'

At Rina's, Giulio found the others drinking ersatz coffee round the stove. Fausto Carrettieri was among them—it was the first time Giulio had met him after his lucky escape from the burning prison. He had been advised to move to Sàvena, as things would be too hot for him in his home province, where too many people knew him; he refused to consider it and had flung himself into the fight with even greater enthusiasm than before. He was now trying to organise groups of young men who could make daring raids on the main towns.

The group was so busy talking that no one noticed Giulio, when he came in. They were discussing what had just happened and were more or less agreed about it: Gabriele summed up their views clearly. Whether or not Mussolini had encouraged his followers to the end, the trial had obviously shown what the desperate fanatics of the Social Republic had decided: for the Germans had not intervened—they were quite uninterested in the internal feuds of the fascists. So if Pavolini, Farinacci, Buffarini and company had not hesitated to kill Mussolini's son-in-law and successor, and with him the eighty-year-old quadrumvir of the March on Rome, there was no longer the smallest doubt that they intended to use crime, terror and any means necessary to stifle opposition and resistance and impose the authority of their evil Republic.

Significantly, the public prosecutor of Verona had ended his speech with the melodramatic words 'Thus have I flung your heads to the history of Italy, and perhaps my own as well, in order that Italy may live.' And this was the mood in which Golfarini was now coming back to Padusa; he had been one of those involved in the trial, and he was ready to carry on in the same way to the bitter end.

The meeting was late starting, because they had to wait for Zanellati and Massarenti, who arrived out of breath, saying that anyone cycling along the main road was being shot at, at the crossroads.

'Well,' said Gabriele, bitterly sarcastic, 'if the nobs took pot-shots at Ciano and De Bono, what's to stop their underlings taking pot-shots at bikes?'

Massarenti said it was now absolutely necessary to set up a united military organisation in the province, and the man best qualified to take command was Fausto Carrettieri, who had shown remarkable qualities as a soldier during the war, and in the last few months had been dynamically anti-fascist.

Everyone agreed; from that moment Fausto Carrettieri officially ceased to exist. To everyone he became 'Commander Giannone.'

At the end of the meeting, Giulio took him aside.

'Well, did you join the communist party while you were in gaol?'

'Why, Giulio?'

'I noticed Zanellati and Massarenti never stopped singing your praises.'

'That's their business. I don't give a damn for parties.' All he wanted, Fausto explained, was to do his duty as a free citizen in the fight against the Nazis and fascists. He realised that anyone who was going to carry on in politics after the war ought to join the democratic parties, but this hardly applied to him. He had reached the age of thirty without ever earning a penny, except in the army, and he must finally either get his degree or find himself a job.

'Hell! Gabriele was dying to get you into the Socialist party.'

'Nothing doing! But if I was forced to choose a party, I think I'd join the communists.'

'But why? D'you know anything about their ideas?'

'Not really, I must admit.'

'You like the men in it, is that it?'

'Those I've met are all quite lowly people, but they've got faith, and a spirit of sacrifice. They may be rough, but they can pass on their feelings to those who join them. It's an interesting party.'

Gabriele, who had followed the conversation from a couple of yards' distance, now burst out: 'But that's no political argument! You've got to choose a party consciously, on the basis of its programme.'

'You're quite right. But that just proves I'm useless when it comes to politics and parties. Didn't I say so?'

LXXXIX

During February, under Fausto's leadership, underground activity in the province of Padusa at last got going. Mario Salatini worked with Fausto, and in spite of his artificial hand he rode an old motorcycle remarkably well.

Salatini was easily excited and easily depressed. At twenty he had been the keenest of his contemporaries to sing the Duce's praises, and now he was keener than anyone in his anti-fascist enthusiasm. Fausto, delighted to have someone so enthusiastic and so ready to become involved, gave him jobs that needed a trustworthy man. The only thing that needed to be checked was his enthusiasm, which was likely to make him rash.

Salatini was responsible for setting up a radio transmitter, which was kept on the move to avoid the Germans, and managed to pass on valuable information to the Allies. Most of this was provided by Mariuccia Cavallari, who was the life and soul of the underground information service. She had volunteered for the most dangerous role—that of double agent. With the resistance leaders' agreement, she had pretended to break off all contact with her brother, and had applied to join the Republican fascist party. She professed to despise anyone who disputed the Social Republic's authority, and was often seen in the centre of Padusa with that grotesque character the Vice-Federal Secretary—the terrified Vashinton Marangoni. A safe-conduct to travel freely by car and see to her farm meant that she could go from Padusa to Guarda nearly every day, and thus keep the various underground groups in touch with one another. Nothing escaped her, and she could hand on news and plans exactly when they were needed. Very soon Gabriele and Massarenti came to admire her without reservations. Russo, who, urged to do so by Mariuccia, had stayed on after September 8th, collaborated with her. The Prefecture was the best place for an observation post and the resistance men found his help extremely important. Through his mistress Russo could tell them even the government's most secret orders at once, and often give them the very plans of the provincial chief.

But he needed daily injections of courage. He seemed obsessed by the fear that he would suddenly be discovered and shot, and he kept pathetically remembering his two daughters in Naples and the need to see to their future. Mariuccia would listen in silence: she knew only too well that what he cared most about just then was his own wretched skin.

Halfway through February, Golfarini had a Socialist party member arrested on suspicion of working with the underground movement. He had never confided in Russo or compromised him in any way, but they were excellent friends, and this was enough to make him tell Mariuccia that he had decided to leave his job. Next evening, when she rang up as usual, on the dot, there was no reply from his flat; next morning Russo failed to turn up at the Prefecture, where he was to be chairman of an important meeting; nobody saw him again.

Golfarini had plenty of other things to think about and

made nothing of it: there was the business of southern workers fleeing south on the agenda, for one thing.

Mariuccia was not particularly upset. She had never been deeply in love with Russo, and lately had begun to despise him—not so much for his cowardice as for his subtle hypocrisy. Left on her own, she flung herself more passionately than ever into the anti-fascist struggle. She got on very well with her cousin Fausto and saw him once or twice a week at the farm, and kept urging him into action, in marked contrast to Dionisio, who damped down Gianni's enthusiasm all he could. It had turned out, in fact, that she and Dionisio had opposing views on the struggle, and the more excited she became at the thought of a pitiless war against the Nazis and fascists, the more Dionisio grew worried. To her, fighting was the most thrilling thing about it. To Dionisio, what mattered was other people and in everything he was determined to spare human life—that of his companions in the fight, and that of his enemies.

Now the time had come, if not actually to listen to Mariuccia's advice, at least to make a timely show of the underground movement's strength by striking at the German and fascist army and police where they were most vulnerable.

In a few days, at the end of February and the beginning of March, Fausto made two successful attacks, using information Mariuccia had given him: without firing a single shot, the partisans set fire to an important military garage and derailed a goods train.

'Is it true you gave orders not to fire except when it was absolutely necessary?' Mariuccia asked Fausto when they met.

'Exactly. As far as it's possible, we're following Dionisio's advice.'

'There'll come a day when you'll stop and bow to your enemies, and they'll sneak out their guns and kill you.'

'Why don't you try and convert Dionisio?'

'Dionisio's a born fighter; but he was born to fight with words, not with guns.'

XC

Fausto's attacks maddened Golfarini. He promised to rip up the entire province in order to uproot the anti-fascist organisation, wanting to show the Duce that wherever he was, the Social Republic's authority was respected. His name and his prestige were involved.

Golfarini's outbursts were by now worrying even the fascists at headquarters. The slightest opposition had him raging, and if he just had a feeling that he was not being strictly obeyed, he would violently attack his officials, high and low. When he was furious he never hesitated to accuse anyone of treachery, and even his close friends went to any lengths to avoid being denounced by him, especially after he had a highly-decorated, trusted official beaten up and imprisoned simply because he had not taken severe steps against café grumblers.

Padusa learnt that during the two big raids at the beginning of March, instead of going to the shelter, Golfarini had rushed up on to the tallest tower in the town hall, and there, taking no notice of the bombs and the anti-aircraft fire crackling around him, he had watched the apocalyptic sight of buildings crashing round him with wild excitement; when the raid was over he had stayed on for a long time, watching the circle of fires that lit up the sky, as if enchanted and fascinated by the destruction.

Minor fascist officials muttered to each other, when they were sure no one else was there, 'He's always been a bit weird, but now he's raving mad!'

One of the first victims of his anger was Vashinton; but the results were luckily not violent.

One morning Golfarini sent for Vashinton at seven o'clock: the unusual hour alone showed that something was coming. There, in the office, he attacked him violently, accusing him of being a traitor who was sabotaging the efforts of the fascist federation by combining with the underground. Finally he flung at him two anonymous letters denouncing him as a double agent. Vashinton luckily found the courage he too often lacked, and defended himself vigorously, realising that otherwise he might lose his life.

[281]

At last Golfarini calmed down. 'You are dismissed from your job as Vice-Federal Secretary from this moment,' he said. 'Go home and wait for orders.'

Next morning Vashinton set off for the mountains.

Golfarini was now hand-in-glove with the head of the political police, Luigi Carpanese, an adventurer who had swooped like a vulture from Milan on to Padusa, his home town, the day after Tagliavini was killed.

Golfarini was a fanatical madman, capable of any crime, but at least he was serving an ideal, even if it was a false and inhuman one; but Carpanese had neither convictions nor ideals. He felt at his best where there was blood and civil war, for he could then give full vent to his instinct for violence. He liked money too, but much less. To his perverted mind slaughter was much more attractive than plunder.

In March Carpanese filled Padusa's prisons and put his famous methods into practice. His secret was torture. The anti-fascists he had arrested were beaten to a pulp, left for days without food, interrogated at night under dazzling lamps, squirted with jets of freezing water. Inevitably, some collapsed and confessed the little they knew.

Halfway through March ten people were quickly tried and shot in the middle of the night by Carpanese's firing squad outside the cemetery wall. The corpses were left there all day. Luckily none of the main resistance leaders was among them, but one of them was a son of Gabriele Palumbo, a brave youngster who had taken part in acts of sabotage.

Gabriele wept in silence, and when anyone tried to console him, he said that he had known from the start that family tragedies were inevitable: this time it had been his turn.

XCI

When Golfarini launched his spring offensive, Giulio had to leave the house at Fuocovivo with Linda and went to hide in Sàvena.

Two days after he left, Carpanese's men turned up to arrest him. In the two rooms he had been living in they found the factor's grandchildren, who had fled from Padusa.

Linda was not well, but she tried to hide it. Since she had been with Giulio she had faced discomfort with surprising energy, but during the last few days she had had long periods of acute melancholy.

One morning Giulio found her looking very pale, her head leaning against the half-open window of the small room they were now living in.

'What's the matter?' he said, taking her face between his hands. 'You look as if you were waiting. . . .'

'Oh, nothing,' she said. 'It's just that horrible pork fat that's upset my stomach a bit.'

Three days later the printer who lived on the floor below stopped Giulio on the staircase as if he had just happened to meet him.

'Tell me, sir, don't you want children either?'

'Whatever do you mean?'

'My wife's a midwife—she's got her brass plate on the door, Vecchi's the name, and she's been to see Signora Linda. But I don't know if she's been able to persuade her not to have an abortion.'

'What?'

'Yes, it's just so: but I wanted to know what you thought about it. You know men understand each other better. I've got no children, but I think the birth of a child is a good thing in times like these—it's an act of faith in life.'

'Yes,' replied Giulio. 'Indeed it is.'

He rushed upstairs, four steps at a time, dashed into the room and found Linda doing the washing at the small sink.

'Have you gone mad?' he said decisively.

She looked at him thoughtfully, without saying a word; she was pale, her face worn.

Giulio was touched, and began to talk lovingly, trying to persuade her. But Linda seemed unshakable. Her teeth were chattering as she said 'How could I stay with you, in all this danger, if I was carrying a child? Our lives—all our lives, but yours especially—are hanging on a thread just now. The fascists may kill you tomorrow, and I'd be left here alone, waiting for a child who'd never have a father. The thought of it makes me shudder, Giulio.'

'But why d'you talk like that? This pessimism's absurd.

[283]

In any case, even supposing a man's got to die, is that any reason for cutting off another life?'

'You think I'm being wicked and selfish; but I can't go go through with it, I just can't.'

Linda started walking nervously up and down the room, biting her lips and staring at the floor; she looked ten years older. They argued for hours, Linda sometimes crying softly, sometimes bursting out hysterically. It was only late at night that Giulio managed to make her drop the idea of having an abortion, and persuaded her to go to her parents in Milan, who would advise her and help her to restore her nerves, shattered by the terrible life she had been leading.

Next day they were in Milan.

XCII

Giulio's nerves were ragged after months of tension, and he felt he needed to rest, and to unwind. But now, instead, he had had this shock over Linda. In order to recover, he suddenly told her that he had to leave in a hurry; but he hid for a few days with his Uncle Fritz, his mother's elderly brother who lived in a fine house on the opposite side of Milan.

For several days he relaxed by walking for miles round the wide suburban streets. Nobody knew him: he was a stranger, like so many others. He might be a fascist or an anti-fascist, a teacher of law, a criminal. Who cared? Everyone was going about his own business. It seemed a paradox, but at last, in a crowd, he felt alone. He used no precautions except a pair of dark glasses, in case he happened to meet fascists from Padusa.

During his short stay in Milan Giulio avoided any contact with the underground. Meeting men who shared his own anxieties would have plunged him into the whirlpool he wanted to escape for a while.

He saw Uncle Fritz only at meals. Taciturn by temperament, as old bachelors tend to be, his uncle would talk briefly about the bad food and the few people they knew in common. Then he would doze in an armchair.

The day before he left, Giulio was unexpectedly joined by

Enzo, who said he had come to buy materials now unobtainable in Padusa. But it was not hard to guess that Uncle Fritz had sent for him, so that he could induce Giulio not to go home.

After the second raid on Padua Enzo had gone to Villanova, a small village nearby, with his wife. Now and then he went into the shop, to avoid trouble with the authorities of the social Republic, but in practice he was hardly working at all: his employees had fled and he was left with just one lad.

'You'll soon have a child,' he told Giulio sadly. 'Don't come back to the abyss—which is what Padusa is now.'

'And if I stay here, what d'you think I should do?'

'You could teach, under a false name. You could earn quite a lot.'

'That would look fine, wouldn't it?'

'But you've done a great deal for the resistance already—more than your duty.'

'We'd be like comic-opera soldiers if we bolted off the minute we thought we'd done enough. The best men stay where they're wanted and it's my job to be there with them.'

'You've all gone mad and think you're indispensable. But you don't realise the Allies are advancing at their own slow pace, following their own plan, and your killing off a federal secretary or blowing up a train doesn't make a scrap of difference to them.'

'You've told me this sort of thing so often, Enzo. So let me say again that we're making an important contribution.'

'Important my eye! The allies encourage you to sacrifice yourselves just for propaganda purposes.'

'But we're building up democracy with what we're doing.'

'You're not building up democracy in the least. The defeat of the Axis is doing that.'

'No, Enzo, we'll never agree about these things.'

XCIII

Halfway through April, on the day that Salatini killed the head of the political police, Giulio went back to the province of Padusa.

The hated Carpanese lived on the outskirts of the town in

a house that had belonged to some Jews, near the silent Porta del Mare, and a hundred yards from the white haze of the suburban apple orchards.

That morning he was to set off from the Prefecture court-yard at six sharp, with ten of his men in an armoured car. A harsh repressive action in a small town of the *bassa* was planned. But Fausto, who had been told about this in good time by Mariuccia, had decided to put an end to the torturer, and had sent his faithful lieutenant to do so.

In the first light of dawn Salatini, with a sten gun hidden under his raincoat, stopped his motorbike outside a dairy, about twenty yards from Carpanese's front door. The street was still empty, and only a very few people slipped by, without looking at him.

Carpanese had got home late the night before, having stayed on at the police station interrogating prisoners and then drink-ing a couple of bottles of brandy with his assistants. Perhaps this was why he had slept badly. He left the house reluctantly, his eyes still gummed with sleep, and in the doorway, as if the light bothered him, he rubbed them before plodding over towards the dairy. Before he had gone five or six steps there was a flash from the sten gun, and he was finished.

Perfectly calmly, Salatini stowed the gun away under his raincoat, glanced at Carpanese's face, already streaked with blood, got on his motorbike and, without hurrying, drove off. The few people who had heard shots in the distance quickly vanished. All the shutters stayed closed, even those in Carpanese's own house.

No one recognised the motorcyclist. Golfarini never got any witnesses to identify the killer.

Two days later a meeting was held in a landowner's house on the river at Alberone, to discuss the possibility of the ecclesiastical authorities intervening on behalf of some harm-less, elderly anti-fascists whom Golfarini wanted to shoot as a reprisal; so they had asked Don Renzo Tedeschi to come along. The other subject for discussion was the underground press, which Dionisio was running intelligently and bravely, writing the liberation committee's small newspaper from start to finish, and organising its printing and distribution entirely himself. The fact that he felt comfortable when dealing with

[286]

print and paper added to his enthusiasm, and although he was quick to call the mildest acts of the partisans foolhardy, he was quite capable of stopping the first German soldiers he met on a country road, and chatting calmly with them while carrying clandestine newspapers in his rucksack. If they gave him the smallest hint of sympathy he plunged straight in and told them plainly that the war was lost and that they should throw in their lot with the oppressed Italians. The first copies of his newspaper were so successful that the resistance leaders were thinking of developing it further.

The meeting was long and excited, as if everyone was in some curious way nervous. When it was over Giulio was exhausted and went up to the modest first-floor study with Don Renzo. Carpanese's death would hardly have worried him if the news had not come at the same time as the newspaper reports of Gentile's murder. Giulio had been as indignant as anyone over this ex-minister's unexpected support for Mussolini's republic, but Gentile was an academic who had never persecuted a soul and had even spoken out frankly against anti-semitism. Above all, his name was illustrious in the field of thought: with Benedetto Croce, he was the only Italian who deserved to be called a philosopher. To the young, who had absorbed his idealistic philosophy and who had been encouraged by his work to go deeply into matters of the spirit, the shot fired at him was a terrible blow to culture itself. Of course, it was a lot better for the old philosopher to die as he did than to end up facing trial after the liberation; but it was still a crime. And Giulio refused to believe that the anti-fascists in a city with a culture like that of Florence could have supported it.

Dionisio, who had been even more shocked than Giulio, had remarked 'Even the finest revolution has its dark pages, and this may be the darkest stain on this new Risorgimento of ours.'

Now, when he thought of the killing of Gentile, Giulio was so shaken that he almost began to doubt some of the values he had for some time thought were quite indisputable, and even Carpanese's killing suddenly seemed to him a matter of conscience, something that deserved consideration. It was a relief to talk to Don Renzo about it.

The priest made a sharp distinction between the two cases. Gentile's killing was a crime, though it might have had a political motive, whereas the death of a torturer like Carpanese set people free—and not only the resistance men. Even the fascists in Padusa would have run ever-increasing risks if Carpanese's regime of terror had been set up.

'But are you sure we have the right to kill coldly, not in battle?' Giulio asked the priest.

'If the man who actually held the gun was interpreting a collective decision, I'd say he was right in the eyes of God.'

'As if he'd carried out a death sentence?'

'Exactly. But even in this terrible struggle we must act responsibly. To Christ human life is sacred.'

XCIV

Golfarini was determined to take his revenge for Carpanese's death, and only five days after it Fausto ran into his men at Casteldoro, and was taken as a hostage. Salatini, who was with him, managed to escape capture by presenting one of the German documents that made the fascists unwilling to inquire any further; but Fausto was imprisoned.

The fascist headquarters at Casteldoro had been turned into a tough political prison, controlled by a sadistic local tyrant, Gilberto Terruzzi, a man who was physically handicapped and burning with hatred for those who had despised him during the forty-five days of Badoglio's regime. There was something medieval in the bullying and cruelty of this small-town despot. As he walked through the streets he liked to read an unexpressed question in people's frightened faces: 'Who will he strike today?'

For some time Terruzzi had been Golfarini's right-hand-man in the district when it was a matter of repressive action, and his masterpiece was this gloomy prison, from which no one came out alive. Here Fausto, whose work in the resistance was well known, was imprisoned with special rigour and closely guarded. During the first days there he was interrogated very harshly about the organisation of the underground movement. Terruzzi spared him no torture, but in the end the warders, less cruel than their master, took pity on his wounds and left him alone.

So, from the small cell where he had been at first, he was transferred to a large cell with its windows almost completely walled up. Here he waited, with about fifteen others, among them, to his astonishment, the ex-fascist official, Mario Braghiroli. This man, who had once declaimed the Duce's speeches, had been accused of betraying the cause by helping the resistance; whereas all he had done in fact was to speak out boldly against some of the bloodthirsty behaviour of Golfarini's followers.

The previous year he had had a mild heart attack, which had somewhat clouded his mind, and had defended himself to Golfarini so clumsily that the false accusation had seemed quite credible; and now he was there, staring about him, wondering from morning to night what he could possibly be accused of, when he had been one of the leading stormtroopers in the Paduan lowlands.

Apart from Braghiroli, there were three other prisoners who looked middle-class: an assistant chief of police who had been in charge under Badoglio, thus making himself an enemy of the fascists, an old Venetian businessman, and a town clerk. The rest were farm labourers, who said they had nothing to do with politics and at most had grumbled at the German bullying and the food shortage. Fausto could not see why the poor fellows had been locked up there, in what looked like the ante-room of death. But perhaps it was just for a personal whim of Terruzzi's.

A prison warder who secretly hated the fascists told him one morning that Terruzzi had asked Golfarini to choose prisoners from Casteldoro whenever anyone was to be shot as a reprisal. Fausto was not surprised.

Seeing his face reflected in a window-pane one day, he looked at his wounds: 'Well, they're healing up. Maybe I'll be quite presentable by the time they shoot me.'

The others heard him in silence.

Occasionally the ex-assistant chief of police would ask the others what he had done wrong—he, whose whole career had been in the police.

'Is it fair? I ask you, is it fair?'

[289]

The businessman, who turned his 'z's into 's's like a true Venetian, said: 'Fair? How can you ask if it's fair? Justice is called Terrussi around here.'

One day, Braghiroli ventured to retort 'But *he* doesn't know what's going on!' *He* meant the slack, melancholy Mussolini.

Fausto grinned at him.

'You can be quite sure he doesn't,' Braghiroli went on. 'If he did, he'd intervene.'

'He cares a lot more about Clara Petacci than he does about us,' retorted the Venetian.

'Hey, boys, aren't we getting any food today?' said a workman. 'Prison's all very well, but at least. . . .'

'Who wants to eat?'

'All very well for you, you had a parcel.'

'That swine pinched mine. . . .'

On April 25th, in the middle of the night, an officer and four militiamen opened the door.

'Get up!'

Barefoot, silent, without breathing, the men rose like robots.

Fausto stared at the officer, whom he had recognised at once in the dim light. He had been at school with him: not a bad fellow, not much brain, a regular officer in the militia just to make a living. When his eyes met Fausto's the officer started, looked down and hastily read out the names of the seven who were to come with him.

'Get dressed!' he said.

'But where are you taking us?' Braghiroli asked.

'Get dressed,' the officer repeated. And he went out into the passage to wait with his men, his sten gun tucked under his arm. One of the men started whistling, and the officer shut him up.

In the big cell they began to dress, without speaking. Occasionally one of them would look at another and then at his shoes, which he could hardly get on to his swollen feet. Fausto combed his hair carefully, then flung the comb into a corner.

'Why throw it away?' the Venetian asked him.

Fausto smiled briefly, without answering.

The assistant chief of police put his tie on under his wrinkled, dirty collar and knotted it. A workman went over to the bucket and urinated; others did the same.

[290]

As soon as they were dressed they turned to the officer.

'Are we going to wash?' asked Braghiroli.

'Don't worry about that. . . . Now!'

They left the cell; first the officer, then two militiamen, then the prisoners, then two more militiamen and a corporal.

Two passages and then the hall. An armed man was ready to draw the bolts, and they all went out into the empty piazza, where they were loaded into a lorry in which other soldiers were sitting.

The officer climbed into the cab beside the driver, who put the lorry into first gear and then started off in the direction of the irrigation canal. It was a fine, cool night and they could breathe. Braghiroli was sitting beside Fausto and murmured 'Maybe they're taking us to Verona.'

'No, we'll stop long before that.'

Sometimes a dog barked as they passed. They went slowly, meeting a few German cars. A motorcyclist, wearing a crash helmet, overtook the lorry, moving fast, and making it swerve suddenly.

'But where are we going?' the Venetian, who had been shaken out of a doze, asked in a worried tone.

'To the cinema,' said a militiaman, and laughed with the others.

Fausto slapped a hand on the assistant chief of police's thigh.

'They may not guess, but you're an intellectual. You do see, don't you?'

'D'you really think. . . .'

'Why, of course! They haven't enough petrol for the war. D'you suppose they're taking us for a joyride?'

Braghiroli asked for a cigarette stub. The assistant chief of police still had some *Africa* cigarettes, and gave him one.

'Why. . . . Look, I've still got four.'

'Half a fag each.'

Six half-cigarettes were passed round.

The assistant chief of police was left with a whole one, which after two puffs he handed over to Fausto.

The soldiers were talking politics. The previous day the *Gazzetta di Padusa* had come out with two bits of good news: '*German counter-offensive in Russia—New weapons soon to be used.*' The youngest of them, a big lad, lit a cigarette and exclaimed, 'Yes, there's still the Germans, God willing!'

Fausto looked at him ironically, shaking his head. The soldiers noticed, whispered among themselves, and laughed. Fausto guessed what it was about.

'Think you'll come to a better end than I will, comrade? Think again, then.'

And no one spoke.

The lorry was running along a small unpaved road beside an irrigation canal, sending up clouds of dust. When they reached a point where the road opened out, the officer in the cab told the driver to stop.

A militiaman unhooked the back flap of the lorry and the seven prisoners got down. The night was turning to dawn—a clear, calm dawn that allowed them to see the bare outline of things against the immense grey-blue background of the sky. The outlines of the trees, roughly sketched on it, seemed to be holding their thin branches up to the sky in desperate prayer. For a moment Fausto remembered the last time his father had said goodbye to him, so sadly.

'We've got here,' he said unexpectedly.

'What?' said Braghiroli.

'Nothing . . . I was just thinking aloud.'

The officer ordered the prisoners to line up on the country road that ran beside the low bank of the irrigation canal. It was then, in the first glimmer of daylight, that the seven men saw two soldiers holding spades, a little way off. Then they saw a hole, and gasped. One of them shrieked, his cry full of rage and terror, and others bit their lips till they bled, to avoid screaming.

The officer ordered his men to line up; a sob burst from Braghiroli, then a desperate scream: 'My God!'

In a few seconds came the order to fire, and then the first volley tore the air. The squad fired a second time and hit the assistant chief of police and a workman, who still stood swaying, fists clenched, arms raised. The bodies sprawled there, untidily. In the shadows their light shirts, streaked with blood, stood out plainly.

Fausto realised he was still alive. When the first volley was fired he had flung himself down and the bullets had glanced over him. So he played his last card. While the officer and those in the firing squad were talking, not far away, their backs turned to the bodies, Fausto clawed at the ground with his nails and dragged himself along the slope, slithering along the dew-wet grass, and when he reached the bank slipped into the canal and shot away underwater.

The men heard him plop into the water: a corporal rushed over to the bodies and counted them. 'Sir, there's one missing, he's escaped! I hope I'm not wrong, but I think it's the most important chap!'

Confusion broke out. The officer was at the canal bank in a few bounds, and saw the water on the left disturbed, then quickly smooth again. The lock gates were not far in that direction, and Fausto must have been making for them, to hide there. This the officer guessed. But he ordered his men to fire the other way, to the right.

'But sir, suppose he went left?'

'I'm giving the orders!' rapped the officer, pointing the sten as if to show that he was ready to fire at the fugitive himself.

A couple of militiamen, furious at the trick played on them, rushed along the canal bank, searching. They fired at random all over the place, and flung a few hand grenades into the water, churning it up here and there.

The dead lay abandoned on the bank, in what was now bright daylight. They seemed to have been forgotten. The air smelt rotten, with the rottenness of dung and stagnant water. Pale and alone, the officer stood on the bank. Far away on the left, beyond the lock-gate, he saw something moving. But he held his fire.

That same evening Fausto was in touch with Gabriele. The underground was told—in such a way that the fascists would hear of it too—that Commander Giannone no longer existed. His place had been taken by Commander Achille.

After what had happened Fausto chose the name of Homer's hero, hoping that his luck would hold.

XCV

Since the beginning of November Dionisio had not ventured inside Padusa. Mariuccia continued to say that she had broken all contact with him, Pina and his parents-in-law told their friends he had gone south. To those in the underground Dionisio Cavallari no longer existed; there was only Doctor Tiberio, the printing-press man. The police were not searching for him, but he was not so ingenuous as to think they knew nothing about him. Too many people knew him, and although he behaved cautiously he could hardly hope that everyone was blind. He thought the fascists were lying low in the hope of catching him red-handed.

From time to time he met Pina at a house in the country. She urged him not to run pointless risks, but dared not dissuade him from living as he did; in the meantime she lived in town with her parents, preferring the dangers of the bombing to the discomforts of flight—particularly since their home was a long way from any military targets, and so in the part of Padusa which was least heavily bombed.

Suddenly, on the evening of May 5th, three Republican guardsmen came to arrest her, on Golfarini's orders. Pina flung a raincoat over her shoulders and followed them in silence, forcing herself not to lose control, while her parents gazed dully at her, swollen-eyed, and the baby, knowing nothing, roared its head off.

At the police station they told her she would go home when they had caught her husband. Then, half ironically and half threateningly, a sergeant asked her if she had anything to say.

'Yes,' she replied coldly. 'I'd like my clothes as soon as possible.'

It was a terrible blow for Dionisio. He felt he had betrayed his wife's love and trust, and reproached himself bitterly for not having foreseen what would happen. But Pina, with her usual common sense, soothed his fears as soon as possible, letting him know through her mother that she would a thousand times rather spend a few weeks in prison—which in any case involved no hardship—than hand him over to the Federal Secretary's warders, who, she knew perfectly well, were quite capable of shooting him on sight.

Dionisio let ten days pass in silence. He wasn't desperate; when the fascists saw he wasn't giving himself up they would free Pina. But Golfarini, having decided to be tough, had no intention of re-examining her case.

Again Dionisio was overwhelmed by a feeling of guilt. He couldn't wait for Golfarini to free her, nor could he turn for help to Mariuccia, who was already in a dangerous position. He thought of Don Renzo, whose noble nature and dedication to the cause of freedom made Dionisio trust him, and whom even Golfarini could not treat with his usual brutality.

Dionisio met him in a country church. There was no need to speak—when Gabriele had asked him to meet Dionisio, Don Renzo had guessed at once what it was about.

'Of course I shan't exactly enjoy meeting a man like Golfarini, but I want to accept the job.'

'Want or must, Don Renzo? I don't want you to do it just out of duty, you know.'

'If a priest did things just out of duty, he'd better change his job! Else what's the point of wearing this cassock? To hear ladies' confessions?'

'Thank you from the bottom of my heart, Don Renzo.'

'Don't go thanking me! When it's over let's both thank God.'

Don Renzo asked Golfarini to see him, and after a few days was received at the prefecture. There had been a heavy air raid the night before, but Golfarini was at work as usual, punctual and imperturbable.

The two men stared at each other: both were men of steel.

Golfarini was the first to speak:

'What have you to say to me, Father?'

'You know I'm here on behalf of the Ferrioli family.'

'Ah yes—a fine family of traitors.'

'That's hardly the word for them, I'd say. They're a quiet family, completely outside what's going on. Now the poor old grandparents have to care for a sickly baby who may in fact be handicapped.'

'Let them thank their ambitious son-in-law, that rebel. . . .'

'They'd thank you a lot more if you'd free Signora Pina, who knows nothing about her husband's activities.'

'That remains to be seen.'

'But it's true! She knew nothing and knows nothing. She can't be the slightest use to you . . . even to make her husband give himself up.'

'I wonder,' said Golfarini mysteriously.

'No, really. Anyway, that's a little trick that just won't work any more.'

'Now look here, Father,' Golfarini exploded. 'These aren't little tricks, as you call them, but matters of policy. We're trying to save our country.'

'By arresting wives when you can't catch their husbands?'

The two men stared at each other, both bitterly proud. For a moment neither spoke. Don Renzo realised he had struck home.

'No, believe me, it isn't the sort of thing an Italian ought to do,' he went on. 'It's not even worthy. . .'

'Tone down your language, Father!' cried Golfarini.

It was not his language, but his manner, that Don Renzo toned down.

'What I meant,' he said, almost sweetly, 'was that it wasn't worthy of you, sir. Everyone agrees you've got courage.'

'Everyone? Even those renegade anti-fascists?'

'Certainly! But why spoil it by acting against defenceless women?'

Golfarini was nervously clutching a paper knife; but he was listening.

'You're a man of culture,' Don Renzo went on. 'Remember how we were moved at school when we read the story of Luisa Sanfelice's martyrdom. . . . She was persecuted, imprisoned, tried and condemned by—'

'By those cowards the Bourbons!'

'Cowards, I quite agree. But. . . .'

'But what?'

'You know what I mean; there's a certain similarity about this situation.'

There was another silence, filled with the priest's anxiety and Golfarini's embarrassment. Then Golfarini rose, thrust out his lower lip and glared coldly at Don Renzo.

[296]

'Right. In a few days we'll free this woman. But I swear that as soon as he falls into my hands, I'll have her husband shot.'

'God willing, this terrible fratricidal war will soon be over.'

'You priests are all against us. You'll be sorry!'

XCVI

A few days later Pina was freed, but Dionisio had to stop meeting her. He knew they were keeping an eye on her, hoping to catch him.

After a week Pina took the baby to a small town near the Swiss border, where an aunt on her father's side lived. Dionisio's father had also left Padusa. The splendid shop, which had been the pride of his life, was half destroyed, and he would have to start again from scratch, a daunting prospect in times like these. And in the last few months Vito Cavallari had aged a great deal. The constant worry over the risks his son was running, and all the disasters brought about by the bombing, had had their effect on him. He put an old employee of his in charge of what was left of the shop, and went off to Milan, which those in the know predicted would not be bombed.

A couple of weeks later Dionisio told a few friends that he was leaving for Milan to meet his wife. As soon as he had gone to the printing press, Fausto stared into Giulio's eyes. 'He won't be back,' he said.

Giulio was silent, and Fausto started talking about Dionisio. No one admired his cousin more than he did: since adolescence, Dionisio had seemed to him a symbol of moral and intellectual probity. Even his anti-fascism had grown up through profound distress. But all his ideas were built on an ideal of freedom and morality—centred on the value of the human person—which weakened him when he was faced with the harsh laws of partisan fighting. 'Man is a great world in himself: people forget this elementary truth,' he often said. He knew it was necessary to fight, and accepted it as a terrible duty that must be carried out to the end. But only a few hours earlier he had said to Fausto, 'How can we spend all day trying to kill? I'm afraid people will get into the habit of it.'

Dionisio could not face these things dispassionately, and the idealistic reasons for the fight, which he believed in so profoundly, could not save him from uneasiness. He thought it an aberration that men should keep flinging bullets at each other like confetti.

'Touch a flower on a bush and it's hiding a mine that'll blow you to bits. Men have made even nature evil!'

In spite of everything, when Dionisio left he was convinced he was not abandoning the fight, but would be back. What he failed to take into account was the fact that, once he had left the invigorating atmosphere of Padusa, other feelings would in the end win him over—shaken to the depths as he already was. Perhaps the fact that his family needed his help so badly would give him a decent excuse.

'He won't be back,' Fausto said again. 'And maybe it's just as well.'

'Of course, he'll keep his hands clean till it's all over,' said Massarenti.

'We'll need a good builder when it's all over,' said Fausto. 'To clear up the mess. And anyway, if the Allies hold off much longer, there won't be many of us left in the C L N.'

'Balls,' broke in Massarenti. 'You intellectuals smother everything in fine talk. You even justify chucking a struggle as decisive as this one by talking about private ideals and other idiocies like that. The sort of rubbish you might expect from women—like talking about making the most of the ruling classes, which simply means keeping the top people in clover so as to stick them in as Ministers tomorrow, while we're risking our lives. As if workmen's lives and peasant's lives didn't count for anything! But oh no, they've got no right to private ideals, or to a family, or to their children, or to the Vatican's protection—they're cogs in a machine that, when you really get down to it, hasn't really anything to do with them.'

'It has,' said Giulio. 'It's theirs in particular. The weakest are those freedom helps most.'

Massarenti had been walking nervously up and down during this outburst, looking at nobody. After it an embarrassing silence fell, with Massarenti alone in the middle of the room and everyone staring at him.

'Sorry,' he muttered, passing his hand over his forehead. 'I'm all on edge. . . . I'd give anything to get home to my parents, myself.'

XCVII

At the end of May Giulio had a letter from Signora Boari, asking him to come to Milan. Linda's nerves were shattered, and only Giulio's presence could restore them. He left early in the morning, in a rickety car belonging to a man who dealt in fabrics, and reached Milan in the evening, after an exhausting journey. There he found a wasted, hollow-eyed woman, who greeted him with floods of tears.

'I'm more and more terrified about this baby, Giulio. Will it have a father? And what sort of child will come out of a woman who conceives in the state I'm in?'

'Don't worry, Linda! Don't make me repeat all the things you already know by heart, all the things your mother must have told you any number of times as well.'

'But couldn't you give up working for the underground movement and come here with me? That's the only thing that would make me stop worrying.'

'You know it would be cowardly.'

'I know, I know, you're perfectly right. But isn't it cowardly to leave a woman in my state, as well?'

'Oh Linda, don't be unfair. Don't say such awful things.'

'You're right, I know I'm not reasonable any longer.'

'Make an effort to calm down: I promise you I'll be careful. And have more trust in life, Linda: in your life, in mine, in the life of our child.'

Linda's face relaxed a little.

'I'll try,' she said, and suddenly fainted in her mother's arms.

Giulio left sadly. He was tormented by the fear that Linda's exhaustion might be hard to cure, but he made an effort to think that when her pregnancy was over she would be restored to health and tranquillity.

When he got back to Padusa he found orders from Fausto to join the partisan formation working in the lowlands.

After months of inactivity the Italian front had at last been pierced and the Allied troops were fast advancing northwards. No sudden change in the political and military situation was expected, so it was thought best to organise many other partisan groups in the lowlands. In view of these coming developments Giulio was put in charge of the whole sector. At first he stood out against this.

'I've never been to the lowlands in my life. Choose someone more suitable.'

'You mean you don't want to?' said Fausto aggressively.

'You don't really think I'm scared, do you?'

'Well, if you're not scared, go on! We're all of us amateurs.'

XCVIII

When he reached the lowlands Giulio had a pleasant surprise —he met a friend he had thought lost to the cause. Under the *nom de guerre* of Aldebaran lurked the millionaire Eriberto, who had joined the partisan group a short time ago. As soon as the fascist party in Padusa was re-formed Eriberto, remembering his recent spell in prison, had let his new masters know that politics no longer interested him and that all he wanted was a quiet life. So he had retired to his large estate at Porto, and had decided to await the end of the war there.

But he had not been able to find peace. In those months of isolation he had wondered continually whether he was not deserting the cause—he who had been an anti-fascist in the days when all his contemporaries were crazy about Mussolini.

When the regime seemed likely to go on for ever he had taken risks because of his own ideas; so how could he busy himself in a farmyard now? He wasn't afraid of death, but the thought of the lice and the filthy earth closet in prison sickened him. Making love to the plump country girls, who liked his city ways and generous presents, was a lot more agreeable; but in the evenings, when he couldn't bear to look at himself in the mirror, his heart sank.

One night he burst out, leaving the factor's daughter warm and sated in bed, and in the first light of dawn, without a word to anyone, took his sten and set off for the not very distant lowlands, determined once again to become the Eriberto he had been.

As soon as Giulio arrived, he began organising the base. On the edge of his territory, where a few partisans were hidden under the command of a youngster called Partenio, there were thick reeds and swampy grasses, with a few paths and some narrow canals going across them. On the ridges there were no houses, only tumbledown straw huts left by fishermen. Food and medicines were taken to a couple of these huts.

About twenty unattached men, nearly all of them foreigners, got in touch with the base just then, and Giulio was not sure whether to be pleased or sorry. He was glad to see the partisans increasing in number, but afraid that too large a group in that small district would attract the Germans' attention; he thought he must scatter his men in very small groups, pushing out along the salt valleys towards the sea. But this was easier said than done, and meantime they stayed where they were.

Food was short and meagrely shared out, and they tried to increase the ration as best they could. But there were few eels in the waters there, fishing was not very successful, and it was only occasionally that they shot a few birds. The only man who never grumbled about the food was Eriberto: perhaps he thought he should be doing penance.

It was a hard life, and some of the youngsters from Padusa who had sheltered in the lowlands to escape military service under the Social Republic suddenly got up and went home without a word. If it had just been a case of tightening their belts, they might have hung on. But what they could not bear was the enervating gloom of that strange watery life, in a country without horizons, under a sky that was always silent. Only hardened, mature men could stand it.

In the local town of Porto everyone knew Giovanna: wives looked scornfully at her, men mentally undressed her, adolescents tried to discover the mystery of her lewd popularity. Among the girls who came to the Sunday market she was easily recognised, cycling casually and boldly along, showing her shapely legs, wearing very tight, bright clothes. When she dismounted she would wander among the stalls, buttocks swaying

[301]

and large breasts much in evidence under the very low neck of her thin woollen jersey. When a handsome boy familiarly stroked her neck and shoulders her eyes would glitter, often restlessly, always disturbingly; and her thick lips would open, promising everything, and her lithe body tremble.

'You're like an electric current,' the boy would murmur.

'Like to plug in?' she would flash back at him.

She was well known for her independence. When she liked a man she showed it; if he was shy her crude, instinctive methods of winning him were hardly likely to do so, but she kept on trying.

People might laugh at her but as a rule they didn't despise her, because she wasn't mercenary. She simply needed to offer herself, paganly, spontaneously, and naturally, without calculation. If she was offered a present she would accept it, but she asked for nothing. They called her Big Tits, and other names, less respectable; her ex-lovers treated her kindly and familiarly, and those she had rejected called her a whore.

She went into the shops and cafés, and even into the *Platz Kommandantur*, and wherever she went she spread a wave of desire. Her home was a small house left to her by her father, outside the town; there she gathered reeds, which she sold in bundles, and kept rabbits and chickens to sell to the restaurants.

On one of those torrid June nights when no one could feel a breath of wind, Eriberto was on sentry duty with Cassiano, a tough partisan from Porto, while the others lay asleep in the hut made of straw and brushwood. Cassiano had boatman's eyes that could see in the dark, and was looking across the marsh and the paths, and sniffing the air, not missing a sound, even that of the eels gliding through the water. Eriberto was dreaming.

'To hell with Mussolini,' he suddenly burst out, turning to Cassiano. 'With these damnable Krauts at our heels, we can't even make love!'

'Oh come off it! Think of your own safety. What's up with you tonight?'

'Are you made of ice?'

'No, but the thought of seeing the S S pop out at any minute makes me shudder.'

'What d'you think I do?' Eriberto was silent a moment. 'Last time I had it was with Big Tits last month. . . . Hell, but that girl certainly raises morale!'

'She goes with you because you're rich, I suppose.'

'Oh, not just with me.'

'But d'you know she's dangerous? She goes with the Krauts as well.'

'Dangerous, my eye! She goes because . . . well, just because! You know what she's like: if she likes a man she doesn't give a damn whether he's from Berlin or Porto.'

'So long as he's handsome, eh?'

'Of course. But the Krauts give her tinned food, and fags, and she hands them on to people round here.'

'Yes, that's perfectly true, she gave my wife a couple of tins without her even asking . . . and some maize flour as well.'

'See? That's what she's like.'

'Well, yes,' Cassiano agreed. 'She's a whore but . . . a loyal whore!'

They both laughed, thinking of her curious loyalty.

Suddenly Eriberto got up and brushed the dust off his corduroy trousers as best he could, holding the gun between his legs.

'What are you doing?'

'Know what? I'm going to Giovanna's. At this hour I'm bound to find her.'

'Are you crazy?'

'No, but I'm going!'

'Are you going to risk being caught just for that? A fine thing that'd be, for a girl like her.'

'Well, she's a girl, at least.'

'You want your head examined, that's what you want! What did they teach you at that university of yours?'

'If all goes well, I'll bring you some fags.'

'And if all goes wrong, you'll come out feet first.'

'Shut up! I'll run all the way and be back in an hour. You know Giovanna's not far, and she's not slow in making up her mind.'

'Well, that's for sure, but. . . .'

'Ssh!'

Eriberto slipped away, as if he had gone behind a curtain

with the soft footsteps of a cat on the tiles; Cassiano heard the reeds closing in behind him, then nothing.

He crossed a couple of small canals by the wobbly planks placed across them, balancing like an acrobat, and reached the path that turned behind a large abandoned house and led straight to Giovanna's hut, two or three hundred yards on. As he went, he thought deliciously of her soft warm skin against his chest; and the thought made him hurry. Yes, he was a fool to do it as Cassiano had said, but the worst was over. . . .

So he reached Giovanna's hut, and around it was total silence. Evidently she was alone. Eriberto went into the yard and through the worn flowered cretonne curtains that barely covered the ground-floor window he saw the light of an oil lamp. Between the window and the lamp, which was standing on a shabby old chest of drawers, Giovanna was having a bath. Suddenly she got up, and the shadow of her naked body lengthened behind the curtain, thrown slightly out of shape by the unsteady flame of the lamp. Eriberto started and moved to the side of the window where the curtain left a gap. Naked, Giovanna appeared to him, humming a wordless tune as she dried her body, and clearly enjoying herself as she rubbed the towel under her armpits and on her belly. In fact she kept on softly and delightedly massaging herself, humming away; sometimes she paused in her song and sometimes hummed more loudly, as if the tune were expressing the pleasure that was beginning to seize her.

Eriberto stood there, too tense to move. Giovanna stepped out of the bath and stood in front of the looking-glass. She went on drying herself with vague, soft movements, her thighs pressed together, the rest of her body swaying, and smiled admiringly at her plump, curved reflection in the mirror.

Eriberto could no longer control himself. To avoid frightening her he left his sten on the window-sill and went in, murmuring gently 'Giovanna . . . don't be scared. . . .'

'Scared of what?' she answered at once, then turned. 'Ah, so it's you, millionaire.'

'Yes, it's me!'

'What a state you're in, a gentleman like you! D'you need anything? . . . Ah, I see, you want a few fags.'

'No.'

'Well, then?'

'I only want. . . .'

'I can well believe it! You've been fasting, haven't you?'

'Yes. Fasting far too long.'

Giovanna went over to him. She stared at him, stroked his hair, and then, with a movement like a wild beast's, tugged it till it hurt.

'Stop it! What's up?'

'Nothing. . . . I want to squash you to bits!'

She said it with clenched teeth, and as if she were already biting him greedily.

The only light on the edge of the marshland was that clumsily lit window. On the sill lay the dark sten gun. Three Germans on duty were searching the area. They were softly singing *Lili Marlene*, but there was no real rhythm in their song: it was more like a lazy murmur, as if the warm night had brought them memories of far-off pleasures.

'Here's where Giovanni lives,' one of them said.

'Yes.'

And they were silent, each thinking of her much-flaunted flesh. And, as if their senses urged them on, they went down the path to her hut. In silence they reached it, and saw the movement of Eriberto and Giovanna.

The corporal turned to the others, winked and indicated with his thumb that Giovanna was inside, making love. One of the soldiers, nodding and smiling mischievously, motioned to him to wait. The other two agreed, and then approached the window, hoping to see more of the scene inside. It was the corporal who first saw the outline of Eriberto's sten gun, and pointed it out to the others.

The Germans' faces suddenly hardened, as if they had heard a command barked out at the barracks. Once they had got over their desire, Hitler's soldiers took over: while the corporal picked up the gun the other two hurled themselves at the door and burst it open.

They heard Giovanna shriek, and through the flowered curtain saw Eriberto leap towards the window. Then the corporal fired from outside, and for a moment the gun flamed.

A thud on the floor: it was Eriberto's body, huddled up as

he breathed his last. Giovanna stared at it for a few seconds, her eyes wide; then, as the only sign of her grief, she started sobbing and trembling.

The corporal went in and glanced at the body, then went over to Giovanna. He put the gun down on the table and took off his belt. Giovanna drew back, first against the bed, then against the wall, her eyes still wide open. The two other soldiers stood speechless, but the corporal grabbed her, flung her on to the bed and muttered in her face, with an ironical smile, 'Come on, Giovanna, give the Germans a bit of love as well! Don't save it all up for the partisans.'

Giovanna reacted in a flash—shoving her feet against his chest and pushing him back as hard as she could till he staggered. Then she seized her chance and leaped up. Anger had now replaced fear and with all the savage strength of her nature she screamed at the three Germans: 'Curse you . . . the lot of you . . . Hitler . . Mussolini . . . murderers, criminals . . . Get out, you rotten Krauts . . .'

And she spat in the corporal's face as he stared at her, his eyes full with rage and shame. Then, seeing tins of meat on the table, she flung them hard at the two soldiers standing motionless in a corner.

'And take your meat with you, you creeps!'

A tin struck one of the soldiers full in the face, and he covered his eye; blood was trickling down his cheek.

The corporal seized the sten gun; pointed it at her, fired.

'You dogs . . . you Kraut dogs . . . may God strike you . . . destroy. . . .'

The final curse stuck in her throat and turned into a brief rattle, which ended in a sigh.

Outside, Cassiano gazed out across the valley, thinking of Eriberto's stupidity. The wind had borne away the echo of the shots, in the opposite direction.

Next morning the others heard about Eriberto. Giulio was silent the whole day.

XCIX

One morning the partisans in the 'command' hut saw a dinghy approaching. Three German soldiers, who must have had orders to search the district, disembarked and walked gingerly towards the hut, their machine guns pointed at it. Five or six partisans crept into the reeds and let them walk on until they were about twenty feet away. Then Partenio signalled to them to open fire. It was an easy target, and the three men in their greenish uniforms fell heavily, streaking the sand with blood.

Giulio and Partenio approached the bodies cautiously. Two men had been shot in the head and were no longer breathing, but the third was wounded only in the arms. He was carried into the hut and roughly bandaged by a partisan who had been a male nurse.

Giulio questioned him, and the man said his commander had sent the small patrol to see if there was a partisan group in the neighbourhood. Now, when his men failed to return, he would ask for reinforcements to scour it. When Giulio asked for information about the German forces there the man refused to reply.

He didn't mind, he said, giving information that might help the partisans to save themselves, but he wasn't going to harm his own comrades. Two of them had already died beside him. In any case, he was sick of bloodshed, and all he wanted was to get home to his family.

He was chatty and sociable, this Paul Müller, and Giulio gave him drinks and cigarettes. Sitting on a cane chair that squeaked under his weight, and won over by his enemy's bright eyes and obvious humanity, Müller at last spoke freely. He realised, he said, that the war no longer had an object, because Germany's only hope lay in its secret weapons, which no sensible Germans now believed in; and he hated Roosevelt and Churchill, because he was sure that in order to surrender Germany needed only an armistice without humiliating conditions attached to it. But those two pig-headed enemies, he said, only wanted revenge, so Hitler would carry on till he was wiped out. Millions of Germans would die pointlessly, and an equal number of innocent victims on the other side as well.

While Giulio listened with friendly interest Partenio was growing more and more obviously angry. After a while he lost patience and asked the man straight out why he obeyed orders from a criminal like Hitler.

Paul Müller was not put out. He said he was a soldier and had to carry out his superiors' legitimate orders. In any case, those who were now the partisan leaders had obeyed Mussolini's orders when he was supreme commander of the armed forces, and when they were wearing the King's uniform, before Badoglio's armistice. Admittedly, he was not on the side of the Axis in this war, but soldiers couldn't judge the justice of their wars and fight only in those they approved of; if they did, all armies would fade away at once.

Giulio began arguing in German about the duty of obedience (and Müller had obviously guessed why he had such a perfect accent), while young Partenio went on doodling in the sand with a thin stick. But Giulio guessed what he was thinking and when he had sent Müller away he slapped him cordially on the back.

'What's on your mind, Partenio?'

'That Kraut. What'll we do?'

'What d'you suggest?'

'I'd get rid of him.'

'But he's a poor devil who's forced to go with the tide.'

'He was quite ready to fire at us, though.'

'Well, he was obeying orders.'

'Exactly—Hitler's.'

'Like all the Germans, good or bad.'

'I'd wipe the lot of them out, if it was up to me.'

'I wouldn't! You've got to discriminate. We're fighting Nazism, not the Germans, just as the Allies before the armistice were fighting fascism, not the Italian people.'

'So what'll we do?'

'It's quite simple. We've got to get out of here at once. Because the Germans'll soon turn up in strength and wipe us out.'

'Right. But what about the Kraut?'

'We'll leave him here. Then he can join his unit.'

'But he'll tell them about us.'

'Who cares? We've got to get out, anyway.'

'I don't agree, but I'll obey. You're in charge.'

'Just like Paul Müller, you see. He doesn't agree with Hitler, but he obeys.'

In a couple of hours they were ready to leave. A long, dangerous march lay ahead.

Giulio took the prisoner aside and spoke to him in German: 'We're off. You're free to act according to your conscience.'

'Thanks, sir!'

And he clicked his heels.

A few days later, when it seemed clear that the Allies were not yet coming, the group was broken up and Giulio had orders to go to Sàvena and operate from there. He was sad to leave his own province, but obeyed without protest.

C

For months the stout resistance put up at Cassino, where the Germans had managed to hold up the Allied advance on Rome, had had a decisive effect on the fascists' morale. The lack of success of the Allied landing at Anzio, where their efforts to surround the capital had also failed, seemed no less significant. All this, the fascists said, proved that the Germans still had plenty of fight in them.

So when, at the end of May, the German defence crumbled dramatically, and the Allies entered Rome on June 4th, the fascists in Padusa were astounded; they had not had time to recover from this blow when, a couple of days later, the even more dramatic news reached them of the landing in France. Fascist officials, high or low, hardly dared look each other in the face, for fear of reading bewilderment there. Many actually wondered if, after the cataclysm, the Germans would stay on in Italy at all: they were afraid they would rush into France to defend the frontiers of their own country, and abandon Mussolini's Republic to its fate.

In these conditions, no one wanted to get involved in setting up the new order, and in particular no one could delude himself that the 'socialising' the fascist Republic had talked about so much was really coming to anything. The ruling classes, who of course refused to give up defending their own interests, had from the start tried to put a spoke in the government's wheel; the Germans, busy with their own war production, were afraid the new provisions would arouse prejudice and kept talking about a bunch of revolutionary amateurs; and the workers, who should have benefited, had never thought this socialisation was anything but a fraud and kept well away from it and from the fascists. Now, with half Italy lost, only Pavolini could delude himself that he was going in for revolutionary reform.

The only people who believed in victory and the Verona manifesto were probably the poor boys in uniform whom the Social Republic had deluded with patriotic myths. Hearts fell as they went by in the streets, half truculent, half scared— singing the desperate song of the Republican fighters:

> Le donne non ci vogliono piú bene,
> perché portiamo la camicia nera,
> perché ci dicon che siamo da galera
> perché ci dicon che siamo da galera . . .

Fascist officials now pretended to keep busy only in order to hide their increasing anxiety. They could see people's dull hostility, sense the growing danger of the empty streets, feel the threat growing as the Allies advanced; most of them sent their families away and not only lived but actually slept in the Prefecture or at fascist headquarters, the last fortresses of their declining power. Anyone who spent the night at home risked ending up like Carpanese, the well-remembered head of the political police.

The only hope of getting out of such a desperate situation lay in a secret weapon. But although the newspapers of June 18th reported, with banner headlines, that German aerial torpedoes were raining down upon England, no one at fascist headquarters believed that this weapon could change the balance of the war; and when, a few days later, Goebbels announced melodramatically that a decisive secret weapon was imminent, few fascists believed him. Most of them were incredulous, and shook their heads, as sceptical as the man in the street, thinking it mere moonshine that science could create a completely new weapon of such immeasurable power as to change the result of a war that was to all intents and purposes already over. No one could have imagined that the atomic bomb had already been conceived: had Hitler dropped it first, the course of human civilisation would indeed have been altered, in a terrible way.

At the beginning of the summer Padusa seemed desolate. The main streets now looked like bloodless arteries—at least half the buildings had been destroyed or damaged, and most of the shops were bolted and barred. After the first two heavy raids families had sheltered in villages, farms, and isolated houses in the country, where danger seemed less imminent, and only a few thousand—the poorest—had stayed on in town. Among the refugees, the only ones seen in Padusa were those who came in briefly to work, commuting hazardously along roads constantly watched by Allied reconnaissance planes.

Troops and police ruled a lifeless city, where even necessary public services were often lacking. Improvised canteens were set up in the Prefecture for clerks and workmen, but often they were left hungry because the van delivering sugar, fat, pasta or the now minute weekly meat ration was attacked or burnt, if not actually re-routed for some unknown destination.

Long queues began at dawn outside grocers' and butchers' shops and delicatessens, and when the local shops were bombed they grew even longer. Food was now a wearisome problem, and the queues were checked and organised by groups set up to control ration distribution. Workmen and the lower white-collar workers, who had no savings, struggled desperately for their own and their children's survival, expressing their terrible anxiety in silence rather than in words.

Those with money could go on the black market, which was more and more openly tolerated, because, whether for good or ill, it was a safety valve. Tucked away in private houses, stored behind shops, or in the loneliest parts of the suburbs, greedy sales were made by unscrupulous people who ventured out into the country, or else by the peasants themselves, who, made cunning by circumstances, brought all sorts of food into town and made profits they had never dreamed of.

No shoes at all were obtainable, but people had to manage

[311]

somehow, so thick cloth, and even rope and wood, took the place of hides and leather. Ersatz materials, which could be bought with coupons, were so poor that they looked like paper. So people went about in worn, patched clothes, and even those who had been elegant before the war now looked like labourers.

Bicycles were ridden on ancient tyres, patched up and bandaged in the most complicated way. But the patches gave out with a melancholy sigh when least expected to, as if ironically mocking the weary labour spent on them. Petrol was not to be found: the few rusty cars authorised to be on the road ran on charcoal, with huge stoves at the back, smoky, reluctant to light, and looking like monstrous kitchens.

Occasionally the German department of propaganda or the Fascist federation sent people of 'proven loyalty' to mingle with the long hungry queues, to hand out hope as well as rations. These people had plenty of big talk about the way the military situation was soon going to change and important lines of communication would soon be opened, which would mean plenty of food again. But people shrugged. How could they believe that the German armies could counter-attack, when it was plain that their equipment was deteriorating daily? By now, it was remarkable to see a tank or an armoured car in working order; military vehicles fell to pieces in full view of everyone, car tyres were rare and precious and soldiers got about on the once-spurned bicycle, as they had done in the First World War. Though they did all they could to keep up appearances, the weary German troops in the summer of 1944 stank of poverty.

Reinforcements from Germany no longer turned up and the German troops had to manage as best they could, living from day to day. Wherever they could find them they took oxen and horses and yoked them to military vehicles, and, to satisfy their most pressing needs, raided the peasants' houses and seized whatever food they could find. Fear, always a bad counsellor, sometimes brutalised the soldiers and made them pointlessly harsh, and an increasing, dangerous hatred was growing up between German troops and Italian civilians.

Notices saying 'Beware of bandits!', which lined the roads near the front, made people constantly afraid of raids. The partisans were now undoubtedly real, and not a day passed without some German soldier dying in the war for the liberation of Italy.

Troop movements took place in the most risky conditions. There was no chance of avoiding the enemy's reconnaissance flights, which calmly watched them, and gave precise orders to bombers or gun batteries. Now and then the front would shift, and fire would rain down on the German positions, sowing destruction, but it met with precious little resistance. It was an event when a German aircraft took off at all. The German planes, which, when they did go up, usually flew in pairs, were nicknamed 'orphans of the storm' by people in the countryside around Padusa.

Allied aircraft controlled even the remotest German outposts without opposition. In full daylight they would swoop down on country roads to machine-gun cars, carts and even bicycles. Trains and out-of-town trams were under constant fire from them, and the airmen were now so sure of themselves that they would sometimes swoop down to a few yards from the ground in a lonely suburban street to machine-gun a couple of soldiers coming back from a meal.

Above the heads of the German soldiers heavy Allied bombers passed uninterruptedly, flying north in close formation. From other directions, too—as they knew quite well—other armies were approaching German soil, to raze the loveliest German cities to the ground and destroy their surviving industries. Many German soldiers came to prefer their own fate to that of their families at home, living in cellars and shelters in a nightmare of terrifying air raids.

How long would it continue? The assassination attempt of July 20th was like an electric shock on a high-tension wire. Fanatics roared their indestructible faith in the Führer, who had survived the attack on his life unharmed; others wondered, in their hearts, whether providence, in saving Hitler's life, had been acting in the interests of the German people.

Occasionally a man would react against the absurd discipline of that hopeless army, defy the firing squad, and desert.

Golfarini saw all this and took it in, but he was not disheartened. Like all true fanatics, he was more than ever determined to carry on to the end. But he was no longer happy in Padusa. He had come there full of confidence, when the neo-fascist authorities deluded themselves that they were undertaking the Verona programme and that fascism would soon rise again; now that the situation was crumbling, he felt himself progressively more embarrassed at the questioning looks of his followers, whom he had promised victory and vengeance, not endless bombs and fear.

So he was quite ready to respond to an appeal from Mussolini's government, who wanted a man of iron to deal with a province where, in May and June, partisan brigades had occupied the mountains. This was exactly what Golfarini wanted; he had always taken to heart Mussolini's exhortation 'live dangerously,' and had always meant to prove it in tasks where others had failed. He was replaced as provincial chief by an outsider just over thirty, Dr Luigi Bassini, who had belonged to the G U F generation and whose only distinction was a prize won long ago in the fascist cultural competitions. Earlier, the choice of such a man for the job would have caused an uproar, but now, with everyone avoiding involvement with a regime that stank of death, he was accepted.

To everyone's surprise, Bassini managed to persuade Francesco Tassinari to accept the job of Vice-Federal Secretary. Till now the brilliant leader of the G U F in its heyday had been living on his large well-irrigated estate, avoiding Padusa as much as possible, and he was generally thought to be unwilling to become involved with the new fascist rulers, though still a party member. Whatever could have made him come out now, when all hope of fascist renewal was lost and a democratic government for the rest of Italy was being set up in Rome? Since boyhood Tassinari had been known not just as clever, but as cunning in the Italian sense of the word. But human action cannot always be logically explained.

CI

Mariuccia's farm was on the provincial road the Germans were now using continually, and one unhappy day a German car stopped and a lieutenant and an N C O got out of it.

Without a word they went into the stable, counted the oxen, and went out again.

The lieutenant, who spoke good Italian, asked for the owner. Mariuccia was away: Brogli, the factor, introduced himself.

'From now on, your animals are for the use of the German command,' the lieutenant told him.

The factor, a fair, balding, fiery little man, tried to protest; but protests and prayers were no use, nor was the fact that the tractors were unusable and so the oxen were needed. A few days later the animals were taken away, and, for fear of further requisitions, those that remained (the animals that had luckily been in distant fields when the rest were taken over) were let loose.

Desperate, the factor went on the black market to find the spare parts needed to get one of the worn-out tractors going; one morning, amid general excitement, the engine fired, and, bucking like a steer, the tractor set off along the farm track. But only two days later a plane swooped down and machine-gunned the poor tractor into a smoking ruin.

The few oxen left were yoked up again. To escape capture and the air offensive they were used at night, but they managed to do less and less and became visibly scrawnier.

Terrified of the machine-gunning, the farm workers fled, and hungry townsfolk seized whatever they could find in the fields—ears of wheat, corn cobs, fruit.

Tirelessly the factor worked on—running the farm, replacing what was missing, foiling thieves. At last he broke down, and was put to bed with violent palpitations of the heart. The doctor ordered him a month's rest.

Mariuccia now had to take over and do her best, inexperienced as she was. For herself, she would have given up the harvest, but it seemed criminal: it was the bread of the poor people in the local town, and the corn lay there ripe and awaiting her. It had to be harvested and threshed.

The terrible days dragged by. There was never an afternoon without an Allied plane flying low over the provincial road and machine-gunning the countryside around it. No one cared to risk his life for his share of the harvest, but Mariuccia managed to persuade the women that it was in their own

[315]

interests to harvest as much as possible. At night the danger was far less, she told them. So, by moonlight, the harvesters cut the corn and took it to the barn.

It was now time for threshing. But the few threshing machines in the district that had escaped being pawned or destroyed were being used by other farmers. Without losing heart, Mariuccia set off to search and at last found one in a village about twenty kilometres away. It had to be brought to the farm, a risky journey when Allied pilots might mistake it for a German tank. The oxen were yoked to the shaft, and Mariuccia, under cover of night, set off at the head of her men.

Threshing presented a new, serious problem. It might be dangerous by day, but would have been just as dangerous at night, because the sparks from the smoke-stack might have been seen by Pippo, the British plane that kept constant watch in the sky there. After a heated discussion in the barn, it was decided to work by day, and Mariuccia, wearing a head-scarf and with her sleeves rolled up, stayed with the men from first to last. And the men drew courage from her glowing eyes.

On the last day a plane flew low overhead. Everyone dived for shelter but there was no bombing or machine-gunning. The pilot had understood.

Mariuccia had won her battle, which was a fight for others: she told the poor people who had fled from the nearby town that corn would be given out free. At Guarda people said no landowner had ever loved the poor as Signora Mariuccia did. A socialist soul, that's what she had. What a shame she'd been a party member!

CII

It was the afternoon of July 6th, Mariuccia's birthday, and the men on the farm at Guarda, who had just finished the thresh-ing, stood round the barn, drinking her health. As they hurriedly drank down the light golden wine, as if merely quenching their thirsts—their worn shirts soaked with sweat, their faces gleaming with it—they seemed weary rather than festive. There was no singing, and little laughter. The cicadas beside the field path, among the thin posts carrying electric wires and the smooth poplar trees, made more noise than the tired men; their obsessive cry sounded like the squeak of unoiled wheels.

At first Mariuccia mingled with the men, joking cheerfully; but her eyes showed that she was not as cheerful as usual. Then she sat down on the doorstep, her legs sideways, her skirt above her knees, careless of a long procession of ants hurrying along beneath them; she stared at a crack in the wall, where a grey lizard had turned over, still as death, in the sultry heat. In the dim hall a useless yellow watch-dog lay on its belly on the red-brick floor, tongue lolling, occasionally looking up at her and then quickly putting its head back between its paws, as if weary with the effort.

How long she stayed there, even after the men had gone, Mariuccia had no idea. But the day was nearly over when the dog ran towards the gate, suddenly excited and barking at Fausto and Gabriele.

Mariuccia arranged her shabby dress, and went slowly towards them, forcing herself to smile.

'Hello. What's up?'

'We're worried,' they said, coming over to her. 'And we'd like to talk to you.'

'Well, darlings, here I am.'

They sat in a circle on cane chairs round a small table a few steps away, and the smell of corn floated out to them from the hall of the house. For a while they sat in silence, while Fausto watched Mariuccia's lovely face, looking worn and tired and with a few faint wrinkles.

'Well,' said Fausto, 'briefly, we've come to say it's time you thought of yourself. You've done a lot already, you know.'

'What?'

'Your double-crossing's becoming dangerous. If they find out you'll be shot at once.'

'You can't be afraid now Golfarini's gone, surely?'

'There's his successor.'

'But he's a frightened little creep.'

'Don't believe that, Mariuccia.'

'All the same, my dears, I'm stopping here.'

Her firmness shook Gabriele, and made him feel almost

ashamed. After a moment's silence Mariuccia went on talking nervously.

'You needn't think I'm like that brave brother of mine, who slinks off to Switzerland just when it really matters.'

'You're not being fair,' said Gabriele. 'Dionisio taught you courage.'

'He taught others and forgot it himself,' Mariuccia said sharply.

'No, no, no,' cried Fausto. 'We're not bound to be totally imprudent. Dionisio was in too much danger—they'd have got him in the end.'

'But you're staying.'

'Everyone's got his duty and his mission. That's true of everyone, even us.'

'Then my mission is to carry on to the end.'

Gabriele was moved. Mariuccia's boldness and courage were helping him to shake off the sense of inferiority that had gradually been coming over him. Since Dionisio and Giulio left he had felt unanchored, unattached, and while the Padusa socialists contributed so much less to the struggle than the Communists did, he could find no peace. But the two cousins were busy getting ready for the future, building up cells in factories and offices and in the country. He tried to do what they were doing with the few helpers he could muster, but it was beyond him.

In the rest of the district it was much the same. The majority of those fighting in the mountains were Communists, and so were the GAP, the groups who boldly terrorised the fascists in the towns. Did this mean that socialism had had its day? Must he admit that a new force had arisen, one which could arouse enthusiasm, as old-fashioned socialism no longer could?

Now, as he read such courage and enthusiasm in Mariuccia's eyes, Gabriele told himself that if a socialist woman could give so much, there was no need to despair of the party. When the time came it would rise to its task. He was not reasoning: it was an act of faith.

For some time now the three of them had been sitting in silence, deep in their own thoughts. Suddenly they heard someone below singing the Axis song *Comrade Richard*, in a fine tenor voice:

Camerati di una guerra,
camerati di una sorte,
dividete pane e morte. . . .

Who could it be? Mariuccia and Gabriele leaped up.

'Don't worry,' said Fausto laughing. 'It's not the Black Brigaders, it's Mario Salatini's theme song.'

Salatini came in with a message for Fausto.

The factor's wife had quickly laid the table, and the four of them sat down to supper, a few slices of ham, white home-baked bread, poorly seasoned vegetables, and plenty of fruit. To Fausto and Gabriele it was a feast, all the more so because there was plenty of wine—a light wine they would once have despised, but which at that moment seemed better than the finest burgundy.

Between glasses Salatini told them how some youngsters had blown up a bridge over an important irrigation canal the previous day. He had prepared the plan himself and was clearly pleased with the result.

'But there's less partisan activity here than in other provinces nearby,' said Mariuccia.

'You're right,' said Salatini. 'But it's not our fault. Could we do any more?'

'Don't reproach yourselves!' said Fausto authoritatively. 'They've got mountains whereas we've just got flat land here in Padusa—flat, flat, flat. That's all.'

Instinctively they looked out of the window. The sun was setting and the wide barn seemed to spread out indefinitely over the flat, black earth, as far as the sun's red glow, now touching the endless horizon. There were few trees and fewer vines: everywhere bare earth, and green crops. Only occasionally did the canals break the monotony of the uniform plain, which, without a change, stretched to the dunes by the sea.

How could they organise large groups of partisans, Fausto insisted, in a country without any unevenness or differences in the landscape, without nooks and crannies and secret places? The only way to escape the German reprisals was to meet just before taking unexpected action. If a partisan formation occupied a village, the Germans and fascists would concentrate their forces and wipe them out at once. Only in the valleys at the far end of the province was there any change in the countryside, and there the permanent partisan groups operated. It wasn't the men's fault, it was the fault of the landscape that they couldn't work miracles, as people were doing elsewhere.

This was all elementary common sense, but Mariuccia was not completely persuaded.

'All the same, I think people haven't quite the temperament for it here. Maybe it's because we lack traditions, or because, if you go back, we're all descended from farm labourers.'

'Hey, what sort of heresy's that?' cried Fausto. 'Aren't they splendid people?'

'Perfectly splendid and I adore them. But they haven't got roots in their own homes, and in their own land, so they're not so constant, and they've got less initiative.'

'Shut up, Mariuccia! If Dionisio could hear you he'd say you were crazy, and tell you to be logical and reasonable.'

'He would! But with all his logic, he's in Switzerland. And I'm here!'

CIII

On the edges of the great valley in a tenant farmer's house at Ostello, Fausto (the fascists' nightmare, commander Achille whom they could never seize), was waiting for Gabriele and the communist Massarenti.

Bundled up in an old overcoat, with a hideous, much-washed woollen muffler and a pair of hefty shoes dropped by parachute by Allied planes a few days before, Fausto felt protected from the cold and damp of November. But he was dying for a smoke. In the morning, the moment he got up, he had collected the last stubs carefully kept in a tin and had made himself a cigarette of sorts with ordinary paper from a notebook. But he would gladly have exchanged even these splendid shoes for a packet of decent cigarettes.

To pass the time he went over what had been happening recently.

Peacetime now seemed to him like a sort of fairy-tale pre-history, and the war, as far as Badoglio's armistice, was already like a childhood memory. Fourteen months had passed since the armistice; and what interminably long months they seemed! Dionisio had only recently said goodbye before going for good, and Giulio had only recently left to join the partisans in the valleys. Yet he had lived through so much since that they already seemed far away, their departures already distant events on the yellowing pages of history.

Was he tired? No, he wasn't, he refused to be. But he was feeling the strain of every month in that terrible year, when every sunrise brought changes. In a short space of time he had lived through and accepted a way of life which no one could have foreseen: the old, solid values had crumbled and new ones had been born of them as if by magic; human nature had been revealed in aspects whole generations had never seen, and finally new men had sprouted like mushrooms.

Yes, he was a new man himself; in his small way he was someone. Who could have foreseen that the lazy womanising student daily lectured by Dionisio would one day become commander Achille, a leader now tipped for work of the highest responsibility after the war, pursued by all the political parties, offered membership of them all on a silver plate, and sent messages by the Allied generals from the other side, as if he were their equal? How could he go back to the university after the war, under teachers who were now used to treating him as some-one of importance? It made him laugh the way some of them, who had once given him such poor marks, now sent messages imploring his protection later on, when the purges came. His degree, he was afraid, was something he must definitely give up —but not so as to fling himself into politics. He was firmly determined not to give way to temptation, not to cash in on his work in the Resistance. Only a couple of days before, Salatini had said persuasively, 'After the liberation, you'll really get on. No one in Padusa's got more right to that than you.'

'What the hell d'you mean? Nations aren't ruled by their generals, still less by jumped-up leaders like me.'

'You underrate yourself, you know.'

'No, I'm judging myself objectively.'

This was Fausto's reply to his inner devil, who now and then

[321]

turned up to tempt him. But Salatini had persisted: 'But Fausto, politics is worth all the rest put together.'

'If you're trying to tickle my vanity, you won't succeed. Nothing seems to me more illusory than political ambition. A man sacrifices himself and his family, loses all inner peace, struggles his way through life, including Sundays and holidays—all so as to get some sort of political post and see his name in the papers a tenth of the size of that of the winner of the *Giro d'Italia* or the *Milan-Sanremo*.'

'Balls, Fausto. Only failures talk like that.'

'It's not balls in the least; you're the one who's deluding himself.'

So politics were out. He would go into industry and, after thirty years of poverty and frustrated longings, finally make his fortune. Why not? What was needed in industry was initiative and organising ability. Initiative he had all too much of, as he had already shown at the front, and his talent for organisation had often been praised by the regional military commands. Yes, the local partisan movement might not be anything very wonderful, but that was due to outside reasons everyone knew about, and was nothing to do with him—he had never put a foot wrong.

Now he looked back at the sudden attacks, all the fights and actions undertaken to save the people. Since Golfarini had left, and Bassini had taken over, the fighting had become much less terrible—which was just as well. The local fascists had realised that the hour of reckoning was near, and, knowing their crimes would soon catch up with them, had started back-pedalling. Fausto had taken advantage of the slackening of tension to build up an organisation capable of saving houses, factories, bridges and irrigation works when the Germans withdrew. He was proud of what he had done, and now that the Germans' collapse seemed imminent, and Allied troops were so close to Padusa, he was anxious to try out his organisation.

A bad few weeks might still lies ahead, but there was no doubt about it, by Christmas he would see Padusa free at last, and with it probably the whole of Italy.

At that moment Gabriele and Massarenti arrived together, looking grim.

'Heard yesterday's proclamation?' Gabriele asked shortly.

'Another from Mussolini?'

'No, from General Alexander to the Italian partisans.'

'What did he say, though, to make you look so furious?'

'We're to cut down our activity, stop large-scale operations, and go on to the defensive.'

Gabriele explained that if Alexander said this to the partisans, it meant that from the date of the proclamation—November 13th—the Allies would be giving up their offensive. This seemed the most ridiculous thing on earth, considering they were within range of the regional capital, and from the liberated Romagna it seemed the easiest thing imaginable to get to the Po. Even the fascists in Padusa were resigned to their Republic's collapse, now that Allied troops had entered Germany on the west and the Russian armies were coming in on the east. How could they fail to see that Hitler's Germany was desperately defending its own soil, and couldn't spare troops for the Italian front, which was now left to its own devices?

'Partisans and patriots everywhere will be demoralised by this proclamation, and it'll only benefit the Nazis and fascists. There's a hard winter ahead of us.'

'What I can't see,' said Salatini, 'is why they've flattened so many of our cities if they're not going to advance.'

'I tell you they . . .' Fausto burst out.

Gabriele slapped him on the back: 'You're both too young to know that there's disappointment in store even for those who are defending freedom and democracy. Just you take it from me.'

CIV

On the night of December 15th Gabriele slept at Rina's. He got up very late, at lunch time, put on his coat and went to sit outside behind the house. During the fine, starry night the mountain had suddenly brought frost into the *bassa*, between the river and the lowlands. Sodden with autumn rain, the dark, loamy soil had hardened, and where it was most swollen it had burst, making cracks all over the fields. The clods were at last breaking up, breathing and cleansing themselves for the coming season.

'See?' said Rina, pleased. 'The earth's healthy and the clods are breathing.'

But Gabriele took no notice, staring at flocks of doves flying high and nervously through the freezing air, looking elsewhere for food no longer to be found in the iron-hard ground. He thought sadly of the coming winter, of the endless war, and the way the people of Padusa would suffer from hunger.

Just as the wireless was announcing that Mussolini was to make a public speech in Milan, the members of the CLN turned up. After the collapse of July 25th, the Duce had made no public speeches, and it had seemed a proof that he had no confidence either in the regime he had created or in final victory. So if he was now going to face his audience again, it must mean something important.

'He's not going to cut the ground from under our feet by announcing general socialisation, I hope,' said Gabriele.

'Not a bit of it: he'll announce an offensive to reconquer Rome,' said Fausto, grinning.

'Laugh away,' said Massarenti, 'but people say he's seriously thinking of acting as mediator between Germany and the rest, as he did at Munich. Crazy bastard.'

'What's more likely is that he'll try and make a pact with the CLN to get northern Italy for himself,' said another.

'Very likely! As if the Krauts would let him!'

But the speech on December 16th announced nothing new and was only a weary collection of clichés. Mussolini tried to defend himself by railing yet again at the king, the generals, and the plutocrats who had betrayed him; yet again vindicating fascism's return to the Republican socialist programme of 1919 and explaining why the new regime had only partly managed to put it into operation. At the end came a vehement outburst: *'We shall defend the Po valley with our nails and with our teeth; the Po valley will remain Republican until the whole of Italy becomes Republican! From Milan must come the men, the weapons, the will and the signal for this uprising!'*

The furious applause of the fanatics in the Lyric theatre came over the radio. But how could ordinary fascists be in-

[324]

spired when, on the only subject that might have raised their
morale, the Duce sheltered in a sort of play on words? When
he spoke of the weapons that would soon restore the balance
of power, all he said was: *'It isn't a matter of secret weapons
but of new weapons that are secret until they're used in the
fighting.'*

This wasn't enough for people at the end of their tether,
who began to see, in this careless, wordy speech—such a contrast to the sharp eloquence of the old days—the melancholy
long-delayed confession that even Mussolini could see no way
out.

Gabriele rubbed his hands.

'General Alexander's proclamation a month ago helped
the fascists. But this speech of Mussolini's might have been
written on purpose to encourage us.'

Everyone agreed, delightedly.

'We've been depressed, this last month,' said Fausto. 'But
that's all over. Full steam ahead from now on!'

'People understand the ideals we're fighting the fascists for
a bit better now,' said Massarenti. 'These recent events and
even the troubles in the partisan movement have helped them
to. Suffering actually makes people more sensitive, when there's
a really strong idea behind their resistance, like freedom.'

Fausto looked him in the eyes: 'Fine, fine, you old communist! It takes a really universal idea to explain why so
many people have changed. Not just me, though I was a good-
for-nothing...'

'Now, no sackcloth and ashes!'

'Right, let's drop it. But there are other men and women
who've changed much more significantly.'

'Who are you thinking of?'

'Well, think of Moro! A failure like that, who's always
been a bit shady, is doing miracles these days. For months he's
been helping the C L N boldly, almost openly.'

'Mightn't it be self-interest?' said Massarenti.

'How on earth? D'you suppose he deludes himself we'll ever
give him jobs or medals?'

'No, I suppose not—he's nobody's fool.'

'And as for that woman of steel, my cousin—you certainly
can't say it's self-interest with her.'

Everyone agreed that Mariuccia Cavallari had marvellously improved once she knew she was fighting for a great ideal. She had been spoilt and wayward, negligent at home, selfish as a wife; whereas now she was an example to everyone. She not only held the most dangerous post in the Resistance with enormous zeal; no one else had made such financial sacrifices for the common cause—she had even sold her own jewellery. And she still gave away her farm products to the people of Guarda. When the others got up to put on their coats, Fausto stayed alone with Gabriele.

'D'you know what's moved me most about my cousin?'

'What's that?'

'Remember when that American parachutist landed on us and everyone was so yellow I couldn't get him taken in anywhere? Well, she got me out of it by offering to hide him at Guarda, and he's still there, you know.'

'Your cousin's a marvel, but you're a fool. Women on their own oughtn't to have men to stay.'

'Same as ever: sex all the way!'

CV

The German command had put up ungrammatical posters threatening death to anyone who sheltered escaped prisoners or Allied parachutists. Probably some radio message sent from his hut by Charles, the American parachutist, had been intercepted. The German commandant had already unleashed his bloodhounds, who were searching the district in alarming vehicles fitted with direction-finding radio sets.

The factor, Brogli, rushed into town to warn Mariuccia that it was impossible to keep Charles hidden at Guarda. 'They'll come in the end and kill the lot of us—first me, then him, and maybe even you, signora.'

Mariuccia felt more desperate than she would ever have thought possible. At all costs she must save Charles. If she could have analysed her feelings exactly, she might not have known whether, in trying to save him, she was acting out of a sense of duty, or out of her need to cherish the love that had suddenly made her seem young again. Brogli, with the peasant

[326]

cunning that never left him, even in the most difficult circumstances, was the one to decide.

'Signora, here in town you've got a pretty safe attic, with several ways out . . . and there's always the roofs to escape on, like cats . . . why not hide him here?'

'Yes, but how can we get him here?'

'It's time to bring up a new lot of wood for the heating. It's already sawn up, luckily. I'll go to the command and get a chit giving me permission to bring it, and I'll make room for him in the middle of the load. It's a good thing he's not very big.'

Mariuccia thought it an excellent idea and realised there was no time to lose. She went down to the garage, and, with Brogli's help, stoked and lit up the 'stove' of the old car. The factor sat beside her, and in silence they set off for Guarda.

During the journey she was thinking intensely; of her unlucky marriage, of her unhappiness and her husband's unhappiness, in his madness. Circumstances now forced her to take the man who had gained her love to the house in which she had lived with her poor husband. Was she wrong?

Brogli looked at her and understood, but in silence. Mariuccia drove carefully, but though her eyes were quick and careful her mind was uneasy, and even her abrupt, slightly violent movements as she drove showed her agitation. Brogli realised he must break through the nightmare silence that weighed on them. Delicately and respectfully, he put his stubby fingers on her shoulder. Mariuccia turned to look at him. 'Signora, we've got to save our skins, as we soldiers used to say in the first war, you know.'

This simple sentence seemed to loosen the tension and give Mariuccia new courage. 'Yes, Brogli, that's true. We've got to save ourselves and what we feel. . . .'

Mariuccia pressed her foot on the accelerator. In half an hour she was in the hut with Charles, talking softly, while outside Brogli pointlessly shifted sacks and tools, to justify his keeping guard there.

'The factor'll prepare the cart tonight and hide you inside the firewood.'

'Fine!'

'Give me the transmitter.'

'No, it's too dangerous.'

[327]

'We'll fix it under the car roof. I can easily get through, because I've got a regular farmer's pass, authorised by the Germans.'

'I can't expose you to dangers like that. You're not a soldier —I am.'

'But don't you see—if they catch you with the transmitter, they'll shoot you.'

She had already raised her voice, but now there was something hoarse and tremulous about it. As she said: 'It's a dangerous game for you, you know,' she was breathing heavily.

'Isn't it dangerous for you?' said Charles.

Mariuccia's eyes filled with tears.

'Oh, I'm up to my neck in it. . . . We Italians are fighting to scour out our souls, to redeem ourselves from dishonour. But you oughtn't to die for us.'

'Why not?'

'What did you know about us, before? When you taught your boys in Iowa, among those cornfields of yours, all you knew was that Rome was our capital city. I bet you didn't know we'd fought for Trieste, and probably Naples meant nothing to you except for its songs.'

'You're right. And marvellous songs they were.'

'Not content with joining up before you were called up, you had to become a sort of supervolunteer and parachute down on top of us. But now that. . . .'

'Now that what?'

'Now that I know you, I'll tell you this: save your life. There's no point in throwing it away on a useless front like this, which isn't going to advance your victory in the least.'

'There's no such thing as a useless front. Everything comes together in this splendid battle for freedom. It was love of freedom that parachuted me into a hemp field.'

'And there you found . . . me!'

Charles smiled. 'There I found you,' he said gently. 'And you want to keep me safe and sound, while you're risking a lot more than I am.'

He took her face between his hands and staring into her eyes asked: 'But why are you telling me all this?'

'Because it's my duty and because . . . well, because I love you.'

[328]

When they had settled all the details, Mariuccia pressed Charles's hand convulsively. He stood quite still, amazed at her dedication, and humiliated at having to stand by uselessly and simply wait to be transported.

Mariuccia drove into town as fast as she could, the transmitter, which Brogli had fixed firmly with thick wire, under the car roof. She was stopped by a patrol, and two Black Brigaders asked her for a lift. She took them in and started chatting.

'A cigarette, comrade?'

'No thank you, signora, I've given up smoking.'

'Quite right too! These cigarettes are like vitriol!'

They laughed, and a friendly atmosphere was established, in which suspicion melted away; the inside of the little car stank of cigarette smoke.

'If we find the American parachutist, we'll make him smoke a whole packet; that'll just about kill him off . . . the dog.'

There was more laughter and Mariuccia joined in it.

'What d'you mean, though?' she said. 'Are there any parachutists around here?'

'They're sprouting like mushrooms! While we're looking in one place they're dropping somewhere else. . . . The Germans are laughing at us.'

'But the creep who was dropped last night won't get into town,' said the other man. 'There's a cordon all round it and a mouse couldn't get through.'

'Oh, couldn't it?' retorted the first. 'Last night a bunch of underground *Avantis* got through under the Germans' noses— the whole town's full of them.'

'But parachutists won't get through, I can tell you.'

A few hours later the parachutist who had been dropped the previous night was in fact arrested; but Charles got through.

Brogli, who always knew exactly what to do, had gone to the headquarters of the Republican national guard in Guarda, and, calmly as ever, said he wanted to take the cart into Padusa.

'Wood for heating.'

'For Signora Mariuccia, is it? Lucky to be able to keep warm!' said the N C O, who had fled from Padusa with his wife and two children.

'Why,' murmured Brogli, 'can't your kids keep warm?'

[329]

'Only when they're in bed . . . and we keep them there all we can.'

'Poor pets! Now listen, Signora Mariuccia said to me: Brogli, she said, if there's any poor soul who's cold let him have a bit of wood. After all, we've got to help each other.'

The N C O looked at him in silence. Brogli nodded and the N C O smiled.

'I'll come with the cart this evening.'

'Right. Bring the shopping basket as well and we'll put a chicken in it. The signora's not going to count them.'

They laughed, and the N C O stamped the completed form, added another stamp saying 'Load examined,' and signed it.

'So long then, till this evening. Everything's nice and quiet, not a soul need know a thing.'

'Right!'

Brogli raised his arm in a slack Roman salute, and the N C O replied by saluting stiffly.

About eight next morning the cart reached Mariuccia's house in Padusa. She was looking out from behind the shutters, hardly able to control her agitation. When Brogli rang at the door, she opened the window, looking carefully casual.

'It's the wood, signora.'

'Again?'

'Well, the cold looks like staying with us, and if there's more bombing, how'll we get through with it?'

'Right, then.'

Mariuccia went down, with Brogli's help opened the big carriage gate, and the load went through.

'Everything all right?'

'Fine.'

They began unloading the wood, and soon Charles's large shoes appeared. He pushed himself out, slithering along the floor-boards of the cart, and then, leaping up like an acrobat, burst out 'All right!' in English. Mariuccia quickly put her hand over his mouth and took him off upstairs, taking two steps at a time. When they reached the attic, which was already prepared for him, they fell excitely into each other's arms, knowing they were free and safe and had got through the danger. Mariuccia then dropped into an armchair and for a long time looked questioningly at Charles.

CVI

For nearly a month they lived in a state of tension, counting the days. By day, Mariuccia went on with her difficult task of passing information to the Resistance. Through her, news and messages reached the attic, and from there were quickly passed on to the Allies, through the transmitter. Mariuccia was just a little paler than before.

After these broadcasts they relaxed for long intervals, finding comfort in their love. Tension vanished, they were both filled with a kind of languid tenderness; and, half awake after making love, memories that were not really distant, yet seemed so, floated before them. It was then that they exchanged their closest confidences.

Charles told Mariuccia about his family.

'My father was German. He emigrated to the States at the beginning of the century and married my mother, who was Scottish. He was a socialist who loved freedom and just couldn't breathe in the military Germany of the Empire. That's why he crossed the Atlantic—not because he couldn't make a living at home.'

'Didn't he ever see his country again?'

'No, never. I thought he'd forgotten it, but when he heard that Hitler had seized power, he cried—I saw him. That was the first time I heard the monster's name.'

'How your father must have loathed him!'

'So much that he never smiled again in the few weeks he survived, either at my mother or at the rest of the family. He was old, you see, and probably what finished him was the horror of seeing a new Germany that was even worse than the one he'd fled from.'

'Now I understand your love of freedom, Charles.'

'Oh, that's nothing special, all Americans feel the same. Maybe it's because everyone who came to our country, from the first colonists in the Mayflower, came looking for freedom.'

'That's very poetic, but the plain fact is most emigrants went to America to make a living.'

[331]

'You may be right. But they were looking for a better world as well. And that's why even now we feel it's our duty to fight so as to guarantee freedom and progress to everyone.'

'If anyone else said that, it might sound like propaganda. But you make it true.'

When Charles's birthday came round, Mariuccia tried to celebrate as best she could. She managed to make a good apple tart and brought a bottle of excellent wine from the now impoverished cellar, and in the silent attic they held a birthday party, tenderly exchanging looks and smiles.

'To your success, Charles!' said Mariuccia, raising her glass.

'To yours, my darling, and to victory very soon!'

'If we're here to see it,' sighed Mariuccia.

'D'you imagine I'm going to die? No fear! I hope for the best with a perfectly *German* pig-headedness!' He laughed gaily. 'As an American of German blood,' he went on, 'I ought to hold out better than the others, and live to see the end of all this horror and barbarism. And so I shall!'

Mariuccia smiled, but Charles noticed that she was twisting her hands together under the table. He got up, and kissed her hair.

'D'you know why I'm hoping for the best? Because in Tunis and in Sicily and at Cassino the bullets might whistle by, but Charles was always left standing . . . I've too many things to do, I haven't got time to die! And you'll live on with me.'

Heartened by this, Mariuccia flung back her head and opened her eyes wide.

'We'll live to do things that are worth doing.'

'Yes, darling. Life's rich, it's full of interest and surprise and sweetness—like finding you.'

'Thank you, Charles. But you love your ideals more than me. Tell me the truth, now.'

'It's the same with you, Mariuccia! Ours isn't ordinary love, just because we believe in so many of the same things, things that matter more than our love, more than our life.'

'Oh yes!'

And Mariuccia flung herself into his arms, her eyes glowing.

The nights were treacherous. Sometimes they heard bursts of firing in the distance; occasionally cars drove swiftly and mysteriously by; and they held their breath when they heard the rhythmic tread of the Nazi and fascist patrols. Every night, before she undressed, Mariuccia, in the bedroom she had once shared with Efrem, sat listening to the sinister noises outside, fists clenched, ears strained, almost enjoying the fear that went so deep into her spirit. Only about midnight, when Charles crept down lightly and silently from the attic, did her nerves relax.

One night, as she waited for Charles to come down after a transmission, Mariuccia sat looking out through a small opening in the shutter. At the end of the street she saw an unusually slow German vehicle approaching, and occasionally stopping, as if the driver were looking for a number or a door. The closer the car came, the more nervous she became. With bated breath she leant forward, and without realising it dug her nails in the wood of the window-sill.

When the car was a few yards from the house door she saw the curve of its radio direction-finding aerial slowly turning. At once she guessed what was happening and rushed upstairs to the attic, where, without a word, her throat paralysed, she jerked the plug violently out of its socket. Then, breathless and staring at Charles, she stood quite still.

'What's up?' he murmured.

Without a word Mariuccia pointed downwards.

'D'you think . . . ?'

With a faint movement of her lips she silenced him, then took his hand and pulled him after her, trying to make no noise. In a moment they were both behind the shutters, and could see the German van parked in the middle of the street outside their house.

'Now d'you see?' Mariuccia murmured.

All they could do now was try to get away.

'Come on . . . hurry.'

They ran down to the ground floor. Mariuccia went over to the car, opened the bonnet, and showed Charles a tin of petrol she kept hidden in the garage as a precaution.

'If we'd got to wait to light the stove with wood, we'd have had it!' she said.

While Charles was pouring in the petrol, Mariuccia ran to the old greenish door that opened on to a small parallel road, which was empty. At the first violent ring of the front-door bell they started, and leaped into the car, he at the wheel, she beside him. The engine fired, Charles went straight into second gear and shot outside. Down the empty road they dashed and came out on to the great highway that led to Porta del Mare, which they drove along without lights and with the accelerator pressed down hard. Soon they reached the outskirts of the town and Mariuccia breathed again. Two kilometres from the old ducal barrier there was a very sharp curve, known to motorists as the Devil's Bridge Turn. In the darkness Charles misjudged the distance and the car crashed into the low wall, zigzagged, somersaulted violently, and plummeted into the canal, its front wheels stuck in the thick mud.

There were no cries, no sound in the night but the lapping of the water.

CVII

At the end of January, when the German defences on the eastern frontiers of the Reich had been broken and the Russians were seventy kilometres from Berlin, even Goebbels had to announce dramatically that Nazi Germany was in mortal danger. What could Mussolini tell the Italians? He tried to divert people's attention with social matters and on February 2nd spoke in a revolutionary tone: *'Fascism is pledged to carry out its social programme, which means socialisation, the solution of a centuries-old historical problem that is now emerging in nearly every country. . . . What this great innovation means is explained in these words, which even the simplest can follow: until yesterday labour was the tool of capital, from today, in Italy, capital is the tool of labour . . . and for this reason we can really say that a new period in human history is beginning.'*

Perhaps Mussolini deluded himself that this would inspire his followers again; its effect, though, was anything but inspiring. If, after pouring scorn on socialist doctrine for over twenty years, Mussolini was now going back to his youthful theories, and actually declaring that the socialisation of the country would open a new period in human history, then it meant that he realised his days were numbered and that, in defiance of history, he was anxiously trying to start again. It was just a further proof that catastrophe was imminent.

In Padusa the fascists were in complete disarray, and many high officials had already begun cutting loose from the party. Those who stayed on were mostly small fry, local officials without too much on their conscience who hoped to get some credit at the end by saving people from German reprisals and preventing bloodshed.

On the other side of the barricades, several rash people had begun behaving as if the Allies were already at the city gates. Among these was Moro. Some months earlier he had thrown up his last German customers and since then he had spent his time collecting funds for the Resistance. Families were beginning to come back to Padusa and Moro buzzed about, stopping to chat with everyone quite casually about the way democratic representation was soon to be set up and assuring everyone in a fatherly tone that he himself would see to it that fascists who had not harmed anyone would be protected.

'I don't want to boast,' he often said, 'but I think I'm fairly well in with the new leaders.'

But he had miscalculated. The Allies were still some way off and were not to arrive for another couple of months. There might be little to fear from local fascists, who knew that collapse was at hand, and worried only about themselves; but the same was not true of outsiders. The Black Brigades in particular were full of adventurers who, pushed ahead by the advance of the Allied troops, had come up to the north of Italy, criminals who would stop at nothing and feared no future revenge, since they were quite sure that at the last minute they could vanish without a trace.

It was these desperadoes who were told that Moro had boasted of being in touch with an underground transmitter, which for several days had been giving the Nazis and fascists trouble. Two Black Brigaders at once rushed round to arrest him and, without going to the prison, took him to a small house in the country recently left empty by peasants, where they could carry out their 'delicate' operations in secret.

In the evening Moro was taken to a room beside the hovel where they had locked him, and to his amazement saw Francesco Tassinari, the ex-secretary of the GUF, sitting at a

[335]

table, looking bored; with him was a fat Black Brigade major who spoke with a Tuscan accent. In dirty uniforms, bearded and sinister-looking, stood the two soldiers who had arrested Moro; they looked quite desperate, as if they would go to any mad lengths to overcome the black fear in their hearts.

When Moro entered, Tassinari gave him a friendly wave and waited till he was seated before speaking. He began talking softly and coolly; but when he recalled the carefree university days, when they had so often been together celebrating what he called 'the successes of our friends and the glories of our country,' his voice became warmer, and he told Moro he had not forgotten their one-time friendship and would speak quite openly.

Moro listened woodenly, looking distracted. Ten minutes passed before Tassinari, clearly embarrassed, wound up his speech. 'I'm here to save you from being shot,' he said. 'But if I'm to do that you've got to give me some definite information.'

'What about?'

'You know what about: this underground transmitter, which seems to be guiding the bombers over us. In particular, tell us anything useful, help us to save these defenceless people.'

'So, in the name of our old student friendship, you suggest I become a spy. Very pretty, I must say!'

'The word "spy" is neither here nor there. You'd just be collaborating with the Republican authorities.'

'The Republic you created, though.'

'It can shoot you, you know, to defend itself . . . whereas I'm offering you a chance of rehabilitating yourself.'

'Rehabilitating myself because of what? Because I wasn't a fascist? But I'm not the least bit ashamed of that.'

'Oh come on, Moro, stop posing and get to the point!'

'Why d'you keep on in that tone? I'm a man of honour.'

'Stop striking these heroic poses!' Tassinari burst out. 'As if we don't all know you're a last-minute anti-fascist, and were perfectly happy to have black-market dealings with the Germans.'

Moro had suddenly turned pale, and wiped his brow with his handkerchief. He settled himself in his chair, then stared at Tassinari and began speaking fast, in dialect, as if the others didn't exist.

'Yes, I was the lousiest student in Padusa, I had dealings on the black market, which was the only way of paying off my old debts. I'm a failure, and in the just world that'll be built by free men after the war, I'd have to struggle to redeem myself. But now that I'm climbing up a bit, why d'you keep suggesting I save my life by doing something that'd throw me down into the depths of unworthiness? Why don't you save yourself, why don't you leave this sinking ship full of madmen and murderers?'

Tassinari gazed at him with tired, hooded eyes, and let him talk. But the Black Brigade major, who had managed to grasp some of what Moro was saying, finally lost patience.

'That's enough of these insults,' he said. 'Tassinari may allow them, but I don't. The choice is simple: either you talk and you'll be freed, or you won't talk and you'll go straight into the next world. Your grave's already dug.'

And he roared with laughter: his sarcastic tone made Moro's blood run cold.

'Well, well, this is a macabre little chat between corpses,' he said. 'I'll be dead tonight and you'll have about another fortnight—because the end's very near. So let's have a bit less arrogance, for heaven's sake.'

'Arrogance!' shouted the major. 'We've been far too patient with a creature like you.'

'You mean I'm not worth much. But now I want to re-habilitate myself in my own way; and I think it's worth it. Betrayal's no rehabilitation.'

'D'you really want us to kill you, then?' Tassinari burst out excitedly.

A long silence followed. Moro gazed into space, the major looked at Tassinari, and Tassinari stared at some insects wandering about on the filthy, uneven floor.

Tassinari had never felt so humiliated as he did then. Moro reminded him of the good old days, when he had been one of the most efficient secretaries of the G U F and seemed all set for a brilliant career in a country that was powerful and feared. Whereas now he had the pain of seeing his poor country brought low, and made into a battlefield for foreign armies, and of seeing himself, once a high official and now without authority, reduced to taking part in the wretched affairs of the police. Since he had supported the Social Republic he had had a feeling that everything he did was pointless. He tried hard to believe that Hitler would be victorious; but in his heart he knew perfectly well what the real situation was. Now only an impossible, miraculous new weapon could alter the outcome of the war.

On the other hand, he felt he must be loyal. He had believed in the 'new order' and, when things were going well and even Churchill applauded it, this was what, for years, he had worked for and supported. So his place, even in this terrible time, was here with Mussolini, who might be just as sad and depressed as he was, perhaps even more so, but who was carrying on. It would be cowardice to abandon him. What he must do was fight on to the end, even die. But why kill a poor wretch like Moro? And, on the point of disaster as they were, what could even that accursed radio they were interrogating him about matter?

Suddenly Tassinari rose with unexpected energy, and spoke firmly to the major and the other two. 'Wait for me outside,' he said. 'Leave me with this man a few minutes. I may manage better on my own.'

The three men dared not object when he spoke so firmly, and they left in silence, looking suspiciously at Tassinari. Alone with Moro, Tassinari stared straight into his eyes and murmured 'I want to save you. And don't think I'm doing it to make the anti-fascists think well of me. Partly I'm staying on here because I'm so revolted by all the coat-turning that's going on just now.'

'Then why d'you want to save me?'

'Because I can't bear the idea of seeing an old fellow-student of mine murdered.'

'But I can't see how you're going to get me out of here.'

'I'm not asking you to betray anyone, but just to tell us a few half-truths that'll put us on the track of the transmitter, even without getting your friends arrested. We could warn them.'

'I realise you're not trying to trick me; but complicated games like that never pay off. In any case, even if I did the dirty on them and betrayed my friends, those gloomy friends of yours would bump me off just the same.'

'I don't think so. I'm here, after all.'

'You're deluding yourself, you don't count any more. They've made up their minds—so let them kill me straight away.'

'But don't you want to live?'

'Who's the Latin philosopher who said it was absurd to fear death because when we're around it's not there, and when it's around we're not there?'

'It was the Greek, Epicurus.'

'There now! I'm already so far above life I can start quoting.'

'Oh, do stop it and listen!'

'Don't feel bad about it, Tassinari. Those creatures are quite capable of bumping you off as well, if you try and save me.'

'Goodbye then,' said Tassinari, and went out sadly.

Moro was alone for half an hour, then the major and one of the soldiers came in.

'Dr Tassinari left,' said the Major. 'He was busy.'

'Or maybe less wretched than you are,' said Moro.

The major looked as if he had been whipped. He became purple in the face, and started vomiting insults at his prisoner. The anti-fascists and the so-called partisans—he shouted— were criminals, often just out of gaol, people who betrayed, stole, ambushed soldiers and killed them, and fought Mussolini after sucking him dry. Of course Moro, a completely amoral man, was one of them. By this time the major was breathless and stopped to recover. Just then they heard machine-gun fire, very close at hand. The major started, then burst out angrily: 'I give you a minute to decide. Speak out, or you'll be shot.'

Moro had become pale; his strength was failing. But he clenched his teeth till they made a scraping sound, and managed to shout, brokenly: 'It's my turn now, but it'll soon be yours—you criminal!'

Then he summoned up the strength to spit his cigarette butt at the major, who stood perfectly still, as if paralysed, staring at him, glassy-eyed, until the soldier stuck his sten gun into Moro's stomach.

[339]

CVIII

After the partisans' flight from the lowlands, Giulio started working in the torrid heat of July with the *gruppi di azione partigiana*, the famous GAP.

Things were not at all as they had been in Padusa. The underground organisation was huge and complex, and there were far more partisans fighting, under first-class commanders who never appeared but made themselves felt unceasingly. In Padusa Giulio had thought himself one of the leaders, but now he felt one of the herd.

All parties and ideas were represented among the partisans at Sàvena, but most of the activists called themselves communists. Ordinary people were widely involved, that was clear, and Giulio realised fully that any great event needs enthusiastic popular support in order to get moving. The local military leader was a communist, once an exile, who had fought bravely in Spain with the republicans. Giulio managed to meet him, and a short talk was enough to show him the man was a born conspirator, who combined a flair for organisation with un-usual coolness. Carelessly dressed and rough-mannered, he was the opposite of the local political commissar, a charming, polished socialist, who daily went to meet death (his was the hardest job) with the relaxed and smiling air of a man going to a dance.

Giulio at once became friendly with Terremoto, an athletic workman of his own age, who commanded the most daring group in the GAP. He too was a communist, and said he had joined the party not for ideological reasons but because he saw it as the party that would fight. Giulio had known many brave men, but none who, like Terremoto, simply did not know what fear was.

'If they torture you,' he said, 'you've got to get it into your head that you're being operated on without anaesthetics. That's what conspirators have to think!' He had already proved he could put this into practice.

One day he asked Giulio to deliver a letter about a very delicate business personally; he was highly suspicious of everyone. 'At 98 Via Santo Stefano, below the bell tower, you'll find the name Amleto Zamboni. Knock three times with your knuckles and when the door opens ask for Bonaventura.'

'I see.'

'Don't forget, three small taps.'

Giulio walked fast to number 98, went into the hall and up two short flights of stairs, and gave the three small knocks rhythmically and precisely. The door opened slowly, and there stood the familiar figure of Professor Fantinuoli, ex-president of the Fascist Institute of Culture. It was like seeing a ghost.

'What. . . . You?' said Giulio, unable to continue.

Fantinuoli stood there, uncertain whether Giulio had knocked at the door by mistake, but perhaps rather more hopeful than dubious.

'Surprised to see me?' he asked in a low voice.

'Yes indeed, Professor, I never thought you were here.'

'Well, as you see, this is where I sheltered. . . .'

'Just sheltered? You're not working, then?'

Fantinuoli looked down.

'Yes—go on, go on!' he said, clearly embarrassed and uneasy: it was now he who seemed like a shamefaced student, trying to justify himself with hesitant replies. Giulio felt he had somehow shrunk, in his humiliation at having to admit himself wrong; and pitied him.

'It's one surprise after another these days, isn't it, Professor?' he said, trying to get over their embarrassment by sounding casual.

'It certainly is! We haven't met since I left Padusa.'

'I'm tremendously pleased to see you again, sir.'

'Remember the fight I had with Puglioli when I left?'

'I certainly do! You were arguing about methods of war propaganda.'

'Yes, but I was on Russia's side. Anyway, you must know I'm in the communist party now.'

'Have you been in it long?'

Fantinuoli hesitated before answering, then murmured something quickly. Crowding up from his subconscious came all sorts of things from the still recent past, fearful and paralysing shadows—respect for the regime, repressed doubts, pride in his position as a fascist official. For a moment he was

[341]

silent, absorbed in thought. Then he shook himself, gave Giulio a sheet of paper and said uneasily 'Give Terremoto Bonaventura's greetings.'

CIX

At the end of August Giulio took part in a dangerous action led by Terremoto. At ten o'clock at night eleven partisans in two cars drove to Sàvena prison, which was right in the middle of town. Three of them, including Giulio, were dressed as Germans, and four, among them Terremoto, were in the uniform of the Black Brigade; the rest were dressed as captured partisans, their faces bruised and battered to give the scene veracity. It was not a particularly new trick, but no one dreamed that such an important prison, guarded by dozens of armed men and not far from the barracks of the Black Brigade, would be the target for such a ruse.

Giulio, who was dressed as a Wehrmacht sergeant and was the only one who spoke German, spoke to the auxiliary police on guard outside the main door. Pretending to translate his impeccable German into Italian, he said he was taking some arrested partisan leaders into the prison. The guards at once gave the agreed signal and the main front door, as well as the secondary door inside it, were opened from within.

As soon as they were inside the four partisans hurled themselves on to the officer in charge of the prison, disarmed a sergeant and three guards, and cut the telephone wires. The fake Germans and Black Brigaders, meantime, had quickly disarmed the guards outside, and other guards who had turned up had got the same treatment in the few seconds' delay while they were puzzled by the fake uniforms. In a quarter of an hour, without losing a man, the partisans were masters of the most important prison in the district.

The warders were shut into the cells, and all the prisoners, including ordinary criminals, were freed. By freeing them all Terremoto hoped to confuse the police searches and give the freed partisans and patriots time to find shelter. The town was enormously impressed: it took a bold action to convince people that the partisan movement really mattered.

[342]

At the end of September 1944, the Allied attack on Sàvena seemed imminent; Allied troops were only about twenty kilometres away. The partisans knew that the local fascist command was uncertain whether or not to defend the city. There were tough men who wanted to defend it, and others, who thought mainly of themselves, who suggested flight. Really strong, bold action from the partisans might influence the fascists' decision in a definite way and save the city from destruction—which was what further defence of it would mean. Terremoto was the obvious man for the job.

'Six of us are going to do something really tough,' he told Giulio before leaving.

'What about me?'

'It's not for a decent chap like you. Anyway, there's only one officer needed and that's me.'

With five partisans and a case of T N T that weighed a hundredweight, Terremoto got out of a car outside the town's main hotel, at one in the morning. The German and fascist commands had set up their headquarters at the Excelsior, and all sorts of important people were living there; and besides this, on that particular evening, Germans, fascists and tarts were dancing in a large ground-floor room to celebrate a young German officer's recent decoration.

Terremoto parked the car outside the front door and got out with three of his men. Two German cars were parked beside it, and some soldiers were chatting by them, but Terremoto and the others went casually over to the hotel entrance, and the Germans seemed not to notice them.

They rang, and the porter came to open the door. Terremoto shoved him into a corner without either the German soldiers chatting outside or the guards inside realising it.

'Keep still and shut up. We're partisans,' he murmured in his ear.

'But you're mad! Don't you know the hotel's crawling with Germans? They'll make mincemeat of you!'

'Leave that to us!'

One partisan took his arm and took him out to the parked car, where he was taken prisoner. The other three went into action. Terremoto went into the office, where, with a pistol, he held up the clerks, while two partisans surprised and disarmed the four guards. A few yards away, in the big room, the fascists and Germans carried on dancing.

The three partisans who had stayed outside took the case of T N T in at the front door and ran up to the first floor with it; there they put it down, lit a seven-minute fuse, and dashed down again.

All the partisans were now back in the hall, and, having no time to tie them up, one of them machine-gunned the guards they had disarmed. Another two went over to the dance hall, held their machine guns level and fired, causing fearful panic; then, led by Terremoto, they all rushed outside. Two or three Germans waiting outside had pushed into the hall, alarmed at the shots; one of the partisans was wounded, but in the struggle managed to get out safely with the others.

Two minutes later the T N T blew up the hotel; but the partisans were already far away.

'My lads did more killing than they had to,' Terremoto said to Giulio next day, when he had finished telling him all about it. 'But war's war and when a man's excited he can't always control what he's doing.'

The attack on the Excelsior, although so successful, did not persuade the Germans and fascists to get out of Sàvena right away. But Allied troops were close to the city and the final attack was expected at any moment. At this point the military commander of the C L N decided to prevent the Nazis and fascists destroying the city before they fled, and he planned to occupy it before the Allies arrived. So he ordered the partisans operating in the mountains and out in the countryside to come into town, and in the second half of September nearly three hundred men crept secretly into the half-destroyed hospital building on the outskirts of the city, near Porta della Lana.

The German commander of the piazza, convinced that Allied troops would be coming into Sàvena in a few days, pretended not to notice. It was hardly worth risking lives against the partisans, who would go to any lengths just to keep control of the city a little longer.

A miracle of organisation had been achieved inside the hospital in the meantime. Everything was done with strict military discipline. There were guard duties, sentries, rations, reveille, plenty of food, and even mattresses; there were duty rosters in all the wards. It was an odd situation, but Giacomo, the political commissar, smiled calmly through it all and managed to persuade the partisans that it was all quite natural. For them, the absurd no longer existed.

Giulio was there, in command of a company; astonished as he watched the steely man who could eat a roll while he fired a machine gun, and failing to see how a partisan base that size could function only a kilometre from the barracks of the Germans and the Black Brigade.

Life in Sàvena was nearly normal. People went calmly about their business through the districts controlled by the partisans, and on to the city centre, where the fascists were still in charge. Thus the whole of October went by. News that the Allies were coming was heard occasionally, but the optimists were always contradicted by the facts.

By the end of the month, the nerves of the partisans shut up in the battered hospital were at breaking point. By then it was clear that the front had stopped and that for the present the Allies were not coming; so the Germans and the fascists, for all their misgivings, were still in charge of the city and were obviously not going to allow them to consolidate a partisan base. And sure enough, at the end of October and the beginning of November, the German command began to patrol the streets near the hospital, helped by the fascists, and to set up road blocks around it. An attack was clearly on the way.

It was then that Giulio heard the news that Linda had given birth to a daughter in Milan. It worried him, this new fatherhood of his; he seemed to feel almost guilty towards the child he had not yet seen and might never see. And his nervousness was vented on the Allies, above all. Everyone knew that the Resistance had decided to concentrate the province's best partisans in Sàvena only because the Allies had given assurances that they would be starting up their offensive again within the next few days; and now their refusal to occupy the city, when everyone knew that the remains of the German resistance could easily be overcome, seemed to Giulio a betrayal.

He remembered what Enzo had said, in particular his final words in Milan. Had Enzo been there, he would have said

[345]

yet again that the Allies reasoned coolly, not impatiently, like the anti-fascists. If the Allied authorities had decided to put off the liberation of the Paduan lowlands until the spring, the capture of Sàvena was quite unimportant. A single city more or less: what did it matter? Admittedly large numbers of patriots and partisans would die there, now and in the months that followed, because they had failed to occupy it. But could the Allied generals—he felt he heard Enzo's voice saying—care about the fate of a handful of fighters, when millions of men of all nationalities had already died in the terrible conflict, and so many others would die before it was over? If anything, the Allied strategists and generals would worry over the lives of their own men.

'They don't give a damn for your life,' he seemed to hear Enzo saying within him. 'And you, like the credulous idiot you are, have got yourself into this death-trap.' In his moments of blackest depression these words went round and round in his head; but he understood the moral value of the task he had undertaken too well to lack strength to hold out against them.

The attack began on November 4th. The Germans concentrated mortars and cannon in the district and began firing heavily and methodically at the buildings occupied by the partisans. They had a couple of old tanks as well, that looked as if they were not mobile enough to be used at the front. Fascist soldiers of the Black Brigade, armed with machine-guns, were lying in ambush all round them.

The German commander of the piazza, who had underestimated his enemy, was counting on burying all the partisans in the ruins. And so he would have done, had the partisan commander, after consulting with his aides, not decided to break out after ten hours of German shelling, which had killed and wounded a great many.

At six in the evening, when shadows were falling over the city, the partisans broke out. Groups of them left by various exits, planning to close in concentrically on Porta della Lana, where the main enemy force was gathered. If they could once get past it they would be free: free to go out towards the mountains, free, if they wanted to, to hide in the suburbs and then, at the opportune moment, re-enter the city walls.

Shortly afterwards a great glow arose from Porta della Lana; it was some tanks, loaded with ammunition, exploding with a terrible roar. The partisans, led by the invulnerable Terremoto, his hair blowing in the wind, had surprised the concentration of enemy troops and thrown them into confusion.

But the small group led by Giulio failed to reach the city gate. Seeing the street barred by a tank his men backed towards the canal bank, which ran north of the hospital; then, hidden in a thick smoke-screen, they dived into the water and quickly reached the far bank. From the smoky opposite bank of the canal someone shouted 'Halt, who goes there?'

'We're Black Brigaders, you fool! Don't fire.'

So Giulio and his companions escaped, and no one in the group lost his life.

But their troubles were not over. At the beginning of December the many fascist troops in Sàvena began an energetic and methodical offensive against the partisans within the city walls, meaning to wipe them out entirely. All roads leading into the old city, which was surrounded by an inner avenue, were closed by walls and barbed wire, and it was only possible to enter at places corresponding to the old gates, where German soldiers, Black Brigaders and police were on guard. Fascist headquarters, the Prefecture, the barracks of the Black Brigade and of the G N R and the most important offices of what could now be considered a stronghold, were protected by barbed-wire entanglements and machine-gun posts. Protective walls, with firing-holes in them, were set up at strategic points.

The German command declared the old city a prohibited area. German soldiers were forbidden to enter, and were rarely seen there.

Faced with the indomitably brave and aggressive partisans in the G A P, who contrasted with the quarrelsome, obstinately cruel fascists who had mostly swept down on Sàvena from central Italy, a German general had the idea, which was not a bad one, of keeping the Wehrmacht soldiers out of the battle altogether. While partisans and fascists killed one another, the Germans could serve elsewhere.

The front was now only a few miles from Padusa and somehow the Germans had to hold it. But the German army had almost collapsed and was now entirely without supplies, so when General Alexander's men made even the smallest attack, things became hopelessly difficult for them. German soldiers moved feverishly along the main road, to and from the front. In the daytime they marched or cycled, often singly; at night they moved in columns, mostly in old vehicles drawn by horses. Grey, silent, and shabby, they aroused feelings of sadness rather than fear.

The police chief, shut up in the impenetrable police building, decided to sell his life dearly. People said that he had tried approaching the CLN in order to prepare a way of escape for the day of defeat, which was now imminent, but that, having been sharply rebuffed, he had grown savage. There was no doubt that he was good at his job and the shrewd action he directed that winter resulted in a great many arrests. In particular he made use of some partisans caught by the police and made to collaborate. Their lives were spared on condition they helped the fascists, and, escorted by staunch Black Brigaders, they patrolled the city streets, having every partisan and patriot they met and recognised arrested.

These mopping-up operations were careful and frequent, and during one of them, on New Year's Day itself, Giulio was arrested. In the evening he was taken to the building belonging to the university faculty of pharmacy, which was used as a prison, and flung into a huge, cold, damp room with a walled-up window. The prisoners—dirty, stinking, ragged— were huddled together for warmth against the far wall, some of them groaning constantly, nerve-rackingly: these were the men who had survived torture.

Giulio flung himself down beside the group, and dozed. After half an hour he awoke, smelling an unbearable stench, and realised that while he was asleep he had been pushed towards a hole in the floor, which, in that disgusting room, was used as a latrine.

He moved away from the stinking corner at once, but could not sleep. In spite of the cold his throat was dry and he needed water. Beside him an old man sat cross-legged on the floor, with a blanket over his shoulders, and Giulio asked him if there was anything to drink.

[348]

'Nothing doing. They bring water once a day. You've got to keep a reserve in your stomach, like a camel.'

At seven next morning two Black Brigaders came in. 'Come along, the last man arrested: Giorgio Bassi.'

Giulio rose and went with them. 'The chief's waiting to question you,' one of them told him. 'And I warn you, don't try and be clever. If you do, you'll be in trouble.'

Giulio was taken into the office, where the captain was standing behind a desk, with a half-empty bottle of wine in front of him and a packet of American cigarettes taken from some partisan prisoner. Beside him stood a Black Brigader, holding an ox-hide whip.

Giulio thought his last hour had come. In any case, since he had been in the hospital at Sàvena he had had a presentiment that he was going to die.

'Are you from Padusa?' the captain asked abruptly.

'How could I hide it? You can tell from my accent, just as I can tell from yours that you're from Tuscany.'

'Who are you, and what do you do?'

'I'm Giorgio Bassi, representative of a pharmaceutical firm.'

'Sure you haven't made a mistake? Aren't you a teacher?'

The man with the ox-hide whip came closer.

'Sir, shall I get going and make him talk?'

'No, wait a bit.'

Just then there was a noise outside, and a young man with his hands tied behind his back was brought in.

'This bastard won't give the names of his accomplices in the attack.'

The captain snatched the ox-hide whip from the soldier's hands, and struck the prisoner violently on the face and chest over and over again, till he swayed and fainted on the floor.

'Bring him back to me when he's revived, and prepare him spiritually. . . .'

Then he turned to Giulio again: 'Well, what about it?'

Giulio knew of Captain Rosi's cruelty, which, since his brother had been killed in the mountains fighting the partisans, had known no bounds: he had heard of it from his fighting comrades, and knew that his men were even worse than he was—using not only ox-hide whips but red-hot irons and icy water hosed on naked bodies. Their special instrument

[349]

of torture, though, was a hermetically sealed gas mask which they put on their victim till he turned purple with suffocation. This they might repeat three or four times, till the wretch agreed to talk.

Some weeks earlier, these men had whipped Terremoto's brother until he lost consciousness, to get a confession out of him. They thought his fainting was faked, so they pulled off his trousers, and made him sit on a lighted electric fire.

Giulio tried to keep calm and behave cunningly: it was now a matter of defending life itself.

'In the war I served with the tanks, like you.'

'A fat lot I care. Tradition doesn't bind me to traitors who kill our comrades.'

'Kill? Me?'

'If you haven't, you're quite capable of it . . . Giulio Govoni. That's your name, isn't it? I'll get you to confess it in the end.'

'Under torture?'

'Certainly, if I have to.'

'That's not fair. Justice proves a man guilty first, and doesn't condemn anyone out of hand.'

'Shut up, boy. I'm not taking lessons, even from a teacher like you.'

'I'm not trying to teach you—I'm just appealing to a much-decorated officer.'

A door opened, and a soldier came in to ask the captain to go into the next room for an urgent telephone call. He was away a quarter of an hour. (It was only the following day that Giulio heard from a servant what the captain had been told on the telephone. At dawn they had found the body of a Black Brigade sergeant, the man who had thought up the gas-mask torture. On a rough piece of cardboard, left on the corpse, was written in red pencil: 'Thus end all hangmen'.)

When he came back the captain's face was furious; he sat down at the desk and made Giulio sit on a stool.

'You appealed to my honour as a soldier. Well, I'll show you I'm a gentleman. We'll send your photograph and documents to the authorities in Padusa. It's lucky they're not far.'

'Now that's what I call sense—'

'Shut up! Don't interrupt me! So we'll see whether you're

Giulio Govoni or Giorgio Bassi. And if you're Govoni—as I have reason to believe—you'll get the bullets you deserve in your back.'

It was several days before the answer came. The authorities in Padusa confirmed that Signor Giorgio Bassi was properly documented in their records; the prisoner's photograph corresponded exactly to his and was not that of Giulio Govoni.

The inquiry sent to Padusa had reached a senior official who was working for the Resistance.

CX

In spite of the reply from Padusa, Giulio was still suspected of partisan activities and kept in prison. From the faculty of pharmacy prison he was transferred to the town's main gaol. There he was just a number: there were all too many cases more important than his.

At first he was alone, in darkness, in a tiny cell. But after a week an ex-priest arrived to share the cell with him.

Ever since boyhood Giulio had thought that unfrocked priests were men who had failed to withstand the temptations of the flesh. He had always been harsh towards what he liked to call the Italian disease of eroticism, so he was naturally highly suspicious of such people. It had never crossed his mind that in many cases when a man gave up the priesthood it might be as a result of some spiritual crisis, and nothing to do with women.

His cell-mate's case had been a spiritual one: Mario Civolani was chaste. He told Giulio that he had had no relations with women, even after leaving the priesthood, and Giulio believed him because it was all too clear from the way he judged human values in ordinary conversation that he was anything but sensual.

Civolani was only two years older than Giulio, but he looked much more. He had left the priesthood at the age of twenty-seven, but in spite of an excellent degree in literature, he had not been able to teach in the state schools, where his real vocation lay. This was a result of the Lateran Pact, as part of which the State had agreed not to allow ex-priests into any job where they would be in contact with the public. So, until war broke out, when in spite of a weak constitution he had been called up, he had lived more or less on the fringes of society by giving private lessons. But he felt no rancour against the Church, which had prevented him earning a decent living, or the private schools, which had paid him so wretchedly, or against the officers who had constantly humiliated him during his military service. He was not a saint, but he was undoubtedly a good man, and a gentle one.

Now he was in prison. He had no idea why, and no one had ever answered his questions. Admittedly he had been against the fascist regime, having ideas that were halfway between the liberal and the socialist position; but he had never taken any part in politics.

When they had become real friends Giulio finally managed to make Civolani speak of his religious upheavals.

'I lost my faith gradually, as so often happens. I felt it my duty to meditate on God, on the soul, on immortality, and also to be in a position to quieten the doubts of my people. Whereas. . . .'

'You were going through a crisis yourself.'

'I was. And the more I felt the sublimity of Jesus, the less I could believe that he was God; the more I was convinced that Christianity's law of love is what brings about every civilising development in society, the less I believed in Catholic dogma.'

'But you must have tried to react against that.'

'For months—for years, till I felt quite helpless and asked the bishop for an audience. I wept like a child before that holy man, who tried to answer my terrible doubts.'

'In a case like that, it's more than a bishop you need.'

'I know. But he didn't try and talk me back into faith. In fact finally he told me he still respected me and that I was to stay on because I'd get over the crisis.'

'Didn't you ever think of doing what he suggested?'

'I felt too ashamed to keep saying Mass without belief.'

Giulio thought it over: Civolani's religious crisis was like his own. If his friend, a priest, had had the courage to solve it, then why could he not face his own sincerely? Why did he keep going to Mass, telling himself that the light of faith would some day remove his doubts? Yet he could not cut the thread that still bound him to his mother and to the creed of his childhood.

After a few weeks together, Giulio had become deeply fond of his cell companion and felt he could not do without him. Then, one night, the guards came to take Civolani away. Giulio saw he was trembling.

'They'll kill me,' he murmured in Giulio's ear, while he hurriedly put on his shoes.

'Nonsense! They haven't even interrogated you!'

'That's true. But storms break over those who don't matter and have no one behind them.'

And in fact, after making him dig his own grave, they shot him a few hours later. Giulio never found out why. But the killers were not concerned with reason. A couple of men were to be killed as a reprisal that night, and someone half asleep had jabbed a finger at a list, and struck Civolani's name.

CXI

On March 15th, shortly before sunset, Giulio was ordered to dress quickly: he was to go for an interrogation at the German headquarters.

To his surprise he was handed over to a German guard in civilian clothes, who took charge of him politely and walked along Via Santo Stefano with him. Without a word they walked side by side, their footsteps echoing under the low arches of the old porticoes. Occasionally Giulio glanced at his guard, who walked fast and confidently, and wondered why this respectable-looking man, who was no more than thirty-five, was dressed in civilian clothes. Could he be a soldier on convalescent leave lent to the political police, who were short-staffed?

Then he remembered that sometimes the Germans had had arrested men accompanied by police dressed in civilian clothes so that other Resistance men would be trapped into approaching them without warning. The streets were crowded, and the chance of meeting someone alarmed Giulio, both for his own sake and for anyone else's.

The prickly, suspicious silence, the fact of walking head down, close to the walls, increased his nervousness. But the state of tension was unexpectedly broken by the man himself, who touched Giulio's arm and said: 'Cigarette?'

Giulio stopped and stared at him. It was the first time since he had been in prison that he had heard anyone speak to him in a human, almost friendly tone. The man understood his surprise, smiled, and, as he was lighting the cigarette, said, in almost perfect Italian, 'Not all Germans are bad, you know.'

Giulio was silent and they set off again. This time it was Giulio who started talking again, still in Italian.

'Are you really German?'

'Yes, I am—I'm from Nuremberg.'

'Ah, Nuremberg. What a beautiful city.'

'Yes, it's very beautiful. At least . . . it was.'

The man's eyes were misted with sadness.

'It *was*; why d'you say that?'

'Because *alles kaputt*: houses . . . families . . . all destroyed in that massacre.'

'Have you had any definite news?'

'There's no one to send it . . . now.'

For a while they said nothing, both of them wrapped round in what was happening to them personally.

'This accursed war,' Giulio said softly.

'*Ja* . . . this accursed war!'

For the first time they looked into each other's eyes, each seeing an expression of profound disgust in the other's face.

'Did you want this war?'

'Maybe, maybe not. No one thought for himself. The Germans all thought alike. When we give ourselves to a leader, he's the master of our destiny. He told us a war was necessary for Germany's life. The Germans said yes, and I was one of them.'

'Then why d'you curse the war now?'

'Because I thought war was different . . . it had to be. Whereas look—I'm taking you from gaol to somewhere worse, and tonight there'll be others killing civilians and others setting fire to towns—burning old people, women, children!'

The man covered his face with both hands, then spat on the ground, as if to eject something horrible.

'Ah . . . how filthy it is!'

Giulio guessed he must have lived through something terrible in order to lose his German stiffness so much that he could talk to an Italian political prisoner in this way. He could not be pretending—the sincerity of his scorn was too obvious. Giulio was just going to ask him why he was so upset when the air-raid siren moaned loudly, and as the few people in the streets plunged into the shelters, the two of them dashed into some houses that were already damaged, with strong outer walls still standing, and a broken but solid archway that seemed to offer shelter. Here they hid and looked up at the flashing sky, while the rhythmical roar of the Allied bomber formations drew nearer and nearer. The first bombs fell at a distance, in the southern part of Sàvena, and the air was full of the roar of explosions and of crumbling buildings.

'There! That's war for you! Nothing but destruction! It's not only soldiers who are killed, but children. And I used to make toys for them. . . .'

'You made toys?'

'Yes. And I often came to Italy as part of my job. Then I came back this way and saw the kids scared when they looked at me.'

'You've done some terrible things.'

'We have indeed. One day, when they know . . . what I've seen, Germany will be hated more than anything else in the world. Yes, it will be! *Über alles in der Welt.* . . .'

He passed his hands over his eyes, as if to remove the tormenting vision from him.

'What d'you mean? The torturing of prisoners in concentration camps?'

'No, something much worse.'

As they lay there, side by side on their bellies, waiting for the storm of fire to pass over them, the explosions of the bombs, the anti-aircraft fire crackling through the air, and the roar of aeroplane engines, all seemed like an obsessive counterpoint to their inner suffering. The German felt he must abandon the discipline of silence to make this man, who was fighting the bloodthirsty Nazi tyranny, understand him; so,

[355]

when the noise was less deafening for a moment, he spoke:
'Marzabotto—d'you know where that is?'

'It's not far from here.'

'And d'you know what happened there?'

'An outrage, as far as I've heard.'

'*Ja*. An outrage. That's the word.'

'Were you there?'

'Yes, I was. I'd joined the 16th battalion of the SS division,
and there were even Italians in German uniform with us.
They told us we must take action against the partisans who
were in control in the mountains. A fighting action, like in
Russia, like in Yugoslavia . . .'

'I see.'

'No, but it wasn't like that. The people who paid for it
were whole families—children, old people, women.'

'And what about the partisans?'

'They fought bravely. A lot of them fell, a lot managed to
escape, and as the action hadn't been completely successful the
major ordered us to wipe out the whole population.'

'Then did you really kill unarmed people?'

'Yes, I did, I did.'

'What an appalling thing for a man in uniform to do.'

'You're right. I'm not ashamed of being German, but I'm
ashamed I was ever a Nazi and humiliated by the thought
that Nazism turned us into killers of women and children.'

'I see.'

'Oh, you can't see completely, only a man who'd seen it
could really understand. Priests killed at the foot of the altar
in front of children gone mad with terror, pregnant women
ripped open, children's corpses with sticks pushed up between
their thighs, panting old women chased through the corn and
killed by grinning murderers, pile of corpses, limbs strewn
everywhere . . . and I was there, and had to fire. What could
I do? I felt I was a wolf in a herd of wolves. I tried to look
away but what was the use? There was always someone who
shot straight . . .

'In the mountain cemetery of Casaglia there was a massacre:
a hundred and fifty women and children crowded outside the
chapel, then, among the gravestones and crosses of the tombs,
they were cut down by machine-gun fire and finished off with

hand grenades. When it was over they left me there on guard, with all that carnage. My head was empty. I tried to persuade myself it was only a horrible dream. D'you know what happened?'

'No.'

'From under the corpses, a child peeped out . . . he dragged himself out on hands and knees, and saw me, but he wasn't afraid, he came over towards me.'

'And what did you do?'

'I was as still as if I'd been turned to stone. The child limped forward and stared into my eyes. I had to run away.'

'It's frightful. . . .'

They were silent, both tortured by feelings which could not be expressed. The raid was over, and in the distance they heard the fire-engine sirens as they rushed where the damage was greatest. Giulio and the German got up in silence and walked on without speaking. Suddenly the German cried 'I can't bear it, I can't. . . .'

Giulio saw him run wildly to the end of the road, and there lost sight of him.

CXII

As soon as he was free Giulio searched for Terremoto, but heard he had been killed in action.

On March 23rd, the anniversary of the foundation of Fascism, an officer of the National Republican guard, who lived in the same building, knocked at the door of Giulio's shelter.

'You're a socialist, aren't you?'

'Why?'

'D'you know about today's meeting of the Council of Ministers?'

'No, what did it say?'

'That from April 21st all firms with at least a hundred workmen and a million capital will be socialised.'

'So what?'

'We're preparing the ground for the socialist party. We're not enemies. . . .'

'Maybe; but you've come to the wrong place, I'm afraid.'

Sadly the officer left him and Giulio thought about the paradox of these latter-day revolutionaries, and the way they were now trying to put through a programme more radical than that of the communists. Among the supporters of the wretched Republic quite a number were deluded enough to think they could make these last-minute approaches, and persuade their enemies to listen and forgive them.

The command at Sàvena, meantime, thought it best for Giulio to return to Padusa. With fascism crumbling all about them, he was most useful in his own province, where he knew everyone and every place to hide. A laconic message from the command read: 'For the common cause, go to Padusa.' Giulio read it and re-read it, and turned it round in his hands, then put it into his pocket, buffeted by his own thoughts. What about Linda and the daughter he had not yet seen? The impulse to rush away to them became stronger, but the command's terse message weighed on him. For a long time sentiment and duty fought in his mind. Wasn't it his duty, perhaps his first duty, to go to Linda and his daughter? He walked absently along the ring road round Sàvena till he found a bench that had survived and sat astride it, thinking.

I must think it over, he said to himself. I must weigh everything up. Then suddenly, like a light, came an obvious idea that seemed to settle everything and release him from his dilemma. Of course, he thought, I can go to Milan and come back again. Ah . . . but who can guarantee my getting there in all this chaos, and when?

The German lines were nearly crumbling, and in those hysterical days any journey, long or short, was an adventure. The least thing—revenge, casual theft, a mistake—might make a man fire at someone he had never seen before. And a dead man meant nothing: he was like a stone that people might trip over, but would not think of pitying. Everyone was in a hurry: such loneliness had never been seen before, among people who needed cunning to survive at all.

Giulio was persuaded that the order the command had given him was reasonable and must be obeyed: it would mean putting off seeing Linda and the baby for only a few weeks. A trustworthy messenger was just leaving and Giulio gave him a letter for Linda, telling her he was free and explaining why he couldn't join her. Then he left for Padusa.

There, a few days later came Linda's laconic reply: 'I'd have been even happier if you could have come, but I know there are some things I mustn't hope for. There are things that matter more to you than me. But remember your daughter has no one but you.' This was followed by an L, which seemed to him mysterious and intimate.

Giulio read the note several times, his heart contracted with remorse.

The day he got back to Padusa he saw Enzo again, after several months apart. They made no fuss about meeting again, both having the sort of shyness that made them easily embarrassed, and so they played everything down—what was happening, the dangers they had run—and said hullo as flatly as if they were just saying good morning. But their eyes showed what they were feeling. During all the past months Enzo's only real suffering had been caused by his fear for Giulio; but this was the last thing he was going to admit.

As always, his first words were admonitory. 'You take care,' he said. 'The Germans may be collapsing, but you may get knocked on the head at the very last minute.'

Although he was glad to see neo-fascism nearing its end, Enzo was afraid that democracy was not the panacea Giulio was hoping for.

'Freedom is all very fine,' he said, 'but Italians have no sense of proportion and won't use it the way the idealists are hoping.'

'Why are you such a pessimist?' Giulio asked.

'Because it was like that even before Mussolini came to power.'

'But experience improves people.'

'Let's wait and see.'

To Enzo, the thought of Russia was a nightmare, and Giulio was astounded to hear him say he was afraid the Soviets aimed to impose Communism by force over the whole of Europe.

'What on earth d'you mean? When Hitler's defeated that'll mean the end of all violence and of all wars.'

'D'you really think so?'

'How can you doubt it? The Allies of the East and West have won the war together, and together they'll rebuild the world.'

'Ingenuous as ever!'

'How can you say that? At Yalta only a few years ago the three great leaders agreed on everything!'

'Giving Stalin complete victory in Poland and Yugoslavia, and as for the rest. . . .'

'Russia's made colossal human sacrifices, and couldn't be left out. But these are details, compared with the understanding on what really matters.'

'And what's that?'

'The task of the San Francisco conference.'

'Heaven knows how long you'll have to wait.'

'No, Enzo! Work's starting there on April 25th, and an international security organisation will be set up.'

'Which won't make anyone secure. . . .'

There was no way of convincing Enzo, who believed only in hard facts and raged above all against Churchill and Roosevelt. Conducting the war in Italy at a snail's pace, refusing to attack the Balkan peninsula, letting the Russians get to Budapest and Vienna before them, and now even to Berlin and Prague, they had handed over half Europe. He thought them both lacking in understanding, puffed up by propaganda.

At this Giulio smiled. His ever-practical brother seemed to him quite divorced from reality.

He was about to leave when Enzo confided in him, in a low voice, that he had decided not to re-open the tailor's shop, but to go into industry. He was sick of seeing people with far less talent than himself easily making fortunes, while he grew old without prospects, sweating hard for the small savings he managed to put away. He realised he had unusual talent as a designer and refused to rot in the shop any longer, measuring the crutch and shoulders of a lot of mean, snobbish customers. Already he had come to an agreement with an old friend who was running an important fabrics factory in Milan; and as soon as the war was over they would set up a firm and start work.

Nothing could have cheered Giulio more than this: he had always urged Enzo onwards and now the enforced idleness of those dreary months seemed to have given him the courage he needed to prove himself. There was a new light in his once-melancholy eyes, which now looked firm and confident. Giulio wanted to ask for details but there was no time. He had to leave on an important mission: a British officer was expecting him.

Captain Wilson had been parachuted behind the German lines—if they could still be called lines. The son of an English diplomat, he had spent three years at school in Rome and spoke good Italian, so he had been chosen for the delicate task of keeping the British command informed about the movements of the retreating German troops. The C L N had given Giulio the job of collaborating with him. They met in a country house a few kilometres from San Biagio, and left together.

Wilson was a real gentleman: cultivated, intelligent, and very friendly. But he was highly suspicious of even the most credible information given him by people who could be trusted. This upset Giulio, and he made it plain to Wilson; who, quite unruffled, would reply 'Trust is good, but mistrust is better. I learnt this proverb in Italy, Machiavelli's country.'

They often quarrelled. Wilson never missed a chance of scoring over the Italians, and often did so rather aggressively; Giulio refused to take it lying down.

One day, when a young partisan who had promised him a bottle of real brandy and had been paid for it in advance sent him a bottle of bad Aquavite instead, Wilson became furiously angry, hurled the bottle out of the window, and, purple with rage, began cursing Italy and the Italians in English. It was monstrous—he shouted—that a youngster who was risking his life for the cause of freedom should sink to cheating a man who had come there simply to help him and his comrades. But plainly it was impossible to trust anyone in Italy! 'Nobody's a gentleman here,' he kept shouting.

Giulio let him pour it all out, but when he saw him a few hours later, good-humoured again, he tried to break the ice. It seemed hardly suitable to pretend nothing had happened.

'So you don't think much of Italians.'

'I do, but I'd think more of them if they were less cunning.'

[361]

'What d'you mean?'

'That they see their neighbour as an enemy to be overcome with cunning; that they make promises they don't mean to keep; and that they make agreements with a mental reservation that they'll find a way out of them later.'

'D'you really think we're all like that?'

'Not all; but too many of you are.'

Caught on the quick, Giulio wanted to retort that this sort of cunning wasn't unknown in Northern Europe, and that if there were now more tricksters in Italy, it was because of economic difficulties, lack of education and so on. But he said nothing. These burning humiliations, after all, were the price that must be paid to the Allies for Mussolini's vulgarity and scorn over twenty years, when, in the name of a superlative Italy conjured up in his megalomaniac brain, he had thundered against the Western nations.

For a good half hour they were silent, avoiding each other's eyes, Wilson doodling on a sheet of paper, and Giulio poking about in his laundry bag. Then a youngster bringing a note to Giulio from Gabriele relieved the tension.

'If I'm not mistaken,' said the note 'today's your 32nd birthday. Many happy returns . . . you've picked a fine day for it. The front's collapsed.'

Giulio said goodbye to Wilson and went out into the half-empty piazza with the lad. They were walking slowly in the soft spring evening, when suddenly the boy from Enzo's shop appeared.

'Sir! Sir, I've been looking for you. . . . Have you heard? Your brother. . . .'

Giulio turned pale, and stopped. The boy's tone and hesitation were all too eloquent.

'What's happened? Tell me, quick!'

'An accident on Ponte di San Giorgio . . . his arms are injured. . . .'

'My God—where is he?'

'At the hospital at Monte Santo, nearby.'

For a moment Giulio stood petrified. Then he shook himself, and, his heart thudding, began running to the hospital, while the boy dashed after him, shouting over and over 'But he's not dead, sir, he's not going to die.'

CXIII

April 15th: the Allied radio announced that the German
army was in confusion, and that liberating troops would soon
be at Padusa.

Fausto Carrettieri had been lying low for several days.
One morning, as he was cycling along the river bank with
his lieutenant Salatini, he was fired at by a small Allied plane.
Even hurling himself off the bank had not saved him—the
tenacious pilot had followed the two men and machine-
gunned them, and Fausto had flesh wounds in the ear and
cheek. He had asked for a week's rest. Even his steel nerves
were beginning to wear thin.

Massarenti took over from him; and Giulio had bicycled
about all day, checking the way orders from the Provincial
Committee of Liberation were being carried out.

Now, with Captain Wilson, he was stuck in a tenant farmer's
house fifty yards from the highway between Argenziana and
Padusa. The house was crammed with refugees bombed out
from a nearby town.

Wilson sat astride an old chair, leaning against the outer
wall of the house, with Giulio beside him, sitting on a stone,
taking advantage of a quiet moment in the twilight to read
a two-month-old copy of *Avanti* from Rome, which had reached
him by crossing the lines. He thought the leading article,
which was by Giuseppe Saragat, important—it interpreted
his own thoughts exactly—and he kept reading the main part
of it to fix its ideas firmly in his mind:

*'The idea of "centre" politics is ambiguous. We stand up
to it with the socialist movement, or rather the socialist idea,
which we propose to make the centre of national life. This
idea means that the various currents of political life and all
the efforts made to raise the country once again must be
allied to the principles of freedom and social justice. We
socialists are not asking to be "top": we ask that, as is logical,
all the deepest aspirations of our country and all the efforts
directed towards its rebirth shall converge upon us.'*

Wilson, who had been reading it out of the corner of his

eye, said smiling: 'Maybe I'd be a socialist if I was in Italy, because everything needs altering. But in Britain our traditions are our pride, so I'm a conservative.'

Giulio stared at him incredulously. Wilson was munching a piece of army chocolate and offered him a square of it.

'Yes, no matter how times change, I'll be a dyed-in-the-wool conservative as long as I live.'

Giulio could hardly help laughing at this attitude of conservatism to the death, expressed in the present whirlpool of destruction.

'If you're talking about conserving your own skin, Captain, then I agree with you.'

'No, I'm not talking about our skins; I'm talking about our traditions, our institutions, our whole system.'

'After this? After everything's been overturned like this? . . . D'you really think Britain can keep her Empire, for instance?'

'Why not?'

'Because those who've smashed Hitler today can't possibly think they can rule Asia and Africa with the whip tomorrow.'

'You mean it's a case of Hitler getting his own back on us, even as he goes down?'

'Yes, in this case it is. Hitler's war machine produced the greatest act of vengeance in history, because the fight against totalitarianism lit a flame of rebellion against all tyrannies . . . all, Captain Wilson!'

Wilson gave a thin smile.

'It's obvious you're a schoolmaster. You like laying down the law, but you needn't think I'm as green as all that.'

'What d'you mean?'

Wilson slowly dusted his jacket and spoke with a casual air: 'One day in Libya, when I was urging the men to stand up to Rommel for all they were worth, a coloured man asked me if we were fighting for people's freedom. I said yes, we were, and he said "That includes India, then?" How could I say it didn't? All the same, it's a bit soon to say the British Empire's finished and done with.'

He smiled smugly and murmured 'Just at the moment it's you who've lost an Empire. The Emperor's gone back to Ethiopia in spite of Mussolini, who gave him such a trouncing.'

'Well, I'm not complaining—that was history's just revenge. But you'll be losing an Empire a hundred times greater.'

Wilson took a tea-bag out of his uniform pocket and smiled enigmatically.

'Well, even if we do. . . .'

'Persuaded, Captain?'

'I was saying that even if we do, it'll be no great loss. The days when you could exploit the natives and really make the colonies pay are over.'

'That's true enough,' said Giulio.

'If black men and yellow men take it into their heads to govern themselves, well, let them try it. Why should we stop them?'

'That way you'll be left without raw materials, like Italy.'

'Nonsense! You've fought Mussolini, but you've still got your prejudices. In a world free from wars and dictators raw materials will be bought anywhere. And they'll be cheaper, at that. Today we're paying political prices to the . . . exploited colonies.'

'I've got a feeling that's a paradox, but basically I agree with you. So the British Empire's folding up, is that it?'

'You still don't follow.'

'What d'you mean?'

'I mean that we may leave the colonies, as you say, but our language, our customs, the civilisation we've given to half the world will remain. That's the real Empire on which the sun never sets.'

'When you put it like that, Captain, I can understand your pride.'

'Yes, I'm proud of being an Englishman. We're the Romans of the modern world.'

'Mussolini said that, years ago.'

'Well, even Mussolini was right on occasions . . . my dear anti-fascist! He knew that the United States was a child of ours, that we'd taken our civilisation—'

'In Morgan's pirate ships?' Giulio said slyly, amused at the idea of embarrassing Wilson.

The Englishman paused a moment, looked into Giulio's eyes and said very slowly, 'Yes, it's true, there have been plenty of pirates in our history, as there were plenty in the

[365]

history of Rome. But they killed and they stole in order to build. . . . Can you deny that?'

Giulio said nothing, but held out a bowl of water that had been heating on a heap of twigs piled round it, while they were talking.

'Splendid!' laughed Wilson. 'Let's have some tea from the old colonies, while there's still time.'

Both of them laughed, completely relaxed, and some peasants came over and sat near them. They too were waiting to see what the flashes not far away might mean.

CXIV

At eight in the evening a column of ambulances passed along the highway, their outlines visible against the clear sky. Soldiers were huddled on the roofs, possibly wounded, possibly not, their legs dangling and bumping inertly about, like the pendulums of ancient clocks that had grown tired of ticking.

'See? The retreat's started,' Giulio said to Wilson.

'But they're only ambulances. Just taking the wounded to Padusa, as usual,' said one of the peasants.

'Wounded or not, they're moving . . . they're off. I was in Tunisia, and I've seen what happens.'

'So it's a retreat?'

'Certainly it is. On the radio they said themselves they were shifting their positions.'

The men laughed and discussed this new method of describing retreat. Then a louder explosion in the distance silenced them and made them listen more carefully.

'We'd better get back—the big stuff'll be passing soon and then we may be in trouble. The others'll come dropping things on their heads and that'll be the end of us all.'

'Getting killed on the eve of liberation would certainly be pretty stupid!'

They went back into the stable and answered the women's worried, silent questions with a vague 'Don't worry.'

'But it's appalling out there.'

'Of course, but that's war, isn't it?'

'But when will it be over?'

[366]

'Soon. They're moving out. They're going north. . . .'

Giulio and Wilson sat cross-legged on the floor; the peasants lay down in the straw, as if to persuade the women they were not worried, but no one slept. Ears were cocked to catch every sound outside the locked door. Some people chewed bits of hay, to hide the trembling of their jaws.

The noise of shots, explosions and shouts was growing. The chaos of a disorderly rout was beginning, as front-line troops withdrew when the Allied vanguard threatened to encircle them. With heavy losses and little mechanised transport, they still hoped to escape annihilation.

The men in the stable, as if suddenly released by a single spring, rushed over to the small window and fought for a position there. They looked out, and, in the growing darkness, saw an apocalyptic ghostly line advancing. Two large puffing Panzers came first, with difficulty. The heavy tanks, those invincible tanks used in Poland, France and Yugoslavia, which had destroyed the freedom of great nations in a few days, now had damaged turrets and sides. Behind them came other vehicles, drawn by oxen.

Wounded and healthy were jumbled together on all of them, while all around them men wearing their regimental flashes were swaying exhaustedly, looking stupefied, plodding along like the oxen. Some of them put their water-flasks to their lips, some lit cigarettes in the shelter of their helmets— all in silence. Further back, orders were shouted by officers and N C Os, but no one heard them—their voices seemed to melt into the night.

A small truck puffed up past the crowd of men and vehicles and stopped. An S S officer got out, and stood in the middle of the road, legs apart, hands on hips. The procession drew up: lazily, smoothly, oxen, vehicles and men stopped. The officer started talking awkwardly, excitedly, and his angry harangue sounded like bursts of machine-gun fire. The men listened, glassy-eyed. One of them moved forward and cried: 'Wasser!'

Then he fell to the ground, striking his head against the officer's muddy boots.

The officer looked scornfully down at this gloomy example of weakness, which a few months before would have seemed to the Nazis like cowardice. Possibly he considered taking his pistol out of his holster and making an example of the man. But two of his comrades lifted him, a slack bundle, on to the Panzer, and the officer merely muttered that real Germans wouldn't be asking for water at such a time but for weapons and a dug-out in which to hold out to the end.

'Victory is still ours: *Heil Hitler!'* he shouted loudly, getting back on his truck. A weary *'Heil Hitler,'* that seemed dragged from the panting breasts of the dying, answered him.

The column continued. The oxen heaved, and managed to shift the heavy vehicles, and the men on foot started up again, heads hanging. Resignation had taken over from initiative: the troops looked more like men being deported than soldiers on active service. No one sang, even softly.

As they now recognised defeat, they looked back over past cavalcades across Europe and Africa, remembering their dazzling victories and comparing them with the present desolation. But more than anything they were probably thinking of the fate of their families and homes in Germany, cruelly wedged between the two armies closing in on Berlin. Now that disappointment had removed all their grotesque trappings,— swastikas, medals, flags and faith in the master race—human feeling was returning, and men who had had to stifle pity for the conquered now had to ask pity from those they had oppressed.

Armoured cars, guns and men moved slowly on, and when they had nearly vanished at the end of the road, planes were heard roaring overhead.

Terror seized the German soldiers. Many flung themselves into the ditches by the road, others rushed pell-mell into the fields. The few Panzers, armoured cars, and other vehicles were hidden in the trees as far as possible, under the small April leaves.

In a flash the planes swooped down on the column, and hell broke loose. Tanks were smashed, wheels and engines hurled into the air, while the petrol in the tanks burnt blue and red and licked at the tree-trunks, wrapping them in destruction. The sides of the Panzers and other vehicles gaped open and the poor oxen fell to the ground, moaning horribly, desperately. One of them, having broken its yoke with furious energy, ran about crazily, bumping into the trees in the smoke and flames, till it was finally struck and fell, almost on top of a couple of soldiers. Dead men's helmets flew about like projectiles, human limbs were flung about the road. In the brief spells between explosions, there were prayers, curses and shouts. It was an inferno.

The wave of planes passed on, and an unreal, fearful silence followed the terrible uproar. Everything seemed dead: men and objects. All that could be heard was the crackling of burning trees and the feeble groans of the dying.

A few moments went by; then, from ditches and fields, came those who had escaped. Silently they gazed about, not knowing where they could be most useful, whom they should first try to help.

The small truck that had been there before dashed back, and the SS officer got out. He looked as harsh as ever as he counted the survivors, lined them up and ordered them to continue. Then he thrust out his arm and cried *'Heil Hitler!'*

But this time no one answered. The truck left, as fast as it had come, and the survivors started out on their sad march again. One of them, as he passed a dead man, cried *'Auf Wiedersehen, Fritz.'*

After a few minutes two wounded men who had abandoned the column reached the stable, where the men were peering through the window. Giulio opened the door and the two came in without speaking, watched by the men, who could still not give way to pity. But two young women got up and brought them wine, and, encouraged by Giulio's eyes, found bandages for their wounds as well.

The men watched their women's compassionate action in silence. Already there was a different light in their eyes. Those frightened boys, broken by their wounds, could not be the enemy.

CXV

From the end of 1944, after the permanent bridges had been destroyed by the RAF, the Germans had set up a pontoon bridge to cross the river at Guarda, a vital point. People shook their heads at the typically German obstinacy with which the command almost daily rebuilt the pontoon, which Allied planes had located with remarkable precision and kept coming back to destroy. 'The Germans have rebuilt the pontoon—we'll have bombs tomorrow,' they said prophetically. And bombs rained down, not only on military targets, but on the town's wretched houses.

In April 1945, the people of Guarda learned of the collapse of the front not so much from the radio as from the number of troops arriving there, and from their confusion and lack of organisation. The pontoon at Guarda drew them all like a magnet; the great stretch of water seemed to provide defence, and beyond it they felt there might be a chance of putting up further resistance.

With thousands of almost undisciplined German troops concentrated in that small space, anything might happen before the Allied arrival, and so, as someone was needed to keep a close eye on the situation, and suggest the right measures for the resistance movement to take, Giulio was sent to Guarda by the C L N. Partisans hidden in the neighbourhood were ready for anything that might happen.

It was a terrible time for the town and its people, exposed to the Allied air offensive on the one hand and to possible violence from the chaotic army on the other. Allied aircraft ceaselessly furrowed the sky and there was no longer any sign of anti-aircraft fire. Wear and tear and the Allied planes had reduced the guns to silence.

The bombs fell on undefended troops who had already lost large numbers, making further gaps in their ranks. Senior officers wondered what was to be done. Pontoons were no longer being built, for in the circumstances it seemed madness to try: yet their exhausted men, their few useless tanks, their mostly unusable vehicles, were faced by three or four hundred yards of water. To those worn-out men the river was like an uncrossable ocean.

Unwashed and unshaven faces, uniforms flung on anyhow, confusion, purposelessness, contradictory orders, the nervous way the most ordinary duties and measures were carried out, all meant defeat. Moral and physical chaos were so terrible that only the absurd seemed to have any sort of meaning. Large numbers of officers and men, realising that defeat was irrevocable, took their own lives, as if, to them, the Third Reich's military defeat meant the destruction of the German people and the end of all civilised existence.

Those who wanted to live often behaved in ways that were no less absurd. Tanks and armoured cars were blown up, stores were burnt; but this was nothing compared with the crazy efforts of deranged soldiers to cross the river—they got into an army bus and drove straight off the bank at top speed. Anything, it seemed, could be used to cross that great stretch of water. Families even had the drawers stolen from their chests of drawers by men trying to get to the opposite bank using improvised oars.

The river swallowed up men and their madness in an atmosphere of appalling chaos. A few peasants, either out of pity or because they longed to see the last of them, helped their one-time masters to get away, and were bewildered by the incredible sight of their retreat; and for days and days, after the liberation, they stood on the river bank gazing at the innumerable bodies thrown up on to the shore.

Bullying and cruelty by German soldiers were far less frequent than had been foreseen, during those terrible nights and days. More likely some exhausted man would turn up at a farmhouse asking for a bit of bread and a glass of wine, and then roll wearily on to the ground.

Giulio was the target for one of the few acts of violence. It was on the last day: the few thousand Germans left were down on the river bank, near the old crossing, and the town of Guarda was free of them.

The partisans had left the country house which had been the headquarters of their small group, and, dressed as harmless peasants, in shabby civilian clothes, had gone ahead to watch the German movements. Giulio had stayed on his own in the empty barn, the silence around him in striking contrast with the uproar at the crossing.

He was sitting on a wooden bench, smoking, and thinking that a great writer could reproduce the atmosphere and make it exciting, could express the whirlwind of human feeling of a defeated army at the very end, when there was no hope of revival and the spectre of the most terrible punishment lay before it. Then he looked up towards the wide farm track and saw a German soldier, without his helmet and with his jacket unbuttoned, swaying towards the house.

He was an athletic young man with very fair hair that hung, unkempt and dirty, over his forehead, and dull eyes that gleamed intermittently and drunkenly under his arched eyebrows. Clearly he had drunk a good deal. He stopped a yard from Giulio, panting and swaying, and the powerful stink of his breath puffed into Giulio's face.

The two of them looked at each other suspiciously. Then the soldier asked for a bicycle, violently, almost shouting. Politely Giulio told him in German that there wasn't one there. But the man refused to believe him: he leapt into the hall like a wild beast and wandered about the house, overturning chairs and pottery.

Then he went outside again and into the barn, where he seized the sub-machine gun and shouted threateningly 'Bicycle or *Kaputt!*'

Giulio suddenly felt lost; but he had the strength to act and he got out of the line of fire by leaping on to the steps outside the front door of the house. He got inside and tried to shut the door but the German was after him and flung himself at it before it was quite closed.

The weight of his body overcame Giulio's resistance, and in giving way, Giulio rolled on to the floor with the German on top of him. Clutching, separating, wrestling again, panting and grunting, they fought until Giulio, who was the weaker of the two but more agile and clear-headed, managed to get away and seize the sub-machine gun which had fallen to one side during the fight. He pointed at the German's chest and the man looked round: when he saw people approaching he put up his hands.

Giulio's torn, bleeding face told the partisans what had happened, and one of them took off the safety catch of his sten gun to shoot the German. But Giulio put a hand over it: 'That's enough shooting. It's over.'

CXVI

On April 23rd Giulio left Guarda, where the German army's tragedy was over, and bicycled to Padusa.

At sunset he reached Porta del Mare, and remembering that Salatini lived nearby he went along to see him. Salatini's mother opened the door.

'You're Professor Govoni, if I'm not mistaken.'

'Yes, signora—good evening.'

'You've come just at the right moment—my son will be here in a minute.'

She sat him down in the dining-room and while Giulio drank 'coffee' made from barley she told him the Germans had left the city without doing any damage. The bishop—a strong man who had made no secret of his hatred of fascism—had persuaded the German commander. For the last few days the fascists had been running away like rabbits. The only one who had behaved consistently was the Vice-Federal Secretary Tassinari, ex-secretary of the G U F, who had shot himself.

After a few minutes Salatini turned up, with a great deal of news to tell him.

'What'll interest you most is that Dionisio's just arrived. At the end of March he came back from Switzerland to Val d'Ossola and stayed there for a while with the partisans, and then came down here just in time for Gabriele, who's been named mayor by the C L N, to make him provincial secretary of the Socialist party.'

'Splendid! No one better.'

'That's what Fausto thinks, too. Only half an hour ago he was telling me this was the time for men like Dionisio.'

'But we need Fausto as well, I'd say!'

'Nothing doing, Fausto's going to retire. The war's over, he keeps saying, and so is his job.'

'Has he really made up his mind?'

'I'm afraid so. The C L N parties yesterday were unanimous in wanting to name him Prefect of the province, but he was quite adamant in refusing. So Melloni's getting the job—he's another non-party man.'

'Melloni?'

'Yes, the landowner, poor Eriberto's father.'

Both were silent a moment, thinking of Eriberto. Then Salatini took some cigarettes out of a drawer.

'And what are you going to do, Giulio?'

'I've got troubles, Salatini: my brother's accident, which doesn't bear thinking about, and my wife, who's not well. I've got to go to Milan and see the family—I'm ashamed of myself.'

'But d'you know what they've got in mind for you?'

'How could I know? These last few days I've been isolated at Guarda.'

'They want to put you in the Labour office. They need three secretaries and you'd be the Socialist one.'

'Me? But that's no job for me—I know nothing about it.'

'But Gabriele and Dionisio want you there. It's an important, responsible job. You're not going to be a fool like Fausto are you?'

'I might accept if there's no one better. We're all in the same boat, and I don't want to look as if I'm opting out. But it's a mistake. . . .'

Giulio stayed at Salatini's that night. He slept uneasily—his thoughts rushing from his brother to Linda and then to the Labour office. In the morning he got up early and found Dionisio at the party's provisional headquarters, surrounded by a crowd of partisans. For everyone he had a smile and the right word, and Giulio envied him for being so relaxed.

They greeted each other with delight, and after a while Dionisio said goodbye to everyone there and they went out together, arm-in-arm, to mingle with the crowd. The city was jubilant, waiting for the Allied troops. About a thousand people were already in the piazza. Giulio at last seemed calm.

'D'you know,' he told Dionisio, 'until the very last minute I had a presentiment that I wouldn't see the end.'

'Nonsense.'

At ten o'clock sharp the first jeep appeared in the cathedral piazza. The church bells rang out and from everywhere—from cellars, bombed houses, air-raid shelters—people came out into the main streets to cheer the Allied troops. The triumphal procession went ahead between hedges of people, while cheers and flowers rained down on them and eyes shone with affection and feeling and the women's waving hands seemed to be blowing kisses.

The huge crowd seemed suddenly to have forgotten all the privations, and to be savouring the joys of freedom and peace completely, greeting everyone and everything, even the military vehicles, which now seemed harmless decorations in a wonderful parade. The Allied soldiers smiled as well, delighted at the people's happiness—big, childish, sportive-looking youngsters who played with the crowd, and lifted children on to the cars as they passed, handed them quickly to their friends and then back to their parents, in a kind of gentle, enjoyable game of rugby. Others held out handfuls of cigarettes and chocolate, and called 'Viva l'Italia!' while they chewed gum.

All these simple things aroused an almost delirious enthusiasm. Most people thought it almost incredible that these youngsters should have emerged from the war so serene, so unmarked by ferocity.

Giulio watched the procession absentmindedly, while bagpipes played gaily. But his thoughts were elsewhere. Suddenly he remembered that same piazza in the evening ten years before, when Mussolini made his speech at the time of the Sanctions; and then later, when he proclaimed the establishment of the Empire, far more crowded than it was now and with a blind, joyful delirium sweeping through it. Close beside him, at his elbow, he still seemed to feel, in the enthusiasm of those distant days, those who had later been carried away by the storm: Tassinari, the G U F secretary, longing impatiently for success, Braghiroli, the little provincial official, with his naïve speechmaking, and Moro, who had been the leader in every sort of hell-raising, even on triumphant occasions like that; and others, too.

He turned to look at Dionisio, and saw that he too was serious and withdrawn. Giulio guessed that he was thinking of those who had died, in particular of Mariuccia. Giulio shuddered when he remembered her, and tried to think of something else.

'Look,' he said to Dionisio, 'here's an Italian troop.'

At the head of it, in captain's uniform, Cavalieri d'Oro, haughty and pale, came riding in a jeep. The one-time racial

[375]

propagandist was the first to come home in the new uniform of the army of democratic Italy.

Pushed ahead by the crowd, Giulio and Dionisio found themselves, without realising it, outside Arlotti's shop. The barber was inside, trying to follow what was going on through the glass left clear of gummed paper, and so was his assistant, a young man who had been active in the Resistance and professed extreme ideas.

'How're things, Arlotti?' said Giulio, after greeting him warmly.

'Well!'

'This looks like a day for celebrating, not for saying *Well!*'

'I can't see clearly. . . .'

'Why not?'

'Because anti-fascism was easy: all you had to do was to say no to those evil men. But now we've got to build.'

'And so we shall.'

'Yes, so we shall, on a table with rickety legs.'

'You're more pessimistic than my brother Enzo. I didn't expect it.'

'Well, Giulio, I'm afraid of everyone, even the anti-fascist exiles. They'll start talking where they left off, in Giolitti's time. But the world's changed in twenty years.'

'But we're here, aren't we?'

'Yes, but the moral collapse of fascism has contaminated everything and everyone.'

'All right, suppose it has. We'll purge ourselves and then, to guarantee everything, we'll have a free parliament.'

'Parliament?' interrupted the boy. 'That's the worst of the lot.'

'Well, what d'you suggest, if you're so clever?' Giulio cried angrily.

'To get Italy on her feet again we need a man like the one I've got in mind. Now, in a few months he. . . .'

'And who might this marvel be?'

The boy smiled knowingly:

'Stalin!'

Arlotti snorted with disgust. 'Better a bad parliament than the best of dictators.'

'You see,' cried Giulio. 'You're on my side.'

'No, my dear Giulio, you're an optimist. Whereas I feel, deep down, that the Italy we're going to get will be only a pale copy of the one you're now dreaming of, in all the enthusiasm of the liberation.'

'Better than it's been, at any rate, don't you agree?'

'Yes, of course. But think of all the broken dreams and the idealists that'll end up cashing in on what's happening.'

'May I give my views?' asked Dionisio, who had listened in silence until then.

'Fire away!'

'You're both right and both wrong.'

'Splendid!'

'Yes, because men are always men, and even now they'll do things that are stupid and lousy. But the ideas we've been fighting for are those that take humanity ahead. Through them and with them, Italy will rise again.'

Appendix

Literal Translations of the Songs in the Text

We are torches of life,
we are eternal youth
that conquers
the future
of armed iron and thought.
By the roads of the new Empire
that spread over the sea
we shall march
as the Duce wishes
where Rome once passed. (p. 12)

Inn number one
paraponzi ponzi po',
a mistress apiece,
paraponzi ponzi po',
Inn number two,
paraponzi ponzi po',
my legs with yours . . . (p. 13)

Duce, Duce, who won't know how to die?
Who will ever deny what he has sworn?
The sword is unsheathed when you wish it;
pennants flying,
we shall all come to you . . . (p. 13)

[379]

A male youth,
with Roman will,
will fight!
It will come,
—the day will come,
when the great mother of heroes will call us . . .

(p. 14)

When we're in Nice, we'll dig ourselves in,
And tell the French we're at home.

When we're in Malta, we'll dig ourselves in,
And tell the English we're at home.

Chorus: bombs in our hands, caresses with our knives
(p. 14)

I started on my way with Giolitti,
I refused contacts with Nitti,
Now I'm a senator,
and Vice-Chancellor of the university

(*last line*) and a stormtrooper of great valour (p. 19)

Youth, youth,
springtime of beauty!
In fascism is the saving
of our freedom (p. 21)

That man who looks so fierce
don't, don't talk nonsense.
Go and tell it to the Kaiser;
maybe he'll believe us. (p. 21)

If the Kaiser doesn't believe us,
go and tell Starace.
that idiot in his uniform
will certainly believe us. (p. 22)

I say goodbye and go to Abyssinia,
dear Virginia, but I'll return.
I'll bring a fine flower from Africa . . . (p. 29)

The Negus's wife
had a male child.
As soon as he opened his eyes
he shouted: Long live fascism.
General Graziani
has been waiting for several evenings
for the skins of Abyssinians
to make black shirts with.
Bombs in our hands,
caresses with our knives (p. 30)

> Forward, o people, arise,
> the red flag will triumph (p. 53)

> Speak to me of love, Mariú . . .
> Speak to me of love, Mariú,
> you are my whole life
> your beautiful eyes gleam
> flames of love glitter (p. 60)

Little black face, beautiful Abyssinian girl,
wait and hope, for the hour is near!
When we are near you
we shall shout hurrah for the Duce and hurrah for the king
(p. 66)

> Inn of learning,
> something indecent happened,
> the Vice-Chancellor in his underpants
> was embracing the girl students,
> go it, pretty blonde,
> go it, pretty blonde (p. 68)

> Gastone, I've lots of women,
> I collect them,
> Gastone,
> Gastone . . . (p. 69)

> Eat lots of potatoes
> don't spoil my nights,
> and you'll see
> the crisis will be over . . . (p. 69)

[381]

Here lies Starace
dressed in his uniform,
greedy in peace,
cowardly in war,
aggressive in bed,
a liar to the people,
capable of nothing,
may he rest in peace (p. 85)

Hail, o king,
emperor!
New laws
the Duce gave
to the world, to Rome,
to the new Empire . . . (p. 121)

To conquer, conquer, conquer!
and we shall conquer on land, in the sky and on the sea.
It is the password
of a supreme will . . . (p. 191)

On the silver Arno
the sky is reflected,
while a sigh, a song
is lost in the distance (p. 199)

Colonel, I don't want bread;
give me fire for my gun.
I've got earth in my knapsack,
which is enough for me today.
Colonel, I don't want water,
give me destructive fire.
With the fever of this heart
My thirst will be slaked.
Colonel, I don't want a change:
no one here goes back.
A metre must be not yielded,
unless death comes . . . (p. 202)

With Mussolini's government
paraponzi ponzi po',
we hadn't got any money
paraponzi ponzi po',
With Badoglio's government
we haven't got bread and oil either.

This is really a lousy world
paraponzi ponzi po',
no women and no bread,
paraponzi ponzi po';
but instead we've got the war,
which sends us underground,
go it, pretty blonde,
go it, pretty blonde (p. 221)

It's he! It's he! Yes yes, it's really he!
The leading drummer of the Affori band,
who rules 550 pipers . . .
What excitement, what a thrill,
when he goes pom-pom . . .
Look here,
as they go,
the geese go quack-quack . . .
When they see him the girls grow shy,
he muddles *Il trovatore* with *Semiramide*.
Lovely daughter of love,
I'm a slave,
I'm a slave
of your whims . . . (p. 228)

Battalions of life,
battalions of death,
he who is strongest always wins,
he who can suffer longest . . .
Against Judah, against gold,
it will be blood that makes history:
we shall give you victory,
Duce, or our last breath!
Red M, similar fate!

black badge for the stormtrooper!
We have seen death
with two bombs and a flower in our mouth . . .

(p. 267)

The women no longer love us,
because we're wearing black shirts,
because they say we're gaol-birds,
because they say we're gaol-birds . . . (p. 310)

Comrades of a war,
comrades of a fate,
sharing bread and death . . . (p. 319)